JASMINE WALLACE

ISBN: 978-1-917087-06-3

Cover design by: Olivia (Fiverr.com: @oliviaprodesign)

# DEDICATION

To all those who ever felt they needed to prove they were worthy of another's love. Your demon is out there.

And their love is unconditional.

# Contents

# FOREWORD

Dear Reader,

***Demon's Faith*** is a MM supernatural romance with some dark topics. It contains content and situations that could be triggering for some readers.

This book is explicit and has explicit sexual content. It is intended for an 18+ audience.

Trigger Warnings include but are not limited to:

- Explicit Language
- Anxiety
- Depression
- Death
- Suicide
- Murder
- Graphic Violence
- Physical and Sexual Assault
- Child Neglect/Abuse

Despite that, I really hope you enjoy my book!

If you do, I would be so grateful if you would review it on Amazon or Goodreads.

Much love,
Jasmine

# INTRODUCTION TO DEMONS

In this book the order of Hell is a culmination of different belief and classification systems.

The inspiration of the seven Princes of Hell has been taken from "Lanterne of Light", an anonymous English Lollard tract often attributed to John Wycliffe. In this the Princes are all assigned to one of the seven deadly sins, with each demon tempting people by means of those sins. This system was also used later in history in the works of John Taylor, the Water Poet.

Lucifer: The Prince of Pride
Satan: The Prince of Wrath
Abaddon: The Prince of Sloth
Asmodeus: The Prince of Lust
Beelzebub: The Prince of Envy
Mammon: The Prince of Greed
Belphegor: The Prince of Gluttony

Other Classifications:
*Incubi and Succubi*: Demons of Desire, born of and overseen by Lilith (Consort of Lucifer)
*Cambions:* Half-demon, half-human
*Natural Born:* Demons born of Succubi or spawn from the lower pits of Hell
*Reaper Demons*: Those charged with the management of condemned or sacrificed souls
*Dealer Demons*: The faces of Hell, summoned accordingly to trade with mortals for their souls
*Rouge Demons:* Those that have abandoned the call of Hell, refusing to engage in the collection of power
*Imps*: Little creatures subservient to their masters, whoever they may be

# PROLOGUE

*Near London: 1,000 years ago…*

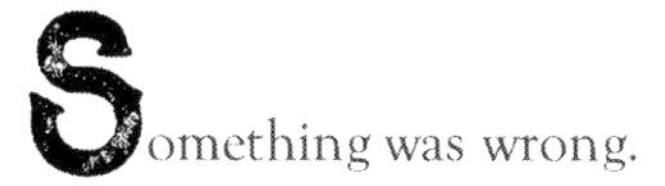

Something was wrong.

He'd felt it as soon as he walked into the house. The air was different. Filled with something he couldn't quite put his finger on, but it bore down on him like a wave crashing against the shore. It was the middle of the night but none of the lanterns were lit. Darkness seeped from every corner, clawing its way across the floor, broken only by the soft rays of silver moonlight that streamed in through the windows.

"William?" he called, stepping further into the hallway. "Are you home?"

Maybe he should have kept quiet. Surveyed the whole house before calling out, but anxiety and fear began to swirl in his gut, making him panic.

The lack of light didn't bother him as he cautiously made his way through the hallway, stopping at each door to crack it open and glance into the rooms. His demonic senses could easily pick out all the shapes in the shadows. Using his powers as well, black smoke that billowed and swept from every pore of his body, he searched the darkest corners feeling for whatever it was he was sensing.

"William?" he called again.

"In the bed chambers."

He exhaled with relief at the sound of William's voice. At least he was home. But his body didn't relax. Withdrawing his powers, he made his way to the bedroom, passing a cautious eye over the remaining rooms before heading inside.

"Are you well?" he asked, noting that like the rest of the house, the bedroom was devoid of light.

"Of course."

He spied William standing by the window, back turned to him, the moonlight offering a soft halo around his frame. His voice seemed off. Its usual warmth was gone, replaced by... *uncertainty*? But why?

"Why are no lanterns lit?"

"Seemed fitting," William said, turning towards him, his face covered in shadows.

"Fitting?" he queried. What was going on? Why was William being so strange? He racked his mind trying to find some explanation for this feeling that was gaining a tighter grip on his chest by the minute. They lived well outside of the boundaries of the ever-developing London and he kept their house shrouded with protection spells so no mortals would find them. "Fitting for what?"

"For this."

The hairs on his neck immediately stood on end as he felt the heat of flames at his back. Before he had a chance to use his powers or transform, a sharp pain radiated from between his shoulder blades. Crying out, he felt the talons at his back digging into his flesh, curling and gripping, keeping him in place. Another hand grabbed his wrist, twisting and pinning it behind him, forcing him to his knees. William had lunged forward and taken hold of his other arm, holding it out as he quickly and deftly carved a rune into his forearm. He desperately tried to access his powers, failing at every turn as the rune pulsed and burned into the very depths of his being.

"What are you doing?" he rasped, searching his lover's face for some hint of what was going on.

"Is it not obvious," William said harshly, grabbing his chin in his grip, bringing their faces a few breathes from each other. "I am taking what is mine."

Craning his neck, he spied the one holding him. Another demon, another cambion like him, who leered down at him, a feral gleam within fire-like eyes. He knew him.

"Kai?"

The cambion sneered. Unlike him and William, Kai was in his demonic form, his skin an ashy charcoal colouring with harsh black markings sprawled across his chest and shoulders. "I warned you that I would take everything from you."

"You mean, *we* would take everything from him," William corrected.

"Of course, sweeting," Kai assured him with a sickly-sweet smile, his long fangs flashing in the moonlight.

Struggling against their holds, he attempted to get his feet under him, trying to ignore the pain in both his back from Kai's talons and in his chest from William's betrayal.

"I do not understand," he ground out, his teeth bared and jaw clenched painfully. "Why, William?"

"Do not say my name with such familiarity," William snapped, his face contorting with rage. "I have endured you long enough. I have broken from my bondage to you. I will endure you no longer."

His heart felt like it was tearing in two, stuttering within his chest as William's words washed over him.

"But you loved me. I felt it," he managed, hating that he sounded like he was pleading. He would not plead for his life. Not even now.

"Love is simple enough to fake, *darling*," William whispered, his mouth twisted in a cruel sneer. "Now, be a dear and let us kill you."

"You are delusional if you believe I will simply *let* you kill me."

The talons retracted from his back, moving to wrap around his throat, yanking his head back until he looked up into Kai's gleaming red depths.

"You are hardly in a position to do otherwise."

Forcing himself to breathe calmly, he kept his gaze locked with Kai's. He refused to show fear, even now. It would not serve him any purpose to give into fear. Silently cursing his lacking ability to heal himself, he tried to steel his body, tensing his muscles, waiting for the right moment.

"You swore I would get to kill him." William's voice seemed far away as he continued to hold Kai's stare.

With an annoyed huff, the cambion looked away. "And you will, sweeting. I only need him to understand the position he is in."

*Now.*

With a grunt, he ripped his arm from Kai's grasp, ignoring the soft pop of his shoulder as it dislocated. He was accustomed to pain, he could cope with this. Wrenching his other wrist from William, he ducked and rolled to the side, easily dodging around Kai as he raced out the door.

He couldn't heal the rune, but he could destroy it. Grabbing a lantern, he smashed it against the wall, placing a shard of glass between his teeth. Slashing through the rune, the spell broke instantly, his powers rushing out of his body as he heard the footsteps of Kai and William behind him. Transforming as he ran, he threw dense balls of smoke at them, trying to gain enough distance to leave. He didn't care about the house. They could have it. They could have everything. What did it matter now? His heart had been ripped from his chest and stamped into the ground. What could he possibly have done to cause William to betray him? They had loved each other... or so he had thought. *Why?*

Red flames, William's fire, rushed towards him. It crashed against him, searing his flesh as it coursed over him. Using the ensuing flames as the perfect opportunity, he gathered the fires of Hell around him and transported himself as far away from them as possible.

Landing harshly against the ground, he rolled onto his back, hissing as the blistered skin on his back protested. His demonic wings twitched beneath him, the taloned tips digging into his flesh, pressed painfully against the ground. Blood pounding in his ears, he forced himself to hear over it, holding his breath as he waited to see if they would follow. After a few minutes he hesitantly pushed himself up onto his elbow, groaning with the effort as he cradled his dislocated arm against his stomach. Not entirely sure of where he landed, he noted that the sky was lighter so had hopefully left England far behind.

Taking a deep breath to brace against the pain, he gathered the fires again, pulling himself just outside a small stone cottage in the mountains. Vaguely, he heard the soft sound of an alarm sounding through the cottage and the rustling of feet rushing towards him.

"Marcus? Marcus!"

Warm, comforting hands gripped at his shoulders, lifting him from the ground. His eyes drifting shut, he allowed the familiar grasp to guide him into the cottage. Fighting against the pull of unconsciousness as best he could, he managed to grind out a final plea before the darkness overtook him.

"Father... I-I am sorry... you... you w-were right..."

# CHAPTER ONE

*1,000 years later... roughly...*

Lounging beneath the vine canopy, Cyrus looked up, blinking softly against the desert sun as it broke sporadically through the leaves. His head rested comfortably in his sister's lap as she ran her fingers gently across his forehead, small spikes of her power that manifested as red lightning dancing across his skin, trying to stem the headache building within him.

"How's that feeling?" Lena asked looking down at him, her dove-grey eyes filled with motherly love.

"Better. It's still there, but manageable," he sighed, reaching up to rub at his eyes.

"How are the dreams?"

"Vivid."

"Tell me about them."

Lena traced her fingers over his forehead again, warmth from her touch washing through his mind, easing the strain behind his eyes. He breathed with relief as the tension in his head started to break.

"They weren't anything new," he sighed, looking up past her face, his eyes unfocused. "Just flashes of past memories. My parents. Some foster placements. Zagan... I don't see them as a single strain anymore. They're convoluted, clashing together, out of order. I can't sort through them. I thought I was over this."

"Our binding is stronger than what you had with Zagan," she explained, moving her hands to rub lightly against his temples, her power licking like waves through his dark blonde hair. "It is pulling out memories that you still need to learn something from. Something that you will need if you hope to break from me in the future."

He chuckled softly, closing his eyes as she continued her work. "Sometimes I wonder if I really want to break from you," he teased, a small smile tugging at his lips.

"You'd better," she laughed, tweaking his nose. "I don't want to feel my brother's emotions for the rest of eternity."

His smile broadening, Cyrus pushed himself to sit up next to her. Lena wasn't really his sister, but they had become as close as siblings. They originally met in foster care when they were placed with the same family. Back then she had been four years younger than him. He'd felt protective of her, but found her meekness at the time to be unbearably annoying, earning her the nickname 'little mouse'. When their foster father had tried to assault her, after nearly beating the man to death, he'd taken an active role in building her assertiveness and strength. They had lost contact for a decade after he aged out of the system and was ultimately sacrificed to a demon. But when she turned up in Hell, a demon herself, they had rekindled their friendship and solidified their sibling-like bond. After Lena became a new Prince of Hell, she took over his binding from their old sire, deepening their connection, but also tying his life to hers.

"Don't worry sister, I don't want that either. I would like to have sex again one day without fear of you feeling it," he smirked at her, looking at her from the corner of his eye.

"Quite." Lena rolled her eyes at him, punching him softly in the arm. "You interested in anyone?"

"You know who I'm interested in."

"Besides him."

"No," he sighed leaning back into the stone wall behind him. "Not that I'm actively trying to find someone anyway. Can't risk dating a human and any demons that show interest are likely only trying to get close to you."

"Fair enough." She nodded pensively beside him.

Together they looked into the enclosed courtyard before them, watching as two demons sparred with each other, their bodies glistening with sweat caused both from their fight and the heat of the sun.

Ambrose was tall, lean, and well built; his arms and chest sporting clearly defined muscles as he grappled with his sparring partner. His broad shoulders strained against his opponent, each trying to find a weakness in the other's stance, to offset their footing.

In contrast, Marcus, although only slightly shorter, had a stockier frame, that when exposed barely concealed his underlying strength. The expanse of his chest was covered in a smattering of tight curls, currently plastered to his skin from his exertions.

"There was a time, I would have loved watching this," Lena mused, drawing Cyrus' attention back to her. "Now I have to sort through both my and your attraction," she laughed, nudging him in the ribs with her elbow.

He chuckled with embarrassment, shaking his head. Ambrose was Lena's partner. Her Consort. Chosen as both her lover and her voice at times when she might be absent as a Prince of Hell. They shared a deep connection, utterly devoted to each other, having once been sire and boundling, as Lena and Cyrus were now. He was incredibly jealous of the love and affection they shared for each other, wanting to feel some semblance of that in his own life. At some point, he had started hoping to find that with the other demon before them.

Marcus was an enigma to him, but one he wanted to figure out. He was fairly certain that the man held similar attractions to him, but as yet had been unable to confirm it. Marcus was a cambion. His father had been a demon who fell in love with a human woman. Their union had resulted in Marcus' creation but unlike most cambions, his mother had survived his birth which made him vastly different to any other cambion Cyrus had known.

Before binding to Lena, Cyrus had been bound to another cambion, Zagan, whose twisted sense of morality and self, had caused endless torment among weaker demons in Hell. In his time as Zagan's boundling, he had been tortured and abused in ways he hadn't imagined possible. Lena had saved him from that fate, although only after herself being subjected to its horrors.

Watching the struggle between the two demons now, he was caught up in Marcus' movements. The sight of him was enrapturing, sending his mind down recesses of desire and imaginings that made Cyrus need a cold shower on an almost hourly basis when around him. The only way he managed to keep his thoughts in check most days was by reminding himself that Lena could feel everything he did through their binding.

"Dammit!" Ambrose cursed loudly as Marcus managed to shift their position, sending the Consort to the ground.

"Best out of thirteen?" Marcus teased, helping him to his feet.

"Not today, my friend," Ambrose sighed, shaking his head. "You win the day."

"You two have been at it for almost three hours," Lena huffed at them. "Give it a rest, would you?"

Ambrose smiled at her, a smile that lit up his whole face and made her sit up a little straighter. *God, how annoying yet infectious their love is*, Cyrus thought to himself as he wondered if anyone would ever smile at him like that. Bounding over to her, Ambrose swept down and planted a warm kiss on her lips. Cyrus watched them with jealousy from the corner of his eye, wilfully ignoring the knowing glance his sister shot in his direction.

"Of course, my Prince," Ambrose whispered to her, as he collected his shirt laying on the bench next to her.

"Ambrose..." she chided gently, a soft smile tugging at the corners of her mouth. Cyrus knew she hated her council calling her 'Prince', all having a close connection and friendship with her. Ambrose knew it as well, but he liked to tease her. He was also the only one who got away with it generally.

"Could *you* two give it a rest?" Marcus chuckled, shaking his head as he walked over to the lounging area, leaving his shirt hanging on the rail. He crossed his arms in front of his chest and leant against a supporting pillar. "How are you feeling, Cyrus?"

Starting at the question, his gaze shot to the cambion, ever still surprised that Marcus would care how he was. "Fine, thanks," he responded hurriedly. "Well, better at least."

Marcus smiled at him. He felt his breath catch in his throat at the sight of it. *Damn*, he needed to figure out how to stop that from happening. "Feeling up for a round?" the cambion asked.

"Oh, give it a break, Marcus," Lena sighed heavily, her head dropping back against the wall. "Between you and Archie, we'd all be training non-stop."

The demonic-trainer was the only other member on Lena's council. He focused on training newborn demons within the pits of Hell whilst also serving as her eyes and ears for all movements and developments down there as she resided over Hell's new domain on Earth.

"*You* want us to be prepared for the Apocalypse. I'm just following your orders," Marcus chuckled at her reaction.

Shaking her head, Lena got to her feet, planting her hands firmly on her hips. "Alright. Bring it on, tough guy."

"Oh no," Marcus held up his hands defensively, smiling sheepishly at her. "I know you'd thrash me. What's the point when I know I'd lose?"

"In failure we learn how to succeed. Did you not say that to me once?"

Studying her, Marcus pressed his lips together. Cyrus looked between them, unable to hide his amusement at the exchange. Glancing at Ambrose, he saw that the Consort was of a like mind, his shoulders shaking almost imperceptibly in silent laughter.

"Fine," the cambion said finally, a slight air of uncertainty to his voice. "You're on, Prince."

"You're an idiot, Marcus," Ambrose chuckled, folding his arms in front of him as he sat down next to Cyrus.

Licking her lips, Lena pulled her auburn hair atop her head into a ponytail, stepping out into the middle of the courtyard, Marcus close behind her. As soon as they reached the centre, she spun on her heel, swinging a right hook at his jaw. The cambion stepped back, the swing missing him by a hair as he tried to regain his footing from the sudden attack. Barely giving him time to recover, Lena stepped with him, her fists trying to land on their mark. Marcus ducked to the side, grabbing at her shoulder and spinning her round to his side, his own fist colliding with her body between her shoulder blades. Staggering forward, Lena dropped her hands to the ground, kicking her feet up in the air so her heel connected with his jaw. The cambion's head snapped back, but he managed to keep upright, even as Lena returned to her feet and landed two blows directly on his chest. Grunting from the force, Marcus caught her arms as they grappled with each other, trying to gain ground.

"Sure you're feeling better?" Ambrose asked, pulling Cyrus' attention from the scene.

"I'm okay," he sighed with a slight nod.

"The dreams still getting to you?"

"Yeah, but Lena's helping me work on those."

Cyrus and Ambrose had always been tense around each other until a year ago when they became members of Lena's council. For a long time, he thought Ambrose didn't deserve to be with his sister, but the devotion the Consort showed their Prince had swayed him. Now, Cyrus felt he could confide in him as much as he could with Lena. He wouldn't go quite as far as calling Ambrose his brother, or at least, not yet, but they had become close friends.

"You know, she still has nightmares."

Shocked by the statement, Cyrus turned his head to look at Ambrose. "About what?" he asked softly.

"About Zagan," Ambrose sighed looking at the ground. "Not as often anymore, but every now and then, she wakes up, screaming."

"I didn't know."

"Probably best you don't let on I told you," he smirked ruefully. "She worries about you. She was with Zagan for a much shorter time than you."

"I was with him a shorter time than you," Cyrus commiserated. Indeed, Ambrose had been a boundling to Zagan some six hundred years ago, taking almost a century to break from his bonds.

"True," Ambrose nodded. "But I was never the sole focus of his... *treatments*. You and Lena were. It was bad for me. It was worse for you."

Cyrus fell silent, merely watching his sire and Marcus spar in front of him. They both moved quickly, easily dodging the other's attacks, recovering just as fast should one actually manage to land a blow. Whilst sparring in the courtyard, they wouldn't use their powers. Lena preferred that such training remain in the pits of Hell, that way they would less likely cause damage to their home. Both Marcus and Lena were adept at spell work and conjuring, having used their abilities jointly to build the home in which all four demons now lived. A home in which Cyrus felt endlessly grateful to be a part of.

Shortly after aging out of foster care, he had moved into his own apartment. He enjoyed the freedom at the time, being able to finally do things on his own without oversight or control from the adults in his life. Sadly, his freedom had been short lived. Whilst he had been in the process of discussing with his social worker going through approval to become a foster parent so he could get Lena away from the placement he had left behind, his last family had kidnapped him and sacrificed him to Zagan. The girl he had been sacrificed with chose for her soul to go to Purgatory despite the silken promises Zagan had made them. Cyrus had chosen to bind to the cambion, the choice feeling better suited to him at the time. He soon came to regret that choice after the first experience of Zagan's 'handling' of him.

But when Lena re-entered his life, then six years older than him as a human, but ten years younger as a demon, he had felt a ray of hope. Suddenly, he had something to live for again. The possibility of having his sister in his life again. The unfortunate event of Zagan overtaking her binding to Ambrose had been difficult for both of them, all of them, but they had gotten through it together.

Following her movements now, Cyrus studied how she stepped across the ground, slowly pushing Marcus back against the limestone wall, the only side of the courtyard not formed by the house. Lena's footwork was perfect, having fought in a number a cage-fighting circuits after she aged out of foster care. Marcus on the other hand, was slower on the ground than when he battled in the air, using his wings in demon form with effortless ease. But he had greater brute strength in human form.

"She's toying with him," Ambrose smirked.

Cyrus laughed softly, stretching his legs out in front of him as he focused on Marcus. The cambion seemed to be fully aware of Lena's tactic in backing him into a corner, but was unable to gain enough ground or advantage to get himself out of the situation. Cyrus was mesmerised by him, watching as his chest heaved with exertion as he tried to find some way of evading the Prince rounding on him.

Smiling wickedly, Cyrus imagined running his fingers over Marcus' chest, brushing them through the soft curls upon it. His breath quickened with veiled desire as he allowed his imagination to pull him further into his fantasies. Biting his bottom lip, he watched with untold amusement as his desire caught on Lena's face, her advance faltering as she picked up on his emotions through their bond. Inhaling sharply, she shot daggers over her shoulder at Cyrus who now ducked his head, suitably chastised under her glare. Marcus noted her hesitation and taking advantage of the situation, stepped forward and landed a solid blow on the side of Lena's face.

"That's cheating, Cyrus," Ambrose coughed, barely containing his own laughter.

"Don't know what you're talking about," he smiled.

Turning with the blow, Lena pulled her leg round, jarring her heel against Marcus' jaw, sending him to the ground with a sickening thud. Planting her foot in the middle of his back, she gripped the base of his neck, holding him still beneath her.

"Yield?"

"Yield," Marcus confirmed with a soft laugh. Lena released him, stepping back as he pushed up onto his knees, shaking his head. "I'm done for the day."

Lena smiled at him, clasping his arm and helping him to his feet. "Finally," she sighed, patting him on the back before turning and walking towards Ambrose and Cyrus. The boundling shifted uncomfortably as she stormed towards him. Her hand shot out, grasping his chin in her hand and lifting it to her face. Drawing nearer she whispered to him, her eyes dark with anger; "Do that again and I'll thrash you, *brother*."

"Duly noted," Cyrus said hurriedly, his eyes wide with tentative fear, despite the teasing smile on his lips. He knew his sister would not really follow through with her threats, but she knew how to be terrifying, even in human form.

"Good," she said, standing up and folding her arms across her chest. "Shower?" she asked turning to Ambrose. Chuckling softly, the Consort got to his feet and followed her inside, leaving Cyrus alone with Marcus.

The cambion sauntered back to the lounging area, finally pulling his shirt over his head, sweat immediately causing the material to cling to him. Cyrus swallowed hard watching him, quickly dropping his eyes to the ground before the older demon caught him staring. Marcus moved to the alfresco dining set, pulling out one of the black metal chairs before lowering himself into it.

"Are you sure you're alright?"

Looking up at Marcus, Cyrus sighed with annoyance. Where before he enjoyed the demon's concern, now it was irritating. He wanted Marcus' attention, but not like this. "You three have asked me that multiple times already today. I have a headache. I'm not dying."

Marcus laughed with sympathy. "Apologies."

The silence that fell over them was relatively comfortable. The heat from the desert was nothing compared to the heat with Hell, but as demons they were unbothered by hot or cold. Regardless, they enjoyed the warmth of the sun and the dryness of the air all the same. Looking up through the canopy again, Cyrus wondered quietly, how much longer he would have to feel lesser than to his other councilmen. As part of Lena's council, they all shared in her power, exalting their station among other demons. But as her boundling, he was subjected to restraints within the council that the others were not. He'd been eighteen when he died and became a demon, and although his body was frozen in time, his mind continued to age. He didn't want to be treated as a child for the rest of his existence, simply because of how he looked.

"Cyrus," Marcus called gently, pulling him from his thoughts. "I, ah..." Looking at the cambion, Cyrus tried to figure out what he was feeling. Marcus' gaze was fixated on the ground, arms folded in front of him, legs stretched out and crossed at the ankles. Yet again, the older demon threw him off guard by his casual good looks. His long sandy blonde hair swept back from his face, its tousled lengths currently held back by sweat, although usually one or two strands would fall in front of his sea-green eyes. As a human, Marcus' skin had his mother's colouring, a natural olive-tan, darkened with golden tones from the desert sun. His lips were a soft pale brown, blending in almost perfectly with his colouring, warm and inviting.

God, how he wanted to kiss those lips.

"What is it?" Cyrus pressed, shifting uncomfortably in his seat as his body flushed with desire.

"Ah, it's just... I understand that us always asking if you are okay can get annoying," Marcus finally restarted. "But it's because we care about you. And, maybe on a more annoying note, if you're not okay, it means Lena is not okay."

Cyrus sighed and dropped his head back to the wall. *Yeah,* he thought, yet again he was reduced to being a boundling.

"One day," he said pushing to his feet, annoyance growing within his chest, "that's going to stop being the case. Maybe then, you can all stop treating me like a kid."

"Cyrus..."

"Don't, Marcus. I don't want to hear it right now." Shaking his head, he turned on his heel and walked into the house. Heading upstairs, he made for his room, slamming the door behind him. Instantly he regretted it, groaning loudly as the sound jarred his ears, aggravating the pain in his head.

# CHAPTER TWO

Marcus watched carefully as Cyrus walked away from him. Closing his eyes, he let his head fall back into the empty space behind him to look up through the vines. He hadn't meant to upset the boundling, but he seemed awfully good at doing that of late.

Sighing heavily, he got to his feet and went inside, intent on having a shower. Possibly a cold shower.

He had no idea what thoughts Cyrus put into Lena's head during their match, but he could guess. He'd noticed the sly glances the young demon had sent his way recently, glances that made his stomach tighten with unwelcome feeling. Cyrus was gorgeous, his youthful looks sending Marcus on a rollercoaster of desire most days, but he refused to indulge those thoughts. Or at least, he refused to indulge in them outside of his dreams. He knew it would take very little encouragement to fall into a whirlwind affair with the boundling, and he was not prepared for that.

Turning his shower on, he stepped into the stream, washing away the sweat coating his skin. Rubbing his jaw, he tried to ease the tension caused by Lena's blows as the water ran over his body. *Hell, she has some force behind her kicks*, he thought to himself. If only he could heal himself as she could. Few had instinctual healing abilities like hers. Most, like him, were reliant on healers when they were injured. Ambrose could heal others to an extent, but he was incapable of healing himself.

Becoming part of her council had been one of the proudest days of his life. As a cambion he was inclined to gravitate towards power, and there were few more powerful than Lena.

For centuries now, he had denied both his desire for power and the flesh. In his early years, his mother had kept him grounded, focusing solely on protecting those he loved. His father, under the influence of his mother, continued that work until he died. After that, Marcus had spiralled, merely fighting to survive following the betrayal of his former lover and boundling, William. It was just after he met Ambrose, he finally gave up on amassing power, settling merely for the friendship they formed. That was, until Lena entered their lives.

Marcus wasn't interested in the power for himself. His desire now was to protect Lena and her position. He didn't want what happened to him to happen to her or Ambrose. They were his closest friends, his family, and he would do anything to protect them.

And then, there was Cyrus...

The boundling was tempting. Infuriatingly so.

He groaned as his body hardened at the thought of Cyrus' doe-brown eyes, sharp jaw line and that dimple he had only on his left cheek. That soft-pink mouth that rested in a permanent pout from the perfect upturn of his top lip, ready to be kissed at any given moment. "Dammit," he cursed to the water, roughly grabbing the taps, turning off the hot and letting the stream run as cold as it could go. What he would do to that boundling if he wasn't afraid of losing everything over it. He had to do something about this. He had to get control of himself again. Never again would he allow his heart of be at the mercy of another. His friends were one thing, a potential lover was another.

Even though the cold didn't bother him, he welcomed the slight shiver the cool water sent over his skin. Taking a deep, steadying breath, he turned off the shower and stepped out. Running his power through his body, the heat of his blood quickly dried him, although he realised too late that practically negated the effects of the cold shower.

After getting dressed, he grabbed a book from his room and headed down to the kitchen to make himself a coffee.

As part of Lena's council, they no longer had to hold to their old designs; their purpose or work in expanding the powers of Hell. However, he still liked to indulge in the occasional deal. When not carrying out their Prince's orders, he and Ambrose still reviewed and managed some of Hell's finances on Earth, mainly now to build on the assets for Lena's purposes. But today, he had nothing but time.

Returning to the outside lounging area, he sipped on his coffee and allowed himself to escape into his book to pass the next few hours. He loved the heat of the desert, the sun and the arid air. When Lena asked him to move in with her and Ambrose, he had jumped at the chance. Living in Hell had suited him until then, but unlike Archie, he had no real desire to remain there. Regardless, there were days he felt out of place among the family unit of Lena, Ambrose and Cyrus.

"Fully recovered, Marcus?"

Startling at the question, he turned to see Lena walking towards him, a warm yet teasing smile on her face. He nodded in acknowledgement to her. She may be his Prince, but she was also his friend. "Some of us don't heal instantly, Lena," he chuckled.

"Hm..." she hummed, her eyes crinkling with delight. "Come on. You're with me today."

Sipping his coffee, he closed his book, leaving it on the table. "Where are we going?"

"To see Asmodeus," she sighed, folding her arms across her chest.

Marcus groaned. The Prince of Lust was not one of his favourite people, demon or otherwise, to visit. "He usually prefers when you take Ambrose."

"Which is why I'm taking you," she smiled sympathetically. Of all her princely siblings, Asmodeus was her favourite, but even she tired of his antics. "I really don't want to have to deal with badly veiled innuendos today." Almost shyly, her gaze dropped to the floor as she pressed her lips together. "That and I may have broken Ambrose..."

"Oh, Lena," he sighed, shaking his head. The two of them were truly incorrigible. Marcus was happy to see them so content in their love, but it could get a little overwhelming at times.

"What?" she asked sheepishly, still unable to meet his gaze.

Rolling his eyes, he put down his coffee, got up from his chair and walked over to her. "Why are we going to see Asmodeus?"

"He's been digging into some information on Raphael for me," she said, looking up at him.

Marcus pressed his lips together in disgust. *Raphael...* an arch-angel who had so rudely announced his existence to Lena shortly after she became a Prince. He was Lena's counterpart on Earth acting under the authority of Heaven. They had not seen him since, but Lena tracked him as best she could without drawing unnecessary attention to herself.

Marcus disliked the angel enormously. "Says he's found something he needs to tell me about. He's down with Lucifer at the moment, but we'll go wait in his domain."

Holding out her hand for him, Marcus took it gently as she gathered her flames around them and transported them to one of the lower rings of Hell. Asmodeus' domain of Lust.

Much like all of Hell, the walls of the junction cavern in which they appeared were carved out of red and black rock, arching high above them. Red dust covered the floor giving it both a sinister and comforting appeal. The smell of sulphur and brimstone quickly filled their nostrils, although they were quite accustomed to it now. The journey had pulled out their demonic features and Marcus, yet again, found himself in awe of Lena's imposing stature.

Her blood red skin shone brightly, illuminated by the streams of lava that ran through cracks in the walls and floor, only contrasted by the four black feathered wings adorning her back, each with spiked talons at their tips. Her hair glowed like the lava within the walls, smouldering atop her shoulders giving an ethereal depth to the black glow of her eyes. Gone was the gentle nature of their usual dove-grey colouring, replaced by a hardness and ferocity that would strike fear into any number of creatures, demons included. A black leather corset covered her torso flaring out to heavy fabric that swirled around her legs, just brushing above her feet. Or rather, smooth black hooves that clipped along the floor, although soften by the dust. Above her head curled four dark red horns twisted like a crown, strands of her lava hair wrapped around their base. Since becoming a Prince, she had added golden rings and chains as adornments to both her clothing and horns, the delicate metal chiming pleasantly as she walked. She was beautiful, although she hated the term; a term used endlessly by Zagan when he had control of her.

In contrast, Marcus felt quite overshadowed. His own colouring was stark black, although angular silver-grey markings trailed over his chest and arms, giving evidence to his lineage as a cambion. Apart from his hair which now sported the same colour as his markings, everything about him was black, including his trousers and open vest. His eyes, bat-like wings and ram-curved horns all matching, aiding in his ability to fade into the shadows, a trait he used in the days after becoming one of Lena's council to carry out her biding against demons that still sought to move against her. Even his power manifested as black smoke, making him the perfect assassin as and when she needed him to be.

"Shall we?" she asked, turning and walking down a corridor to their left.

"Do we not need to get to Asmodeus?" he asked as Lena walked away from him down the corridor. Jogging slightly, he caught up with her, falling in step slightly behind her. He thought they were going to transport straight to the Prince's chambers.

"We will," she said nodding her head, her lava hair falling over her shoulders. "I would like to talk with you for a moment first."

Confusion swept over him as he gazed at her. Her face was unreadable, her eyes shut as they walked. "What about?"

"You."

Marcus stopped in his tracks, simply staring at her back. Lena halted as well, her wings puffing out slightly as she took a deep breath before turning round to look at him. Pulling his own wings in tighter, he dropped his gaze and coughed uncomfortably. "What about me?" he asked.

"Are you okay?" she asked, warmth and concern in her voice.

Caught completely off guard, he took a step back. "Of course," he assured her. "Why do you ask?"

"Why are you afraid?" she queried calmly, tilting her head to the side. "I can smell your fear. You know you don't need to be afraid of me."

"I'm not af–" he started but found himself unable to continue. His breathing came rapid as he tried to sort his thoughts. He was afraid. The fear gripped tightly at his chest. Why was she asking this? What reasons did she have to question him? Had he not given her everything? His loyalty and devotion. Swallowing, he told himself he was overreacting and forced himself to continue. "I'm not afraid of you. I'm afraid where this questioning is going."

"Ah," she said knowingly, stepping towards him. "Marcus, your position on my council, your position in my life, is always guaranteed, regardless of your answer. I'm merely asking if you're okay? If there is anything you need to talk to me about? I am here to guide my council as much as they are to guide me." Reaching out, she cupped his face in her hands, lifting his gaze to hers. Marcus searched her face, relieved to see the genuine truth of her words in her eyes. "You are my friend and more than that, you have been my mentor and greatest warrior. I can feel when something is bothering you, as I can with all my council. I need to know you are okay."

Sighing with relief, he raised his hand and gently touched his fingers to the back of her wrist. "I'm fine, Lena," he said, closing his eyes, simply feeling the strength that emanated from her. "I promise you, what is bothering me, is of no consequence to you or your council."

"Oh, Marcus," Lena sighed, dropping her hands. He looked at her, wondering what was wrong. "I care about more than just my council. I care about my friends. My family. But I won't press further."

She turned on her hoof and restarted down the corridor. He trailed behind her thinking over her words, a deep churning in his gut as he stared at her wings. They shortly came upon a larger cavern, two tall black doors imposing against the red rock, blocking off unwanted visitors to the chambers behind that belonged to the Prince of this domain.

Coming to an abrupt stop in front of the doors, he stared at Lena, trying to figure out what she was thinking. "I've upset you," she said after a while, her head dropping forward although she did not turn to look at him. "I'm sorry."

"Lena..." his voice trailed off, unable to continue as a lump formed in this throat.

Her brilliant black eyes glanced at him over her shoulder. "Hm?"

"Ah... nothing," he said, dropping his gaze to the floor. "Don't worry about it."

Lena sighed heavily, turning back to face the doors. "I will always worry, Marcus. But I won't force you to tell me anything you do not wish to." She paused for a moment, a heavy tension between them. "Unless, of course, I have reason to believe it is something I need to know."

Marcus knew she didn't really mean her last sentence as a threat, but it was there all the same. She needed to have absolute faith in her council, or else its stability would be threatened, questioned by the other Princes. If she couldn't trust them implicitly, what was the point.

Raising her taloned hand, Lena pushed at the doors, her red lightning dancing across its surface, announcing her presence to anyone within as they entered the chambers beyond.

"Sister, Marcus. Thank you for coming."

Lena turned her head sharply to the right as her brother, the Prince of Lust, strode towards them. Unique to demon-kind, his eyes glowed like blue fire, filled with a deep intelligence intermingled with a permanent gleam of desire. Above them, sharp, jagged horns protruded from his brow, twisting and curving towards the back of his head. Unlike his sister, Asmodeus' dark skin was mottled and leathery, like cracked obsidian laced with silver strands, although muted and dull even with the firelight of the torches around the walls. Muscles that could only be carved from power and dedication rippled beneath his skin, barely containing the Prince's strength.

"Hello, brother," Lena greeted him warmly, kissing his cheek as he embraced her. "I wasn't expecting to find you here yet."

Asmodeus pulled back. Marcus was surprised to see such a serious expression on the Prince's face considering his usual frivolous nature. "This cannot wait," he stated earnestly.

"You said you had something concerning Raphael?"

"No, not about Raphael. But someone just as important. Please come with me," Asmodeus ushered his sister towards another door before pausing to look back at the cambion. "Marcus, would you wait here?"

"Of course, my Prince," he said with a bow.

Lena smiled at him as she followed her brother. "I'll be back soon."

Marcus took up a place by the door, leaning into the wall behind him, losing himself to his own thoughts. Lena never came to Hell on her own anymore, but she would almost always see her siblings alone. Discussions between the Princes were of paramount confidentiality. It was her choice if she wished to disclose the conversations with her council, but they were all aware that there were some things she had to keep secret, even from them.

He was no longer as ambitious as he once was, but he did not relish the thought of possibly losing everything he had. If Lena was concerned about him, did she still have faith in him? Did she still have confidence that he could guide her in her role as Prince? He would admit he questioned it himself a few times in the beginning, but he vowed to stand by her, to help her. That meant growing and learning alongside her as to how best to support her. He'd had a reputation among other cambions for being weak. His role on Lena's council had swiftly brought that to an end when she had sent him to weed out any remaining loyalty to Zagan within their ranks. The fighting had been brutal, but he had succeeded and, in the end, all cambions had pledged themselves to her. *He* had done that. *He* had slaughtered his own brethren for her. And he would have done that a thousand times over to remain by her side. What possibly could she be feeling from him that would make her question him? Did she feel his uncertainty around Cyrus? He would never allow that to threaten her. He would never allow himself to do anything that could affect her.

*Is this how Cyrus feels,* he asked himself, *when we ask him if he is okay?*

The time passed fairly quickly as Marcus stared at the ground, the fire from the torches creating flickers of light that danced in front of him, captivating and ensnaring his mind. He jumped slightly as the door the Princes had gone through reopened abruptly, his Prince storming out, a thunderous look on her face.

"Lena?" he queried.

"Not now!" she barked at him, her wings fluttering anxiously behind her. Marcus straightened at the harshness of it, but took no personal offence.

"Sister!" Asmodeus called after her, rushing out. Lena rounded on him, gnashing her fangs in annoyance, but he didn't flinch. "Do not act rashly."

Lena said nothing, her teeth gritted as she restrained herself, simply turning on her hoof and racing out the door.

"That went well," Asmodeus said cheerfully although his face had a different story to tell. "Good to see you again, Marcus."

"Hm," he mused, staring after Lena but finding himself unable to move.

"Marcus!" Lena shouted from beyond the doors, her voice barely containing her ire.

"You'd best go after her," the Prince of Lust sighed giving him a sympathetic smile.

Marcus nodded as he quickly went to rejoin his Prince. What could Asmodeus possibly have said to her to cause this reaction?

She stormed through to the corridor, causing Marcus to have to jog to keep up with her. As a demon, she was only slightly shorter than him, but the strength in her hocked legs gave her greater speed.

"Lena, wait!" he called for her as they neared the junction. It would not do for his Prince to enter a chamber without him on the chance other demons with unknown intentions may be there. "Lena!"

She halted in her tracks and he could see her shoulders rise and fall as she took a deep breath. He came to a stop behind her, but said nothing, simply waiting for her to speak. He heard her exhale sharply before she turned to look at him. Her expression unreadable, but her eyes looked tired, dulled by some weighty knowledge.

"Do you remember when Ambrose and I thought we were being sneaky around you?" she asked wearily.

Marcus chuckled. She was trying to divert her mind. Her avoidance of serious moments was well known within her council. "Yes," he nodded, smiling at her. "Fondly. You were not very good at it."

"No, we weren't," she sighed, shaking her head. Her small laugh was barely audible and had an undertone of sorrow to it. Marcus took a step towards her cautiously, wanting to provide her with comfort but unsure as to how to go about that. After a moment she lifted her head and smiled at him. "When are you going to find someone?"

"I don't want anyone," he replied, crossing his arms in front of him hating the defensive feeling he had around her of late.

"Well, I know that's not true."

*Oh no...* dread washed through him, but he swallowed it as best he could before responding. "And how would you know that?"

"Asmodeus told me," she shrugged.

He sighed heavily and hung his head, trying to ignore the pit in his stomach. "This is why I don't like seeing him."

"This is why no one likes seeing him," Lena agreed, turning back down the corridor and heading towards the junction. He fell in step with her, thanking her silently for the slower pace. "I'm pretty sure Ambrose is the only one of my council that can tolerate him. But come on, Marcus. Of all people you can tell me."

"Please don't, Lena," he said softly, a quiet plea in his voice. "Please don't pry into this. I don't want to be with anyone. Can we just leave it at that?" *Please,* he begged internally. He did not want to confess that he was attracted to her boundling. Not now.

"Alright."

Surprised at her quick agreement he stared at her from the corner of his eye, regarding her sceptically. "Really?"

"Yes. Why are you surprised?" she asked, a small smirk tugging at her lips.

"Because that felt too easy..."

"Okay. How about, 'alright, for now'?"

"That sounds more like you," Marcus laughed, allowing himself to find amusement in the situation despite his fear of the topic.

Lena shut her eyes as they walked into the junction, placing her hands on her hips, her brow furrowed in concentration. "Let's go home," she said finally, holding out her hand for him. "I need to discuss something with you and Archie."

# CHAPTER THREE

There had been an unbearable tension in the house after Lena and Marcus got back from seeing Asmodeus. Cyrus may not have been able to feel Lena's emotions in the same way she felt his, but he knew something was bothering her. She, Marcus and Archie had been locked away in her altar room for a couple of days discussing whatever it was she had learnt. He and Ambrose were not privy to the conversations for the moment, although he was pretty sure that the Consort knew what was going on as he too had been walking around on eggshells since her return.

Needing some respite from it all, Cyrus had spent more and more time in the hellhound den he was keeper for. For the past decade he had managed and overseen this den on his own, but a new keeper had joined him a few months ago meaning he no longer needed to spend as much time there as he used to. But he still loved the beasts and found quiet solace in their company. Regardless of them being beasts, they accepted and trusted him for what he was. They held no expectations nor did they look at him with constant concern in their glowing red eyes.

"Hey Cyrus!"

"Oh, hey Jess," he greeted the other keeper as he walked into the den. "Sorry, I didn't realise you would be here today."

"Oh, the more time I can spend with the hounds the better, really," the girl smiled as she fussed over some of the young pups in the centre of the den. "It's good to see you, though."

Jess was a boundling to a demon named Titus. A dealer demon like Marcus and Ambrose, although, unlike them, he offered almost all of his sacrifices to opportunity bind to him, keeping as many as he could near him, practically hoarding them. Titus was part of Lena's inner circle although not part of her council. He had been invaluable in her and Cyrus' escape from Zagan and continued to support the Prince with the aid of his boundlings even now. Jess was a rather exuberant demon, her happy and smiley disposition making her stand out from her generally gruff sire. Like Cyrus, Jess' demonic features were fairly simple, with dark red skin, short red horns and gleaming black eyes. However, compared to the ashy-red of Cyrus' skin and dark blonde hair that practically concealed his crown of horns, she was striking.

"How are you?" she asked as Cyrus made his way to one of the alcoves where a pregnant female was resting.

"I'm okay, thanks," he responding, forcing his body not to bristle at the question. Of course, she meant nothing by it other than genuine interest. He was simply fed up of people asking him *that* question. "How are you getting on?"

"Fine, thanks," she said cheerfully, shooting a wide smile at him.

Cyrus felt sorry for the girl. She'd only been sixteen when sacrificed so looked incredibly young compared to most demons. In time, as she came into more of her own power and spent more time in Hell, her face would change slightly to give her an older appearance, but for now, she still looked like a child. He knew that was part of his problem as well, having been eighteen at his death, he still had quite young features as a human. His demonic face had hardened somewhat, in some part due to the treatment he had endured under his old sire.

Kneeling down beside the hellhound, he inspected her belly, feeling for the pups, noting their size and number.

"How are Zamira's pups settling in?" he asked over his shoulder, as the hellhound stretched out under his touch. Zamira was Lena's hellhound and under Cyrus' personal care. She had imprinted on Lena shortly after the Prince had become a demon. All hellhounds were bound to find a demon they would serve for the remainder of their life, but not all demons were fortunate enough to gain a hellhound of their own. Just over a year ago, Zamira had a litter of five pups who stayed with their mother and mistress until they were old enough to live in the den on their own. One of the male pups, Sollis, ended up imprinting on

Ambrose so remained at the house with his mother. The other four returned to the den their mother had grown up in a few weeks ago.

"They're good," Jess said, walking over to the entrance of the alcove. "One of the females, Luna, I think, wasn't settling too well. She's moved to another den. The others are fine though."

"Good to know," he nodded, giving the hellhound before him a scratch under the chin.

Hellhounds were incredibly large compared to breeds on Earth, generally standing at the same height as an average man. They could grow larger depending on how powerful their demon was, having no powers of their own until they imprinted. Zamira was huge, even for a hellhound, requiring an entire wing in the house for her leviathan-like form. Sollis, whilst now towering above his siblings, was still smaller than his mother. Their bodies were shaped almost like a greyhound, although their snouts were more rounded and filled with deathly sharp teeth, ready to rend flesh from bone on their demon's command. Most had a black coat but some had tones of grey and white mixed in.

"You sure you're okay?" Jess asked innocently. "You seem off."

Cyrus sighed heavily before getting to his feet and turning to look at her. "No offence, Jess, but please don't ask me that. I'm sick of hearing that question."

"Sorry," she said hurriedly, her face falling form hurt. "I didn't mean–"

"I know you didn't," he assured her. "As I said, no offence. I just came here for some peace and quiet, that's all."

"Ah, okay. I'll leave you alone then."

Before he could say anything, Jess spun on her heel and walked off to tend to some of the other hounds. He shut his eyes briefly, taking a deep breath, before moving off to a different alcove where they kept the food and fresh hay for the hounds. It was covered with a faux wall so the hounds couldn't simply get to the food as and when they wanted. He coursed his power over the surface, opening it for him to pass through. He filled up their troughs ensuring, as well, there was sufficient water for them. Lost in his own thoughts, he simply busied himself with checking over the hounds and the den. He didn't even notice when two demons came to the entrance.

"Who are you?" Jess asked, drawing Cyrus' attention towards her. He quickly spied the demons who had arrived, growling slightly as he recognised them. Tucked away in an alcove they hadn't noticed him yet, but he was not going to leave Jess to face them on her own.

"Where is he, girl?" the smaller one asked, jumping down from the ledge into the recessed den. *Damien...* a cambion who had once been closely aligned with Zagan. He lacked in height compared to most demons, but the definition in his muscles beneath his sienna-burnt skin gave evidence to his strength. As per his birthright, deep black markings scrawled across his chest starting from the centre of his collarbone and travelling down over his ribcage. In Cyrus' opinion, they lacked elegance and beauty compared to Marcus'. "Where is Cyrus? We know he's here."

To her credit, Jess stood her ground, neither flinching or balking as Damien stepped towards her. She had moxie, Cyrus would give her that.

"What do you want, Damien?" he called, stepping out of the alcove.

Damien's eyes shot to him, a cruel sneer forming on his lips. "There you are."

Sighing heavily, Cyrus forced himself to walk towards the cambion. He could already feel his skin crawling merely at the presence of Damien. But if he didn't want Lena to get involved, he had to keep calm. "What do you want?" he repeated, moving to stand in front of Jess. "Do not make me ask again, I'm not in the mood."

"Careful, Cyrus," Damien sneered at him, walking closer, his voice barely louder than a whisper. "You may be a Prince's boundling now, but you are still a weakling demon."

Glancing over to the other demon who remained by the entrance, Cyrus noted that he was one of Damien's boundlings, Balo. He'd been bound to Damien for almost five decades now and their reliance on each other was well known. They were rarely far apart from the other to the point where Cyrus had begun to question if there was not more going on between them.

Rolling his eyes, Cyrus folded his arms across his chest. "I'm losing patience, Damien."

"I just want to talk."

"Uh-huh..."

Damien closed the final distance between them, his face mere inches from Cyrus'. Feeling the bile rise in the back of his throat, the boundling pressed his tongue to the back of his teeth, fighting the instinct to swallow. A single finger trailed along Cyrus' jaw, red eyes travelling up and down his body. "Perhaps, you'd like to come back to mine," the cambion sighed, "like old times. We could talk privately there."

*Bingo.*

Slight amusement grew in his chest as he saw Balo shift uncomfortably at the entrance. Possessiveness was a common trait among demons and rarely were younger ones good at hiding it. Even Ambrose had struggled to control his over Lena and he had been six hundred years old when they met.

"The only reason I ever set foot in your place was because Zagan compelled me to," Cyrus retorted. "You're insane if you think I'm going to go there willingly."

"Don't you remember all the fun we used to have?" Damien said licking his lips.

"'Fun' is not the word I would use to describe it," he exhaled sharply, his patience thoroughly spent. "Regardless, I doubt Lena would be too thrilled to feel what you used to do to me."

"Prince Lena can take that up with me if she likes."

"I'm sure she would."

Damien's expression grew dark, his red eyes smouldering with hatred. "That woman you cling to is a pathetic excuse for a Prince of Hell. Surely, you'd be better off binding yourself to someone like Zagan again."

Cyrus couldn't help the snort that escaped him, no longer caring if he pissed the cambion off. "What, you mean someone like you?" he jeered. "You are nothing compared to Zagan. And more over, you are nothing compared to Lena." His smile grew as he saw Damien bristle at the remark. Cambions may have yielded to Lena following her ascension, but not all were happy about it and resentment ran deep within their ranks.

"What about you, girl?" Damien smirked turning his eyes towards Jess. "Titus is hardly worth your time."

Cyrus' body flushed with anger as he stepped to the side, placing himself directly between Damien and Jess. "Leave her out of this, Damien," he warned, a quiet threat in his voice. "Jess, get out of here."

The smile that formed on Damien's lips was cold and menacing. A look that Cyrus had become all too familiar with in his years as a demon. "Oh, so you do want to be alone with me?"

"Hardly," he scoffed haughtily. "Jess—"

"I'm not going anywhere," the girl said firmly.

Moxie, yes. Smart, no.

"Fine," Cyrus sighed. No point in trying to argue with her in this situation. Damien had the advantage as the only fully-fledged demon in the den. Of course, he couldn't compel Cyrus or Jess, but like Jess' sire, Damien hoarded boundlings and Balo was in the prime position to go get more of them if needed. Keeping his eyes locked with Damien's, Cyrus tilted his head to the side, sizing up the shorter demon as best he could. "Now I know you didn't come here just to try and get into my pants, Damien, so what do you want?"

The cambion huffed, folding his arms across his chest. "I want you to take a message to that precious Prince of yours."

"I'm not your errand boy," Cyrus spat at him.

"You will do this, if you don't want to find yourself thrown in the Pit after your old sire," Damien threatened, holding up a finger, the point of his talon just barely touching Cyrus' nose. "The Princes kept their noses out of the dealings of Hell for centuries before Lena came along. She would do well to learn from their example, so tell her to back off. I don't care if she is a Prince or not. She slaughtered cambions and, regardless of who may have pledged to her, we will not allow that to stand. She had better watch her back."

"And you couldn't say that to my face, because?"

The air in the den shifted and Cyrus closed his eyes, both savouring and cursing the familiar feeling of his sire's power filling the room. Lena was here. Her voice ethereal as it floated around the den, echoing off the walls. Flames burst to life to the side of the facing off demons. Damien blanched, taking a step away from Cyrus as his gaze locked on the fire. Without a word, Lena and Titus stepped through the flames, her wings raised proudly behind her.

"P-Prince Lena," Jess stammered, bowing slightly. Cyrus smiled at her reaction. His Prince certainly was one to command respect but she didn't stand for formalities too often. "Titus?"

"Jess, come here. We're leaving now," Titus commanded. The black bands of Jess' bindings glowed and with a sigh, she obeyed.

Seemingly summoning what little bravado he had left; Damien's gaze followed the girl. "See you around, little one," he smirked even as Titus and Jess disappeared in flames.

His anger boiling, Cyrus grabbed Damien by the throat and slammed him back against the recessed wall. He saw Balo from the corner of his eyes start to make a move towards him but halted when Lena cleared her throat. "You lay a finger on her, and I'll rip your throat out," Cyrus whispered to the cambion, his claws digging into the red flesh beneath them, relishing the soft gleam of fear forming in his eyes. Sure it was likely present because Lena was now there but the boundling drank in the sight all the same.

"Cyrus," his sire called to him, walking closer. "Let him go."

Shocked, he looked over his shoulder at her. "Lena?"

"I said, let him go," she repeated, nodding her head in confirmation. She didn't compel him as Titus had Jess, but Cyrus knew if he pushed back, she would.

"Listen to your Prince, twinkle," Damien goaded him even as he gasped for breath under Cyrus' grip.

"Insult him again, Damien, and I won't stop him from killing you," Lena snapped, irritation clear in her voice. "Cyrus, let him go."

Snarling with disgust, the boundling pushed away from Damien. The derogatory nickname the cambion had given him made him irrationally angry, but there was little he could do to act on such anger at this point. At least he knew his sister wouldn't stand for further insult to him.

"Wait outside for me," Lena ordered him. This time she did compel him, although he wasn't exactly sure why. His bindings resembled lightning, thin jagged lines refracting over his arms, shoulders and back as if he had been burnt by her power. They glowed softly at the command as his feet began to move towards the entrance of the den. He didn't fight so felt no pain, but let his anger build within him as he walked into the corridor and came to a stop a few strides from the archway. From the corner of his eye, he spied Balo taking a similar position on the opposite side, his sporadic, angular bindings glowing from his own commands.

Swallowing against the lump in his throat, Cyrus leant back against the corridor wall. Lena didn't compel him often and when she did, she usually had good reason to. But he was struggling to understand her reasoning here. Why did she have to interfere? He could have handled the situation. As part of her council, he had more than enough power now to deal with the likes of Damien. Why couldn't she give him the chance to show her that? To show her that he could handle himself.

After a while, Damien strode out of the den, thunder on his face. He turned down the corridor, not even glancing at Cyrus, pulling Balo along with him. Lena exited close behind him, her gaze watching closely as the cambion and his boundling disappeared from view. Cyrus braced himself as Lena turned and looked at him, walking towards him slowly.

"You didn't have to come for this, Lena," he said as calmly as he could manage.

"Of course, I did," she said, coming to stand in front of him. As demons their eyes were almost level, with hers only slightly above his. Times like this, he much preferred to talk to her in human form where she was smaller than him. "I can't have demons thinking they can do whatever they want when it comes to my boundling."

"I was handling it."

"It didn't look that way to me."

"You didn't give me a chance."

Lena sighed and hung her head, her hands on her hips. "I knew the moment Damien came into the den. I could have intervened a lot sooner, but I didn't."

Until then his anger had been directed generally at the situation. Now it was focused solely at his sire. "I am not a child, Lena!" he shouted, his fists clenched painfully by his sides.

Shock washed over her face as she took a step away from him. "I know that," she said calmly, her brow furrowed in confusion. "Cyrus, I know."

"Do you?" he pressed on, but he forced his voice to a more reasonable volume considering their location. He'd kept quiet for too long now. He needed her to understand. He needed her to hear him. "Because all of you treat me like I am! All of you treat me as just a boundling. Could you just for once, look at me and not make me feel like I am lesser than you?"

"Cyrus... I... of all my council you—"

"I know I am the weakest," he interrupted, his nostrils flaring as hurt and self-hatred coursed through his chest. "But you don't need to remind me of it every day."

"That was not what I was going to say," Lena snapped, stepping forward and pushing against his chest, forcing him back against the wall with a thud. His anger flaring, he lunged forward and swung at her, his fist only connecting with air as she deftly ducked under his arm and slammed her palm into his ribs, sending him stumbling to side. "Enough!" she shouted. His bindings glowed forcing him to obey the command, his rebelling mind causing pain to sweep through him at his defiance. Pinching the bridge of her nose, she took a deep breath to steady herself. Cyrus knew his anger would be affecting her, but he could no longer control it. "I'm sorry," she said finally. "I'm sorry if I make you feel that way. Above all, you are my brother. More so than the other Princes. And maybe, I'm a little protective of you because of that."

Cyrus huffed with annoyance, throwing his hands in the air. "Can't you understand?" he cried. "I used to protect you. You were my *little* sister. You are not meant to protect me!"

"Why?" she yelled, her eyes gleaming with his anger. "Why can't I protect you? Why can't I protect what I love?"

"You can. Of course, you can," he sighed, a sense of defeat creeping in. She was right, of course. As his Prince and sire, she could protect him from almost anything. And she was good at it. She proved that time and time again. But he didn't have to like it. "I... I just don't want you to think that I can't protect you like Marcus and Ambrose can because I'm bound to you or because you see me as your brother. I want to protect what I love too."

Silence fell over them, but Cyrus was thankful that at least it was not uncomfortable. With a heavy sigh, Lena stepped forward and took hold of his hand, pulling his gaze back up to hers. Her eyes were gentle and warm, as she gathered her flames around them and took him back home.

# CHAPTER FOUR

There was a tense hum in the air, shifts of power causing vibrations to bounce off the walls of Hell as Ambrose and Marcus made their way through the corridors to Archie's chambers. They didn't speak, feeling no pressing need considering the situation they were facing.

Since becoming Lena's Consort, a few of Ambrose's demonic features had changed, most notably his height as he now towered at just over eight feet tall. His dark red skin and the black tattoo across his chest remained the same. He was not a cambion, but Zagan had marked him with the tattoo as a boundling for reasons that Marcus had yet to find out. However, where Ambrose's horns on his head and arms used to have a simplicity to them, they now twisted and curled with jagged edges that could be used to tear at his enemies as efficiently as the long talons at the end of his fingers. After his ascension, horns had burst from his back, matching those already formed on his shoulders and upper arms, running down his spine protecting him from attacks from behind. His black hair which he generally pulled into a short ponytail as a human, formed into a long braid down his demonic back, swaying gently as he walked, the tie brushing along the waistband of his trousers. There were certainly demons with more terrifying features, but Marcus appreciated the regal elegance of his friend, especially so with the position of power he now held.

Coming to a stop before a stone door, almost invisible within the red rock of the residential cavern, Ambrose lifted his hand and knocked loudly. Marcus shifted closer to him, eyeing the demons cautiously that ambled around the cavern. Lena and Ambrose, as relatively new Prince and Consort of Hell, were still prime targets for demons seeking to gain power for themselves. They never ventured to Hell alone for that reason. The door opened and Archie welcomed them inside, quickly closing the door behind them.

"Ambrose," Archie said, clasping his arm warmly in greeting as a friend and comrade. "Marcus."

"Hey Archie," Ambrose said walking further into the room. "What's up?"

Archie's red skin was lighter than Ambrose's, although it was difficult to tell in the light afforded by the torches. His black horns were smooth, gleaming in the torchlight like polished ivory, coming to sharp points above his head. Bright red wings pulled close to his back even as the three men sat at his table. "How much do you know at the moment?"

"Lena brought me up to speed last night," Ambrose confirmed, leaning back in the chair and folding his arms. "She's down with Asmodeus and Mammon at the moment."

"Good, she's safer down there."

"Safer?"

The demon sighed, closing his red eyes for a moment before explaining. "After Damien's approach of Cyrus the other day, I've had Titus following him for a bit. He's amassed more of a following than we first thought. More than Asmodeus warned Lena about."

Marcus chuckled at the absurdity of the thought, although the gravity of the situation was not lost on him. "Zagan was the only one we knew who was capable of successfully coordinating the cambions. Damien barely registers on the power scale after him."

"And yet, he's managing it," Archie said pensively. "He was Zagan's right hand, after all. It seems the cambions' believe he will best continue Zagan's work."

"Making cambions the ruling race," Marcus sighed heavily, rubbing at his temple. *Idiots*. The Princes ruled Hell. Disregarding Lena's origins, Lucifer used to be an angel and the others were born from the deepest fires of Hell. None of the Princes were cambions. So why did they think they had any greater right than the most powerful demons known to exist?

"Apartheid is not exactly a new concept down here," the Consort shrugged. "I'm pretty sure Hell invented it to be honest."

The demonic-trainer chuckled slightly. "We did. And no, it's not."

Ambrose clicked his tongue, a look of concern etching into his features. "How worried do you think we really need to be?"

"Personally, I don't think it's anything we can't deal with."

"What about the cambions that pledged to her after the Cleansing?" Marcus asked, leaning forward on his elbows, raising his wings slightly as Archie's chair dug painfully into them. How in the hell did he like these chairs? Marcus had spent a number of years finding armchairs that comfortably accommodated him and he refused to move anywhere where those chairs didn't follow.

"Most of them are still loyal to Lena," Archie shrugged, turning his gaze to the cambion. "They won't risk getting on her bad side. Regardless of their desire for power, they are scared of her, which is just as persuasive an argument as the next one for them. But there are enough powerful cambions siding with Damien, that they might be swayed if we don't act swiftly. Unless Lena wants to wipe out their entire race—"

"Hey," Marcus cried with mock offence, barely keeping the smile threatening to form on his lips at bay.

"Present company excluded of course," the trainer continued with a warm smile, his eyes crinkling with good humour. "I think we should find a way to shield her from any possible fallout. She has enough to worry about with Raphael top-side, she doesn't need to be watching her back in Hell as well."

Ambrose sighed heavily, halting the conversation for the moment. His eyes were shut and his brow furrowed as he retreated into his thoughts. "Well, Lena and I are due to spend a few days in the lower ring with the other Princes and Consorts soon. Perfect opportunity for you two to do what you do best."

It was Marcus' turn to sigh as he stared at the top of the table, images of his rampage against the cambions a year ago playing out in his mind. He held no regrets for what he did back then. He'd done what he needed to do to protect his Prince and his family. There was no shame in that. And he would do it again in a heartbeat if he needed to, but perhaps another approach was needed now. "I'm not sure recreating the Cleansing will be as effective as it was last time. We should have killed Damien back then."

"Lena hoped by sparing him, any that were silently loyal to Zagan would fall into line," Ambrose said, although nodded in agreement.

"I know, but its backfiring on us now," he said, resting his chin on his hand, trying to reason through in his mind what steps they should take. "The problem is, taking him out now will make him a martyr among cambions. We can't just kill him."

"So, bring him to our side," Ambrose said, leaning forward. "Get him to publicly pledge to Lena. That should quell the other voices. If he is indeed leading the dissent, then gaining his favour would destroy that."

"And how would you propose we do that?" he scoffed. Naturally, it was the right course of action, but how in the Hell did Ambrose expect them to pull that off?

The Consort laughed softly. "How would I know?"

"You're the politician."

Archie threw back his head and laughed loudly; a deep, belly laugh that brought tears to his eyes. Ambrose and Marcus stared at him in shock. The demon was not known for outbursts of emotion.

Joining in his laughter, Ambrose shook his head. "You insult me, Marcus," he chuckled. "Everyone has a weakness, something that can be exploited to persuade at the very least, obedience." He paused momentarily, chewing his bottom lip in contemplation. "Start with Damien's boundling, Balo. They've been inseparable even before the Cleansing. Oh, and bring Cyrus in on this. He knows more about Damien than any of us. See what he thinks."

Marcus felt his body flush at the boundling's name. "Are you sure?" he asked, looking at his friend.

Archie also appeared to have his reservations. "Should we ask Lena first?"

"Lena and I have already talked about this. She wants him involved more, anyway," Ambrose continued without pause, either not noticing or ignoring their hesitation. With a sigh, he got to his feet, Marcus and Archie following suit. "Ignore the fact that he is her boundling, he lived with Zagan for a decade."

"You lived with Zagan for a century," Marcus said, folding his arms across his chest.

"Five hundred years ago," the Consort scoffed. "No, Cyrus needs to be involved. He is a fellow council member after all and his life is directly tied to Lena's survival. Bring him in."

"I'm not sure–"

"Marcus, do not question me on this," Ambrose interrupted harshly.

"Take it as an order if you need to."

Turning on his heel, the Consort made his way to the door. Nodding to Archie, Marcus quickly followed his friend out. It wasn't that he had anything against the idea of bringing Cyrus in, as such. But the boundling was a hot head and was not very good at keeping his temper in check. Of course, demons needed a fire in their belly to survive Hell, but they also needed to learn how to control it, and use it as and when needed. To learn how to not be controlled by it. Cyrus was too young to have learnt that. He may be older than Lena, but she had gained the full knowledge and experiences of her Princely siblings when she became a Prince, so had the temperament of a demon much older than she was.

And then, there was his attraction to deal with.

So far, he and Cyrus had very little to do with each other directly. They were fellow members of Lena's council, but they served vastly different functions. Dealing with threats to their Prince, such as Damien and the other cambions, was Marcus' role. Bringing Cyrus in, even just for his opinion, would mean that he could no longer avoid the young demon on a regular basis. However, that did present the enticing prospect of finding out more about the boundling. Of finding out if the glances he had been sending Marcus' way were just glances, or something more. Of perhaps, finding out if Cyrus' desires aligned with his own.

Staring at Ambrose's back as they walked, Marcus tried to deny the small seed of excitement that settled in his belly at the possibility.

A few days after his argument with Lena, Cyrus was hiding out in Zamira and Sollis' wing, giving the younger hound a bath. Well... *attempting* to give him a bath. The result so far was that Cyrus had been splashed with more water than the beast.

When he and Lena had gotten back from Hell, they had tried to talk, but she had been swiftly called away by Archie, leaving Cyrus to once again feel like he was being left out. Like he was being pushed to the fringes because he couldn't handle whatever they were dealing with. What was it going to take to get them to see him as an equal? How much longer was he going to have to suffer their babying of him?

"Sollis, come on!" he cried, chasing the beast round the outskirts of his den. "Don't make me get Ambrose. *Please.*"

At the mention of his master's name, Sollis looked back at Cyrus, forgetting where he was going and slammed into the wall with a yelp. Zamira had been sleeping in the corner but at the whimpering of her son, raised her head to growl at him. Cyrus chuckled at the silent exchange between mother and son, lifting the cloth as Sollis sauntered over to him, his snout practically dragging along the ground.

"Cyrus, are you in here?"

"Yeah," he called back, turning his head to the door. "Hey, Ambrose."

Stopping in the doorway, the Consort took in the scene before him. "Sollis..." he groaned, shaking his head as he made his way further into the room. The young hound bounded over to his master, who with wide eyes, quickly flamed out of the way, reappearing beside Cyrus. "No, sit!" The beast skidded to a halt before letting his hind haunches fall to the floor in obedience. "I have no desire to be covered in wet fur today, thank you."

Cyrus laughed, dropping the cloth he had been using into the bucket. He let his black flames course over his body, quickly drying his clothes. "I should have gotten you sooner."

"Yeah," Ambrose sighed, shaking his head as he turned to face the boundling. "Cyrus–"

"Don't ask me if I am 'okay'," he quickly interrupted.

Ambrose laughed heartily before clapping him on the back warmly. "I wasn't going to. Your sister would like to see you."

Groaning loudly, Cyrus looked up at the ceiling. He'd been avoiding her the last few days. He felt bad about what he said to her, but also didn't feel like he needed to apologise over it. It was perfectly valid for him to feel as he did. *Right?* "She still pissed at me?"

"She was never pissed at you," Ambrose assured him.

Looking along his nose at the demon, Cyrus regarded him sceptically. "Do I need to be worried?" he asked cautiously.

"No," the Consort said, smiling at him. "But you should hurry. I think you'll be happy to hear what she has to say." Sighing, he turned and lifted the cloth out of the bucket. "Guess, I am getting wet fur on me today. I'll take over washing Sollis."

"Thanks," Cyrus chuckled, making his way to the door as Sollis raced over to his master, his bright red tongue hanging out of his mouth. Where Zamira was a stoic, lady of leisure in her demeanour, her young son was a mischievous rascal. "Where is she?"

Scratching his hound under the chin, Ambrose wrung the wet cloth over his back, scrubbing in the soap with his fingers. "Her altar room. Where else?"

His mind racing, Cyrus made his way upstairs to Lena. Her altar room was placed in the eastern corner of the house. A perfectly square room with rows upon rows of shelves lining the walls, holding up various jars and vials filled with magical herbs and elixirs. In the centre of the room, Lena's conduit, a crystallised book sat proudly atop an ebony lectern. Seven black candles infused with sage and camphor burned constantly in a circle around the stand, their flames muted, casting no light or shadows.

"Hey, Lena," he called, taking a deep breath as he walked inside, careful to remain outside of the circle.

"Hey," she smiled at him as she looked up from her work. The power she had been coursing over the book receded into her. With the conduit she could see through different realms and realities, viewing both the past and glimpses of the future. She could track and view current events as well, making it the perfect tool for both her creation of cursed objects and spying on her enemies. "Come in, I want to talk to you about something."

"What is it?" he asked, walking over to a small table she had set up in one of the corners of the room for meetings. Her altar room also functioned as her office, where she would meet with her council and other demons as needed. Pulling out a chair, he sat down, regarding his sire carefully.

She was quiet for a moment as she simply looked at him. "You were right," Lena sighed finally. Holding his breath, Cyrus stared at her, his brows pulled together at he tried to gauge what she was thinking. "I have been treating you like a child. I want to stop doing that. Sometimes, I forget that you have been a demon longer than me." Turning towards him, he saw sadness in her eyes, their usual warmth replaced with a cold regret. "But I need you to understand, that as my brother, I can't help that I worry about you. I worry about all my council. You are my family. I want to protect all of you. But I also realise that I can't be everywhere all the time. *And...* I can't look over all of you, all the time. So, I want to offer you something. Ambrose and I will be away for a few days. It is the year anniversary of my becoming a Prince and we will be in the lower ring with the other Princes and Consorts in celebration." She stepped towards him as Cyrus tried to slowly let out the breath he had been holding. "I will leave you here as my voice for that time."

Forget about slowly, his breath expelled sharply, shocked at her declaration. "Not Marcus?" he asked, considering the cambion was essentially her favourite general.

"No, but he will be your guide for that time. As will Archie," she said, folding her arms across her chest. "Marcus and Archie have been carrying out some work for me within the cambion ranks. There are some that, despite Marcus' efforts last year, are still sowing dissent against me. Still trying to resurrect Zagan's work in marking them as superior to other demons. Something that Damien alluded to you the other day, but we've now confirmed to be true. They have been undertaking reconnaissance missions, reporting back to me on things they have seen and heard, then guiding me on what my next action should be. I would like for you to take that over in my absence." Sighing, she let her gaze drop to the floor before continuing. "You lived among cambions for ten years and were subject to one of the most powerful cambions Hell has ever known. As such, I believe your experience and your opinions will be invaluable. Marcus is the perfect assassin and as a cambion himself, he is well versed in their nature. Archie is a brilliant tactician and understands the movements and motivations of the factions. Listen to them, follow their guidance. But remember," she said firmly, holding up her finger to drive home her point, "*you* are in charge. Do not let them push you around."

Cyrus could barely believe what he was hearing. Was she really going to entrust this to him? "I'm assuming you are going to tell them not to," he said reproachfully.

"No," she said shaking her head, pulling out a chair next to him and lowering herself onto it. "Ambrose has already told them they are to consult with you. I will tell them the rest of my instructions, but I will leave it to you to assert your authority. Otherwise, I might as well still be treating you like a child."

"Lena..." he breathed, leaning forward and taking one of her hands in both of his. She squeezed his hands tightly, her motherly warmth finally returning to her eyes. "Thank you," he said earnestly.

"You're welcome," she smiled. Leaning to the side, she pulled a small crystal from her pocket and pressed it into his palm. Looking at it, he could feel the power vibrating from it. Lena's power. "If anything does go wrong and you need me, break it. In the lower ring I will not be able to feel you as easily as I do up here. The crystal will call me back."

He chuckled. "Fair enough."

"Good luck."

After leaving her, Cyrus headed to his room, laying down upon his bed, going over what she had said to him. She was finally giving him a chance to show her that he could still protect her, like he had when they were kids. He knew he had to keep his emotions, and his temper especially, in check during this time. But he vowed he would. He would not disappoint her or give her any cause to lose faith in him. He would show her, show all of them, the rest of the council, that he could be relied on.

# CHAPTER FIVE

After Lena and Ambrose left, Cyrus found himself sitting in the outside lounging area with Archie and Marcus, as they talked him through the current situation with Damien. He could tell that Archie was not overly happy with the prospect of taking orders from him, but Marcus seemed more at ease with the idea than he had expected.

"Damien has gotten the support of at least five high power cambions," Archie explained, lounging happily on the bench along the wall. The little sunlight that broke through the canopy danced across his face, his eyes closed as he enjoyed being top-side for a period. "Whatever they are planning we are not yet sure of. We're assuming, based on what Asmodeus told Lena, that they are planning an assault on her of sorts. Something to destabilise her position with the other Princes."

It wasn't often Archie came top-side, so Cyrus was not used to seeing him in human form. His brown skin was perfectly highlighted by the desert sun, gleaming with warm tones of chocolate and molasses. Flashes of red could be caught within his long dark hair as it sprawled around his head on the bench.

Cyrus folded his arms across his chest, leaning back into the chair by the railing, the sun bearing down on his back and neck. "Do you really think they could threaten her position with them? They were all ecstatic when she took up the mantel of the eighth Prince."

"Personally, no, I don't think they could," the demonic-trainer said, shaking his head slightly. "My feeling is that Asmodeus, Mammon and

Abaddon would support her without question. Even Satan to a point."

"I highly doubt Lucifer would turn on her," Marcus added, his elbows resting on the table in front of him, his eyes locked on some distant point no one else could see. "Belphegor and Beelzebub are a different matter."

"How so?" Cyrus asked.

"At the time, they were in agreement that Lena remain bound to Zagan rather than be returned to Ambrose."

"I didn't know that."

"Only Lena and Ambrose knew that until a few days ago," the cambion sighed, his eyes refocusing as he looked at the boundling. "They hadn't even told me. Mammon was also of that opinion but as she benefits more than anyone from Lena's object creation, I can't see her jeopardising that relationship now."

Cyrus inhaled deeply, dropping his head back against the back of the chair, looking up into the canopy. "Okay. But they need her to find the ninth Prince. And it took them so long to find her. Would they really risk throwing her out and restarting their search?"

Marcus shook his head. "Lena doesn't think so. She's certain that her siblings would not fall for Damien's ploy to make her look weak."

"But we think it's best to look at everything with a healthy amount of scepticism," Archie groaned as he swung his legs off the bench and pulled himself into seated position, resting his elbows on his knees. "Lena may be turning a blind eye when it comes to her siblings."

"Our role as her council is to think of and anticipate things that she may not. Head off threats to her, even if they turn out to be nothing," the cambion explained.

"Good point," Cyrus conceded. He knew that the two demons did a lot for Lena, but he hadn't fully appreciated how much. They saw and thought of things, he hadn't even considered, regardless of the fact that he should have. He was smart, and saw things that most didn't, generally speaking. Perhaps he'd been letting his irritation at being treated differently to the rest of the council cloud his judgement...

More than ever, he felt the sting of having been left out when it came to protecting their Prince. He had promised her as kids that he would for the rest of his life. It hurt, realising, that she had been deliberately keeping him from fulfilling that promise. Especially considering what they had gone through together with Zagan. But she was trying her best to rectify that. So, he had to try his best now.

"Ambrose said you know Damien better than any of us," Archie said, drawing his attention back to the conversation. "And I'm inclined to agree. So, tell us about him."

Huffing slightly, Cyrus contemplated his answer. "He's arrogant," he said, staring at his ankles crossed in front of him. "Although, I know that's a well-known fact about him. But he's also scared of Lena. I saw that the other day in the den."

"If he's scared of her, why would he be moving against her?"

Cyrus shrugged, not because he didn't know the answer, but because the answer seemed as obvious to him as the question. "He was the same way with Zagan. To his face, Damien was the perfect subservient, but behind closed doors he would get overly mouthy." Taking a deep breath, he had to force himself to continue, trying desperately to keep his mind focused on his explanation rather than the memories from which it was formed. "Zagan would send me to Damien frequently for... well... for whatever he wanted really." He shifted uncomfortably, closing his eyes as he pressed on. "Once alone, it was almost like Damien would forget that Zagan could force me to tell him everything that happened or was said to me. And he would. It was how Zagan kept an eye and ear on all of his so called 'allies'. He didn't trust any of them. He commanded respect through fear. Damien forgets himself when he's around demons he considers lesser than him. And he considers most demons lesser than him simply because he is a cambion."

"So, he's easy to get talking," Archie sighed, leaning back against the brick wall, folding his arms across his chest.

"Absolutely," Cyrus nodded, "if you have the right person for him to talk to. I doubt he'd talk to me the way he used to, anymore. Although, he does still seem to think he could get me into bed with him again. Don't suggest that as a possibility," he said hurriedly, staring harshly at Archie and Marcus pre-emptively. "I refuse to go there."

"Wasn't going to," Marcus chuckled, shaking his head.

There was a slight pause from Archie before he smiled and shrugged. "I mean..."

"Archie," the cambion warned, shooting him a dark look. Cyrus furrowed his brow, wondering what that meant.

"Sorry," the demon apologised, suitably chastised, holding up his hands in defeat. "I didn't really mean it."

"Good," Cyrus snapped, irritated even if it had been meant as a joke.

"Because it's not happening. *Ever.* The only reason I used to sleep with him is because Zagan compelled me to and I can't see Lena compelling me to do the same, can you?"

"I'm sorry, Cyrus," Archie said earnestly, his face softening. "Truly. I know what it is like to be used that way."

Both Cyrus and Marcus straightened, surprised at the confession. Cyrus knew that his experience was not unique for boundlings, but with the way Archie carried himself, it was difficult to imagine someone using him in the same way. "You do?" he asked uncertainly.

Archie nodded, a rueful smile on his lips. "I was a boundling once and my sire acted in much the same way as Zagan."

"I'm sorry."

The demon coughed and shook his head noting the apology was not needed. "Let's just move on, shall we?"

Cyrus sighed, hanging his head, swallowing against the guilt rising in the back of his throat. He hadn't meant to upset Archie. "Yeah," he said softly. "Um, Damien's closest boundling is Balo. I've suspected for years that there was something more between them. Balo confirmed my suspicions the other day."

"How?"

"Damien wanted me to come back to his when he came to the den. Balo's possessiveness kicked in. He looked at Damien the same way Ambrose looked at Lena when she first saw me again."

Marcus laughed, finally breaking the tension that had settled over the trio. "Well, that's damning evidence right there," he managed between fits of laughter. Ambrose had really not done a good job of hiding his emotions in the early days of his and Lena's relationship. Even less so as he became more attached to her.

Cyrus smiled before continuing. "I don't think we can get to Damien directly. But I do think we could get to him through Balo. Damien is sloppy in the wording of his commands. Leaves loop holes that can be exploited."

Archie shook his head, not in disagreement, but in confusion. "If Balo is in love with Damien, or whatever he might be, why would he betray him?"

"I'm not talking about betrayal," Cyrus clarified. "But Balo could be persuaded to talk to Damien and I think Damien would listen. If the aim is to get Damien to pledge publicly to Lena, Balo could be used to implant the idea that by doing so, Damien would be securing his position and power. They've basically been joined at the hip for the last fifty years. With how many boundlings Damien has, he certainly seems to favour Balo above all others."

"Would we possibly not be better simply approaching Damien with an offer?" Marcus asked, wiping the last few tears from his laughter away.

"No." Cyrus shook his head emphatically. "He's stubborn. He won't accept an offer from Lena directly or otherwise. But if he thinks it's his idea and he approaches Lena with an offer which she accepts, he'll see that as a victory."

"Not bad," Archie mused with a soft approval in his voice. Cyrus was surprised at the warmth that washed through his chest hearing it. "So, what kind of idea do we want to implant."

"There's only one thing Damien wants," he shrugged. "Control of the cambions."

"That's unlikely to ever happen," Marcus scoffed.

"No kidding. But perhaps, if the idea that he could have a high-ranking position, supported by Lena, were presented, he might see this as sufficient to give up on his other pursuits."

"Okay, but who should talk to Balo?"

"Not me," Cyrus chuckled ruefully, letting his head again fall back onto the chair. "He's was jealous of me even when I was bound to Zagan. He wouldn't listen to a word I say."

"Could we ask Titus?" Archie asked.

"Oh no. Damien's boundlings aren't allowed to go near Titus without him present. Not after Titus took two boundlings from him. Willingly, of course."

"Ha!" Marcus burst out, his voice full of satisfied glee. "I didn't know about that."

"Yeah," Cyrus sighed. "It didn't go down well."

"I bet."

"Pasha."

"Huh?"

"Pasha could talk to him," Cyrus nodded. "Regardless of her known allegiance to Lena, she helped raise Damien in the nurseries. He's got a soft spot for her. Balo would listen to her."

"Alright. I like it," Archie said, leaning forward. "What do you think Marcus?"

"It's a good idea," Marcus agreed. "Not simple, but good ideas are rarely simple."

"Okay," Archie huffed as he pushed up to his feet, placing his hands in his trouser pockets. Looking at Cyrus, he asked; "Are you happy for me to speak to her or would you prefer to?"

Cyrus sighed, closing his eyes. Why did the question feel like a trap? "What did Lena say to you?" he asked, firmly believing she had involved herself beyond what she told him she would.

"Nothing," Archie assured him. "Cyrus, you are young and I don't know you very well yet. Not like how I know Ambrose and Marcus. But Lena has left you in charge and I trust her judgment. This was your idea, and for what it's worth, I think it's a good one. So, tell me what you want to do."

Still eying the demon sceptically, Cyrus shook his head. "I don't know Pasha very well. Zagan didn't care for her. You go."

"Okay," Archie nodded, stepping out into the courtyard. "I'll be back soon."

Once clear of the canopy, Archie disappeared in flames, leaving Cyrus and Marcus alone.

Pushing himself up to his feet, Cyrus walked to the edge of the canopy and the courtyard, leaning against the pillar, letting the heat of the sun bear down on his face. He could feel Marcus watching him and wondered if the cambion knew how obvious he was being. Enjoying the sensation, Cyrus made no move to bring attention to it, allowing himself simply to retreat into his thoughts, replaying the recent conversation.

There were always other options of bringing Damien and the cambions into line. He agreed that sending Marcus to reenact the Cleansing would have little to no effect anymore. The cambions had learnt all they would from such actions. Cambions desired power but they weren't stupid. They knew that Lena could wipe them out if she truly wanted to, which is why they yielded to her so quickly after her defeat of Zagan. She had no love for their kind, other than Marcus, and even those that had pledged loyalty still clambered for her continued favour. So why did Damien seek to move against her now? A year had passed without incident. Cambions were thriving, other demons were thriving, all due to the massive influx of power when Lena ascended. What had changed?

"Why now?" he asked suddenly, staring into the sun.

"What?"

Smiling, Cyrus could tell he had pulled Marcus from some deep thought. "Why now?" he repeated, turning to face the older demon. "It's been a year since Lena became a Prince and Damien is choosing *now* to make a move. Why? It's got to be the worst possible time. Demons that are loyal to Lena will be revelling in the celebrations. Demons that are afraid of her will be remembering her wrath from the days following. Emotions are too high, too raw. It doesn't make sense."

Marcus sighed heavily and rested his chin in his hand. "Good questions. I'm not sure," he pondered. "For so long the Princes have been absent, simply letting the rest of us do as we wish. Lena's arrival has changed all of that. Suddenly, the Princes are overseeing things again. I would guess, that with Lena and the other Princes being in the lower ring, they feel they can move freely for the next few days."

Only Princes and those they took with them could enter the lowest ring of Hell. The domain for Lucifer, it was a kind of fallout shelter for the Princes. The aim was for them to co-ordinate the Apocalypse from there, protected from any attacks by the forces of Heaven. But a side effect of that meant that the Princes were, in a way, blocked off from the dealings of Hell. They could not as readily observe or intervene in the actions of their demons. It was why the Princes needed their councils. Demons they could trust to continue carrying out their orders in their absence.

"We'll need to think of a way of controlling Damien, should he fall in line with our plan," Cyrus said, turning back into the sun. "Publicly pledging to Lena is not enough. He'll get everything he wants and we'll have no way of ensuring he only uses that for our purposes."

"We could use Balo to control him, if they really are as close as you think."

Cyrus bristled at the idea, regardless of its merit. "You thinking of getting Lena to overtake his binding?" He felt sick at the suggestion. Do to Balo what Zagan did to her? He couldn't imagine her agreeing to that.

"No," Marcus said, getting to his feet and leaning on the pillar opposite him. "Lena would never do that. And I'm not sure she'd cope with two of you."

Allowing himself to find the humour in it, Cyrus joined in Marcus' laughter. He knew it was driving Lena insane with how much she could feel from him, never mind dealing with another set of emotions. Whether or not she would feel as much from another boundling was uncertain, but she was desperate enough for him to break from her.

"It will depend, I guess," the cambion continued, "on, firstly, if Balo goes for suggesting the idea to Damien and secondly, if Damien listens to him. Let's wait to see what happens. There will be a time of negotiation in which we can assess how best to assert control."

The pair fell silent, each embracing the sun's warmth. As discretely as he could, Cyrus studied Marcus. The sun gave the cambion's olive skin a warm glow, perfectly complementing the golden tones of his hair. The green of his eyes sparkled like emeralds, brilliant and glinting with both a wealth of intelligence and life experience. Mingled within their depths, however, was a pained loneliness that Cyrus desperately wanted to extinguish one way or another.

A slight breeze passed over them, catching at Marcus' hair and tousling the strands across his face. Biting his bottom lip, Cyrus had to fight against himself, forcing himself to not to reach out, wanting nothing more than to run his fingers through the golden tresses.

Sighing heavily, he looked at the ground, folding his arms across his chest, hoping that would help him keep his hands to himself. "You really think it's a good idea?"

"I do," Marcus nodded, turning his face towards the boundling with a warm smile. "Have faith in yourself, Cyrus. It's bad form for a demon to second guess themself."

"I'm not second guessing myself," he said looking up and locking his gaze on the cambion. "I am second guessing yours and Archie's ready acceptance of it."

Marcus raised a brow, but if he was offended it didn't show. "Please, say what you think," he smirked, pressing his lips together.

"Yeah, I'm not stupid enough for that," Cyrus chuckled darkly, pushing off from the pillar and heading off across the courtyard. He found himself suddenly needing space from the older demon. His infatuation with him was becoming too much. He needed to breathe, to think clearly, and Marcus' proximity made that exceedingly difficult.

"Who on earth said you were stupid?" the cambion called after him.

"Forget it."

"Cyrus?"

"I said forget it, Marcus," he snapped over his shoulder. "Let me know when Archie gets back."

From the corner of his eye, he saw Marcus start after him, before halting only a few steps from the canopy. "Where are you going?"

Sighing, Cyrus reached the opposite wall and opened the door. "I'll be in with Zamira and Sollis. They need a walk." Forcing himself not to look back, he strode inside to the hellhound's den, pulling the door shut behind him. Leaning back against the door, he let his head fall back with a thud against the wood. Sollis bounded up to him, the young hound eagerly awaiting his attention. Closing his eyes, he wrapped his arms around the hound's snout. At least here, he could relax.

# CHAPTER SIX

Pasha had been more than willing to help out with Cyrus' idea. After Archie had spoken with her, she came back with him to the house and together, they had all built on the conversation she was to have with Balo.

In the meantime, Marcus was still running reconnaissance, making sure he knew where Damien was and who he was talking to at all times. But he was getting tired and if he didn't want that to make him sloppy and risk being caught, he needed to sleep soon. When living in Hell, transformed demons could go almost forever without sleep, sustained by the souls that fuelled the fires, unless they exhausted themselves either by overexerting their power or sustaining substantial injury. Living top-side, and in human form, so much meant he was subject to human aliments. He couldn't get sick, but hunger, thirst and exhaustion became common place.

Flaming into the courtyard after his most recent run through Hell, Marcus sighed heavily, breathing in the hot arid air, relishing the cleansing feel as it burnt the scent of sulphur from his nose. It was night, the soft moonlight turning the usually orange and pink granite pavers a soft peach tone. The cacti shrub arrangements were muted, their sharpness softened by the desert haze. Heat still radiated from the red brick and limestone walls, even as a cool breeze tugged at his shirt.

The courtyard had many entrances into the house. From beneath the canopy of the lounging area were two doors, one that led to the kitchen and the other into a storage shed that was not connected to the rest of the house. Opposite was the entrance to the wing for the hellhounds, connecting to the lower hallway. Finally, glass doors that could open the full length of the wall facing the entrance gate encompassed the hallway which ran along the inner length of the house. Situated on the lower floor of the house was the library and offices for Ambrose and Marcus. The upper floor housed the bedrooms which faced into the courtyard with the interconnecting hallway running on the outside wall. Ambrose and Lena had the wing above the hellhounds, separated from the other rooms by Lena's altar room. Marcus' room was on the opposite side, Cyrus' in the middle with one room remaining empty since it had been vacated by Archie. Currently, it was being used as a sort of storage and overflow room.

Marcus loved the house. It was one of the favourite places he had ever lived, reserving the favourite for the cottage he and his parents used to live in. But this house was comfortable. Large enough that the four occupants could move around for their own purposes without disturbing the others, but also small enough they could easily find each other when needed.

Heading to the kitchen, he grabbed a pastry from the counter, quickly devouring it as he made his way up to his room. He hoped he could get a couple of hours sleep before having to check in with Pasha and Archie as to how things were going. He supposed he should also check in with Cyrus at some point.

The boundling confounded him recently. His idea at gaining Damien's compliance was brilliant and not something Marcus had expected to come from the young demon. Refinement was needed, but they had time to sort that out. But since he had stormed off into the hellhounds' wing, he'd been avoiding Marcus which was all the more perplexing.

He was certain now that Cyrus held some attraction for him. The boundling's attempts at slyly studying him were less than discreet and Marcus would secretly admit to studying the demon himself when the opportunity arose. More than once now, he had caught himself actively fantasising about Cyrus, despite his previous reservations. He refused to act on such desires, but gave up on trying to suppress his imagination. Perhaps, if the attraction was still there, he could actively explore some of it once Cyrus broke from his bindings. Marcus had no desire to subject Lena to what he wanted to do to her boundling. Maybe it was because she was absent, and in the lower ring thus removing the threat that she would feel it as acutely, he allowed his mind to conjure up images of Cyrus within his bed. They could likely get away with a kiss without her knowing or feeling it, but considering how strong their bond was, going much further would almost certainly reach her, even down there.

Contemplating whether it would be a good idea to check if Cyrus was at least home, he stopped in his tracks as the object of his thoughts walked out of his bedroom.

Locking eyes, they simply stared at each other for a moment. Marcus felt the magnetic pull of the doe-brown eyes upon him, coughing quickly to hide any uncertainty on his part.

"Hey," Cyrus said softly, walking over to him, hands in his pockets. "When did you get back?"

"Ah, just now," he shrugged, straightening his back as the boundling came closer. "Damien's been in his chambers for a while now so I thought I would use the chance to catch up on some sleep."

"Do we know how Pasha is getting on with Balo?"

He shook his head. "No. Or at least I don't. Hopefully okay. I think she and Archie are going to come by in the morning."

Cyrus nodded, dropping his head forward slightly. "Um, I wanted to say, I'm sorry."

Shocked, Marcus studied the boundling. "What for?" he asked quietly.

"For my reaction the other day," he sighed, rubbing the back of his neck. "It wasn't fair of me to think you and Archie were only humouring me."

Marcus shut his eyes and pressed his lips together. "Cyrus, I can tell you are a smart kid. But you need to have conviction behind your ideas." Opening his eyes, he tried to convey to the boundling the earnest nature of his words with his gaze. "A certain amount of reservation is healthy, but you also need to stop thinking the rest of us are out to get you, or trying to discredit you. You are a member of the same council and you did a fantastic job of protecting Lena last year. But you let your temper get the better of you. We all do, time to time. You just need to learn when to let the anger out and when to use it quietly. When to turn it into a tool or weapon rather than letting it control you." Cyrus was silent, merely absorbing what was being said to him. Marcus saw the slight glint of hurt in those brown eyes and cursed himself for yet again causing it. "I'm sorry for the lecture. It's just," he sighed, trying to find the right words. "I think... I *believe*, you have a lot of potential, and I don't want to see you fail to grasp it by letting your doubts in yourself win."

Cyrus coughed, dropping his gaze and shifting on the spot. "Lena said you were a good mentor."

Smiling, the cambion felt a wave of warmth course through his chest. He was proud of Lena's accomplishments in her short time as a demon. He was even more proud that she seemed to attribute some of that to him.

"Well," the young demon said, inhaling deeply. "I'm about to head out, so you'll get some peace and quiet for a bit."

"Where are you going?" he asked, surprised at the concern that washed through him, suddenly worried about the boundling's safety considering recent events.

Cyrus' eyes narrowed, studying him. Marcus forced himself not to look away. There was nothing odd about him asking that... was there?

"I'm going to the hellhound den," Cyrus said, his head tilting to the side. "I haven't been there since my run in with Damien. I need to check on them."

Chewing the inside of his cheek, Marcus' eyes grazed hungrily over the boundling's neck, the light tan of his skin inviting him to kiss and bite along its curve. What was wrong with him? He had to be tired if his thoughts were getting the better of him this much. He swallowed quietly before taking a deep breath hoping to fortify himself.

"I'm not sure it's a good idea for you to go by yourself at the moment," Marcus said finally, dropping his gaze to the floor.

"Why?"

"Just thinking that the last time you went, Damien cornered you, and Lena is not around at the moment to step in if needed," he explained as gently as he could. "Also, if anything happened to you, she would flay me."

Cyrus chuckled softly, causing Marcus' eyes to snap up to his face. "I can take care of myself, Marcus."

"I know," he said hurriedly. "I know you can. Um..." he trailed off, rubbing the back of his neck, trying to figure out how to word what he wanted to say without insulting the young demon. "I know you don't like hearing this, but as Lena's boundling you are a way of getting to her.

I can't stop you from going, and I'm not going to force you to, but I do think you should consider taking someone with you, just in case. Just whilst we're dealing with Damien."

"How about you then?" the boundling asked, the flirtatious invite clear in his voice.

Marcus' heart pounded loudly in his ears, beating against his ribs painfully, excited by the idea. But instead, he shook his head slightly. "I'm exhausted. I really need to sleep. You should ask Archie or Titus."

"Alright," he smiled warmly. "Sleep well."

The smile on Cyrus' lips was enthralling, brightening his entire face. He was so close. Too close. His scent and warmth were overwhelming. Marcus knew he had to get away, but he couldn't bring himself to leave, captivated by the demon in front of him. Cyrus looked up through his lashes, the dark brown depths of his eyes ensnaring the cambion, pulling him into their gravity.

His mind went blank, unable to resist, as he stepped forward and caught Cyrus' chin with his hand. Pushing him back, Marcus crushed their lips together in a ferocious and hungry kiss, ignoring the sound of surprise from the young demon. They slammed into the side table behind them, Cyrus clutching the edge of the wood to steady himself as Marcus leant over him, placing his palms flat on the surface, confining the boundling between his arms. Pressing their bodies together, Marcus felt a deep desire awaken within him as Cyrus' youthful body hardened against him. Flicking his tongue against the demon's bottom lip, Marcus growled with approval as his lips parted for him. He delved into the warmth of the boundling's mouth, meeting his tongue in a frenzied dance, hungry to explore every inch of the young demon's body.

What spell had Cyrus cast over him? What power did he possess that made Marcus want to forget everything but the feel of his kiss? *This kiss...*

A loud shattering startled him from his assault on Cyrus' mouth. Breaking the kiss, the pair looked towards the cause of the sound. The green and white vase that had been on the table, jostled by the sudden actions, now lay in pieces scattered across the floor.

Pushing away abruptly, Marcus stared at Cyrus, his chest heaving as he tried to regain control of his breathing. He could only imagine the look of shock and confusion on the boundling's face mirrored his own.

He needed to leave.

*Now.*

"I'm sorry," he managed to blurt out, as he gathered his flames and transported to his room.

Falling back against his door, Marcus lowered himself to the floor, placing his head in his hands. What did he do that for? He'd managed to stop himself from doing something like that for months. Why now? His breathing was still rapid as he strained his hearing to try and determine if Cyrus was still in the hallway. He heard footsteps, shuffling closer but they halted outside the door. Closing his eyes, Marcus swallowed. *Don't knock*, he begged silently. *Please don't knock*. If Cyrus knocked, he would open the door, and God knows what that would lead to.

He exhaled sharply as he heard the igniting of flames. Finally alone, he remained where he was, trying to calm his heart, the pounding of it deafening within him. What had he been thinking? Fantasising was one thing, but to actually act on it was insanity. Lena would kill him if he got involved with her boundling, he was sure of that.

Well... maybe not *kill*, but it was very unlikely she would take kindly to it.

Not to mention what she would do if they did get involved and it ended badly. Her and Ambrose were one thing, but him and Cyrus muddied the waters. It would destabilise everything if they ended up in a situation where they could no longer get along.

As his heart finally returned to its normal rhythm, Marcus pushed himself to his feet. He eyed the bed ruefully, almost disappointed he hadn't just let his desirous instinct take control and lain Cyrus upon it. His chest tightened as the image conjured in his mind. Shaking his head to clear it, he turned away and headed into the bathroom.

Cold showers had worked in the past. Surely, they would work again now.

Turning on the shower, Marcus stripped off his clothes, tossing them in a heap in the corner of the room. Unfortunately, the heat from the day meant the water wouldn't run as cold as he wanted, but he sighed with relief as he stepped into the luke warm stream. He had to do something about this. Lusting over the boundling was becoming unbearable. Either he had to get the boy out of his system or get away completely. He supposed he could drive Cyrus away, put a wedge between them, permanently. Of course, as they were both on Lena's council they couldn't avoid each other forever, but he could put an end to the glances and flirtations. But that would mean hurting the boundling and Marcus couldn't bear to do that. That would make him no better than any other cambion and for some reason the thought of Cyrus looking at him with disgust, anger or hurt, made his stomach twist with anticipatory shame.

No, driving Cyrus away was not going to work. But indulging in a relationship, even just a physical one, was also not a possibility. Or at least, not whilst he was still bound to Lena.

Licking his lips, he could still taste Cyrus on them. The boundling smelt like the smoke from a smouldering fire as it cooled in the early morning mist, mixed with hints of straw and leather. A scent bestowed on him from his work with the hellhounds. Despite the cool water, Marcus' body was hot and hard, desperate for release from the excitement of the kiss. This, at least, was something he could deal with.

Placing one hand on the wall to steady himself, Marcus wrapped the other around his cock, stroking as he closed his eyes, remembering the feel of Cyrus pressed against him. The young body had been as firm as he had imagined it to be. The soft fabric of his shirt had done nothing to cushion the ridges of the muscles carved into his stomach. His lean hips had moulded snuggly against the cambion, shifting instinctually when Marcus wedged one of his knees between his legs. He'd felt the hardened length of Cyrus pressed against his thigh, and was certain the boundling had felt his own in a similar fashion.

If only that vase hadn't fallen, he would have pulled the young demon back into his room and torn his clothing from him, exposing the beauty of his body to his eyes. He would have lain Cyrus over the bed and explored every inch of him with his hands and mouth. He wanted to devour the boundling, consume him in the same way he felt consumed by his infatuation.

Remembering the feel of Cyrus' lips, the permanent pout they had when he wasn't smiling or talking, Marcus wished he could taste them again. Taste his kiss. He'd been so willing, so eager, to allow the cambion's tongue inside. The warmth of his mouth had been intoxicating and Marcus wanted to feel it wrapped around his cock, to watch as the boundling knelt before him with those wide, chocolate-brown eyes looking up at him. His cambion nature pushed him to dominate in the bedroom and he could easily imagine the young demon allowing him to fully indulge in this side of him. He wanted to hold Cyrus down and take him over and over throughout the night, to hear him moan and cry out with pained pleasure.

With a loud groan, Marcus found his release, the warm ropes of his cum firing against the tiled wall of the shower. He was panting from the force that pulsed through his stomach. Grateful for the support of his hand on the wall, Marcus stared at the evidence of his desire, his body calming as the spray from the water against his shoulders began to wash it away. If his imagination had caused such a reaction, what would the real thing do?

After cleaning himself, Marcus stepped out of the shower, drying himself with his power as he strode over to his bed. Not caring about dressing, he fell on top of the covers, burying his face gratefully into a pillow. He really had to get a handle on this. *Or let Cyrus get a handle of me*, he thought masochistically to himself, a rueful smile on his lips.

Sighing heavily, he rolled onto his back and stared at the ceiling.

There had been a time he had wished to find someone, to have some semblance of the love he had seen and been part of between his parents. He'd even thought he'd found it once, much to his misfortune and bitter regret. He forced himself to remember William and the pain he'd felt following his betrayal. How could he be certain that allowing himself to indulge in Cyrus would not end in the same way? He didn't really think that Cyrus would betray him like that, but then he hadn't expected William to either, so maybe he wasn't the best one to judge. And that didn't stop other demons from taking advantage. Not all demons could be as fortunate as Lena and Ambrose, and even they had their trials in the past. Whatever this was, whatever he was feeling for Cyrus, it was dangerous.

But that kiss...

He'd never experienced a kiss like that. One that set his body aflame with desire. Not even with William.

Squeezing his eyes shut, Marcus forced himself to find the quiet comfort of sleep, knowing full well he was going to dream of that kiss. As his consciousness began to drift, a soft smile formed on his lips, welcoming the dreams wholeheartedly.

# CHAPTER SEVEN

*Darkness was closing in around him as his body was pushed roughly into the coarse stone of the wall. Taloned fingers dug into the back of his neck causing a visceral fear to grip at his chest, fully aware of what was coming and yet unable to prevent it. His bindings, harsh angular spirals, glowed and pulsed, sending waves of white-hot pain up his arms, attacking his mind as he tried to fight against the commands whispered into his ear. His sire pressed up against his back, fangs sunk into the flesh of his shoulder. Black fire danced over his skin, desperately trying to heal the damage being done to him, but unable to get ahead of the swift fury. The warmth of his blood ran down his spine as his body was slammed repeatedly into the harsh rock. He couldn't scream, couldn't cry, his mouth clamped shut, commanded not to speak. Compelled to silence.*

*Pain ripped through his side as the talons of his sire dug into his ribs, their sharp points carving a power rune into his red skin. The rune vibrated, burning into him, charged with black lightning that kept his flesh from healing. He couldn't breathe, couldn't think for the malicious actions being taken out upon him. He couldn't move away from the pain, forced to endure it. Closing his eyes, he tried to shut down his mind, to leave his body behind.*

*"You are worthless," his sire whispered to him. "You are beyond worthless. This is all you deserve. All you will ever be good for." His sire's voice was ethereal, barely there yet so loud in his ears, echoing over and over in his mind.*

*The room spun and he fell into the abyss beneath him. At least the pain had stopped. A cold hand gripped at his chest, pulling him further into darkness. Flashes of blue and white light spiked and danced across his vision in waves.*

*There was the sound of sirens, loud and blaring, intermingled with the screeching of tires and a woman's scream. A baby's cry...*

*Lightning flashed in the sky, the deafening thunder causing him to drop to the floor, hands clamped over his ears. "No, no, no!" he screamed, trying to drown out the baby's wail. His head was caught in a whirlwind, unable to focus or find solid ground on which to form a singular thought.*

*"Please," a small voice whimpered. "Please, leave me alone."*

*Panic washed through him as he scrambled to reach the door now before him, its dark green looming over him like a wave threatening to drown him. He had to get to her. He had to save her. That was all that mattered. The monster that stalked her was grotesque, turning to face him as he ripped the door open. The girl sat hunched in her bed, the covers clasped tightly under her chin. Grey eyes pulled him in, gripping at his heart as his body slammed into the monster.*

Cyrus cried out, sitting bolt upright in his bed, sweat dripping from his brow as he pulled his mind from the dream. *Not again*, he groaned internally, dropping his head into his hands, pulling his knees up and resting his elbows upon them.

The dreams were becoming more and more vivid without Lena there to ease his mind. Awake the lingering feelings of the dreams didn't bother him as much, but the images took time to fade. Lifting his head he studied his arms, relieved to see her lightning-like bindings and not the angular spirals of Zagan. They ached slightly, like the memory of his dream had activated his old commands. The red star in the centre of his chest, marking where the knife that had killed him had plunged into his heart, tingled like a healing sunburn.

Looking over to his bedside table he saw Lena's summoning crystal. He needed her. He needed her warmth and comfort. Her guidance. But a nightmare was not sufficient cause to call her back from her celebrations.

Throwing the covers from him, Cyrus pushed himself to the edge of the bed, planting his feet firmly on the floor. The solid wood beneath his feet was comforting, the sweat coating his body cooling even in the warm air. Sighing heavily, he pushed himself up and walked to his bathroom. He needed a shower.

Closing his eyes, he let the water beat down over his shoulders, cleansing him of his dreams. Cleansing him of his fear. The words Zagan had whispered to him still caused him doubt. He knew deep down that Lena did not think of him in the same way. He was not worthless to her.

But whether she had meant to or not, lately he had been feeling worthless. This chance she had given him had lifted that somewhat. Now he wanted to banish it completely. Hopefully, if things went well with Damien and Balo, he could finally let that go. He could finally be free of the memory.

The second part of his dream was easy enough to place. It was the night his parents had died. He had been a little over two years old when they were in a car crash. A crash only he had survived. The crying baby had been him. He didn't consciously remember anything of the crash, but part of binding to a demon is the resurfacing of old or forgotten memories to harden one's mind to the trials of Hell. Hearing his mother's scream before the impact always tore through him, but there was nothing he could do about it. It was just a dream after all.

Finally, the girl... she was Lena, when she was only twelve years old. When their foster father had tried to rape her and he had nearly beat the man to death. It had been the birth of their sibling-like relationship. Of his desperate need to save her, to protect her.

Shaking his head to dispel the thoughts caused by the dream, he attempted to distract himself by remembering the events of yesterday instead.

He'd gotten back from the hellhound den to find Marcus gone. He hoped that the cambion had actually gotten some sleep, but was disappointed he hadn't gotten the chance to ask him about what had happened in the hallway. The kiss had been so sudden but he hadn't minded. It had been wonderful. The final confirmation he needed that Marcus felt something for him. His initial reaction of shock had almost immediately been replaced with longing. He hadn't wanted the kiss to end. He wanted Marcus to take him then and there, disregarding the potential of someone walking in on them in the hallway. The way with which Marcus had held him against the table had been so unbelievably hot, feeling his hardened cock pressing into his hip, their lips crushing together in abandon. God, he wanted more.

But the look on Marcus' face when he pulled away had been one of pure shock, mixed with fear. Cyrus hadn't known what to make of it, so had simply stood there dumbfounded. Why would Marcus be afraid? He had never seen the cambion be afraid of anything, even when Lena had almost decimated the training pits last year.

Letting his head drop back, his face settled into the stream of water, his mind unable to sort everything out now. At least he knew there was a chance something could happen. He would work out the rest later.

Stepping out of the shower, he dried himself before getting dressed. The sun was starting to broach over the walls of the courtyard outside his window. Archie and Pasha would hopefully stop by shortly. Taking a deep breath, Cyrus turned his focus to the matter at hand. Bringing Damien into line. He had to think of some way to control him should he be swayed by the idea of gaining Lena's support. Simply having her favour would not be enough. They needed something they could use to put pressure on Damien if needed. Balo seemed the prime target, but that would mean lowering Lena to the likes of Zagan. Something he couldn't imagine her ever agreeing to. So, he had to think of something else.

He made his way to the kitchen to grab something to eat. Normally, he could go a few days without food, but with the intensity of his dreams of late, he needed both food and sleep more often than he was used to. It had become rather bothersome.

Devouring a bowl of cereal, he caught a flash of flames form the corner of his eye. He walked towards the doorway, looking out into the courtyard to see Archie and Pasha standing in the centre. What he didn't expect to see was Balo standing between them.

"What's going on?" he asked, swallowing the last of his mouthful. Why on earth did they bring Balo here? This was not the plan.

"Ah, Cyrus," Archie said, nodding in acknowledgement to him. "Fortunate timing. Balo wants to talk."

"Uh-huh..."

Dropping his bowl into the sink, Cyrus walked over to the trio, sceptically regarding the other boundling.

"I know you've been left as Prince Lena's voice," Balo said with a curt nod. "You want my help with Damien, I'll speak with you directly."

Glancing towards Pasha, she shrugged. "He's a bright kid. Figured out what we wanted pretty quick."

"I've tried talking with him," Archie said, striding to stand next to him. "He won't speak to anyone but you."

"Compelled or not?" Cyrus asked, directing the question to Balo.

Balo held up his arms showing that his bindings remained their stark black colouring, giving evidence to a lack of commands. At least, currently.

"Alright," he huffed, placing his hands in his pockets. "Come on then. We'll speak in Ambrose's office." Turning on his heel, he walked back into the house, Balo following close behind him. Archie and Pasha took up a seat under the canopy, settling in to wait until the two boundlings were finished. Looking over his shoulder as they walked, Cyrus asked; "Aren't you concerned Damien is going to find out you've come here?"

Balo shook his head, his human blue eyes gleaming in the desert sun like clear spring pools. But there was no warmth to them, their icy depths piercing. "Damien doesn't tend to compel me to tell him where I've been. As long as I don't go back reeking of you, I should be fine."

"Well, there's little risk of that," Cyrus chuckled haughtily.

Holding open the door to Ambrose's office, Cyrus studied Balo as he walked into the room. The boundling's Scandinavian heritage was prominent in his features. Almost pure white-blonde hair adorned the top of his head in a messy swept up style suited to models and celebrities. His skin was pale, but flushed with soft tones of gold and pink. He was attractive, Cyrus would admit, but his desires no longer found Balo's beauty as alluring as he used to. The blonde of his hair was too light, his skin too fair. His slight and slender frame held no comparison to the one Cyrus truly wanted.

Joining Balo in the room, he leant against Ambrose's desk, folding his arms in front of him.

"So, what do you want to say?" he asked cautiously.

Now they were away from the other demons, Balo sighed heavily, his body relaxing somewhat, closing his eyes as his head hung forward. "Look, I'm going to help, if I can," he said, much to Cyrus' surprise. Shifting against the desk, Cyrus straightened, his brow furrowing, wondering what Balo was playing at. "I've already decided it's in my best interests to do so. I have nothing against Prince Lena, in fact, I quite like her." Balo opened his eyes and looked up at him. There was a simple honesty to them. "The fact that a former boundling became a Prince of Hell," he sighed, shaking his head with a slight laugh, "it's incredible. With the way cambions run around like they are the superior demons, it's nice to see that it wasn't one of them destined for that role."

Cyrus smiled at the other boundling. He agreed, it had been nice to see Lena ascend to her throne. Especially knowing that Zagan had once been a candidate for the position. Seeing him be passed over for her had been sweet justice.

"Added to that, I'm also terrified of her," Balo admitted. "I honestly think Damien is being incredibly stupid trying to move against her, regardless of the pressure he's under from other cambions." He sighed and moved to one of the armchairs near the desk. Sinking into it, he crossed his legs and rested his head on his hand, elbow propped on the arm rest. "I wanted to speak with you, because I'm not sure he'll listen to even me on this."

Chewing the inside of his cheek, Cyrus pushed off the desk and sat in the opposite armchair. "If he doesn't listen to you, Lena will be forced to repeat the Cleansing. Starting with Damien."

"Do you think she really would?"

Cyrus nodded. "She would prefer not to, but she will if she has to."

"I was afraid of that," Balo groaned, leaning his head back against the chair. "I'm assuming as you orchestrated for Pasha to speak with me, that you've figured it out. Damien and me."

Chuckling slightly, Cyrus nodded his confirmation. "Honestly, Damien does a good job of hiding it. You, not so much."

Balo laughed, a genuine smile on his lips. "Fuck, it's actually nice to find out that someone knows."

"I am curious though. You and Damien," he started, wondering how to phrase what he wanted to ask. "When Zagan would send me to him, why would Damien even bring me in, considering how close you seem to be?"

The hurt that flooded Balo's eyes was unmistakable. "I'm truly sorry about that, Cyrus. He never wanted to. Damien didn't want to touch you. But he didn't have a choice. Much like how you were compelled to go to him. If he didn't... if he... it was all to protect me. If Zagan found out that Damien didn't want you because he had me, then..." Balo's voice trailed off, his chest heaving like it was trying to shake a heavy weight that lay upon it. "Even that day in the den was just for show. I lost my composure, but he didn't really want to do anything with you. Like all cambions, he has to show he is in control, that he doesn't care for what others think."

"You don't have to explain further," Cyrus said softly. He understood what Balo was trying to say. It was a common fear among all demons that had someone close to their heart. Relationships put you at risk. They could be exploited and twisted to bring you to heel. To force submission and obedience. The exact thing Zagan had put Lena and Ambrose through the year before. Even his sibling relationship with Lena had been used as a method of control by the cambion. "Also, I appreciate the irony that we are essentially leveraging your relationship to ask this of you."

"I don't care about that," Balo said flatly. "Not coming from someone like Lena. It's common knowledge now what she and Ambrose went through, so I believe… I *have* to believe, she wouldn't go too far with it. I also believe that this is in both Damien's and my best interests and as such, worth the risk. So, I will try to talk to him," he sighed as he leant forward, resting on his elbows, his gaze locking with Cyrus. "But I need to ask something first."

"What?"

"If I help you, if I can plant the idea for him to pledge to Lena, can you promise me that Damien will be safe?" he asked, his eyes piercing through Cyrus, quietly begging for reassurance. "Will he be protected? In the same way Lena protects her circle?"

Biting his bottom lip, Cyrus considered what his answer should be. He may have been left as Lena's voice, but it wasn't really his place to make such promises. Certain things, yes. But to promise protections for a demon who was actively seeking to threaten her position was far too big of a thing for him to agree to.

"You were honest with me, so I'll be honest with you," he said finally, looking towards the other demon. "Lena doesn't like Damien. At all. As such, I can't promise that she would protect him." Balo hung his head, but didn't seem all that surprised by the information. "If he pledges to her, publicly, if he can quell the dissent of the other cambions, then maybe. But she will never trust him."

Exhaling slowly, Balo scratched at his neck, falling back into the chair. "Yeah, I figured. It was worth asking though." The two boundlings fell quiet for a while, each lost in their own thoughts. "Well," Balo said after a moment, slapping his hands on his knees as he pushed himself to his feet, "I should get going. Damien doesn't *tend* to ask where I've been, but if I'm gone too long, he might."

"Fair enough," Cyrus sighed, standing as well. "I'd shake your hand, but as you need to avoid '*reeking*' of me, I suppose I should refrain."

Balo laughed heartily, a warm smile on his lips. "Touché, Cyrus. Touché." They both moved to exit the room. Pausing just before the door, Balo looked at Cyrus, a gentle expression on his face. "I truly am sorry for everything Damien and I did to you. But, I'm glad to see where you are now. That Prince Lena has such faith in her boundling."

Cyrus nodded appreciatively. "Thank you," he said. "As nice as this exchange has been, I think we'd be best to act like we still can't stand each other outside of this room."

"I think I can do that."

Exchanging a final smile, Cyrus took a step towards the door putting distance between him and the other boundling as Balo hardened his expression. Opening the door, Cyrus did not expect for them to come face to face with Marcus.

"What the *hell* is going on?"

Rooted to the spot, Cyrus could only stare at the cambion, instantly remembering their kiss the night before. *Dammit*, he chastised himself, this was not the time. Balo may have been open about his relationship with Damien, but he did not want to give away his attraction for Marcus.

"Marcus, hey!" Archie called from the courtyard. The cambion's head snapped round to look at the demon as he ran over from the lounging area. "Hey, wasn't sure when you were going to get back. Balo just wanted to talk to Cyrus."

"So, you left them alone?" Marcus asked harshly, rounding on him.

"Ah?" Archie stopped in his tracks, tilting his head to the side in confusion. "Balo asked to speak with him alone. It's not like anything could have happened in the house."

"Cyrus is Lena's boundling," Marcus stated loudly. Cyrus bristled at the statement, pressing his lips together to stop himself from reacting vocally. "You cannot put him at risk like that. You cannot put Lena at risk like that."

Raising his brows, Cyrus stared at Marcus' back. There had been a poignant pause between the last two sentences. This was an interesting reaction from the cambion. After agreeing that Cyrus could take care of himself the night before, why was he now so angry that he'd had a private conversation with Balo? Of course, the demon's concern could solely be for Lena, but as she was still in the lower circles, she was as safe as anyone could be.

"Marcus?" Archie queried, his expression utterly dumbfounded.

"Forget it," the cambion snapped, turning on his heel and disappearing down the hallway.

The tension remained even after Marcus' departure, Cyrus, Balo and Archie all staring after him, confusion evident across all their faces.

"That common around here?" Balo asked tentatively.

"Not really," Cyrus replied.

"You and he?"

Cyrus forced a laugh. "Hell no," he lied. "You honestly think I would be with another cambion after Zagan?"

Balo joined in his laughter, nodding in understanding, before striding past him and into the courtyard. "See you round, Cyrus. I'll check in with Archie if I get anywhere with Damien."

With a flourish of flames, Balo disappeared.

"I'll go check on Marcus," Archie said turning to head down the hallway.

"No," Cyrus said quickly. Possibly a little too quickly considering the startled look on Archie's face. "I'll go talk to him."

"You sure?"

Cyrus nodded. "Yeah. I need to talk to him about something else anyway."

"Alright," Archie nodded, making his way back to the courtyard where Pasha was waiting for him. "Good luck."

Chuckling, Cyrus headed off after Marcus, firmly believing he was going to need all the luck he could get. Considering the cambion's outburst just now, maybe it wasn't the best time to ask him about the kiss, but he was desperate to see if there would be a repeat so wantonly threw caution to the wind.

# Chapter Eight

What was he doing?

Marcus strode into his room, slamming the door behind him, his heart beating wildly in his chest. When he got home, he'd heard the laughter from Ambrose's office so went to check on it, barely noting that Archie and Pasha were in the courtyard. Seeing Cyrus and Balo alone inside had caused some fierce emotion to rip through him. Something he couldn't put a name to, but it had made his body flush and shake with rage.

What was wrong with him? Had he completely forgotten how to control himself?

The few hours of sleep he had gotten had been filled with dreams of Cyrus. Wonderful, sensual dreams that had left him more frustrated than rested when he woke. But by God, he had enjoyed them.

Sinking onto the edge of his bed, he groaned as he dropped his head into his hands, digging the heels of his palms into his eyes. This was becoming excruciating.

Jumping slightly, his gaze snapped to the door at the soft rap of someone knocking. Cautiously, he got to his feet and crossed the floor, hoping it was Archie coming to question his reaction. He could handle that. Opening the door, his breath caught in his throat as the cause of his recent torture stood before him.

"Cyrus?"

The boundling raised a brow at him, an amused smile on his lips.

Those soft-pink, pouting lips, inviting him in whether they intend to or not. Swallowing hard, Marcus rooted himself to the spot, unable to look away or react as every fibre of his being screamed with want.

"Care to explain what that was about?" Cyrus asked, tilting his head to the side.

Annoyance flushed through him at the question helping to ease the enchanting nature of the boundling enough for him to look away. Taking a deep breath, Marcus turned and walked back into his room. Cyrus stepped into the doorway, leaning into the room as his hands gripped the top of the frame.

"It was nothing," he sighed, trying to fortify himself as he turned back towards the boundling, shoving his hands into his pockets.

"Uh-huh," the boundling said sceptically, eliciting further annoyance from him. "Like that kiss yesterday was nothing?"

His chest tightened with desire at the memory. The casual beauty of Cyrus in his doorframe was sinful. It took all of Marcus' strength to stop himself from crossing the floor and claiming him then and there. He tried to say something, he had to say something, but he had no explanation. There were no words that could describe why he did what he did. Nothing but his lust for the boundling and he couldn't admit to that.

As if sensing his thoughts, Cyrus' eyes drooped and darkened, as he stepped into the room and kicked the door shut behind him, the soft click of the latch echoing through Marcus' mind. Without a word, the boundling strode towards him until they stood a breath apart.

Unable to look away, Marcus' chest heaved with anticipation as the young demon reached up and trailed his fingers along his jaw, letting himself fall into the warmth of the brown eyes that locked with his. Involuntarily, his lips parted, his mind going blank as the boundling took a final step towards him and pressed a gentle kiss to his mouth. Sighing into the kiss, the cambion shut his eyes, simply taking in the sweetness of it. And sweet it was. Unbearably so as the warmth of Cyrus' body melded with his own.

Fists clenched in his pockets, Marcus willed himself to remain still. If he moved, even a little, he was sure he would lose control. There would be nothing stopping him from pushing Cyrus onto his bed and climbing atop him. Where the kiss yesterday had been full of raw desire, this kiss was blissfully seductive, slowly stripping him of his self-control. His body was frozen, but his mouth responded hungrily, opening to allow the languid exploration of Cyrus' tongue, meeting it with his own. The boundling tasted divine, his feel and scent permeating every sense.

"Hm," Cyrus hummed against him. "Still going to say that's nothing?"

"Cyrus, you need to stop," he whispered softly even as his own cock hardened painfully at the thought of laying the boundling down on the bed beside them.

"Why?" the demon asked, stepping impossibly closer and nibbling along his jaw. "Are you really going to stand there and tell me you're not the slightest bit attracted to me? After how you kissed me yesterday?"

Growling, Marcus grabbed Cyrus' shoulders and pushed him back, putting some space between them. "It's not about attraction, Cyrus. You are Lena's boundling. She will feel everything."

"I am not just a boundling," Cyrus snapped at him, pushing his hands off from his shoulders and stepping towards the cambion again. He grabbed a fistful of Marcus' shirt, a wave of excitement coursing over the older demon's chest at the gesture. Smiling playfully, Cyrus leant into him, his upturned top lip inviting Marcus to draw closer. "But if you want, I could be your boundling. At least for today."

Cyrus' eyes were glazed with desire, further chipping away at Marcus' resolve. "Dammit," he ground out as he moved his hands to the demon's neck, pulling him closer and crushing their mouths together. Their lips met hard as Cyrus took hold of his wrists, letting him take control. Marcus darted his tongue out to trace over Cyrus' bottom lip, growling with satisfaction as they parted obediently for him. Sliding his tongue into the warmth of his mouth took the last bit of restraint he had.

Tearing his mouth from the boundling, Marcus stepped back, ignoring the hurt on the bounding's face. Cyrus was a brat, of that he had no doubt. But he wondered how the young demon would react when pushed. Commanded. Dominated.

"Get undressed," he ordered.

The expression on Cyrus' features changed instantly, the hurt replaced with surprise and darkening with desire. His chest heaved as he pulled his shirt over his head, casting it to the side. Unbuckling his belt, his trousers fell easily to the floor which he pushed away with his foot. His cock stood proudly, the head pointed invitingly towards the cambion. Letting his gaze wander over him, Marcus' breath came rapid, his chest tightening as Cyrus' beauty overcame him. The young demon was perfectly formed, the lean, muscular body reminding the cambion of Grecian statues of young athletes and warriors. The boundling was Adonis personified.

Stepping towards him, Marcus trailed his hand over Cyrus' chest, brushing tenderly over the red star, his death mark, before continuing down the demon's stomach, his fingertips grazing over the hard and defined muscles. The boundling had those delicious ridges from his hips trailing to his groin, enticing the eye to his surprisingly impressive length. Marcus fleetingly thought what it would feel like to have the young demon within him, but decided to table that desire for another day. He wrapped his hand around Cyrus' shaft, stroking gently and watching intently as the beautiful man turned to a frenzied mess before him. He wanted to deny his attraction for the boundling, or at least to wait until he broke from his bonds before indulging them. The thought that Lena would feel every action done to her brother made him wary. But the soft moans and irresistible feel of Cyrus were intoxicating, causing Marcus to throw caution to the wind.

"Cyrus, listen to me," he said softly, his hand stilling in its movements, although he didn't let go. "This is all this will be. Do you understand? I am not looking for a relationship. This is just sex." Even though Cyrus nodded, the cambion knew he wasn't listening. He had to try one last time, taking hold of the boundling's chin and turning his head towards him. "Cyrus?"

"Just sex. I got it," the demon sighed breathlessly, raising his hands to pull at the older demon's shirt. "I don't care, just take me."

A seductive smirk spread on Marcus' lips as he let his hand fall from Cyrus' silky shaft. "On your knees."

The young demon obeyed willingly, slowly lowering his body before him, looking up through his thick brown lashes. Marcus undid the top of his trousers, letting Cyrus pull them down for him to step out of, as he pulled his shirt off and tossed it aside. His anticipation grew as brown eyes travelled over his body, before coming to rest on the rock-hard evidence of his desire.

Before Marcus could say anything, the boundling took his cock in his mouth, sucking and licking along his length without hesitation. His jaw dropped at the sensation, the warmth of Cyrus' mouth enveloping him completely, sending waves of building pleasure through his body. Tender fingers stroked and massaged his balls as he tangled his hand through the dark blonde hair.

This is what he wanted. Never had he seen a more beautiful sight than this gorgeous young demon kneeling before him, kissing him in the most intimate way possible. His mouth was impossibly warm, the suction drawing everything from him, even things he had not wanted to give until today. Until right now. This was his dreams come to life and the feeling was so much better than he had imagined it to be.

"Enough," he rasped, pulling Cyrus' head back suddenly. "On the bed." His control was disappearing fast, unable to say more than a few words of instruction. Cyrus turned on his knees and pulled himself onto the bed, laying down on his stomach. Marcus looked at his position and shook his head. "No, on your back."

Looking over his shoulder at the older demon, surprise was evident on the boundling's face before he slowly turned over and rested back against the pillows. Marcus could not deny that Cyrus was gorgeous. His body youthful but firm and chiselled in divine detail, pulling the cambion towards him like a magnet.

"This may just be sex, Cyrus, but I do not want to fuck you like a dog," Marcus said, lowering himself on top of his soon to be bed-fellow. "Not yet, anyway," he smirked playfully.

The smile that formed on the demon's face was bewitching. Knowing it would be his undoing, Marcus claimed his mouth as their cocks pressed together between them. Maintaining the kiss as their tongues danced together, he began to move his hips, rubbing their lengths along the other, their pre-cum mixing against their bellies.

"Marcus," Cyrus moaned against his mouth, wrapping his arms around his shoulders. "Fuck me. I want you to fuck me. Please."

Not that he had expected to be able to stop at this point, but his name on the young demon's lips completely decimated any resolve he had left. His primal desires taking control, he pushed back onto his knees, grabbed the lube he kept in his bedside table and emptied a good portion onto his fingers. Pulling one of Cyrus' knees up, he guided his fingers to the tight hole, circling the lube around it. Slowly, he let one of his fingers slip inside, feeling the tightness of the gorgeous body as the boundling gasped. After a moment, when the tension around his finger relaxed, he pushed another inside, stroking and stretching the tight ring.

Cyrus moaned, his head dropping back on the pillow, pushing his shoulders and chest into the air. Marcus let go of his knee and traced his hand up the young demon's thigh, over his stomach and chest to circle his thumb over one of the small peaks of his nipples. He could feel Cyrus' body shiver beneath his touch, causing his own cock to twitch painfully, wanting to plunge inside the eager young body before him.

Unable to hold back any longer, he removed his fingers and nudged the head of his cock against the opening, lowering his body to cover the boundling beneath him. Cyrus placed his hands on Marcus' neck, gazing up at him, pupils blown until his brown eyes were almost black.

"Ready?" he asked even as he pushed his hips forward.

"Yes," Cyrus panted, desperation ringing in his voice, his grip tightening and lifting his hips to allow better access.

Slowly, he inched forward, pulling back when he was met with resistance allowing the young demon to adjust to him, before pushing forward again. Cyrus' mouth hung agape, eyes shut as Marcus finally buried his full length within him.

"Ah, Cyrus," he groaned, dropping his head into the crook of the boundling's neck. "You're so tight." It took every remaining shred of self-control in him not to come at that moment, feeling the gorgeous body pulse around him.

"You're huge," Cyrus counted, his warm breath washing over his neck and shoulders.

"Oh god, you need to relax," he managed to grind out from behind gritted teeth as the boundling clenched around him painfully. It was a welcome pain, but the grip on his cock was too much for him to start moving. He felt the young demon take a few deep breaths, the tension in his body finally easing and releasing its almost death-grip hold. "That's it. Good boy," he sighed, pressing a tender kiss to his neck.

Smiling as the boundling gasped at the praise, Marcus pulled his hips back slowly, keeping a steady pace as he pushed back inside, revelling in the feeling as Cyrus continued to relax beneath him. He lifted onto his hands, increasing his pace as the young demon grew accustomed to him, intently studying the fascinating display of pleasure and desire now dancing across his beautiful bed-mate's face. The boundling kept hold of his biceps, as if to hold himself in place as Marcus drove their hips together. Cyrus' cock rubbed between them, throbbing and twitching in time with his movements.

"Kiss me," Cyrus pleaded, his eyes locking with the cambion.

A low growl pulled from his throat as Marcus lowered his head to comply. Their lips met with hot passion, their tongues swirling and dancing within their mouths. Cyrus was panting when Marcus broke the kiss, smiling wickedly as he grabbed the boundling's hip and neck, rolling to the side to shift their position, pulling the boundling atop him.

Cyrus' eyes widened as he now straddled Marcus' hips, bracing himself by placing his hands flat on the older demon's stomach. Needing no encouragement, the boundling began to move his hips, lifting up, tilting forward then falling back against Marcus, controlling the pace. The cambion reached between them, fisting the demon's cock and pumping in time with his hips.

The boundling was beautiful, the light tan of his skin glistening with a fevered mist, glimmers of sunlight dancing across the definitions of his muscles. The flats of his palms burned into Marcus' abdomen as the young demon found a tantalising rhythm that bewitched the cambion. With each movement, the range of motion increased. Cyrus' hips lifted until only the head of Marcus' cock remained within him, before crashing back against him with desperate need.

Marcus was mesmerised, all his dreams and fantasies could not compare to the feeling of the boundling wrapped around him now. He had no idea how he was going deny the demon in the future. And currently, he didn't care.

"Have you even thought of what you're going to say to Lena when she sees you next?" Marcus teased, not really caring about the answer. "She's going to have felt all of this."

"You really want to talk about her whilst your cock is buried inside me and mine is in your hand?" Cyrus asked breathlessly, a coy smile on his soft pink lips.

"Good point," he chuckled as he drove his hips up to meet with the boundling's.

Cyrus' moan echoed through the room, his head flinging back to cry out towards the ceiling. His cock hardened and twitched within Marcus' hand. Letting go, the cambion grabbed his neck roughly, pulling him down to his chest, wrapping his arms around him and pinning the young demon's arms to his sides.

"Not yet," Marcus growled into his ear. "You can come when I say you can. You're going to be a good boy for me, aren't you?"

Groaning plaintively, Cyrus nodded against his cheek as Marcus lifted his knees and took control again, pumping his hips furiously upwards. The young demon whimpered against his neck, sending shivers across his skin as the sound met his ears like silken promises. He could feel the boundling's body tightening, his ragged breath giving evidence to his efforts to comply with Marcus' order. He was so close, but he wanted to draw out the experience as much as possible, knowing he could not allow this to happen again.

"Fuck," he groaned, "you don't even need your dick played with to come, do you? I can feel it throbbing against me. You're going to come just from me fucking you, aren't you?"

"Yes! Marcus," Cyrus moaned, his fingers digging into Marcus' hips as if to pull him deeper inside him. "Please, come in me. Please, let me come," he begged, his hot breath quickening as his body stiffened.

"Not yet," the cambion repeated, biting along Cyrus' shoulder, increasing his pace, barely keeping his own needs in check. The tension in his abdomen built painfully as he forced himself to hold back. He wanted to memorise every inch of the boundling's body, feeling it mould against his in perfect union. When he was sure that Cyrus was beyond ready, he ran his hand through the young demon's hair, pulling his head back to whisper in his ear. "Now," Marcus growled, letting his own body release the tension in his gut, his cock pulsing within the boundling, his climax releasing the hot flood within.

Cyrus cried out, his body convulsing as the older demon held him tightly, the warmth of his release pooling between them.

Marcus kept the boundling pressed against him as their breathing slowly returned to normal. Cyrus had managed to pull one of his arms from his hold, his fingers now running through the cambion's long hair. He shut his eyes, enjoying the peaceful bliss of the moment. It had been a long time since he'd felt like this. His desires sated although not gone. He could easily roll the young demon onto his back and repeat the experience, his body already preparing for just that. But this had to end here. Now.

With a heavy sigh, Marcus rolled them over, placing the boundling on his back. Withdrawing, he got to his feet and walked into his bathroom to clean up. He heard Cyrus shift on the bed and felt those brown eyes on his back. Grabbing his briefs, he pulled them on roughly, before finally looking back at the demon. The soft confusion on his face did nothing to detract from the glory of his body, his skin shining with the sweat from their entanglement.

"You should go," Marcus said gruffly, barely managing to deny the desire to fall back into the bed with him. Ignoring the tightness in his chest as confusion and pain washed over Cyrus' beautiful face, he turned away moving to grab the rest of his clothing. He heard the boundling push off from the bed and make his own way to the bathroom, picking up his clothes as he went. When he returned to the bedroom, dressed, the young demon had a thunderous look on his face.

"I know you said 'just sex', and that's fine," Cyrus snapped at him. "But I'm not some fuck-buddy whore you can just throw out when you're done."

"You came to me. I did not seek you out," Marcus said pointedly, staring blankly at the boundling despite the guilt that swirled within his gut.

"I didn't hear you complaining whilst you fucked my arse."

"Sex is sex, Cyrus," he snapped back. "Cuddling after, that's a relationship which I told you I do not want."

"Fine," the boundling huffed, walking to the door and opening it. "Use your hand next time," he said over his shoulder, slamming the door behind him.

Marcus shut his eyes, exhaling sharply. He returned to his bed to sit on the edge. Cyrus' scent still thick in the air, enticing the memories of how he felt wrapped around him. But he was Lena's boundling. A Prince's boundling. A Prince they both served as trusted council. He should never have let things get as far as they did. It was inevitable that Lena was going to find out, regardless of her hesitation to compel Cyrus to tell her anything, they were friends. Siblings. He would likely discuss it with her anyway. Marcus let his head fall into his hands with a groan.

This had the potential to go very wrong, risking both their safety and position. Even Ambrose didn't know about his preference for men. He had never been attracted to the Consort in any way other than as a friend, so it hadn't mattered. His own father, despite the love they had for each other, constantly pushed him to find a human woman to have a cambion with and continue the bloodline. Sure, he'd helped Marcus when his relationship with William had gone so terribly wrong, but there had always been an undertone of disappointment that it had not spurred him towards women. But Cyrus was different. He had managed to stir something within Marcus, he had thought was long dead.

And it had felt wonderful.

# CHAPTER NINE

Cyrus walked through the house, heading to his room, anger coursing through his body. He was perfectly fine with just having a physical relationship. He'd had them in the past with other demons. But he'd never been tossed aside so carelessly, or so immediately after. That is, if he didn't count Zagan or those he had been sent to. He'd thought with Marcus it would be different. Not that he thought he could have an actual relationship with him, regardless of how much he hoped for one, but he'd assumed they would be able to be more open with each other that he might have been with others. They had certain privileges and protections as part of Lena's council. Any relationship between them would not be as great a risk as it would be without that.

Racing inside his room, he stilled, ice washing through his veins as he saw his sire standing by the window.

"So," she said turning towards him, an amused smile on her lips. "Did you have fun?"

"Lena, ah... when did you get back?" he asked cautiously, stepping further in to the room.

"About half an hour ago. We're going to play dumb, are we?" she chuckled, leaning back against the window frame. "Like you didn't just send me on a rollercoaster of sexual desire as well?"

"No, sorry," he shook his head. "I'm sorry, Lena."

"Don't apologise," she smiled. "I'm happy for you. Marcus is a good man."

"How did you...?"

"Putting aside the crush you've had on him for the last year and that I feel what you feel, Cyrus, occasionally, without trying, I get glimpses of what you see." She paused momentarily as the horrific realisation began to dawn on him. "I saw his face."

"Oh god!" Cyrus cried, slapping his hand over his face in embarrassment.

Lena laughed, walking over to him. "Don't be embarrassed. I think this is great."

"Yeah, well," he sighed, moving over to the bed, sitting on the end. "It won't happen again."

"Oh?" she said shocked. "Why? Of course, if you don't want to tell me, I won't pry."

"He's not after a relationship and I don't want to be used as a sex doll," he spat harshly, although not directed at her. "I had enough of being used like that by Zagan."

"Cyrus," she whispered. Her voice was full of concern and sadness.

He looked up at her, pain gripping his chest at the compassion in her eyes. They didn't talk much about their time with Zagan, but Lena was fully aware of his history with the cambion and he knew it caused her untold pain.

He smiled sadly at her and reached out to take hold of her hand, squeezing it between his fingers. She stepped towards him, wrapping her arms around his shoulders. Returning the embrace, he placed his hands on her back and buried his face into her neck. Her warmth was comforting against the turmoil within his chest. He'd missed her. Regardless of their bond as boundling and sire, she was his big-little sister, and he needed her in every sense that implied.

"Well," she said, pulling back slightly, touching his cheek tenderly. "That may not necessarily be a bad thing."

Cyrus looked at her, confused, waiting for her to explain.

"I would never stand in your way of pursuing a relationship with anyone. And especially not with Marcus if that's what you really want," she clarified quickly. "You are afforded with great position and respect as part of my council, and as long as you do not break the trust that entails, you are free to be with whoever you want. At least with Marcus, you would not be forced to keep secrets from him. But even with that position, there is an element of risk that may not have occurred to you. We are all of us, only as strong as our weakest link." She sighed as she pulled away fully and walked back to the window, looking out at the courtyard below. "Ambrose is my weak link. If anything happened to him, I could not continue my work. I would be lost without him, and I would destroy everything for him." Turning back to Cyrus, her gaze turned serious. "If you and Marcus did form a relationship, you risk becoming each other's weak link. A weakness others could exploit to infiltrate our council. I also need to know that you two can continue to work together, without letting your personal feelings get in the way. I will support you, whatever you choose to do, *but*," she emphasised, "make sure if you do pursue him, that you want him for more than just physical attraction. Attraction is important, but it is a poor basis for a relationship."

He stared at her silently, letting her advice sink in. Slowly he nodded his understanding. "When did you become so wise, little mouse?" he asked, smiling softly at her.

Lena returned his smile and made her way to the door. "I had all of Hell's history poured into my mind when I became a Prince, remember. I'm still sorting through it, but it does give for some fascinating life lessons." Opening the door, she looked back over her shoulder at him. "I mean it though Cyrus. I will not get involved, but I will support whatever decision you make."

"Thank you," he said softly.

"When you're feeling up to it, can you come to my altar room? We need to talk about Damien," she said as she walked out of the room, shutting the door behind her.

With a heavy sigh, he fell back onto the bed, staring at the ceiling above him.

Maybe Lena was right, and it was best to just keep things physical, or end them entirely. He had, in a way, hoped that his tryst with Marcus would get the older demon out of his system. Let him move on to others, ones that would come with less complications. But his body remembered the feeling of Marcus within him and ached for more. He'd never been fucked like that, being able to see the face of the one taking him. It had been amazing. One of the best experiences he'd had, if not the best. And he wanted more.

"Dammit," he groaned, resting his arms above his head. He wasn't done with Marcus. Not by a long shot.

He might not be able to convince the cambion into a relationship, but perhaps he could show him, that sex could be more than, well, just sex.

It had taken a while, but after many questions, Cyrus had managed to fill both Lena and Ambrose on his plan with regard to Balo and, by extension, Damien. He had replayed his conversation with Balo over and over in his mind and after analysing it with Lena, they both agreed that for now, it was best to simply trust the boundling. Unless they had cause to suspect otherwise, it would seem that Balo was on their side. Lena had been very surprised to learn about his thoughts over her becoming Prince. Completely unique in all of Hell's history, she had not been a boundling for very long, so hadn't thought herself as truly one of them.

After their conversation, Lena and Ambrose had retired to their room. Apparently, the celebrations with the other Princes had been exhausting, although Cyrus was fairly sure they had ulterior motives to finding some seclusion. He decided to make his rounds among the hellhounds, first checking on Zamira and Sollis before heading to the main den for a bit. Thankfully, he had been alone, able to use the time to unpack his recent escapade with Marcus without interruption.

Looking back, he was sure that Marcus had enjoyed it in more than just a physical gratification sense. If his interest was purely physical, then he wouldn't have fought against it so hard. Right? Cyrus had prepared for rejection when he knocked on Marcus' door. There had been every possibility that the cambion would have simply slammed the door in his face.

But he hadn't.

After a restless night of flitting between his usual nightmares and pleasant dreams about Marcus, he wanted to talk to someone about it, but didn't really have anyone he could open up to like that. Talking with Lena or Ambrose came with issues and complications he didn't need. When he was bound to Zagan most other demons avoided him, not wanting to come under the scrutiny of his then sire. And now, bound to Lena, he couldn't fully trust that anyone seeking to be his friend did not have ulterior motives to get close to her. Which pretty much brought his options down to one of the other Princes or Archie. Although both came with the risk of their conversation getting back to Lena. But Archie made the most sense. He might tell Lena, but he wouldn't tell anyone else.

So, Archie it was.

Knocking on the demonic-trainer's door, Cyrus hoped he would be in. He could have just flamed in as Archie had told him and the rest of the council, they were free to do so at any time, but unless he was with one of the others, it felt... *weird.* Just the thought of it dug up unpleasant memories from last year when he and Lena had run to the trainer when escaping Zagan. After a moment, the door cracked open and he exhaled sharply with relief.

"Hey, Cyrus," Archie said with a small smile, opening the door further to let him in. He quickly stepped inside, his body remaining tense until he heard the door click shut. "How are you?"

"Hey, I'm fine," he returned the greeting, even as he bristled at the question. "Sorry to just drop in on you, but do you have a moment?"

Nodding slightly, Archie ran his clawed hands through his hair, pulling it back into messy knot on top of his head, his blue flames licking around his fingers drying his hair as he went. Evidently the trainer had just had a shower, his usual clothing draped over the back of a chair so that he was only wearing his trousers. His horns glistened against the light from his fire, seemingly luminescent compared to the rest of him. "This about yesterday?"

"Yeah," Cyrus nodded. "You just got back from the pits?"

The trainer chuckled. "Yeah. Give me a sec." Hurriedly, Archie pulled his leather vest on, flames coursing over the back so that it magically formed around the base of his wings. "Anything to do with what happened with Marcus?"

Pressing his lips together, Cyrus inhaled deeply through his nose, Hell's burning scent of sulphur giving him an odd reassurance. They were demons for fuck's sake. It's not like Archie would judge him. "Surprisingly," he sighed, moving further into the room, "that question has a very complicated answer."

"Oh?" the trainer asked over his shoulder as he busied himself at a makeshift kitchenette making two cups of coffee. Even demons liked their creature comforts. Suddenly, his hands stilled on the mugs, his head snapping round like he had just been slapped. Red eyes pinned Cyrus to the spot who simply stared back, suddenly very unsure he'd made the right choice of coming to speak with Archie. "*Oh!* Well, it's about fucking time."

His eyebrows practically shot into his hair line as he stared at Archie's back. It wasn't until the demon shoved a mug of coffee into his hands, he managed to find his voice again. "What?"

"Well," Archie sighed, gently guiding the boundling to the table. "Maybe I should ask what happened first before jumping to that conclusion," he said as they both sat down.

"What conclusion?" Cyrus asked, even though he knew exactly what conclusion had been reached.

"You two did fuck right?"

All air expelled from his lungs and he struggled to remember how to fill them back up. *What the fuck?* Surely, they hadn't been that obvious that even stone-cold Archie had picked up on things. "Ah..."

"Statement stands," Archie said with a warm smile that looked very out of place on his harsh features. "About fucking time."

"Ah..." Cyrus cursed himself inwardly for being unable to say anything else. Why now of all times was he rendered speechless?

"No one's said anything to me if that's what you're thinking," the trainer assured him, taking a sip of his coffee. "And you two actually do a pretty good job of hiding it, but I've been around both of you long enough to see what was going on."

Feeling his shoulders relax a little, Cyrus gave him a meek smile. "Right... yeah." Coughing slightly, he brought the coffee to his lips and focused on the heat and bitterness of the liquid as it washed over his tongue, trying to calm his mind.

"So, what did you want to talk about? Not sure I'm the best person to speak to about relationships."

"Um, I... I just needed to speak to someone that doesn't live in the house. And someone I knew wouldn't use this against us."

"Fair enough," Archie chuckled, tapping his fingers idly on the surface of the table. "And logical."

"I understand if you would prefer we didn't."

"I don't mind. So, what's happened then?"

Taking another sip of his coffee, Cyrus forced himself to speak. He'd come this far, after all. "Yes, we fucked yesterday. But he basically threw me out after."

"Ah," the trainer sighed. "So, he's still in denial."

"Am I being stupid, Archie?" he asked, not entirely sure he really wanted the answer. More than anything he longed to be seen as an equal among Lena's council. If he was chasing after something that wasn't there, what right did he have to serve her? What right did he have to ask for her to trust him? "Am I seeing something that's not there?"

"I don't know, Cyrus," Archie shook his head. "Sorry, wish I could tell you otherwise. Marcus is an incredibly private person. He's never opened up to either me or Ambrose about relationships or anything really." The trainer shifted uncomfortably in his seat, his wings adjusting restlessly in the air behind him. "I know he went through something pretty bad a few centuries ago. Before he met Ambrose. And it really messed with him."

"What happened?"

"Ah, it's not something for me to say," Archie said apologetically, scratching his cheek with a single talon. "I'm sorry, I'm terrible with these sorts of things but I would think, if he's let you in even just a little, there must be at least something. Whatever it is, it has evidently been enough for me to pick up on."

"Ha, yeah," Cyrus laughed under his breath. For anyone else that might have been an understatement, but not for Archie.

"If I were you," the trainer continued, "and this is assuming a lot because I don't know how you truly feel about him, I wouldn't give up. You look good for whatever did, or didn't, happen yesterday."

Gaze snapping to Archie's, he studied the demon to see if there was any hint of teasing or mocking in his eyes. A lump formed in his throat when he saw only sincerity. Swallowing around it, Cyrus nodded appreciatively.

"Thanks, Archie."

"Well, maybe I have a knack for this relationship stuff after all."

"Don't go inflating that ego too much."

"Ha!" Archie snorted loudly, the sound bouncing around his chamber walls. "You kn—"

In an instant the air in the room changed seeing both demons surge to their feet, coffee forgotten, as flames burst to life in front of the door. Blue and black flames licked up their arms waiting to see who would dare to enter Archie's chambers unannounced. An alarm sounded for a moment to indicate that whoever it was, was not part of Lena's circle.

Cyrus pulled his brows together, his mind racing as for some form of an explanation for what was going on as Damien stepped out of the fire. *Had Balo told him?*

"You got a lot of nerve flaming in here, Damien," Archie barked, rounding the table so that he and Cyrus stood shoulder to shoulder. That was if you ignored the fact that Archie's shoulder stood at the same height as his head.

"Trust me," Damien drawled, his hands stuffed in his pockets, "if I had another option, I'd have taken it. Especially if I had known twinkle wa—"

A duet of growls emanated from the two demons at the term, silencing the cambion.

"Watch it." The silent threat in Archie's voice that had dropped to a barely audible whisper was clear for all in the room. "Cyrus is a member of a Prince's council. You will not insult him."

"Calm down," the cambion sneered at them, although raised his hands in a show of compliance. "I only flamed in because I didn't want anyone seeing me knock on your door. And like Hell I'm going to Prince Lena's house. She'd kill me before I got the chance to speak."

"What makes you think we won't kill you?"

"I just want to talk, Archie. The sooner you let me, the sooner I leave."

"Then talk," Archie sighed, his blue flames dissipating from his hands, motioning to a chair in silent command for Damien to sit down. Cyrus followed suit, but kept his power beneath the surface, ready to be used if needed. Didn't matter what Damien was here for, he would never trust the cambion. "But if we don't like what we hear, you may not be leaving."

Cyrus and Archie exchanged a glance. This was too soon. Far too soon. Unless Balo had spilled everything to Damien, then there was something else going on. But for now, they would just listen. Judgement came later.

# CHAPTER TEN

Gazing along the shelves, Marcus studied a jar full of White Baneberry, the small white buds with black specks dotted along bright red stems looking eerily like eyeballs jammed against the glass. They were certainly not the strangest thing that Lena had lining her altar room, but they always drew his attention for some reason. With a long exhale, he sunk lower into the chair next to the small table whilst his Prince flittered around the room, stopping here and there to grab a jar and take out a small portion of its contents, throwing them into a large wooden bowl resting on her hip.

"So, I'm to give my support to Damien as long as he pledges publicly to me," Lena said, her back still to him.

"Yes," he sighed, his head falling back onto the chair, arms folded across his chest. "And that he persuades any that still seek to move against you to back down."

There was an interlude of silence between them as Lena continued to pull various jars from the shelves. She was preoccupied with preparing an infusion for her Prince-sibling, Abaddon, but they had to speak about Damien, so their conversation was somewhat jagged. Marcus didn't mind. He was more than happy to spend as much time as needed with her. It was better than other possibilities at the moment. At least in her altar room, he didn't run the risk of running into a certain boundling.

Staring at the ceiling, he wondered if he should say anything to her about Cyrus. He didn't want to. Not really. But he also didn't want to keep secrets from her. That would almost guarantee losing her favour. He hated this feeling of uneasiness around her now. He used to feel so comfortable around her, able to tell her and Ambrose anything.

Surely, Hell needed a Prince of Guilt, because this felt worse to him than any other sin he had ever committed.

"Hm..."

Raising a brow, Marcus shifted his gaze to Lena. She had placed the bowl, now full of various herbs and roots, on a long workbench that was pushed against the far wall. Her shoulders were tense as she placed one hand on her hip, the other gripped firmly around the rim of the bowl. Pulling himself back up in the chair, he studied her, trying to gauge her thoughts.

"What is it?" he asked cautiously.

"Damien gets a lot out of this," she sighed, turning to lean her hip against the workbench, her arms and ankles crossed. "We get almost nothing, other than peace of mind, if you could even call it that."

He nodded in agreement, chuckling quietly to himself as he recalled Cyrus saying something similar. The adopted siblings really thought a lot alike. Noting she was still talking about Damien, he allowed himself to sink back into the chair. "Our thoughts were, if he brings the idea to you, he is more likely to keep to end of the agreement."

"He made an agreement with me when I spared his life last year," she scoffed, shaking her head with a grim smile on her face. "So far, he has not kept to it."

"Because you offered it. This time, he will feel in control, although he won't actually be."

With a huff, Lena turned away, gripped the edges of the bowl and poured her lightning over it to mix with its contents. The herbs disintegrated, forming a coarse powder infusion. Carefully, she scooped up small portions of the powder into some vials placed along the workbench. She placed three on her shelves and with a loud click of her fingers sent the other two to Abaddon, the small flames bursting from the bench surface. Walking across the room, she slumped into the chair opposite him, her brows furrowed.

"Do you think we can trust him?" she asked quietly, her gaze locked on some distant point only she could see.

"Hell no," Marcus chuckled, shaking his head. "Which is why we will need another way of controlling him, just in case. But, at least in the beginning, this will allow us to keep a closer eye on him."

Studying her from the corner of his eye, he watched her hands open and close in her lap as if she was trying to grasp onto something that wasn't really there. It was something she had done the entire time he had known her. A way of her sorting out her thoughts. "And this was all Cyrus' idea?"

He nodded, turning his head to look at her fully. "Yes. He's smart that boundling of yours."

"He should be," she laughed softly with a fond smile forming on her lips, despite the maintained dip of her brows. "He taught me how to play chess."

Surprise hitting him square in the chest, Marcus pushed himself up in the chair and rested his forearms on the table, leaning towards her. "I have never won a game of chess against you."

"And I've never won against Cyrus."

He made a mental note to watch the next chess game between Lena and Cyrus if there was going to be one. He'd give anything to see the Prince lose that game. "We don't give him enough credit, do we?" he sighed.

"No," she agreed. "And unfortunately, I am very much included in that. Seeing him in his eighteen-year-old form, it's easy to forget he's still older than me." Tapping her fingers on top of her thighs, she turned her face to look at him, their eyes locking. Marcus shifted slightly, feeling uncomfortable under her scrutiny. Did she know? He knew it was inevitable that she would find out, but he'd hoped that Cyrus would wait a little while before telling her. "How are we planning on controlling Damien once he has my support though?" she asked breaking him from his thoughts.

Coughing slightly, he shrugged in response. "We're still working on it."

"So, no ideas at all?"

"Did Cyrus not speak to you about that yesterday."

"He did," she said with a small nod, "but only about the plan with Balo to speak to Damien. And his conversation with Balo. So?"

"We had an idea," he sighed, letting his gaze drop to the surface of the table. "But we don't think you would like it."

"What is it?"

"Cyrus seems to think that Balo may be in love with Damien and has a suspicion that those feelings might be reciprocated."

"Balo confirmed that to Cyrus yesterday."

"Oh?" Marcus raised his brows in surprise before quickly pulling them together in confusion as both curiosity and jealousy coursed through his chest at the further reminder of Cyrus and Balo alone in Ambrose's study. Swallowing, he squeezed his eyes shut briefly, pushing the memory from his mind.

"Mm-hm," Lena hummed, nodding softly, seemingly unaware of the emotional turmoil of her councilman. "So, what was the thought with that information?" she continued.

He sighed heavily, squaring his shoulders before scrubbing his hand over his face. "We thought that maybe taking over Balo's bindings would give you control over Damien."

"Well, you were right," she chuckled darkly, "I don't like it. I have no desire for a second boundling. One is bad enough."

Returning her laughter, Marcus smirked at her. "That's what I said."

Silence falling between them again, Lena crossed her legs, tapping her fingers on the top of her knee, her lips pursed from deep thought. "Still, it does present an interesting possibility," she said after a time, rolling her head to the side, eliciting a soft click from her neck.

"Hm?"

"If Damien does indeed feel as strongly for Balo as insinuated to Cyrus, the boundling could still be used for exerting control without taking him from Damien."

Her eyes were locked on the ceiling, allowing Marcus to stare at her unabashedly. "In what way?" he asked, curious as to her thoughts.

"I guess it depends on what is more important to Damien. Power or Balo?" she shrugged nonchalantly.

"Would you really go down that train of thought?"

"I will do what I have to, Marcus," she said, her tone harsh but not unkind. Her gaze turned to him, pinning him with their grey depths. Lena had all the warmth and love of a mother but in an instant, she could push all of that aside and exude a darkness that seemingly had no end. "You of all people should know that."

He nodded. Of course, he knew. He'd witnessed firsthand the extent of her vengeance. Even as a mortal she had been tough, but, as with all souls that fall into Hell, her demonic nature had made her ruthless. She needed to be to survive being a Prince.

"But to threaten a boundling?" he asked, holding her gaze.

"I'm not talking about threatening him," she sighed, shaking her head. "I'm talking about offering something to them that they may want more than anything. The ability to be together without fear of someone taking advantage of their relationship."

"By taking advantage of their relationship," he quipped, grinning at her.

"Well... yes," she laughed, returning his smile. "In a manner of speaking."

"It's not bad. But how would you present it?"

"I will need to think about that," Lena said quietly, her eyes dropping to the table in contemplation. "In the meantime, if you or Cyrus come up with something else, let me know."

*Cyrus...*

Exhaling heavily, Marcus leant back in the chair, folding his arms in front of him. He had to tell her. It would be better if she found out from him. And if she already knew, surely, she would appreciate that he was being honest with her and not trying to keep it a secret. Right?

"Ah, Lena..." he started, bracing himself for her reaction. "About Cyrus–"

"Nope," she interrupted quickly, practically springing to her feet and rushing over to her workbench. "No. We are not having that conversation. I am aware of what happened and I am not getting involved."

Ah, there she was. The Lena that avoided serious personal conversations like a plague. "Fair enough," he sighed with a soft smile. "Can I say 'I'm sorry'?"

"I'd rather you didn't," she said turning back to him, her hands on her hips. "I think, however, it goes without saying, if you hurt him..." she trailed off, her threat unvoiced but there all the same.

"I don't want to hurt him," he said softly, getting to his feet and pushing his hands into his trouser pockets.

"Good. Keep it that way."

Pressing his lips together, he nodded in confirmation at her command. "Do you still need me?" he asked.

Before Lena could answer, there was a soft knock at the door.

"Come in," she called.

Marcus felt his breath hitch as Cyrus and Archie entered the room, both with amused smiles on their faces. Flashes of memories of the boundling lying beneath him invaded his mind's eye, which he hurriedly stamped down, taking a step backwards to place the table between him and the young demon like a barrier.

"Hey," Cyrus said, nodding towards him, no hint of the hurt he had shown yesterday in his eyes. Relief washed through Marcus' chest, glad to see that the boundling did not seem to hold any resentment. Or at least, was hiding it in the presence of their Prince.

"Hi," he responded, hoping that his greeting would be seen as directed at both Cyrus and Archie.

Lena coughed slightly, shuffling along her workbench, brushing off remnants of the infusion as she went. "What's up?" she asked over her shoulder.

"We have some good news," Archie replied, walking over to her, leaning against the end of the workbench and folding his arms across his chest. Marcus felt certain that he was purposefully avoiding looking at him, but couldn't figure out why. Surely, Cyrus wouldn't have spoken to him about yesterday. It's not like the boundling and trainer were particularly close.

"Okay," their Prince said, trying to prompt further explanation.

"Damien came to visit me," he said, his smile broadening to a grin.

"And?"

"Well, he had some interesting things to say."

Marcus chuckled inwardly. Archie was teasing her. A bold move to make, especially considering the conversation he and Lena just had, not that the trainer would know that.

"Are you going to make me guess? Or do I have to beat it out of you?" Lena teased back, leaning next to Archie, her gaze darting back and forth between Marcus and Cyrus. The cambion didn't miss the mischievous gleam in her eyes as her lips tugged to the side in a coy smile. At least she didn't seem upset that he bedded her boundling.

Cyrus smiled at his sister, as he sauntered over to the table and sunk onto the chair she had only recently occupied. Marcus stared at the boundling, desperately trying to keep his thoughts in check, silently cursing his lack of control yesterday and the floodgates that had opened in his mind.

"Balo, it seems, was more persuasive than we thought he would be," the young demon said, stretching out his legs and crossing his ankles. His shirt clung tightly to his lean frame and Marcus had to practically tear his eyes from the way it formed over Cyrus' stomach, doing nothing to soften the ridges of his abs. Catching slight movement from the corner of his eye, he looked at the boundling's face, swallowing as their eyes locked momentarily. Cyrus smirked at him, his brown eyes twinkling with some unspoken mirth. But as quickly as he saw it, the younger demon looked away, back towards their Prince. "More persuasive than he thought he would be," Cyrus continued.

"Damien offered exactly what we hoped," Archie said, nudging Lena with his shoulder. "Well, with one slight addition. He pledges allegiance to you, in return you support his control over the cambions."

"But he also wants a place in your inner circle," the boundling finished, with a dramatic roll of his eyes.

The Prince scoffed at the notion. "Well, that's not happening. Any mention of Balo?" she asked, looking up at the trainer.

"No," he shook his head. "Balo also wasn't with him."

"Do you think he knows Balo told us about their relationship?"

Now Cyrus shook his head. "No, I don't think so."

"Neither do I," Archie agreed.

Lena pursed her lips, looking at the floor in contemplation. "Well, I guess it's a step in the right direction at the very least."

"What's wrong?" Cyrus asked, leaning forward as he looked at her, concern etched on his face.

The Prince shook her head slightly. "Not sure. Feels too quick. You only spoke with Balo yesterday after all."

Archie and Cyrus exchanged a look. Darting his gaze between them, Marcus felt like he was missing something. He had to swallow against the rising jealously burning the back of his throat.

"We thought the same thing," Cyrus said softly. "I don't think Balo will have let on to Damien that we spoke with him."

"But," Archie continued for him, "we have no way of knowing if Balo was compelled to tell him."

"Hm..." Lena hummed.

"Even if he has been, Damien is still making the offer," the boundling smiled, a glint of fire entering his eyes. "And I've had an idea on how to control him."

"You have?"

"He has," Archie chuckled. "And it's a damn good one."

Marcus frowned at the demonic-trainer. It wasn't like he didn't believe the idea was good, but he didn't like the affectionate grin Archie sent the young demon's way.

"Well, it has to be better than taking over Balo's bindings," the Prince huffed with an amused smile. "Well, spit it out."

Leaning back in his chair, Cyrus clasped his hands behind his head, a smug grin on his face. Marcus swallowed, forcing himself to look away as the muscles on the boundling's arms flexed enticingly.

"We force him to reduce his number of boundlings," the young demon stated confidently. "Dealer demons gain power from their boundlings. Take them away and he'll be dependent on your support. Without it he will have nothing."

Marcus' brows shot to the ceiling. It was an elegant idea. Perfect actually. It would force Damien's hand completely. It didn't threaten the current boundlings and secured his future compliance. He couldn't stop the small smile forming on his lips as he took in the look of pride on Cyrus' face. Glancing towards her, he was pleased to find that Lena shared a similar expression.

"I like it," she said. "I really like it. Well, I'll leave it to you and Archie to sort the finer details."

Cyrus' chest puffed slightly as he grinned at his sister, his eyes gleaming with joy.

Pushing away from the workbench Lena made her way to the lectern and ran the tips of her fingers across the surface of her conduit. The crystals glowed red with her power, her dove-grey eyes fading to a brilliant white as her mind looked through the voids between realities.

"Marcus?" she called to him.

"Yes."

"I want you to follow Balo for a while. Don't let him out of your sight for a few days. I'll get Titus to focus on Damien."

"Of course," he nodded his head in acknowledgement of his orders. "Do you want me to go now?"

"No," she shook her head. "Give it a couple of hours. Let him and Damien breathe for a bit. Let them feel like their plan is working, whatever it may be."

"Will do."

"Can one of you find Ambrose for me, please? I need to speak with him," she said turning her body fully towards her book, effectively dismissing the men.

Leaving her altar room, the three men stood almost awkwardly in the hallway, glancing between each other in a silent and uncertain conversation.

Archie coughed, breaking the tension as he rubbed the back of his neck. "I'll go find Ambrose," he said with an uncomfortable smile. "See you both later." Without a second glance, he turned on his heel and made for the stairs, heading to check the offices and library for the Consort.

Moving down the hallway sightly, Cyrus seemed to make his way to his bedroom. Marcus watched him intently, unsure if he should say anything or just let the boundling go. His mind screamed to let things be, to simply let the young demon leave and to let the events of yesterday remain a fond memory. But his body wasn't on the same page. From the moment Cyrus walked into the altar room, his cock had been painfully hard within his trousers, pushing stubbornly against both his briefs and the zipper. His untucked shirt was the only thing hiding it, although even that wasn't doing a fantastic job. Seeing the side table where he had kissed the boundling only two nights before, now devoid of any vase or arrangement on its surface, did nothing to ease the heat coursing through his veins.

His breath caught in his throat as Cyrus turned back towards him, standing only a few steps from that damned table, a cautiously hopeful look in his brown depths. Marcus didn't know what to do with himself in that moment, wilfully ignoring the stray thought that maybe he should allow Cyrus to tell him what to do. That the boundling would be better at handling him than anyone else right now, including himself. He should just go to his room, or the library, or his office to hide until he had to find Balo.

"Marcus?"

Cyrus' voice startled him from his thoughts. Clearing his throat, Marcus turned his gaze to one of the windows, trying to let the lust haze clear from his mind. "Hm?"

"Can we talk?" Cyrus asked, his voice soft and unassuming. "Just talk."

Damn whatever this power the boundling had over him was. But he supposed he owed Cyrus a conversation at the very least. He looked back at the young demon and nodded, stepping towards him as he opened the door to his bedroom. Hoping he wasn't about to make a colossal mistake, Marcus made to follow him before some semblance of rationality finally made its appearance.

"Ah," he hesitated, glancing over his shoulder back towards Lena's altar room. "Perhaps, we should talk in my office. Ambrose will likely be coming up soon." That and he doubted he could be trusted to not make a repeat of yesterday in a room where there was a bed.

Cyrus looked past him but seemed to agree with his conclusion, nodding slightly before pulling his bedroom door back shut. Once Marcus reached his side, they both made for the stairs at the other end of the hall, keeping some space between them at the headed downstairs. The cambion took a deep breath as Cyrus walked past him into his office, the warm leather scent of the boundling filling his lungs. Hopefully, whatever the result of this conversation was, he would be able to finally relax around the young demon again.

*Doubtful...*

# CHAPTER ELEVEN

Marcus' office was the mirror image of Ambrose's, except where the Consort liked dark wood with red and gold accents, Marcus preferred pale birch with opalescent inlays around the built in book shelves. Black and silver-grey drapes hanging from the corners almost like a symbol of rooms owner. The furniture was simple, the grey oak desk standing proudly near to one wall, a large black leather chair sitting behind it. Marcus' laptop lay closed on top of the leather desk cover, a paper notepad and two pens arranged neatly beside it. The cambion's favourite armchairs that he had for centuries sat in front of the desk, their velvet green covering with gold studs magically maintained against wear and tear.

Standing by one of the chairs now, Cyrus turned to look at the older demon as he pulled the door shut behind him. They eyed each other in silence for a moment, green eyes locked with brown as they waited for the other to speak. Swallowing tentatively, Cyrus shifted on his feet, not quite sure how to start. He had wanted this conversation, but now that he was alone with Marcus, all he wanted to do was kiss him. All other thoughts fled his mind. Maybe this had been a bad idea and he should have left it for another day. But if the cambion was going to be following Balo for a while then he didn't know when they would next see each other, and he might have talked himself out of it by then. They needed to talk. To figure out how to move on from yesterday.

"Cyrus."

"Marcus."

Cyrus grinned sheepishly as they spoke simultaneously, rubbing the back of his neck and dropping his gaze to the floor.

"Sorry," he said hurriedly. "You first."

"You're the one who wanted to talk," Marcus chuckled, shaking his head slightly. His tone was light and indulgent. Cyrus relaxed a little at the sound.

"Right, yeah," he sighed, shoving his hands in his pockets, his pointer finger digging into the skin around his thumbnail. "I'm sorry, for how I reacted yesterday."

"Don't be."

Caught off guard, Cyrus' gaze snapped to the demon. Marcus was looking at the ceiling, rubbing his jaw with the back of his fingers, the delicious length of his neck on full view. The boundling balled his fists in his pockets, desperately fighting to keep his urges in check. This conversation would come to an abrupt end if he acted on his desirous impulses.

"I, uh..." Marcus started, bringing his gaze back to Cyrus, a strange mix of emotions swirling in his green depths. "I didn't handle yesterday very well either. So please, don't apologise."

"Marcus," he said softly, walking towards the cambion. He halted still two or three steps apart when the cambion held up his hand. At least, he didn't step away.

"That doesn't mean I've changed my mind," Marcus said sternly and with such command that Cyrus felt his spine straighten, a shiver running down it. "I'm not trying to be cruel here, Cyrus. I'm trying to be practical. I don't want to hurt you, but I can't see how this could end without one of us being hurt and by extension make it very uncomfortable for us to work together on Lena's council."

"What makes you think it would end?"

Marcus sighed heavily, stepping forward and closing the distance between them a little. "I'll grant the hypothetical that it could work. I don't believe it would, but for argument's sake, sure," he shrugged, not dismissively, but almost with an air of uncertainty, like he didn't really believe that it wouldn't work. Cyrus' brow furrowed as he intently studied the cambion's face, trying to gauge his thoughts. "Say *we* don't hurt each other, but something else could happen. We could find ourselves in a similar position to Damien and Balo, someone leveraging our relationship for God knows what."

*Okay, that stings a little,* Cyrus thought, although he made similar rationalisations to himself last night. Swallowing against the lump in his throat, he managed to speak. "It's not like we're lower-level demons, Marcus. I don't particularly like the idea of hiding behind them, but Lena and Ambrose wouldn't let that happen to us."

"Yet another point as to why it couldn't work," the cambion said. "What relationship would it be if it was dependent on others to maintain it? To protect it? Lena and Ambrose are powerful enough to protect themselves."

"Are we not? You certainly are and I think I've proven in this last year that I am. Our powers increased tenfold when we became part of Lena's council."

"I don't understand why you're fighting so hard for this, Cyrus," Marcus snapped, annoyance evident on his proud features. The scowl that formed on his lips was so unbelievably kissable, Cyrus had to dig his nails into the palms of his hands to keep them to himself.

"I don't understand why you're fighting so hard against it," he retorted. "Are you honestly telling me you haven't thought about how good it felt? Are you telling me you haven't thought about doing it again?"

"Cyrus."

The warning growl was unmistakable, but Cyrus couldn't stop himself. Not now.

"I think you're scared," he challenged.

"Careful, Cyrus."

"What?" he snapped, closing the final distance between them and pushing his chest against Marcus'. The heat from the cambion washed over him, their noses practically touching as he angled his face up slightly to keep looking into his eyes. Marcus was only an inch or so taller than him, so it would only take for Cyrus to lift his chin slightly for him to be able to kiss those stubborn lips. "What will you do that you didn't do yesterday?"

"Don't," Marcus growled, his eyes darkening with both desire and anger, his body instinctively leaning into the boundling.

Cyrus felt his breath catch, knowing he was bucking up to someone who could very easily hurt him physically, but he didn't believe that

Marcus would ever do that. Hurting him emotionally, sure. But physically, no. *Well, maybe...* at least not maliciously. But if he didn't push now, he might never get the chance again to see how far he could go. Maybe it was a stupid game considering the stakes, but it was one he currently wanted to play.

"You, yourself said you don't want to hurt me," he breathed, his gaze dropping for a moment to the cambion's parted lips before returning to his eyes. "And you wouldn't do that to Lena. So, what will you do, Marcus?"

He felt the vibrations through his chest as Marcus practically snarled at him. "Back off, Cyrus."

"No. I won't back off, because I don't think you really want me to. I think you want me to push you. Or do you want me to beg you? Because I'll do that if that's what it takes to get you to admit you lik—"

"Enough!" Marcus roared at him, his strong hand snapping out and grabbing the boundling by the front of the throat. "I've tried, Cyrus. I've tried to push you away gently, but there is only so much patience I will afford you. I don't want to hurt you, but I will if I have to."

He knew he should be scared. The look in the cambion's eyes was all too familiar to him. One he had seen reflected endlessly in the eyes of his old sire and countless other cambions that had used him and his body. One that he saw in his nightmares. But where their eyes had only been filled with anger, malice and hatred, Marcus' was softened with desire and even a hint of affection. This man did care for him, regardless of what he might say. Sure, the threat was there, but rather than scaring Cyrus, it made his skin tingle with heat and longing.

*Well, that's new...*

"You want 'just sex', fine," he said, pulling his face close to Marcus to whisper against his lips. "But do not lie to me and say you do not want me. If you had just wanted to use me for your own gratification, you wouldn't have fucked me the way you did. I have been used by others that way for years, I know the difference."

"Cyrus," Marcus warned again, his grip on his neck tightening, making him gasp for air. "You are too young. You do not understand."

"I understand that I want you," he said huskily. "I can't change the way I look, but I am not eighteen anymore."

"I am fifteen hundred years old, Cyrus," Marcus retorted.

"So, you're experienced," he teased, smiling playfully at the cambion.

"I like that."

In a swift motion, Marcus spun them around and pushed him back against the wall by the door, pinning him with his body. Cyrus welcomed the painful kiss that crushed against his lips, as the demon bit into his flesh. He kept his hands flat against the wall, steadying himself as Marcus' free hand roamed down his body, roughly cupping him through his jeans.

"Is that what you want?" the cambion growled against his lips. "To be claimed and taken by someone who can control you?"

"No," Cyrus whispered, causing Marcus to pull back slightly in surprise. "I had enough of being controlled by Zagan. But I want you, desperately. So, if being controlled by you is all I am going to get, I'll take it."

Marcus' lips parted, his face softening and his breath quickening. Both his hands relaxed and moved to cup Cyrus' face between them. The cambion's thumb traced over Cyrus' bottom lip. Opening his mouth, he sucked Marcus' thumb inside, laving a warm kiss upon it, their eyes locked together. The sea-green depths of the older demon washed over him like waves along the sand, sending ripples of anticipation across his skin. Never had he wanted another like he wanted this demon. Every inch of him burned for his touch, wanting more with ferocious longing.

"Cyrus," the cambion breathed, leaning forward and brushing a soft kiss over his now swollen lips. The tenderness in the touch was painfully exquisite to Cyrus as he moaned softly into the kiss, closing his eyes and raising his hands to trace along Marcus' jaw. The kiss seemed to last an eternity as their tongues explored the other in slow abandon, pulling them further into the heated desire that radiated from their bodies. He could feel the hardness of Marcus' body pressing against his stomach, as his own responded in kind. He cried out in denial as cool air washed over him when the older demon suddenly ripped his mouth away and took a few steps back. "Cyrus, we can't," Marcus said shaking his head and turning away. "We can't do this. You need someone who can actually give you what you want, and that's not me. I- I can't do this."

Hurt flooded Cyrus' chest, gripping his heart painfully within an invisible vice, as he stared at the demon's back. He took a deep breath trying to slow his breathing, before pushing away from the wall. "Why not?" he asked. "How do you know you can't give me what I want? That I can't give you what you want? What you need?"

"You know nothing about what I need," Marcus sighed walking across the room to put more space between them. "I have spent almost a thousand years denying my desires, in preference for staying alive. Staying safe. Keeping others safe. My sole purpose now, is protecting Lena. In helping her in her role as a Prince of Hell. How can I do that if I get into a relationship with her boundling?"

"I have the same purpose, Marcus," Cyrus replied, placing his hands on his hips. "Even more so as my life is dependent on her staying alive."

"All the more reason we should not entertain whatever this is."

"Bullshit!" he shouted. "You want me, as much as I want you. I know you do. Otherwise, what the fuck was that kiss just now? Do not hide behind Lena as an excuse."

"Don't worry, that won't happen again," Marcus said turning to face him, hands in his pockets, a dark expression on his face. "This is not just about us. Anything we do, affects Lena. Affects her council."

"You think I don't know that?" he snapped. "You think I don't know that every time I think of you, every time I want you to kiss or touch me, Lena feels it. She's my sister, Marcus. I don't particularly relish the fact that she is fully aware whenever I get horny. But that would happen if it was with you or someone else."

Marcus sighed heavily, dropping his gaze to the floor. "I'm sorry, Cyrus. I truly am. I wish I could make you understand, but I cannot do this. I cannot be what you want me to be. Who you want me to be."

"Then help me understand, Marcus," he pleaded, again stepping towards the cambion if only to emphasis his desire. "Please. Just tell me why?"

"Cyrus, *please*. Just let this go."

"I can't. I wish I could, but I can't. I've tried," he admitted. "I had hoped that with yesterday, I could maybe live with just that. Get you out of my system. Get you out of my head. But I can't." Cyrus felt desperate now. A desperation he had told himself he should never show to anyone, but he didn't know how to hide it anymore. Not with Marcus. Not when he wanted Marcus more than anything. "So, if you want me to let it go, to give up on you, you're going to have to tell me why."

"I have given you multiple reasons."

"No, you've given me excuses, but not reasons."

"Is there a difference?" Marcus huffed with clear annoyance dripping from his harsh tone.

"In this instance, yes," Cyrus said, folding his arms in front of his chest. "Lena is an excuse. My being her boundling is an excuse. A reason would be that you don't want me. That you're with someone else. Or actually explaining why you don't want a relationship, because that seems to stem from something well before you met Lena or Ambrose."

The cambion's eyes narrowed. "Fine. I don't want you. Now will you drop this?"

"Yeah right," he said rolling his eyes dramatically. "That's why you've jumped me three times in as many days. Because you don't want me."

Marcus flinched at the statement, but otherwise held on to his cool exterior, his hands planted firmly on his hips.

"So, what is it?" Cyrus continued, realising the older demon was not going to respond. "Because knowing what I do about you, I highly doubt there is someone else and I don't buy that you don't want me. I also know that despite their best efforts, not a single demonic faction has ever been able to gain your favour. Until Ambrose that is, and you have never looked at him the way you looked at me yesterday, so there's nothing there. Which means you only hung around Ambrose because he was one of the few people that you could actually care for without giving too much of yourself away. One who expected nothing of you."

"You're assuming I only like guys."

"Alright, let's analyse the women in your life then. The only woman you hang around with now is Lena and you would never go there because that would hurt Ambrose. Then, *maybe*, there's Tegan, but *she's* not into guys so again, no dice. Others may not know much about your personal life, but you lived in the cambion caverns for centuries and we both know, generally speaking, cambions are indiscriminate as to taste, so they wouldn't care seeing men or women come and go from your chambers. They also wouldn't talk about it, because they do the same thing so who cares right? What does get talked about is that you never had anyone. Not a single demon, man or woman or otherwise. I'm guessing you went to them, if you went to anyone. You've never let anyone in. You've never let anyone get close. So, what? Someone hurt you, right? And now you avoid relationships like a plague. Which is also why you can only imagine this ending badly."

The cambion laughed. Actually laughed. Like Cyrus had said something hilarious. Pursing his lips, the boundling swallowed against his own annoyance at the sound.

"Lena said you were smart. And I knew you were, but fuck, Cyrus," Marcus shook his head, almost in defeat. "I can see why she loses to you at chess."

Annoyance made way for pride at the praise, his chest puffing out despite the inappropriate timing considering the nature of their conversation. The pair fell into an uncomfortable silence. Cyrus could almost see the wheels in the older demon's head turning, but he refused to be the first to say anything. He had set the board; it was Marcus' move now.

"I won't lie," Marcus said finally, raising his gaze to meet with Cyrus'. "I do want you. I want to lay you down on my bed and never let you leave it. But I can't. I can't indulge those fantasies."

Cyrus swallowed, choking back the hurt he wanted to throw at the cambion. Why tease him with that knowledge? Why torture him further? Although, he guessed he only had himself to blame for that. That's what he gets for pushing so hard, right? "I can't accept that, if you can't tell me why," he said softly, his heart beating painfully within his chest.

"Accept it, or don't," the older demon said, turning away. "Regardless, this ends here."

"No, it doesn't. You don't get to dictate how someone else feels about you."

"But I do get to dictate how I respond to those feelings. This is over, Cyrus."

"For now," the boundling whispered as he turned on his heel and walked out of the room, not waiting to hear any response Marcus may have and pulled the door shut behind him.

Well, that couldn't have gone worse if he'd tried...

# CHAPTER TWELVE

The next few days passed relatively quickly for him as Marcus kept close to Balo, keeping as close of an eye on him as possible. Hell had few shadows he could utilise as cover seeing as most walls were laced with streams of lava, but he had other means of avoiding notice. So far, he was fairly certain that Balo had not betrayed them. That he had not divulged all of their intent to Damien. But then, it wasn't like he could watch them when they were in their personal chambers. At those times he would return home and Lena would spy on them as best she could through her conduit. Everything seemed to be going smoothly. Although, maybe a little too smoothly, causing his senses to be constantly on guard, waiting silently for any hint of something that wasn't right.

The more he thought about it though, the more he started to convince himself he was only feeling this sense of unease because of the situation with Cyrus. He hadn't seen the boundling for any significant length of time since their conversation, passing him occasionally in the hallway or the courtyard. Still, he couldn't help the sharp pang of guilt whenever he would catch Cyrus' eye and see the remnants of hurt and sadness within their chocolate-brown depths. On at least two occasions, he had to stop himself from wrapping his arms around the young demon and apologising or making empty promises.

And the promises would be empty. He couldn't give more than that.

He couldn't put himself in a situation again like he had with William. There was just too much at stake. And it was too painful for him to even entertain the idea. He'd been telling himself that he was protecting Cyrus, and by extension protecting Lena, by keeping the boundling at arm's length. But the longer he ignored and was ignored by Cyrus, the more he realised he had really only been protecting himself. Physical needs could be indulged, sure, but with each day he realised that physical would not be enough for the young demon. And possibly, not even enough for him.

He wanted love, he wanted affection. He wanted some iota of what he saw between Ambrose and Lena with each passing day, but he had long since accepted that something like that was not on the cards for him. What Cyrus didn't know was that when he did need some physical need met, he sought it from the incubus brothels on Earth. No strings attached and bound to secrecy; they were the perfect companions in that regard. He very much doubted that the boundling would understand that.

Flaming back to the house after Balo had retreated to Damien's apartment, Marcus steeled his resolve as he made his way to Lena's altar room. There was no other choice anymore. He needed to put distance between himself and Cyrus.

"Lena, can we talk?" he asked walking into the room.

Her back was turned to him as she poured over her book, her lightning covering her entire body. Her head tilted slightly at his voice so he knew she heard him, but he didn't press further as he sat down at the table. She would acknowledge him when she was ready. Slowly, her lightning receded into her body as she turned to face him, a warm smile on her face, brightening her eyes. He drank it in, knowing he was about to do something that would take that smile away.

"Of course," she said cheerfully, settling down into the opposite chair. "What is it?"

"I mean, can we talk and it not leave this room?"

And with that, the smile vanished, a serious expression of surprise and concern mixing upon her features. "Alright," she said cautiously with a small nod. "Yes. I promise I won't repeat anything you say to me. What's wrong?"

"Um, it's about Cyrus," he sighed, shifting in the chair uncomfortably. "I know you don't want to talk about it, but..."

"It's alright," Lena assured him, leaning forward to rest her forearms on the table.

"Has he talked to you about it since?"

"No," she shook her head. "Not directly anyway. But he's bound to me, Marcus. I feel what he feels."

"I know." He scrubbed his hand over his face, unsure of how to continue. He hoped that Lena would help led the conversation for now until he found an opening to ask what he had to.

"Moreover," she continued as if reading his mind, "the connection between Cyrus and I is particularly strong due to our history before becoming demons. Without needing to focus, I occasionally see what he sees."

His stomach bottomed out, abject horror and embarrassment filling every part of his body that now flushed with heat. "Please tell me, you didn't..." he trailed off, groaning into his hand.

"Oh, I did," she said softly, a faint brevity to her voice serving only to heighten his embarrassment. "And I am sorry about that. Try as I might, I can't always control it."

"Oh hell," he sighed, his head falling back onto the chair so he stared at the ceiling. "I'm sorry, Lena. I'm so sorry. I've tried to stop it. I've tried to push him away."

"Why? There's obviously something there. Why deny it?"

"Because I have to," he hung his head, still avoiding her gaze. He couldn't risk losing his nerve. Not now. "I don't have another choice. I can't... I can't be with him. Not in the way he deserves. Does Ambrose know about this?"

Lena shook her head. "No, I don't think so anyway. I haven't said anything to him and I don't intend to," she assured him. He exhaled slowly, slight relief helping to dispel some of the unease in his stomach. "Although, I don't know why you don't speak to him about it."

"I don't want him to think..."

"You know he won't judge you."

"I know he won't," Marcus sighed, squeezing his eyes tightly shut, not wanting to delve too deeply into the fears he harboured over this particular topic. "It not about that. I don't want him to suddenly question all of our previous interactions. Our friendship. I never had any interest in Ambrose. Not as anything more than a friend."

As if sensing his inner turmoil – although she likely could *actually* sense it – she leant forward and took one of his hands between both of hers, giving it a reassuring squeeze. "You know he wouldn't do that."

"I… I can't take that risk, Lena."

His chest ached, knowing she was trying her best to provide him with comfort and reassurance, pained that he couldn't just accept it. Why couldn't his father have just accepted this part of him? Of all people, he would have thought a demon wouldn't have cared who their children chose to sleep with. For centuries now, he kept this part of himself secret, despite knowing that most demons would not care, all because his father had. It had meant that even when Ambrose, his *best* friend, had been open with him about his feelings for Lena, Marcus had never felt safe enough to do the same. Even now, he wasn't going to the one person he trusted more than anything. Yes, he trusted Lena implicitly, but they didn't share a history like he and Ambrose did. And he knew he still wasn't telling her everything. Yet again, he felt compelled to keep a part of himself back. Locked away behind an impenetrable wall. Why couldn't he just let go of his fears and be open with both of them? Truly open with them.

"Well," Lena said after a long pause, breaking him from his thoughts. "I promised Cyrus I wouldn't get involved."

"So, Cyrus has talked to you about it," he said, keeping his gaze firmly fixed on the top of the table, simply focusing on the feel of her hands around his, using the sensation to keep his thoughts grounded.

"I have talked to Cyrus about it," she sighed. "Small but important difference."

"And?" he asked, almost masochistically wanting to know her true thoughts on the matter.

"And nothing," she said, again squeezing his hand, her tone firm yet reassuring. "I have no issue with it, but I can see you do. You can be open with me, Marcus."

"I know," he breathed with relief. Some part of him had believed that she would be accepting of this side of him. And to an extent accepting of his encounter with her boundling. But the larger and more vocal part of him still ran rampant with fears and doubt that she would have ridiculed or rebuked him for it. The sincerity in her voice pierced his heart like a lance, chipping away at his resolve. Taking a deep breath, he shut his eyes, forcing the next words to leave his mouth. "I came here to ask you something."

"Oh?"

"I need to be released from your council."

Her hands pulled away from his, the loss of contact crashing in on him as harshly as one of her infamous kicks.

"W-what?" she stammered.

"Lena, I love you," Marcus said, dropping his head forward to rest on his hands, which he now brought up to cover the shame building on his features. "You and Ambrose are my dearest friends. I will not risk your safety and the way..." he sighed, pushing himself to meet her gaze, flinching at the shock and hurt now burning like a wildfire within. "The way I feel about Cyrus risks that. He is *your* boundling, I should never have let myself give into him in the first place. I should never have indulged something that directly affects you. I cannot serve you appropriately if I am caught up in whatever Cyrus wants this to become."

She simply stared at him, unmoving, frozen as he watched a range of emotions pool within her eyes. "Marcus—"

"Please, let me finish," he interrupted, knowing he had to before he had a chance to change his mind. "Your purpose, your work, is more important than a fling or errant desire. I have to leave you, to protect you. I'm sorry," he ground out, shaking his head, "but I can't see any other way of dealing with this."

Lena's entire body slumped into her chair, unformed tears brimming in her grey depths. Marcus wanted to carve his heart out, seeing the pain and sorrow behind them. He wanted to claw the words back and swallow them, retract everything he had just said. But it was too late. The damage was done and now he would suffer the consequences. As long as Lena and Ambrose were safe, he would suffer this a thousand times over. As long as they were protected from his foolishness, his lack of control, it didn't matter. They would heal. They would survive. That's all that mattered to him.

"Is leaving my council what you really want?" she breathed, her chest heaving shallowly, like she couldn't quite catch her breath. "To lose everything I have given you?"

"No, of course not, but—"

"Then, no."

"Lena—"

"No, Marcus!" she cried, jumping to her feet, her eyes now burning with fury. A fury that poured from her body in palpable waves, hitting him like the fires of Hell itself. "I will not release you. I don't care if you are with Cyrus or someone else. I don't need you to protect my work. I don't need you to protect me. What I need is your guidance, your wisdom. And I do not believe that Cyrus has had any effect on that. So, no, I will not release you from my council. And I will not entertain this conversation further."

She turned from him, stalking over to her workbench, placing her palms flat on its surface as if to steady herself. Marcus pushed to his feet, needing to do something other than sit in witness to her agony. He wanted to go to her, to apologise. But he had to see this through. He had to make her understand.

"Lena, please," he pleaded. "I don't know how else to handle this."

"Then figure it out!" Lena yelled at him, turning back to face him, her lightning sparking across her arms, causing him to step back from her, visceral fear building in his chest. Rarely did she lose control of her powers these days. For her to do so now, her emotions were getting the better of her. Guilt punched him in the gut, weighing heavily on his shoulders, chest and limbs, knowing he had hurt her deeply. He didn't fully understand why, but he knew he was the sole cause of it. Something that would haunt him for possibly centuries to come. "Because I promise you, running away will not solve your issues," she continued. "Trust me, Marcus, I speak from personal experience here. No matter where you run or hide, whatever you are running from will find you. Have you thought about what Cyrus would do if he knew you asked to leave because of your fear of affection?"

He flinched at her question, wishing he could be angered by it, instead feeling more and more demonic with each passing second. "That's not fair, Lena," he hissed through gritted teeth.

"What you are asking is not fair," she spat harshly. "I said I would not get involved, but you are directly involving me by threatening the stability of my council."

"My staying will threaten its stability," he pressed, throwing his hands out uselessly, trying to and emphasise his point. "This *will* end badly and then neither he, nor I, will be able to serve you. He needs someone else. Someone who can actually care for him."

"But he wants *you*," Lena said, taking a step towards him. "And from what I have felt, you want him. So, what's the problem?"

"I can't, Lena," he sighed, shaking his head. Closing his eyes, he pushed his hands in his pockets, hoping to hide the way they shook as she drew nearer. "I just can't. I can't explain why."

"Then you don't really know." Her voice was barely louder than a whisper, but the sorrow within it pulled his gaze to her. She was back at the workbench, leaning back against it, her arms wrapped around her waist. She looked so small, nothing like the strong Prince he had come to know and was honoured to serve. He'd taken her spark and he wanted to kill himself for it. Suddenly, she exhaled sharply and squared her shoulders, fire returning to her eyes as they locked with his. A shiver ran through him as she stared into the very depths of his being, her gaze hardening with resolve. "Take some time if you need, but you are still part of my council," she said dismissively, firmly implying that he had no say or choice in the matter. "I need you here. Come back when you're ready."

Realising nothing he was going to say would change her mind, Marcus nodded and left the room. He made his way to his bedroom, walking to the far wall from the door and bracing his hands against it, his breathing heavy as he squeezed his eyes shut tight until his vision started to spot. His shoulders heaving, he slammed his fist into the wall with a loud roar, pouring his anger, pain and frustration into the blow. The satisfying crunch of his knuckles grounded him. The physical pain coursing up his arm was nothing compared to the vice constricting his chest.

He punched the wall again, cracks forming in the surface under his blows, before pushing away from it with a grunt. He needed to leave. To get as far away from the house as possible, knowing he was ripping a part of himself out as he did so. Ignoring the dull ache in his hand, more than likely having broken something, he grabbed a bag stuffing some items into it. He would go find a healer shortly, but he had to leave now, before he changed his mind. Without a second glance around the room, he gathered his flames and transported himself to the mountain ranges of Serbia.

Before him stood the stone cottage he and his parents had lived in. The same cottage he had fled to after William's betrayal. Closing his eyes and breathing in the cool air, he walked inside, dumping his bag on the table in the centre of the front room. Although, he didn't come back here often, the last time being almost a century ago, he had set up a number of spells that kept the cottage maintained and clean. He didn't like the memories the place evoked in him, but it served him well when he needed to escape for a while. He'd given up his chambers in Hell, and for some reason he didn't quite want to go to Hell just yet anyway.

Sighing, he collapsed on the daybed in the corner. The cottage was small, consisting of only two rooms; the front room which housed the kitchen, dining area and sitting area, and a bedroom with ensuite bathroom towards the back of the cottage. He'd installed the bathroom and hardwood floor, but otherwise the cottage still had the same decor from when his mother had been alive. It was like stepping back in time and Marcus could almost hear his parents' voices drifting on the air as he shut his eyes, letting his mind drift, replaying both his conversations with Cyrus and Lena, hoping to, as his Prince put it, 'figure it out'.

# CHAPTER THIRTEEN

The sun bore down on them as they lay spread over blankets upon the golden sand. A soft breeze fused with the salt from the sea moved around them, tugging at their hair and sending warm shivers over their skin. Lena had brought them to the beach in the morning, having seen something in her book calling her here. Her council didn't mind, happy to have a day of sunbathing and relaxation under the pretence of an outing with friends. The pretence of being human. Being normal. They may all love being demons and the power that came with it, but they had all been human once, and to live in the illusion every now and then was… nice.

Cyrus lay back with his hands clasped behind his head, his eyes closed as he drank in the beach sun, content on listening to the casual bickering of his sister, Ambrose and Archie around him. Marcus was absent, having disappeared a couple of days ago. Cyrus wanted to ask Lena about it, having heard an argument between them coming from her altar room shortly before the demon left, but figured it was better to not press the issue. Not yet anyway. As much as he wanted the cambion, as much as he wanted to see him, the space had been a relief. Tensions in the house had eased and it had given him the opportunity to truly assess how he felt about everything.

He cared about Marcus. More than he probably should, but there was no helping that now. Sure, he desired him physically, and Cyrus wanted to explore more of his sexuality with the cambion, but he also wanted to care for the man. To help ease the darkness that obviously consumed him.

He'd been with a couple of guys when he was alive, but much like with Zagan, they had been overly dominant, only seeking to control him and he had allowed that being completely inexperienced at the time. After becoming a demon that had continued, although notably only because he had no other choice than to obey.

He wasn't entirely sure he wanted to be dominated and controlled again. But at the same time, he had enjoyed the authority Marcus exuded over him. And he reasoned that being dominated didn't mean he couldn't enjoy it. It didn't mean he couldn't have a consensual dominant-submissive relationship that didn't cause his body to shut down in panic. The encounter with Marcus had made that abundantly clear to him. The cambion wanted to dominate. It was in his nature. But he hadn't taken anything that what wasn't freely given or offered to him. Marcus had made sure that he enjoyed their time in the bedroom. And Cyrus wanted to see what else he could experience at the hands of the demon. It may have started out as sex and relieving some of the tension between them, but now he wanted more. So much more.

Lena's laughter brought him out of his thoughts, the clear chime of it forming a warm smile on his lips. She had been through so much in her life. So much pain and trauma. Hearing her so happy, filled his heart with joy.

"I'll miss places like this," he sighed, peeling his eyes open to glance at the infectious grin on his sister's face.

With a giggle, she swatted at his thigh before sinking back into her Consort's embrace, her back pressed into his bare chest as he braced on his hands. "The Apocalypse is not going to destroy places like this," Lena said cheerfully, instinctively knowing what he was talking about. "It is merely going to cleanse them. They may change for a time, but nature will survive. The Apocalypse is a battle of morality. To see which side is purer in its design and purpose."

Archie scoffed from his other side. The red highlights in his hair ever more prominent under the blaze of sunshine as he rested his arms atop his knees. The rich umbre tones of his skin darkening by the minute. "Heaven wants to eradicate demons."

"But they know they can't," she responded, her eyes closing briefly. "Their light cannot exist without our darkness. Only Earth and mortals will be truly affected. Heaven and Hell are bound to always exist, ever since God split morality. We are utterly codependent on the other."

Pushing up onto his elbows, Cyrus looked over the sea, the waves coursing over the sand. "So why even have the Apocalypse?"

"Because we need to reset," she continued. "The Earth needs to reset. Heaven and Hell have gotten too big. The Apocalypse will affect both sides, diminishing our powers, forcing us, and them, to rebuild. It is in that time myself and the ninth Prince will conquer all. Earth is my domain. Heaven is theirs."

"Will we really place a Prince in Heaven?"

"That's the aim."

Lena sighed, tilting her head until it came to rest on Ambrose's shoulder. With an affectionate smile, he kissed her temple before burying his nose into her hair. Cyrus saw the way the Consort breathed in her scent, her body melting into his as he did so. Ambrose shifted slightly, putting his and her weight onto one hand, sliding his now free hand around her waist, pulling her closer to him.

With a slight cough, Cyrus looked away, not wanting to impose on their moment. It was unwise for demons to display their relationships publicly, but Lena and Ambrose's bond was well known among all demons so they happily indulged in public displays. A luxury only really afforded to Princes and their Consorts. Swallowing his jealousy at the thought, he became aware of Lena's gaze on him. But he couldn't look at her. He didn't mind too much about her sharing in his emotions, but every now and then it became bothersome. Admittedly, more frequently these days than in the beginning.

"So, why are we here anyway?" he asked, pushing up onto his hands so his back was to his sister.

"If I knew, I'd tell you," Lena chuckled. She was as clueless as the rest of them. "My book refused to show me anything else but this beach this morning so I have to assume there is a reason. Hopefully, whatever it is will make itself known soon."

"Well," Archie sighed, rolling forward onto his feet and standing up. "I'm going to get us some drinks whilst you figure it out." He grabbed some money from the beach bag.

Cyrus picked up on the hushed exchange between his sister and Ambrose behind him, laughing internally when he heard the Consort grunt. Lena had more than likely sunk her elbow into his stomach.

"Hold up Archie, I'll come with you," Ambrose huffed, scrambling to his feet and dashing after the demonic-trainer. As humans, the two were of a similar height and build, their long black hair fanning across their shoulders. Only the manner of their walk and the contrast in their skin tones defined them as they made their way across the beach to a bar.

Once the two demons were far enough away, Cyrus felt Lena shuffle closer to him, smiling at her when she laid her head on his shoulder. Despite his recent frustrations with regard to his role on her council, they were in a good place at the moment. Turning slightly, he kissed the top of her head before resting his cheek against it.

"Are you okay, Cyrus?" she asked, hugging her knees to her chest.

"I'm fine," he answered. The question bothered him less than normal. He knew why she was asking and it had nothing to do with her confidence in him. "Where did Marcus go, by the way?" he questioned, continuing to watch the waves crash over the sand.

The shake of her head was almost imperceptible but he felt it on his shoulder. "Don't worry about him," she said softly.

"Who said I'm worried?"

"Cyrus."

"Lena."

"Love you."

"Love you too," he chuckled, nudging her with his shoulder. "I know you're avoiding my question."

His sister glared at him from the corner of her eye, confirming he was right. She was avoiding the question, but he assumed more than likely because she didn't know the answer either. He smiled before again kissing the top of her head. He wasn't going to push for answers. She relaxed into him, evidently picking up on his contentment through their bond. They were closer now than they had ever been and Cyrus didn't want to jeopardise that for anything.

Lena scanned the beach, her gaze wandering over the multitudes of people likewise soaking up the sunshine. Falling into a comfortable silence, he forced his mind to stay in the moment, refusing to let it drift to Marcus. He didn't need Lena feeling his frustrations at the cambion right now. She'd gone into 'Prince-mode', as he liked to call it, trying to find whatever it was that had called her here. He didn't want to break her concentration.

"Drinks!"

Ambrose's voice pulled them from their trance, Lena quickly straightening, a wide warm smile on her face as she took her drink from him. Archie handed Cyrus a can of beer which he immediately opened, allowing the cool, hops liquid to course over his tongue.

"Thanks, swee–" Lena started to thank her Consort before something snagged her attention, her head quickly snapping to the shore line. Exchanging a look with Ambrose, Cyrus wondered what she had spotted. "Oh my..." she breathed, her voice trailing off. Even Archie raised a brow in curiosity at her current state.

"Lena?" Ambrose asked tentatively, sinking down onto the towel next to her, making to reach out for her.

"Oh my God!" she cried suddenly, scrambling to her feet, her drink spilling across the blanket as she did so. In her haste to grab her kaftan, sand was thrown over her council.

"Lena!" the Consort exclaimed, shielding both himself and his beer from the shower.

"Sorry," she mumbled hastily, barely managing to pull the fabric over her head, her arm getting caught as she hopped on the spot. "Ah... stay here," she ordered them, holding up her hands as she turned and hurried off down the beach.

"Where else would we go?" Cyrus laughed, shaking his head at her back.

Ambrose joined in his laughter before scooting over the blanket towards him, righting whatever was left of Lena's drink and brushing errant sand off. Moulding a small hole in the sand to stand his can in, Cyrus helped the Consort as best he could. Archie rested off to the side, leaning on one hand as he kept his gaze on their Prince.

Lena beelined for a young girl that was chasing the waves along the shore. She diverted last minute and made her way to a woman who was watching over the girl. The two women seemed to strike up an immediate conversation, polite smiles exchanging effortlessly.

"Does she know her?" Archie asked, bringing Cyrus and Ambrose's attention to the women.

"How would I know?" Ambrose answered with a shrug.

Cyrus huffed a soft laugh. "You sleep with her," he sniggered, earning a snort from the demonic-trainer and a punch in the arm from the Consort. "Ow," he mocked with a half-smile, rubbing his arm. Like his sister, he possessed instinctual healing abilities, his power already chasing away the pain from the hit.

"Do you know how long it would take to go through the list of everyone she and I know?" Ambrose shook his head at him, but returned the smile regardless.

"When are you and Lena going to start have children anyway?" Archie asked.

"Never," the Consort responded flatly, indicating the conversation would not go any further than this. "Neither of us want them and we performed a barren ritual on her way back."

"Drastic."

"Maybe, but it's what she wanted."

"Fair enough."

Cyrus knew exactly why Lena didn't want children and he couldn't blame her for it. Until he met her, he had not suffered any abuse at the hands of foster parents, but the homes they had lived in together opened his eyes to the pain many foster children experience. And Lena had experienced more than most. She would rather die than potentially subject a child of her own meeting a similar fate.

The three men watched their Prince as she continued to speak with the mystery woman. She crouched down to converse with the young girl briefly before making her way back to them, waving at the woman and child as she did so.

"Well, that's interesting," she smiled, settling down on the blanket, leaning into Ambrose's embrace.

"What?" the Consort asked, his arm pulling her closer to him.

Lena's smile grew wider like she had a delicious secret she could barely contain. And she did, Cyrus' head reared back in surprise as she answered; "She's a nephilim."

"What?" he blurted, unsure he heard properly. Archie choked on his beer and Ambrose went completely still.

She nodded, confirming he had heard correctly. "The forbidden offspring of an angel and a human."

"Damn," Archie said, a faint impressed air to his voice.

"And here comes her father," Lena said nodding to an all too familiar face stalking towards them, a thunderous look on his arrogant features.

"No way..." Cyrus said under his breath.

If looks could kill, the arch-angel, Raphael, would have them all buried six-feet under. If they weren't already dead that is...

Lena smiled. Or sneered. The curve of her lips sinister and taunting, her eyes gleaming with wilful intent. A look she only had when her demonic nature simmered beneath the surface. A look that would send most scurrying for their lives. Only her council had nothing to fear when she looked like that. It made Cyrus' skin pebble with anticipation, waiting to see her next move, eager to learn.

Raphael stopped a few strides from their blankets, his windswept black hair fanning over his tense shoulders. His deep olive tanned skin shone golden in the sunlight, darkening the thin white shirt that hung loosely around his frame. His gaze searched the four demons, carefully assessing each one before returning to settle on Lena. A quiet rage vibrated through his body, fire burning beneath the brown depths of his eyes. His chest heaved with laboured breath; his fists clenched either side of his hips as he fought to control himself.

Cyrus grinned in amusement. Who would have thought an angel could be so... *emotional.*

"Good to see you again, emissary," Lena greeted, her voice clipping around each word.

The angel practically snarled at them, his eyes staring daggers towards their Prince. "You and your harem need to leave, now," he spat.

In an animalistic flourish of movement, Cyrus, Archie and Ambrose shot to their feet, their bodies coiled tightly as they stepped around Lena and formed a wall before her. Ambrose growled menacingly, his eyes growing dark with possessive fury, heat practically rising from his shoulders as his breath came shallow and quick. Likewise, Cyrus pressed beside him, his stomach tightening with the desirous need to defend Lena. Regardless of her position as a Prince of Hell, he would not allow anyone to insult his sister in such a fashion. It made him glad to see the glint of discomfort form in the angel's brown eyes.

The Prince laughed darkly behind her men. "I wouldn't insult them, angel. Trust me, you won't fare well against them all."

Raphael quickly recovered his composure, glaring around the men to once against look at her. "I said leave, demon," he hissed, his voice quiet, filled with unease.

"No," Lena said firmly, rising to her feet. With a gentle hand, she pushed against Ambrose's bicep, directing him to step to the side so she could stand between him and Cyrus. At no point, did either men's gaze leave the angel. "Unlike you, demons freely walk on Earth. Angels rarely deign to visit that which they profess to love. Yet, here you are, a third visit in less than three months. Can't possibly think why?"

Her gaze travelled beyond Raphael causing him to turn and follow her line of sight where it settled on the girl still playing in the waves. His body flinched, a slight shudder passing through his arms before he spun back wildly to face Lena.

"Stay away from her." This time the angel did actually snarl, the sound so broken the words barely took form.

"Don't worry, angel. I don't hurt children," the Prince smiled slyly at him, although no light touched her eyes. "You've been a bit naughty though, haven't you? Nephilims are considered abominations in Heaven. I wonder what your brothers would say if they knew. Now, I know they hurt children."

"I'm warning you, Lena—"

"Don't make threats you can't keep, Raphael," she spat, her smile vanishing in an instant. "I am aware you've been trying to find a way into my home without tripping my alarm systems." Cyrus noted both Ambrose and Archie faltered slightly at her statement. Likewise, he hadn't been aware of that particular fact. "I know your secret now. You want it to stay a secret, back off. If you come near me, my council or my home again, I will tell your brothers about your daughter."

"You say you do not hurt children, but you would threaten one?"

"Oh no," Lena said shaking her head. "I'd save your daughter, protect her as my own. I'd leave you to your brothers."

Raphael blanched at her promise, but managed to keep his body rigid with his inner rage.

"Grand design or no, I will destroy you," he threatened, malice dripping from each word.

"Bring it on, angel," the Prince taunted.

The angel opened his mouth as if to say more, but seemed to decide better of it. His mouth snapped shut with a loud click of his teeth, sufficiently audible that Cyrus was sure he cracked a tooth. With a huff, Raphael spun on his heel and stalked away from them, his body vibrating with barely contained rage.

"Do you think it wise to threaten him?" Archie asked, his voice dangerously low as Ambrose and Cyrus drew deep breaths attempting to calm themselves.

"Probably not, but the opportunity had to be taken," Lena sighed as she bent down and started to pack some of their things away into the beach bag. Forcing his shoulders to relax, Cyrus made to help his sister, picking up one of the blankets and shaking the sand off it as she continued talking. "Raphael has been skulking around recently and I need it to stop. Now, I have the advantage."

"When were you going to tell us?" Ambrose asked, an irritated tone to his voice. "Before or after he broke in?"

Looking at him apologetically, Lena's shoulders slumped. "I'm sorry. I didn't want to distract you, any of you, from the situation with Damien. Raphael is my concern."

The Consort shook his head, moving closer to her to grip her chin, lifting her face to his. Sighing softly, Lena melted into his hold, her eyes dartling back and forth between his. Slowly, he leant down, touching their foreheads together. She touched the inside of his wrist, a silent conversation passing between them before he let go, placing a fleeting kiss on her cheek.

"We should probably confer with Marcus," the demonic-trainer said, gathering the mostly empty beer cans. "Get his thoughts on how to handle any retaliation Raphael may bring."

Lena paused and Cyrus didn't miss the way her body tensed and her jaw clenched at the cambion's name. That was interesting. "We... can't..." she muttered from behind gritted teeth. *Very interesting.*

"What? Why not?"

"Marcus has..." she started the tension in her body only easing when Ambrose placed a hand on her lower back. He grabbed the bag from her and hoisted it over his shoulder. "He's taken a leave of absence for a while. He has some things to work through." Cyrus pulled his shirt over his head, watching his sister as discretely as possible. "I will speak with Lucifer tomorrow. He needs to know about the child."

An unfamiliar feeling settled within Cyrus' gut as he took in his sister's reaction. Not quite guilt, but it felt just as heavy. Mixed with sorrow. He already suspected that Marcus had left to avoid him, and her reaction all but confirmed his suspicions. Sure, he'd accused the cambion of being scared, but he hadn't expected that the demon would actually run away. Maybe there was something else going on, but it seemed too convenient for Marcus to essentially disappear so soon after their conversation in his office. He'd left without even saying goodbye and it certainly seemed like his departure had upset Lena. The boundling's brow pulled together as he looked at his sister, wishing, not for the first time, that their bond went both ways. He couldn't help but notice that she avoided his gaze.

"Lucifer will want her brought to Hell," Ambrose said, pulling Cyrus from his thoughts.

The group looked over to the girl, watching as her mother spun her around in the air, Raphael drawing closer to them. The woman smiled when she spotted the arch-angel, the girl squealing and running towards her father. He scooped her up in his arms, casting a furtive glance over his shoulder at them. The mother touched his arm, pulling him into a hushed exchange as their daughter returned to splashing in the sea.

"He'll support my decision to leave her here," Lena said turning away and making her way up from the beach. The three men followed close behind. "Here she serves my purpose. Let's go home."

Making their way to the small side street they had arrived in, they made sure no one could see them before gathering the fires of Hell and transporting back to the house. All the while Cyrus stewed over why Marcus had left, wondering if there would be anyway of tracking the cambion without Lena's help. If Marcus had truly left because of him, then that was cause enough to continue their conversation.

# CHAPTER FOURTEEN

*Serbia; 1,000 years ago...*

With a heavy sigh, Marcus looked out over the mountain ranges, his arms folded defensively over his chest. The warm steam of his breath puffed out in front of him, mixing with the cold air. Small patches of snow still clung stubbornly to the peaks even as the days grew warmer. His mind and heart warred with each other, his stomach rolling with emotions he couldn't quite name, causing an ever-present nausea to settle within it. He was angry. Furious, even. But had no notion on how to deal with or alleviate this affliction. He couldn't go after William. Not directly. Not whilst he was protected by Kai. But he wanted to. He wanted to tear his lover apart for the betrayal. His whole body vibrated with the need to inflict as much pain on William as had been inflicted upon him.

Sensing movement behind him, Marcus tilted his head to the side slightly, a small acknowledgement as his father came to stand by his side. Lucien had been almost forty when he became a demon, however, despite the slightly older look to him, he and Marcus could easily pass as brothers. The cambion was taller than his father, but they had the same colouring. The only difference between them was their eyes. Marcus had been blessed with his mother's eyes where his father's were a deep ocean blue.

"Are you well?" Lucien asked.

"Do not fear, father," he sighed. "I will not stay long."

There had been a tense air between them since his arrival a few weeks prior. His father was his greatest support, but he had never approved of Marcus' relationships with men. He'd never understood the cambion's desires, no matter how many times Marcus had tried to explain it to him.

"You are my son, Marcus," his father said softly, placing a warm hand on his shoulder. "You may stay as long as you need. I want you to stay."

He chuckled heartily, knowing that eventually he would drive his father insane if he took him up on that offer. "You say that now."

"I will always say that."

"Please, father," Marcus said flatly, turning and heading back inside the cottage. "Not now."

"Then when?" Lucien pushed, following him. "It has been almost a month since you arrived here, burnt and bleeding. When will you finally speak with me?"

"I have already admitted you were right," he sighed, moving around the kitchen, drawing some water from the kettle sitting over the wood-fire stove, pouring it into a cup filled with nettle and cleaver herbs. "What more do you want me to say?"

Shaking his head, Lucien rounded on his son, almost slamming his palm on the wooden workbench by the stove. "I do not care about that," he snapped. "You are your own demon, you make your own choices. I may not have liked or trusted William, but he has hurt you and regardless of how I felt about him, I want to make sure you are well."

Rubbing the back of his neck, Marcus hung his head, unable to meet his father's gaze. Ever since his mother died almost five hundred years prior, their relationship had steadily become more and more strained. They hadn't realised how much of a grounding effect she had on their lives. How much she had held their unusual family together. Regardless, he loved his father and he didn't want the strain between them to become unbearable. But Lucien was not a cambion and his demonic nature was not as encompassing, as consuming, as Marcus'. He tried to keep it at bay mostly, remembering the soft words of his mother, but that could only assuage his rage for so long.

"I am fine," he managed, closing his eyes and moving to sit at the table.

"You are healed, yes," Lucien nodded, pressing his lips together in frustration as he took the chair opposite. "But you are not fine."

"Father..."

"Marcus."

"Leave it be, old man."

"I may be your father, but I can still trample you into the ground, boy."

Chuckling at his father, Marcus smiled as he sipped gingerly at his tea. They drove each other insane more often than not, but light-hearted exchanges such as these made him realise how lucky he was to have a family. One that actually cared for and loved him regardless of their differences. Very few demons had the opportunity to experience what they had. "I would like to see you try," he smirked.

Lucien returned his son's smile, but a sad gleam hinted within his ocean eyes. "Please, Marcus. Speak with me."

The cambion sighed, his breath shuddering out of him as he gathered the courage to fully open up to his father, something he rarely did. "I..." he started, coughing slightly as his voice caught in his throat. "I do not understand what happened. I felt what he felt. I felt his love. How could he do this? How did I not notice?"

"Love can make us see things that are simply not there," his father shrugged, tapping his fingers on the surface of the table.

"But I felt it," he said, letting his head fall back so he stared at the ceiling. The sage wisdom of his father was not exactly what he wanted right now, regardless of how true it might be. "Before he broke from bondage, I felt it."

"Perhaps, you felt what you wanted to feel," Lucien sighed, cocking his head to the side, a sympathetic smile on his lips. "Marcus, what your mother and I had is exceptionally rare for demons and perhaps even rarer for cambions."

"What do you mean by that?" he asked, locking his gaze on his father, his tea lying forgotten even as the steam snaked up into the cool air.

"I mean, that you live between the two worlds. Turned demons, ones who come from bondage, learn to leave their human life behind," Lucien clarified, leaning forward to rest his forearms on the table, folded in front of him. "Cambions never have that chance, which is why they are meant to be raised in the nurseries and barracks, to force you to embrace your demonic side only." His eyes dropped to the table, a pained expression on his features. "Maybe, your mother and I did you a disservice raising you here–"

"No," Marcus interrupted harshly, shaking his head. "Do not think that way, old man. I would take this pain a thousand times over for the life you and mother gave me."

Lucien smiled ruefully at his son, a smile that didn't quite meet his eyes. "What I am trying to say, is that you will have to make a choice. You can either cling to your human self, in which case I will suggest again, find a human woman to love, or man if you truly insist on that–" Marcus growled, interrupting his father, his brow furrowed with annoyance. Lucien smirked at him, shaking his head, but held up his hands in defeat and apology. "*Or*," he continued, "embrace your demonic nature, be a true cambion, caring for no one or anything. William and Kai may have taken everything you had built for now, but you are more powerful than you realise, my son. You can rebuild."

Marcus sighed and hung his head, grabbing his tea cup and holding it firmly between his hands, letting the heat from the clay cup seep into him. "Even if I did embrace my cambion nature, I will always care for you, old man."

"I will not be around forever, son," Lucien shrugged.

"We are immortal. Yes, you will."

"Very well," his father chuckled warmly. "Let me rephrase. I do not wish to be around forever. I miss your mother."

Looking at his father, Marcus saw the soft gleam of sorrow in the blue depths of his eyes. "I know," he commiserated. "I miss her too."

"I am weary, Marcus," Lucien sighed heavily. "I may not have liked William, but I had hoped that perhaps, if you truly had found someone to share existence with, I could find peace with that and find a way of moving on. I do not wish to leave you behind, but I am spent. I have no desire to serve Hell any longer."

"You are not becoming a rouge are you, father?"

"No, boy. Not yet, anyway."

Pressing his lips together, Marcus let his father's words settle over him. The weight of them sat like an anchor in his stomach, as he realised that one day he would be left alone. He held no affection for other cambions and his power had been built on his ability to survive on his own. Everything he had done had been leading to this even if he hadn't realised it. But perhaps this didn't have to be the final outcome. Perhaps he could find companionship without giving too much of himself away. Without putting himself in danger of again losing everything he built.

He just needed a different goal.

"I will make you a deal, father," he said finally.

"Oh?"

"Stay with me for now. Or rather, let me stay with you. I will rebuild. Take my revenge on William and Kai, and then, I will help you see mother again."

Lucien smiled at his son and tapped his fingers lightly on the table, nodding slightly as he did so. "I accept."

*Present day...*

"Marcus? Are you listening to me?"

Pulled abruptly from his thoughts, Marcus startled slightly, shifting in his chair as he stared at the man talking to him. "Huh?" he murmured, blinking to refocus his mind to the moment. "Oh, sorry, Henry."

"What is wrong with you?" his uncle asked, his head tilting to the side.

Marcus shook his head, again shifting in his seat, letting his head fall back with the loud thud against the wooden back. "I just have a lot going on at the moment," he sighed, staring at the ceiling.

"Is that why you're here and not with your Prince?" Henry asked, pouring them two glasses of whiskey and placing the clear crystal on the side table between the armchairs. Marcus shot him a withering look practically daring his uncle to continue that line of questioning. "Well, that's a look and a half," Henry chuckled. "Fuck, Marcus. What's wrong with you? Did you get kicked off her council?" he teased, a wicked smirk on his lips.

"Joke or not, I'll still kick your arse," the cambion snapped.

"Sure, you will."

His uncle settled into the chair next to him as they stared into the fireplace before them. Marcus had spent nearly a week at the cottage, but found the solitude after living at the house for so long, unbearable. He arrived at his uncle's mansion the night before and Henry had welcomed him without question. But Marcus knew the man's curiosity would get the better of him eventually and it seemed less than twenty-four hours is all it took.

Henry was his father's biological brother and identical twin. They had been sacrificed together around four hundred years before Marcus' birth. Together, they accepted the binding to become demons. Unlike his brother, Henry had fully embraced being a demon, becoming a council member for dealer demons and keeping any and all lovers at arm's length. Or at least that's what everyone thought. Marcus knew that his uncle's heart was hook, line and sinker taken by a medic-demon, Jacinda, but they hid their relationship perfectly.

Before Marcus had ascended to Lena's council, he had begrudgingly reported to Henry on all deals he made. He was well respected and feared among demons. It was somewhat surprising that he was not yet part of a Prince's inner circle. Something that now was even less likely to happen, considering Henry had been in favour of taking Lena away from Ambrose before she became a Prince. As such, Lena and Henry did not generally get along and Marcus had kept away from his uncle as a result.

Feeling his uncle's ocean-blue eyes boring into the side of his head, he rolled his head to the side to glare at him. "What?"

"Nothing," Henry smiled, shaking his head. "You just sound so much like your father when you talk like that. So, what *is* wrong with you?"

"Just possibly contemplating digging myself an early grave," he joked, smiling to himself, realising that he actually wasn't far off contemplating such a fate.

"Ha!" his uncle blurted. "Fifteen hundred years is not an early grave, Marcus."

"Says the almost two-thousand-year-old demon."

"Fair point," Henry smiled, raising his glass in toast. "So, what is making you think this?"

Marcus sighed heavily before taking a sip of his drink. "The fear that I might be repeating past mistakes."

"I'm going to need more information," his uncle huffed, running his hand through his dark blonde hair, just barely disturbing its usual neatness.

"Fuck, how many mistakes do you think I've made?" he asked, glaring at his uncle.

"I'm your uncle," Henry shrugged with a teasing smirk. "I think everything you do is a mistake. It's my job."

"I thought uncles were meant to be supportive."

"Human uncles maybe. Not demonic ones. Come on, boy—"

"Don't call me 'boy'," Marcus snarled, although he tried to keep any harshness out of his tone. He knew his uncle was goading him and he didn't wish to feed into that but he would tolerate the teasing only so far. "Only father could call me that."

The look on Henry's face shifted immediately to something dark and menacing. "I might have cared about your opinion on that if you hadn't killed my brother," he spat.

"He asked me to, Henry," the cambion snapped, practically slamming his glass down on the table. "I'm not going over this with you again. It was seven hundred years ago now. You know what, this was a mistake." Shaking his head, he pushed to his feet and turned to leave the room. "I'll see you around."

Henry sighed behind him. "Wait. Marcus, wait!" he called, quickly chasing after him. His uncle caught him, a firm grasp on his shoulder preventing him from leaving. "I'm sorry. You're right," he apologised. "Regardless, you are still my nephew and I do care for you. So, talk to me."

Giving his uncle a withering glare, he allowed himself to be led back to the armchairs. They had never seen eye to eye over Lucien's death. His father had been an exceptionally powerful demon. The idea that a demon like that wanted to die was a foreign concept for many. Henry had tried to understand his brother's position, but Marcus suspected he struggled with the thought he was left behind by his twin. However, unlike Marcus' mother, Jacinda was immortal like Henry, so he would never have to deal with her loss. He'd also never had to deal with a loss or betrayal like Marcus had.

"I've... met someone," the cambion finally said, resting the cool surface of the crystal glass against his temple.

Henry pressed his lips together and drew in a harsh breath. "Oh dear."

"Yeah."

"And?" his uncle pressed.

"And," Marcus shrugged. "Well, it's fucking idiotic of me to even entertain it, but..." he trailed off, suddenly unsure he wanted to admit this to his uncle. But he needed to speak to someone. "I can't get him out of my head."

"Who is he?"

"I can't tell you."

"Marcus."

The tone in Henry's voice was almost like a warning, but he knew his uncle only meant it to assure him, to push him to open up. Something he shied away from doing for so long. But if there was anyone he could be open with about these sorts of things it was his uncle. Unlike his father, Henry had never judged him for his preferences. He had encouraged the relationship with William and apologised profusely for that in the aftermath of the betrayal. Henry had even helped him hunt William down all those centuries ago.

"I know," he smiled warmly at the other demon. "But I really can't. More to protect him than me."

"Alright," Henry conceded, nodding knowingly. "I understand. So, what's the problem?"

"You know what the problem is. What if I'm just repeating what happened with William?"

"And if you are?" his uncle asked contemplatively. "Are you not in a substantially better position to weather such an outcome than you were back then?"

"Power wise and position wise, yes," Marcus agreed. "But... I'm not sure I would want to survive if it went badly."

"Look, Marcus," Henry said bluntly, twirling his glass between his hands. The cambion regarded him cautiously. Rarely does good news or advice start with 'look'. "You survived what William did to you and you killed him for it."

"I never got Kai though," he sighed.

"Yes, but Kai is another cambion. It would have been complicated."

"I could have killed him last year in the Cleansing."

"So, why didn't you?"

"Because I wanted to see him bow to Lena more."

"There's that cambion fire," Henry laughed, knocking back the last of his whiskey. "What I mean is, you already survived it once. You will survive it again if it happens. But what if it goes right? What if you finally get to have that life you used to be so desperate for? I know what Lucien used to tell to you. It doesn't have to be one or the other, Marcus. You can have love and power. They do not have to be mutually exclusive."

Staring into the depths of his glass, swirling the burnt-golden liquid around the clear walls, he tried to reconcile both his father's and uncle's words in his mind. Could he have both? Could he have that with Cyrus? Even if it was possible, if he let himself fall into a relationship with the boundling, he knew he wouldn't survive it if it went wrong. He wouldn't want to survive it. It wasn't like he hadn't thought about it. He had. He'd thought about how nice it would be to find Cyrus waiting for him each night in bed, or simply being alone with him in the library, or having breakfast together in the courtyard. He'd thought about it all. But each thought was laced with fear that one day those moments would end and he'd be left alone. Again.

But maybe they could indulge a little, he reasoned with himself. That had to be better than living with the constant sexual torment he'd been thrown into over the last few weeks. Anything had to be better than that. Maybe, they just needed a little more time to fuck each other out of their systems. Then at least, he'd be left with blissful memories rather than bitter regret.

*Right?*

# CHAPTER FIFTEEN

Hands clasped together behind his head, Cyrus sighed as he stretched out his legs, looking across the courtyard, working on building the energy to go check on the hellhounds. He'd had a rather lazy morning of ambling around the house. Lena was busy off tracking the nephilim whilst Ambrose and Archie negotiated with Damien. After discussing it with them, they all agreed that Cyrus should remain out of the negotiations, at least for now, as Damien used the time to insult him more than make productive conversation. He was happy to be as far away from that cambion as possible. Lena had faith in his plan of controlling Damien, and that meant more to him than actually being involved in the discussions.

Pulled from his thoughts, he raised his brow as he watched Marcus flame into the courtyard before him. "So, you're back then," he huffed, a teasing smile forming on his lips.

Marcus glanced towards him, hoisting the bag he was carrying higher on his shoulder before slowly walking over to the canopied area. "I am," he nodded, a guarded look in his green eyes.

"Are you going to tell me why you left?"

"Bloody hell, Cyrus. Could I have ten minutes before I have to try and defend myself from you?" the cambion snapped, striding purposefully past the boundling and into the kitchen.

"Nope," he said cheerfully knowing it was going to annoy the other demon, quickly springing to his feet and following Marcus inside. "Why did you leave?"

"Just leave it, Cyrus," Marcus groaned over his shoulder as he practically raced up the stairs heading for his room.

"Already told you I can't do that," he smirked with amusement. He never thought he would see the cambion run away from him. "So, you might as well stop avoiding the question."

Marcus sighed, flinging his door open with a bang, trying to grab it to close it but not before Cyrus managed slipped into the room behind him, leaning against the frame. "I'm not avoiding it. I'm declining to provide an answer, because I don't owe you one," he said, moving to the bed and dumping his bag at the foot of it.

"For fuck's sake, Marcus!" he snapped, sudden annoyance getting the better of him. "Can you act like a decent human being for once?"

"But I'm not human am I, Cyrus?" the cambion snarled at him, finally meeting his gaze. "And neither, in point of fact, are you."

"Why did you leave?" he repeated, folding his arms across his chest, keeping his eyes locked with Marcus, refusing to be the first to look away.

"Circling back to that are you?" Marcus chuckled, firmly planting his hands on his hips. The smile on his lips didn't meet his eyes, their green depths harden with badly veiled anger.

"Still not answering, huh?" Cyrus said, pushing off form the wall to stand, but not moving across the floor. "Fine. I'm guessing you left because of me."

Marcus shook his head, dropping his gaze to the floor. "You going to call me a coward again?"

"I never called you a coward. I said you were scared. I still think you are."

The cambion stalked towards him, a fine tremble to his arms that most would have missed. But Cyrus had spent so much time studying the demon before him, he noticed it with ease, realising he had hit a nerve. He should have been scared. But he wasn't and he could no longer wait for answers.

"Do not push me, Cyrus. I am not in the mood," Marcus growled.

"So, answer the damn question. Why did you leave?"

"Cyrus, let it go."

"I told you, I can't. Why won't you just answer me? Why did you leave?"

"Because of you!" the cambion practically roared, his fists balled at his sides, fury marring his proud features. "Is that what you want to hear?

Yes, Cyrus. I left because of you. Because I can't get you out of my fucking head! Because for whatever fucking reason, despite all of my concerns, I keep coming back to *you*. And you're right. I am scared. Scared that this, *us*," he spat harshly, motioning between them, "is going to fuck everything up with Lena and our lives here and anything else that could possibly go wrong."

An indescribable warmth coursed through his chest. So, Marcus wasn't as indifferent to him as he made out to be. Of course, the cambion had already admitted to wanting him, but this was more than just desire. This was more than just wanting to fuck. "I knew you felt it," he smirked.

"Seriously?" Marcus snapped throwing his hands in the air, closing the distance between them, his face contorting with rage. "You're going to act smug right now? You fucking brat!"

"I can be a brat if you want," Cyrus smiled at the demon, straightening his spine and firming his resolve. He knew he was playing a dangerous game, pushing like this. He'd already pushed hard during their last conversation, but he knew he could push further. He wanted to push further. He wanted to push until the tension between them snapped, leaving only the fierce pull he had been feeling for the last few weeks. Knowing now that Marcus was as drawn to him as he was to the cambion only heightened his desire to do so.

"Dammit, Cyrus." Marcus closed the last bit of space between them, leaving only a hands gap between their chests. Cyrus could feel the waves of heat pouring from the demon before him, crashing over him like the desert air. He was so painfully aware of the primal power this man had and he wanted to experience everything that came with it. "Why do you have to be so fucking stubborn?"

"Because only a stubborn person could put up with the constant whiplash they get around you," he retorted, making to push their chests together, feeling perhaps a little too confident in the moment that he was finally getting under the cambion's skin. With a low growl, Marcus' hand snapped out, closing around his neck in the way that made his heart skip and slam into his ribs at the same time. Practically sneering at the demon, he breathed; "Case in point."

"What the fuck have you done to me?" the cambion snarled, the anger that had brightened his green depths giving way to darkening desire as his pupils enlarged with lust. "Why can't I just keep away from you?"

"I could ask you the same thing," Cyrus breathed, leaning into Marcus' hold of him, relishing the dominant nature of the grasp. "But I know what you did to me. I dream about it every night. And I think you know why. Because we would be so good together. I know it and you know it."

"Fuck you, Cyrus," Marcus spat, pushing the boundling against the wall.

"That's all I want," he said ruefully, a spiteful smile on his lips. "I want you to fuck me, Marcus. I want you to fuck me over and over, until I can't walk. I want you to fill me with your cock and your cum, until I forget what it's like to be empty. I want to be taken over by you, until there is nothing left of me. I want—"

His words were cut short as Marcus crushed their mouths together, their tongues clashing in passionate anger. The cambion pulled at his shirt, untucking it from his jeans. Large hands wandered beneath the fabric, trailing up his stomach and chest, the shirt rising with them. Pulling back from the kiss only long enough to lift the shirt over the boundling's head, Marcus quickly returned to the assault on his mouth, sucking Cyrus' bottom lip between his teeth and biting softly. Sighing into the kiss, the young demon cupped Marcus' face between his hands, revelling in the sting on his lips.

With a soft growl, Marcus whipped his own shirt over his head, returning to press his body against Cyrus. The soft curls on the cambion's chest brushed against his skin, causing thrilling shivers to course over his entire body. Wanting more, he pulled at the band of Marcus' trousers, fumbling with the clasp. In a swift movement, the cambion grabbed his wrists, stopping him in his tracks, and pinned his arms above his head.

"Marcus," he whimpered, his body painfully hungry for the demon that held him. The demon that had somehow managed to fuel his desire to unimaginable heights despite his constant rejections.

"Shh," Marcus hushed him, holding his wrists with one hand, as the other trailed over his bare chest, pinching one of his nipples. Lowering his head, the cambion flicked the peak with the tip of his tongue causing the boundling to gasp at the action, his back arching with pleasure. Marcus caught the nub between his teeth, teasing it with light pressure, as his free hand traced slowly over Cyrus' ribs and waist, moving to his lower back to pull him closer. Sighing with desire, the young demon closed his eyes, intent on enjoying the attentions the cambion now afforded him, whose tongue now swirled around his nipple in enticingly warm circles.

With expert ease, Marcus undid the top of his jeans, pushing them down just over his hips, before slipping his hand inside and wrapping his fingers around the boundling's cock. Cyrus moaned at the touch, his hips bucking forwards even as the cambion pushed back with his body, keeping him pinned to the wall.

The older demon smiled, dropping a row of kisses along Cyrus' jaw and neck, his hand running smoothly along the silken shaft. "I've missed your moans," Marcus murmured against the hollow of his neck.

"They're yours," he sighed, straining against the hand still holding his wrists, wanting to touch the cambion in the same way. "Whenever you want them."

"Hm... what a delicious thought," the demon growled, pulling his hand from his jeans, chuckling at the boundling's cry of disappointment. "Don't fret, gorgeous. I may be angry with you, but even I am not cruel enough to leave you like this."

Cyrus stared at the older demon, soft surprise on his face. "No one has ever called me that," he whispered, hoping he had not misheard.

With a soft smile, the cambion pressed a long, tender kiss to his lips, pulling a soft, longing whimper from his throat. "You are gorgeous," Marcus sighed against him. "Your body is the most enticing thing I have seen and tasted."

Warmth flooded his belly, anticipation building within his chest as Marcus pulled at his wrists, guiding him towards the bed. They fell onto the bed together, Cyrus revelling in the weight of the man atop him, wrapping his legs around his waist, not wanting to give the older demon a chance to change his mind.

"So eager," Marcus teased, claiming his mouth with his own. He let go of the young demon's wrists, tracing his hand down his arm, bringing it to rest on Cyrus' jaw, gently pulling his mouth open to dip his tongue inside. The boundling moaned into the kiss, snaking his arms around the cambion's neck, never wanting the moment to end. This is what he wanted more than anything.

Marcus pulled back from the kiss, forcing Cyrus' legs from his waist so he could pull the jeans from his hips. The young demon lifted his hips, assisting in the removal of the remainder of his clothes. Fully naked now, he watched Marcus' face, trying to discern what he was thinking, as the older demon traced over his thigh before letting his hand come to rest on Cyrus' throbbing cock.

Speech stolen from him, he could only watch, enthralled, as Marcus lowered his head and sucked his cock into his mouth, his stomach tightening with both shock and excitement.

"M-Marcus? Wh- what are you doing?"

The cambion looked up at him through hooded eyes, widening as he took in the boundling's confusion. Lifting his head, Cyrus immediately missed the contact of Marcus' mouth around his cock.

"I would think it's pretty clear what I'm doing, gorgeous," the older demon stated, tilting his head to the side, his blonde hair falling across his eyes.

"You..." the boundling started, clearing his throat as his voice caught within it. "You d-don't... I know..." he trailed off not sure how to phrase what he meant.

"You know what?" Marcus asked, lifting himself back up to lay his body over Cyrus, their breath mingling between them.

Swallowing, Cyrus looked away briefly so Marcus couldn't see his embarrassment. "I know cambions prefer to be dominant. You don't have to..."

"Has no one ever done that for you?"

Squeezing his eyes shut, he managed to shake his head slightly. It was true. No one had ever done that to him. For him. He had never been on the receiving end of such attentions.

"Cyrus, look at me," the cambion said softly, cupping his cheek. At the contact, Cyrus complied, brown meeting green. "Being dominant, doesn't mean that only my pleasure matters. And trust me, sucking your cock is not only pleasurable for you," Marcus smiled at him, rubbing his thumb tenderly over Cyrus' cheekbone. "So, if you have no further objections, let me take care of you."

Cyrus barely nodded his agreement before Marcus travelled back down his body, licking and biting along his abs as he went. Returning to the position between his thighs, the older demon again lowered his head, taking the boundling's length within his mouth. The warmth of his tongue caused Cyrus to drop his head back against the mattress, a low moan pulling from his chest. He sighed as his body writhed with the building sensations. Marcus' hands held onto his thighs, forcing his hips to remain still as his tongue swirled around the head of his cock, pressing against the soft flesh just beneath it. It was amazing as every nerve in the lower half of his body fired with pleasure, forcing Cyrus to forget his earlier hesitations. Pressure grew within his belly, his breath quickening and his moans grew louder, echoing through the room. His cock throbbed painfully inside Marcus' mouth, as the cambion sucked him deeper into his throat.

"Marcus!" he moaned, louder than he intended as he grabbed at the demon's hair, trying to gain some control. "Marcus, if you keep going, I'm– ah!"

His stomach tightened as shockwaves of pleasure rippled up his body, his release flooding into Marcus' mouth. The older demon growled with satisfaction as he swallowed and licked all that the boundling had to give. Cyrus' body convulsed as his climax subsided, his mind blissfully blank and unfocused, barely aware as Marcus discarded his trousers before climbing atop him.

"Cyrus," the cambion said softly, pulling his attention back to the moment. Cyrus met his gaze, any remaining rational thought dissolved as he saw Marcus' green eyes darkened to a sea storm from desire, pupils blown so wide the colour was almost gone. "I want to hear you cry out for me and only me. I want to make you moan until it's the only thing you can do. May I have you?"

Cyrus could only nod in answer, as he reached up to hold onto the cambion's neck. Marcus leant down, pressing a tender kiss full of yearning upon his lips. He could taste the bitterness from his release, still in shock at the experience that had been given to him.

Grabbing the lube, Marcus sat back on his knees, pouring some onto the head of his cock before positioning himself between Cyrus' thighs. No words were needed as the older demon pushed inside the tight hole, stretching it around him.

"Fuck, gorgeous," Marcus groaned as he rocked his hips slightly, gaining further depth with each small thrust. "You're taking me so well. How much more can you take, baby boy?"

Cyrus' head tipped back against the pillows, unable to answer even as his own cock twitched at the sensation, hardening again as Marcus finally buried his full length within him.

The older demon caught one of his knees, pulling it up and against his chest, hooking Cyrus' leg over his shoulder. "Arms over your head," he ordered as he started to move his hips. Eager to comply, Cyrus practically threw his arms above him, the wondrous sensations emanating from his arse pulling endless moans from his throat. "Yes, baby, like that," the cambion said gruffly, increasing his pace as his hips rammed forward. "Fuck, you're tight. Tell me how you feel."

His body, already over-sensitised from his climax, could feel every move, every touch, every inch of the demon that now claimed him. His arsehole was insatiable, desperately wanting more as Marcus reached a depth within him as yet unexplored by anyone else. Anything, he vowed silently to himself, he would give anything to be able to feel like this for eternity. To feel this way at the whim of Marcus.

"Amazing!" he cried, as his fingers dug into the pillow above his head. "You feel so fucking good, Marcus," he panted. "Your cock is amazing. I've never felt like this. I want everything you can give me."

Confusion ripped through him as the cambion withdrew, until he found himself flipped onto his stomach, Marcus' warm body pressing against his back. Sliding back inside effortlessly, Marcus slammed his hips against Cyrus' arse as the boundling gasped out with surprise and pleasure. The cambion trailed his hands over his shoulders and up his arms until their fingers intertwined above their heads.

"Wait," he rasped, trying to hold back against his desperate need for release. "We need a towel."

"I can change the sheets," Marcus growled into his ear. "Now unless you're screaming my name, be a good boy and shut up."

Cyrus whimpered beneath the demon, his body winding tighter as he was forced closer to the edge, shivering with pleasure at the command. He may like pushing Marcus' buttons and being a brat in general, but he wanted to be good for the older demon. He wanted to be so good for him. And if being good meant that he got to continue to experience what it was like to be taken by Marcus, he would happily put aside his bratty ways and be the best of boys for him. Just for him.

But he needed more.

"Marcus," he half groaned, half moaned around the name, revelling in the heady feeling overtaking him as the cambion growled with approval at the sound. "More, please."

"You want more, baby boy?" Marcus rasped, biting along the boundling's shoulder.

"Yes."

"Call me, 'sir', and beg me for it, gorgeous."

"Sir," Cyrus breathed, pressing his forehead into the pillow. "Please, sir," he begged. "Please, fuck me harder."

The cambion cursed under his breath, wrapping strands of smoke around the young demon's wrists, keeping them pinned above his head. Marcus pulled them to their knees, placing a large hand on the back of Cyrus neck, holding the boundling firmly in place as he brutally slammed his hips forward. Despite his history with the kind of hold, Cyrus thrilled at the dominance of it, his toes curling as pressure built within his abdomen again. Something with Marcus felt different. He felt calm. He felt... safe. Lost in the building tension as the cambion worked his body closer to the edge, rather than the darkness of his memories. He could feel Marcus' cock throbbing inside him, the sensation only serving to heighten his own pleasure. Oversensitivity caused him to flinch as he felt a strong grasp wrap around him, stroking firmly with each thrust of the older demon's hips.

"Come for me, gorgeous. Let me feel you come."

If he'd been on the edge of the cliff before, the demon had just thrown him off it. Cyrus' cry echoed through the room, his cock and arse pulsing as waves of desire coursed through him. Marcus followed suit, his fingers flexing against the boundling's neck with a groan, emptying his hot release, filling Cyrus completely.

Slowly, as their bodies stilled and their breathing calmed, Marcus rolled to the side, taking hold once again of Cyrus' hands and gently pulled the boundling into his arms, away from the mess on the sheets. Confused, he stared at the cambion, unsure of how to react to the gesture as Marcus wrapped his arm around his shoulders, holding one of his hands against the soft curls covering his chest.

"Marcus?" he asked softly, as he tentatively laid his head on the older demon's shoulder.

"Don't read anything into this, Cyrus," Marcus said gently. "You said you wanted me to fuck you over and over and I fully intend on doing just that." With a sigh, he rolled Cyrus onto his back and lifted onto his elbow to look down into the boundling's eyes. "I can't give you the kind of relationship you are looking for. I've been there, done that and it almost killed me. I won't go there again." Cyrus felt his chest tighten with grief, but stared silently at the demon, not wanting to push the subject. Tenderly, Marcus ran his hand down his side, brushing his fingers along his ribs and hip before resting on the curve of his bottom. "But I will no longer deny that I desire you, and it has been a long time since someone pursued me as stubbornly as you," he chuckled softly. Despite the acute sorrow in his chest, Cyrus smiled joining in with quiet amusement. "Even though I still think this is a bad idea, until you find someone else you desire, I am happy to fulfil your needs."

Sadness washed through his body as he knew, he would never want anyone but Marcus. Everything within him was now primed for his touch, his mouth, his cock. No one would ever again be able to make him feel the way that Marcus so effortlessly did. But he would take the offer, if that was all he would get. He willed his face to be expressionless, hoping to not give himself away. Slowly, he reached up and touched the cambion's jaw.

"Okay," he said softly, nodding his head. "I can live with that."

Marcus nodded, before lowering his head and capturing his mouth with a firm kiss. Cyrus felt an icy hand grip his heart, painfully squeezing it within his chest. Trying desperately to ignore it, he lifted his arms to wrap around the cambion's shoulders, focusing on the warmth of the body that pressed against him.

"Lena is going to kill me when I see her," Marcus sighed against his lips. "I was hoping to find her first, but..."

"Got distracted."

"Deliciously so."

"You're a bastard, Marcus."

"And you really are a brat," the cambion smirked. "Well, gorgeous, if I'm going to face the wrath of your sire, I'm going to get my fill of your body first."

Cyrus smiled, nuzzling his face against Marcus' cheek until their lips found each other. It might not be quite what he wanted, but at least he would get to enjoy Marcus' affections for now. He could only hope that one day, the walls would come down, allowing him inside. Or that someone else might steal his attention, setting his heart free of this hot and cold game he, admittedly, started. Both seemed like an impossibility, so Cyrus decided he would focus on the here and now. And here and now, he was being willingly devoured by the one he so desperately wanted.

# CHAPTER SIXTEEN

Marcus tried to ignore the heavy feeling of unease forming in his gut as he, as gently as possible, extracted himself from Cyrus' embrace, leaving the boundling sleeping in his bed. He had to find Lena. He could no longer put off the inevitable conversation with her and although it was enticingly tempting to remain curled up with Cyrus, he needed to remove the dread at her reaction to this development.

After their time in the bed, Marcus had taken the young demon to the bathroom, reverently washing and caressing the gorgeous body. He wanted nothing more than to allow his hands to wander over every inch of sculpted skin. Cyrus brought out a side of him, he hadn't indulged in a long time. Taking care of someone after sex wasn't necessary to him when the only encounters he'd had until now were with incubi. More often than not, they left him before he had a chance to even catch his breath.

But taking care of Cyrus was something special. Something... beautiful. It warmed him, like a fire spreading from the very core of his being. The boundling melted into his touch, sighing with contentment as Marcus worked the tension out of his muscles. Tension that the cambion had worked into them. And he had worked Cyrus hard. Almost as if he was making up for lost time, which he supposed in some ways, he was.

After the shower - and after what they did in the shower - Marcus carried the half-asleep boundling back to his bed. It almost surprised him when he crawled in behind Cyrus, pulling the gorgeous body against his, breathing in the boundling's scent. He'd missed this. Those moments of contented bliss and calm where his mind simply fell silent. Where his pain and internal turmoil were like a distant memory. But like all good things, they must come to an end.

Now re-showered and dressed, he glanced at the sleeping demon, a soft smile on his lips. Hopefully, Cyrus would not be too upset to find him gone, but he would speak with him further once he got back. With a sigh, he left the bedroom, certain that he would be faced with yet more questioning from the boundling, regardless of what he did.

Once in the courtyard, he closed his eyes and concentrated on where Lena might be. The link they all shared as part of her council meant they could find each other as and when needed. He had feared that she may have pulled away from him, dampening their connection, but he found her with ease, a warmth spreading through his chest as her aura called to him. Bracing himself, he gathered his flames and transported to her side.

Confusion settled over him as he found her leaning against a tree, her gaze locked on a house on the other side of the street from her. A young girl, maybe six or seven years old, played in the front garden. A woman, the girl's mother he assumed, based on their matching blonde curls and blue eyes, sat on the balcony keeping a careful watch on the girl.

"Hey, Lena," he said softly, not wishing to startle her. Regardless, she flinched slightly at his greeting.

"Marcus?" she questioned, looking over her shoulder at him. "What are you doing here?"

"I needed to talk to you," he said, making his way over to her side, shoving his hands in his trouser pockets.

"How'd you find me?"

"Perks of being part of your council, remember?"

"Right, yes," she nodded with a tight smile. "Right... Sorry. What did you need to talk about?" She paused slightly before pinning him with a hard glare. "Please don't say Cyrus."

"No," he chuckled under his breath, shaking his head. "Not about him."

"Thank Lucifer," she sighed, her shoulder's relaxing. "So, what about then?"

"I heard Damien's coming by tomorrow for final negotiations. I just wanted to catch up in private over what's been happening whilst I was away."

"Oh, okay. Yeah, sure." She sounded uncertain. He peered at her from the corner of his eye, noting she was again transfixed on the girl. "Now's not really a good time though. Could it wait until I get back to the house?"

"Of course." He made to leave but his curiosity got the better of him. That and he didn't really want to leave. He hadn't realised how much he'd missed her. How much he missed just being in her presence and he wanted to spend some time with her. He also wanted to find out what she was doing and why she was so focused on a child. She didn't want children as far as he was aware, so it seemed very much out of character for her to take such interest in one. "Do you want me to leave you alone?" he asked hesitantly.

Lena shook her head, turning towards him slightly with a sad smile. "No," she said softly. "I could actually do with the company."

Marcus smiled despite himself. "What are you doing?"

"Watching."

"I can see that," he said with soft, indulgent laughter in his voice. "What are you watching?"

"The nephilim."

The breath knocked from his lungs as his head reared back in shock at her declaration. "The *what*?" he gasped, his eyes wide and locked onto the child. "Nephilim?"

"Oh right, you were away when we found out about her," she sighed dismissively, a hint of distain to her tone. Marcus winced at the sound, realising that there was a long way to go before they would return to how they were before he left. Dropping his gaze from the girl, he quickly glanced up and down the street, realising that no one was paying them any mind, despite the fact that his Prince wasn't exactly being discreet in her spying. As if picking up on his thoughts, Lena chuckled slightly and shifted against the tree. "We're shrouded. No one can see us," she assured him.

"Good thinking," he nodded. "It might come under suspicion for two adults to be staring at a... 'child'?"

"Ha!" she laughed, throwing her head back, a wide smile on her lips. "Yeah... no ordinary child though. She's Raphael's daughter. Found out about her around a week ago. I've been trailing her and her mother since."

Being a nephilim was shock enough, but the arch-angel's daughter? He would never have seen that coming. "Raphael's daughter, huh?" he mused. "Well, that's an interesting twist."

"No kidding."

They fell into a comfortable silence for a while. Marcus stood contently beside her, his gaze watching the crowds behind them, playing on the field opposite the house whilst Lena continued to study the girl. He was itching to speak with her about Cyrus, but didn't want to jeopardise the calm between them right now. But perhaps he could ease them into the conversation.

"So why are you trailing her?" he asked, moving to lean on the neighbouring tree. There was only a metre between them so they could still converse without needing to raise their voices. "You going to bring her in for Lucifer?"

Lena shook her head. "No. I need her where she is," she sighed, shifting slightly so her back was against the tree and she could move her gaze between the girl and Marcus. "I've spoken to my siblings about her and they have all agreed to leave this to me."

"All of them?" His brow raised in surprised. It was rare all Princes held a unanimous opinion.

"Mm-hm," she murmured in affirmation.

Studying her, Marcus saw her face morph into one of sorrow, a deep-rooted pain emanating from her eyes as she looked back towards the house.

"What's wrong?" he asked softly.

The Prince took a deep breath, exhaling slowly before she answered him. "Her mother is sick," her voice barely louder than a whisper.

"What do you mean?" he queried, his gaze snapping to the woman as she called out to her daughter. The girl bounded up the stairs and put something in her mother's outstretched hand before returning to the garden. The woman smiled warmly, intently studying the gift her daughter had given her. "She looks okay."

"She's dying," Lena explained. "I would estimate she has maybe a year at best. Most likely only six months. The nephilim is constantly emitting power. Like water leaking out of a cracked pipe. She is literally poisoning her mother. Our powers are toxic to mortals after all and that child is giving her mother a daily dose."

"Shit," he muttered under his breath, realising the underlying cause of his Prince's sorrow for the child. "What will happen to her once her mother dies then?"

Lena shrugged. "Raphael can't care for her without raising suspicions. It would risk other angels finding out about her. She can't go to Heaven. They'd kill her. Foster care most likely," she sighed with a harsh grimace. "She's grown up in a mortal life so..."

If Lena could change anything about the mortal world it would be how the foster care system functioned. Her history with the system was certainly not the worst, but it formed deep emotional scars for her. Something that fed the ruthlessness of her demonic nature. Marcus' heart had broken for her when she had told him and Ambrose her life story and the abuse she suffered both at the hands of her mother and foster parents. With his own mother having been so accepting of his demon half, he found it hard to understand how parents could be so cruel to their children. His father may not have understood him, but his love had never been in question.

"Can anything be done for the mother?" he asked.

"No. Other than a deal maybe," Lena huffed, crossing her arms in front of her. "But I can't risk getting close to her. Raphael has increased his visits to her now he knows I know about them."

"Can't Raphael help her?"

"She's dying from angelic power. He would only succeed in speeding up her death. She would need demonic power to counteract it."

"Why do you need the girl to stay here?"

Lena scoffed and hung her head in exasperation. "That's a lot of questions, Marcus. If you'd been around, you would know most of this."

The niceness of the moment was gone as guilt slammed into his chest, practically knocking all breath from him. He knew he had hurt her when he asked to leave her council and even more so by actually leaving. He doubted that it would have helped that immediately on his return he got caught up in her boundling. Taking a deep breath, he braced himself for her scrutiny, knowing it was long overdue by this point.

"Sorry," he breathed, his voice quieter than he would have liked. He coughed slightly, forcing himself to meet her gaze. "I'm sorry, Lena. You were right. I shouldn't have left."

"After everything we did together during the Cleansing, everything we went through. The blood we spilt..." She looked at him with an almost pleading look in her eyes, like she desperately needed him to understand the meaning behind her words. "I worried at the time that you would hate me for sending you after the cambions. I still worry."

"I don't," he said, emphatically shaking his head, pushing away from the tree to draw closer to her so she could see the truth in his eyes. "I could never hate you, Lena. I happily carried out your orders because I knew I was protecting my family by doing so. And I would do it again, in a heartbeat, if you commanded it. You and Ambrose are my family."

"Until you and Ambrose, everyone left me," she sighed, dropping her gaze to the ground. "My father. My mother. The rest of my family abandoned me to foster care. I even lost Cyrus for a time, regardless of what happened, it hurt all the same."

Finally, he understood her pain. She thought he had abandoned her, like everyone else before. Regardless of his intentions to protect her, he had hurt her in the worst way possible. Swaying on his feet, Marcus felt sure that even a slight breeze would knock him on his arse. That possibility when he asked to be released hadn't even crossed his mind. He knew he had risked her questioning his loyalty to her. It never occurred to him that he would shake her belief in his devotion to her as well. He wanted the ground beneath him to crack open and swallow him whole as he shut his eyes tightly, wondering how in the Hell he was going to fix this. She sniffed, drawing his attention back to her as he tried to stamp down the shame he felt at the pained expression on her face.

"When I ascended, this council became my family. *You* became my family," she continued. "Cyrus is a part of that family, too. I don't care whatever arrangement you have made with each other, but I need to know that *if* it does go wrong between you, I won't lose you both."

"You won't. I promise," he said with such conviction he almost believed it himself.

"I rely on you, Marcus. A lot," Lena sighed, holding out her hand for him. He caught it eagerly, giving it a reassuring squeeze, wanting to impress his commitment to her again through their touch. "I need you by my side. I don't think you realise how important you are to me."

"You can still rely on me," he assured her.

"Can I?" she asked a hint of derision to her tone. "Or will you just run again when things get hard?"

"No," he shook his head again. "I swear to you, Lena. I won't ever leave you again."

"Good," she gave him a curt nod, tightening her hold of his hand.

He moved to stand beside her as they both leant against the same tree, their shoulders pressed together. After a moment, Lena's gaze turned back to the house as they watched the woman start to corral her daughter inside, the sun beginning to touch the horizon behind them. "I need her here because she serves a purpose for me here. Leverage over Raphael. There's something else, but I can't quite put my finger on it yet. I'm drawn to her. Similar to how I was drawn to Ambrose when I first met him. She's... important somehow."

Marcus stared at his Prince, a soft indistinguishable gleam illuminating her grey eyes. Her gaze upon the child was filled with both warmth and curiosity.

"What's her name?" he asked quietly.

"Hope," Lena whispered, the name sounding like a sacred promise falling from her tongue. "Her name is Hope."

# CHAPTER SEVENTEEN

If he ground his teeth together anymore, he was going to wear them down to his jaw.

Forcing himself to relax, Cyrus twisted his neck forcing loud cracks from it. His jaw clicked as he loosened it, exhaling sharply as he did so. Lena looked at him warily, a warning in her eyes that he needed to gain control of himself before Damien arrived. He nodded to her in understanding and apology. Of all days, she didn't need to be distracted by his emotions. The intensity of their binding, compared to what he had with Zagan, was bothersome. There were days he honestly believed they would be better off if he were bound to someone else. But who on Earth, or in Hell, would be able to override Lena's binding? Only another Prince of Hell, unless she voluntarily relinquished him and he knew full well that would never happen. Bothersome as it was, Cyrus liked the closeness the bond gave them. He didn't want anyone else to be his sire, even for all the difficulties it came with.

They hadn't talked about what happened between him and Marcus the day before. He doubted his sister wanted to talk about it so would only raise the subject if she did first. It had bothered him to wake up and find Marcus gone, although he supposed he should haven't been totally surprised by it. It would have made more sense if they had been in his room, but waking alone in Marcus' was... odd. He felt like he'd been imposing on the space. He left almost immediately when he realised Marcus wasn't there, flaming to his own room to shower and dress in preparation for Damien's visit.

Now, he and said cambion leant against the same wall in Lena's altar room, only a small space between them, but to Cyrus it felt like a canyon. Sure, they came to an agreement yesterday, but they needed to talk further. To figure out how they should interact outside of the bedroom. Marcus may know how he wanted things to work, but Cyrus felt clueless, and the uncertainty was going to drive him insane.

Shifting against the wall, he swallowed hard, pushing the thoughts of their agreement from his mind. Now was not the time to delve into it. Ambrose and Archie sat leisurely at the table. Lena leant against her workbench. They were all waiting on Damien and, supposedly, Balo.

"He's late," Marcus huffed, folding his arms over his chest.

Lena pursed her lips in annoyance. The tension in the room was close to breaking point. If Damien didn't get there soon, Cyrus had every faith that Lena would find him and drag his cambion arse through the deepest fires of Hell.

"Maybe he got caught up," Archie mused with a teasing smile.

"In Balo," Ambrose chuckled under his breath despite the fact everyone in the room could hear him.

"Ambrose!" Lena snapped.

Marcus' shoulders began to shake with quiet laughter and Cyrus pressed his lips together to hide his own smile. They shared a knowing look and the boundling felt himself relax slightly. At least Marcus wasn't outright denying their attraction. He may not want to declare it openly, which was fine, but he wasn't exactly hiding it either.

"But seriously," the Consort continued, meeting Lena's glare. "How long are we going to wait for him? If he doesn't want to deal then..." he trailed off, leaving the obvious question to simply hang in the air.

The Prince shrugged. "Then he leaves me with no choice. He either deals with me, or he dies. I don't have time for insignificant power struggles."

The nephilim was the priority now. Damien was a distraction.

As if sensing her patience was wearing thin, the soft chime of their alarm sounded, alerting them to a new presence in the courtyard. Archie and Marcus quickly left the room to collect their guests. It wasn't long before they returned with both Damien and Balo between them. Cyrus, despite his less than subtle grin, had to look away to stop himself for searching for signs that they had, in fact, gotten caught up in each other.

Marcus returned to his side and hissed quietly at him; "Tame that grin, gorgeous. Or I'll tame it for you."

His eyes widened at the statement as he coughed to cover his gasp. *Fucking hell...*

Lena pinned them with a glare that would have set them on fire if it were possible. Marcus leant against the wall as cool as a cucumber. Thankfully, their guests didn't seem to notice as Archie guided them to the centre of the room to stand before their Prince.

"Prince Lena," Damien greeted cooly.

"Damien," she returned, taking a small step towards him.

"So, I get the whole reception today, then?" the cambion sneered, looking around the room.

Cyrus bit the inside of his cheek, keeping his face emotionless as Damien looked over him. In human form, the demon was even less impressive with ashy-toned hair and muddy-brown eyes. Why the cambions seemed to be listening to him was a mystery to the boundling.

"Well, then," Damien huffed turning back to Lena, "shall we get on with this?"

Lena hummed as she licked her lips. "There's going to be a slight addendum to the deal discussed with my council. An addition to the already agreed terms."

Cyrus' brows bunched together in confusion. What was she doing? He glanced at Marcus from the corner of his eye and saw a similar expression pass over his features momentarily before schooling back to serene calm. Archie caught his gaze, a small frown on the trainer's face, but he shook his head slightly, silently telling him to keep quiet. It would not be good for Lena's council to voice any form of opinion that contradicted her in front of Damien. Or anyone for that matter. Breathing in deeply through his nose, Cyrus forced his face to relax.

"What?" the cambion breathed, his composure wavering for a moment before he set his face in a hard stare. "What is this?"

"Nothing has been solidified yet, Damien," Lena said waving her hand dismissively. "We are still negotiating."

The air in the room felt unbearably heavy, thick and full of tension. A knife could cut through it. Or it might snap. Cyrus felt a pit form in his stomach, swirling like a storm threatening to throw him over the bow of a boat. He hadn't been directly involved in negotiations recently, but he was aware of everything that had been said. Everything that had been agreed and Lena had left it to him to decide when the terms were sufficient. Why was she changing things now? Why hadn't she talked to him about this? Was she really that wrapped up in the nephilim, she couldn't even take five minutes to fill him in on her plan?

"What are the new terms?" Damien asked, taking a deep breath as he stared at the Prince.

"You are going to give me one of your boundlings."

*Oh shit.* Cyrus' blood ran cold. No way she was doing this. Why would she do this?

"What?" the cambion snapped, his brows skyrocketing into his hairline.

Lena sighed, pinching the bridge of her nose. "This is going to take forever if you keep asking that question. Do I really need to repeat myself?" She paused, looking pointedly at Damien, waiting until he finally shook his head confirming she didn't. "Good," she nodded approvingly before continuing. "You are going to send one of your boundlings to live with me, here. They will still be bound to you, and in that way, if you step out of line, I can bring down upon you a world of hurt and I don't even need to touch you. They will serve me, you will instruct them as such, and they will be removed from your control. I will provide you with the appropriate wording for the command and you will give it as directed."

Damien shifted on the spot, his breath coming ragged and shallow as he fought to contain his anger. "Why would I agree to that?"

"I am preparing to give you sufficient power to control all of the cambions. Excluding Marcus, of course," she chuckled. Marcus huffed a small laugh, but Cyrus could feel the tension pouring from his body. "Do you really think I would do that without an insurance policy?"

The cambion looked like he wanted to explode, his fists clenched beside him, his whole body vibrating with quiet rage. "I'm assuming you have no preference in boundling?" he ground out.

"On the contrary," Lena practically purred, a feral grin forming on her lips. Cyrus swallowed quietly knowing whatever she had planned would likely pop the tension in the room like a pin to a balloon. A balloon filled with hydrogen with a pin lit on fire. "You will leave Balo with me."

*Boom.*

"What?" Damien blurted, stepping back slightly like her words had been a physical blow. "No!"

"Tell me, Damien," she sighed, stepping towards him, lowering her voice as she drew closer. "What is more important to you? Balo," she taunted stepping to his side and between him and the boundling in question, "or the position and power I am going to give you?"

The demon was silent, his gaze following the Prince as she circled around him, visibly chewing the inside of his cheek as he contemplated her question.

"Damien?" Balo pressed him, evidently no longer content to remain silent as his fate was decided without him.

"Quiet," Damien snapped at him. Cyrus noted curiously that no command had been triggered, Balo's bindings remaining their stark black. But the boundling clamped his mouth shut as instructed.

"Balo will be protected with me," Lena continued returning to her position in front of her workbench, once again leaning against it. "No one will touch him, unless you give me reason to. How long do you think you can continue to protect him now that I know how much he means to you?"

"I could just go to the other cambions. Continue the dissent."

"But you wouldn't," Lena shook her head, her smile never leaving her lips. She walked back towards him. Closing the distance, she lifted a hand and poked her finger into the centre of his chest. Damien flinched slightly under her touch, but Cyrus would give him credit as the cambion held her glare. "Because in order for them to continue to follow you, you'd have to explain why you declined my offer. And that would mean exposing Balo to them. The cambions that *are* loyal to me have already started spreading the rumours of the terms you presented to my council. There would be no lying to them," she sneered at him. "Not anymore."

Forget a pin dropping, a feather could have fallen and everyone would have heard it for the silence in the room. No one was breathing as the expressions on Damien's face morphed from anger to pain to contemplation and back. Lena had him cornered, with no alternatives available to him, he had to accept. Or lose everything.

Cyrus stared at his sire, unable to comprehend what would have driven her to making this change. They had agreed that Damien was going to reduce his number of boundlings by not taking any new ones, having to seek Lena's approval before offering, forcing him to be reliant on the power she was going to give him to maintain future control. Power she could always take away. He couldn't understand why she would also seek to drive the two demons apart. And why did it seem like none of her council knew she was going to do this?

"What do you plan to do when he breaks?"

"He will continue to live with me under the same conditions," the Prince said flatly, waving her hand as if it was obvious. Raising a brow at the cambion, she smirked. "Do you doubt my ability to keep him here?"

"No," Damien said after a moment, his shoulders slumping with defeat.

"You may have a day to think about it if you need. But you do not get my support if I do not get Balo."

"Will I..." Damien started before his voice faltered, ripping through the tension like a razor blade. He coughed slightly before continuing. "Will I be allowed to see him?"

Cyrus felt like a knife had been stabbed into his gut at the question, guilt racking his body. He'd told the others of his suspicions about Damien and Balo. Now he felt directly responsible for tearing the lovers apart. Sure, his current fling with Marcus was not a relationship, but his heart stuttered in his chest at the thought of being torn apart from him like this. The same way Lena and Ambrose had been torn apart the year before. Which made it all the more shocking that she was taking this action.

Lena sighed, folding her arms in front of her. "You may visit once a fortnight to see each other. At which point you will also report to me all movements of the cambions. Any more than that and I'd get sick of seeing you," she drawled as if she was bored with the conversation. She wasn't. Cyrus knew that. But she was putting on a show. Doing what was necessary to rattle Damien. "I am giving you everything you want, Damien. Are you really going to turn back now?"

The cambion swallowed audibly and when he spoke, his voice was broken. "Alright. I accept."

"Damien! No!" Balo blurted, hurt flashing across his face as he stepped towards his sire.

"Control your boundling, Damien," Lena snapped, waving her hand dismissively as she turned away.

"Bal, stop," Damien ordered. Balo stepped back in shock, his bindings glowing as the command took hold. "I'll fix this."

"And how do you propose to do that?" the Prince asked, rounding on the cambion. "I'll tell you what, if you can prove yourself to be trusted, if you can prove you can control the cambions, *if* you can prove

I do not need to keep... Bal? May I call you that?" she directed to the boundling.

"I'd rather you didn't."

"Fair enough," she shrugged, turning her gaze back to the cambion. "Prove to me I don't need to keep him from you, I will return him." Her words hung heavy in the air. Even Cyrus could see that it was a very big 'if'. Lena did not trust Damien at all, and he very much doubted there would be anything that the man could ever do to earn her trust. "You have my word."

"I thought I had the word of your council," he spat at her.

"You did," she nodded. "But my council is not me. I am free to change any terms they may present. With immediate effect, Balo will remain here. Tomorrow, you will publicly pledge your loyalty to me in front of all the cambions. Only then, will I provide you with the power you require. Deal?"

The hesitation was tangible but only lasted for a moment before Damien ground out, baring his teeth; "Deal."

With a triumphant smile, Lena held out her hand waiting for Damien to take it. He stared at it like it was a snake, coiling to bite him. Licking his lips, he took hold of her hand, her lightning coursing over his arm leaving faint markings in his skin that faded after a moment.

The deal was bound.

"You may say goodbye," the Prince said with a curt nod, turning away and walking to her workbench, picking up a leather cuff as she continued speaking. "You will then command Balo to follow my orders, whatever they may be. Archie will then show Balo to his room. Balo, you will stay there until I come to see you." Turning on the spot, she tossed the cuff to the boundling who caught it impulsively. He turned it in his hands, inspecting it, obviously aware it was an object Lena had made. "Put this on, now. You will not be able to use your powers or transform whilst wearing it, nor will you be able to remove it. Do not try to leave, or I will kill Damien. Do you understand?"

Balo swallowed, his eyes closing as he accepted the inevitability of his fate. Taking a deep breath, he finally looked up at the Prince, slipping the cuff on as he did so, the runes in the leather glowing momentarily as it contracted to fit perfectly around his wrist. "Yes," he said quietly.

Archie pushed to his feet, motioning for Damien and Balo to leave the room before him. Cyrus watched them leave, anger building in his chest. Desperately waiting for the door to close, his clenched his fists, arms still folded, gaze locking onto Lena once Damien, Balo and Archie were out of view.

"The hell was that?" he snapped as soon as the door clicked shut, pushing away from the wall and stepping towards his sister.

"Cyrus," Ambrose said softly, but with no real authority to it. The Consort glanced towards the door, evidently more worried about Damien or Balo hearing than stopping him from arguing with his sister.

Lena looked at him, leaning against her workbench, a silent questioning in her eye, daring him to continue.

"Did Archie and Marcus know you were going to do this?" he asked, instantly wondering if this whole time she had led him to believe she trusted him, he was only being humoured by the others.

"No," she said without hesitation, shaking her head. "But you should have."

Rage flared through his chest, his lip curling from his teeth as he snarled at her; "What does that mean?"

"What was your plan?" she asked, stepping towards him, barely a breath of space between them. "Once Damien agreed to the deal, what was your plan to control him? Did you really think that simply providing him with enough power and slowing weeding him of boundlings was going to be sufficient? In the long run, maybe. But whilst he still has his numerous boundlings, we needed something with immediate control."

"No. I knew we would have to keep an eye on him. I had thought of this," he said waving his hand round in emphasis, "but I didn't think it was something you would have agreed to."

"Then you thought wrong."

She might as well have hit him, the way he almost fell on his arse at her dismissal. He wished she'd hit him, then at least she would also be in pain. He wanted to shout at her, but the acute sorrow that coursed through his chest dampened the urge. "Lena?" he managed, hating how small his voice sounded.

"Cyrus, someone like Damien cannot be controlled simply by checking in on him from time to time," she said, her eyes pleading with him to understand. "We needed leverage, and now we have it."

But he couldn't understand. He knew that becoming a demon altered a person's morals. His own had very much been affected. He didn't even bat an eye when she ordered the Cleansing of the cambions. He'd helped, intent on inflicting the same pain on them that they had inflicted on him for years. But this was different. To tear apart a bond between a sire and a boundling was incredibly frowned upon in Hell. When it happened to Lena and Ambrose it nearly started a civil war among demons. How could she do the same thing?

"You are doing to them what Zagan did to you and Ambrose," he growled at her, barely noticing as the Consort got to his feet and Marcus stepped away from the wall. It wasn't like he would ever do anything to harm his sister, regardless of how pissed off he was with her right now. It wasn't like he could. He was no match for her, he knew that. But of course, their instinct was to protect her. It became an overriding drive of all Princes' councils.

"Where do you think I got the idea from?" she snapped, lifting her chin, bringing their faces closer together. "But at least they can be comforted in the knowledge that I won't be carving into Balo's flesh every day. Balo will not be living here with the constant threat of being raped or abused or beaten. Unless Damien gives me reason to, Balo will be living in positive luxury compared to what we experienced. Can you say that Zagan treated us or anyone with the same courtesy?"

"Are you really okay with doing this?"

"No, I'm not," she sighed, retreating from him slightly to pinch the bridge of her nose. "But I no longer have the time to figure out an alternative. I will do what is necessary to protect myself and my family."

Before he could stop himself, Cyrus practically yelled at her; "You are still treating me like a child."

"Then stop acting like one!" Lena shouted at him, fire flashing through her eyes, illuminating their grey depths with demonic energy. She closed her eyes as she collected herself. "It was a good deal, Cyrus, and I'm proud of you. But you lacked the conviction to follow it through."

Drawing a deep breath, he forced himself to keep his hands by his side, desperately holding his desire to take a swing at her in check. Before he could say anything that he would likely regret, he gathered his flames and transported to his room. He couldn't look at her. He couldn't speak to her. What had been the point in giving him this chance to prove himself if she was just going to throw it all in his face?

With a roar of frustration, he slammed his fist into the wall, relishing the fact that she would feel his pain.

"What did the wall do to you?"

# CHAPTER EIGHTEEN

"What did the wall do to you?" Marcus asked, although he regretted the question as soon as it left his mouth.

Cyrus groaned and the cambion was fairly sure the boundling rolled his eyes, despite not being able to see his face. *Brat.* Flames coursed over his body and Cyrus disappeared, evidently not in the mood to talk. *Fucking brat. Well, too bad*, Marcus thought as he stepped forward and focused on the trail the young demon had taken. After Cyrus had left the altar room, Lena had pinned him with a hard glare and he knew she wanted him to go after the boundling. He was going to regardless, but he hadn't expected he was going to have to chase the young demon.

Gathering his own flames, he followed the boundling through the fires of Hell, reappearing a few metres behind him as Cyrus strode off down an empty alleyway. Marcus wasn't entirely sure where they'd come but he took off, chasing the demon.

"Cyrus!" he called after him, easily catching up. "Come on, stop. You know you're not getting away from me."

"Leave me alone, Marcus," the boundling snapped over his shoulder. "I'm not in the fucking mood."

"Well, I wasn't suggesting that," he smirked.

The demon groaned again, his head falling back even as he continued to walk away. "Marcus..."

"Sorry," the cambion smiled, hiding it quickly. "Just trying to lighten the mood."

"Fine," Cyrus sighed, finally stopping and turning towards him, placing his hands on his hips. "I'm not *fucking* in the mood."

"Yeah," he shrugged, "I can't do anything with that."

"Can you just leave me alone?"

"Nope," Marcus said, with an emphasising pop and he took a step towards the boundling. "I tried to leave you alone and you forced your way in. You're stuck with me now."

Cyrus scoffed, one of his brows raising in question, a teasing smirk on his lips. "Oh?"

"Not like that," the cambion said pointedly, raising a finger in emphasis. He realised how what he said sounded, but that had not been his intention. "But I am going to make sure you're okay."

"I'm fantastic," the boundling snarled. "Can't you tell?"

"Cyrus..." Marcus trailed off with a groan of exasperation.

"Don't 'Cyrus' me," he snapped. With a huff the demon turned on his heel and started off down the alley again. Marcus had no issue keeping up with him, his gaze pinned on the young demon's back. "I can't believe she did that to me."

"She didn't do anything to you."

Cyrus snorted with derision. "She threw the fucking curveball of the century."

"But not to you," Marcus said firmly. Apparently firmly enough for the boundling to stop and look back at him. "She did it to Damien. And she's right, Cyrus. I hate to say it, but this is the perfect way of controlling him."

"You, Archie and I all agreed she wouldn't do this."

"No," he sighed, shaking his head. "We agreed she wouldn't take over Balo's bindings. And she hasn't. She's found the next best thing though."

Silence fell between them as they held each other's gaze. Marcus could almost see the thoughts working behind Cyrus' eyes, their chocolate brown depths yet again enchanting him. Seriously, what was it about this man that drew him in so much? Something about the way Cyrus looked at him, something within their dark colouring, gripped at his chest and stubbornly refused to let go. It almost made him wish he could let go of his pain and reservations and actually fall into a relationship with the boundling. Swallowing past the lump in his throat, he coughed, dispelling the dangerous thought from his mind.

"Did you know?" Cyrus asked suddenly, pulling him back to the moment.

"No."

"Don't lie to me."

"I'm not lying, Cyrus," he said earnestly, stepping forward to close the distance between them. Regardless of his hesitations, everything in him wanted to be close to the boundling. "I didn't know she was going to do this. I don't know about Archie or Ambrose, but I'm pretty sure she kept this close to her chest."

Cyrus blinked at him, unshed tears forming in his brown eyes making Marcus want to take the young demon in his arms and leave their world behind. "Why couldn't she just trust me?"

It would always come down to this. No matter what was said or done, Cyrus always felt inferior. A deep-rooted pain forced upon him, likely from his treatment at the hands of Zagan. He would always see the concern of others as being treated differently, or like he was breakable, not noticing that the others were often treated the same way. Like Lena, he had never had a stable family, so didn't know how one was supposed to act. Not that Marcus really knew how a family was supposed to act.

"She does trust you," the cambion sighed, stepping closer until they were in arms reach of each other, although still not touching. "But at the end of the day, Lena is a Prince of Hell, and that comes with secrets, even from us. You have escorted her to meetings with the other Princes. We don't know even half of what they must talk about, I can guarantee that."

"Ambrose knows."

"Ambrose is her Consort," he said with a soft smile. "They are essentially a single entity. It's not the same and definitely not a fair comparison." They fell again into a comfortable silence as Cyrus looked at the ground, simply letting Marcus' words settle over him. He took the opportunity to look around them, taking in the Mediterranean style of the surrounding buildings. The alley was bright with moonlight, illuminating off the white washed walls either side of them. The road was a cobble and flagstone mix, softened in the moonlight only by the fine layer of ashen dirt over it. He could hear the faint sounds of nightlife reaching them from one end of the alley, brightened by street lamps and house windows. But no one that passed the alley's entrance came within it. Evidently it was not one that led anywhere of importance. "Where are we by the way?" he asked, his curiosity spiking.

Cyrus chuckled. "A little town in southern Italy," he said looking down the alley with a warm affection in his eyes. "I grew up here."

"You're Italian?" Marcus asked, his eyes wide as he turned back to the boundling.

"No," Cyrus shook his head. "But I lived here until I was eight. Until I went into foster care."

"You didn't go into foster in Italy?"

"I'm not Italian," he shrugged. "Not a national. I got sent back to my country of birth. Same as Lena." His smile dropped and his eyes returned to the ground. The anger appeared to have left him, but the pain and sorrow were still there.

"Cyrus," Marcus called gently, waiting until the boundling looked at him. "You know she didn't do this because she doesn't trust you, right?"

"She doesn't trust me," Cyrus snapped, hurt flashing in his eyes as he ran his hand through his hair, tugging at some knots that snagged on his fingers. "Fuck. She made me think she cared about what I think and then she threw it in my fucking face."

"No, she didn't," he said emphatically, keeping his gaze steady hoping his eyes alone could convey his conviction to that statement.

"Yes, she fucking did," the boundling snarled at him.

Sighing, he stepped forward, raising a hand to reach for Cyrus. "Come here."

"Marcus," the young demon sighed. "I said, I'm not in the mood."

Smirking at the boundling, Marcus grabbed the nape of his neck, pushing into him with his body until they fell against the wall, placing his free hand on the surface beside Cyrus' head. "And I said, I'm not suggesting anything like that," he whispered, their lips almost, but not quite touching.

"So, you push me against a wall to what? Talk?" Cyrus challenged, his own lips curving into a wicked grin, hands gripping at the side of Marcus' shirt. He might protest to not being in the mood, but the cambion knew he could make the boundling change his mind with only a few words.

Marcus growled, barely keeping his desire to kiss the demon senseless in check. "Do you have any idea how hard you make it not to go full dominance on you?" he asked, licking his lips as Cyrus' eyes drooped and darkened with desire. "Keep your bratty ways up, gorgeous, and I swear I'll be punishing you every fucking day."

"Oh? And what would you do, tough guy?" the boundling asked, his eyes focused on Marcus' lips.

"Behave, gorgeous. I'm not trying to turn this into a thing, but I'm not above fucking you in this alley," he chuckled darkly. "And believe me when I say, if I do, I won't be letting you come. I'll take my pleasure from your body and leave you teetering on the edge for as long as I wish. I'll tie you to my fucking bed so you can't do anything to relieve yourself until I feel you've learnt your lesson. So be a good boy and listen to me."

Cyrus swallowed, his breath hitching, but he returned his gaze to Marcus' eyes, relaxing against him. "I'll be good."

"Good boy," Marcus nodded approvingly. He sighed, rubbing his fingers against the back of Cyrus' neck, their eyes locked together. He kept his voice low as he spoke, impressing the importance of what he needed to say. "You and I both know that you and Lena need each other. Not just because of your binding. Siblings are made to piss each other off, but at the end of the day you love each other. No matter how pissed you get at her, can you honestly say you would have it any other way?"

A shallow breath stuttered out of the boundling, his eyes wide, but soft. "No," he breathed without hesitation.

"I didn't think so," the cambion smiled. "Lena did not make this decision to directly hurt you, or in anyway because of you, or what you did for her. Finding the nephilim has changed things. She is doing what she needs to do as a Prince of Hell. Stay angry at her for a while if you need. But maybe think about what you would do if you were in her position."

Cyrus' eyes fluttered shut and Marcus took the opportunity to rest their foreheads together. Their breath mingling, he could sense Cyrus trying to reconcile the words with his emotions. Nothing else needed to be said at the moment. He knew it was best to wait for the boundling to indicate when he was ready to talk further. Content in the moment to just hold him, Marcus leant in harder against the young demon, breathing in his smokey-leather scent. Their bodies were flush with each other, Marcus' leg snug between Cyrus', their warmth melding together.

Eventually, the young demon opened his eyes, a glassy sheen from withheld tears to them, but with a shaky breath, he raised his hand and cupped Marcus' jaw. "Thank you," he whispered, his thumb tracing over the cambion's bottom lip.

Marcus smiled, kissing the pad of Cyrus' thumb. "Now," he sighed, "we need to talk about how things are going to be around the house."

"Oh?" the boundling said uncertainly.

"I shouldn't have teased you the way I did today," Marcus said, shaking his head slightly, but not enough to move away. "It was reckless. If Balo is going to be living at the house, we need to be careful. *Very* fucking careful."

"You don't want to just..." the demon trailed off as if he didn't want to finish the question. Marcus waited patiently, urging with his eyes for Cyrus to continue. "You don't want to just stop?"

"No," he said, possibly a little too quickly for his own good. "Cyrus, I meant it when I said I can't get you out of my fucking head. I still want you in my bed, but from now on you flame in, or I will flame to your room. *Or* we go somewhere away from the house entirely, which is probably the best idea as the only spare room for Balo is the one between ours." Desire flashed in the boundling's eyes and Marcus felt his body respond in kind. This demon was going to be the death of him, he was sure of that. Doubt began to creep in as, yet again, he wondered if this was the right thing to do. Their arrangement may have been his idea, but perhaps he hadn't though it all the way through. If Cyrus did ever find someone else he desired, would Marcus be able to give him up? He was no longer so sure he would. Wilfully ignoring the errant thought, he threaded his fingers through the boundling's hair. "If Balo is around, we stay on opposite sides of the room. Outside of the bedroom, we act like we did when we first moved into the house. Inside the bedroom... well then, gorgeous, you are all mine."

A helpless sound pulled from Cyrus' throat, something Marcus knew he hadn't meant to make. He smiled, wondering if he would be able to get the demon to make that sound again.

"Lena is going to kill us one of these days," the boundling groaned, his head angling so their lips brushed against each other.

"As long as it's when my cock is buried in that perfectly tight arse of yours, I'll die a happy demon," Marcus sighed, revelling in the fleeting touches of Cyrus' soft lips.

"Fuck's sake, Marcus," the young demon chuckled as their mouths crashed together.

The cambion growled into the kiss, his fingers digging into the boundling's scalp as if to pull him closer. He demanded entrance to Cyrus' mouth with a firm thrust of his tongue, sweet warmth flooding his body as the demon complied eagerly. He was reminded of their first kiss and the heat of it as their tongues danced with a frenzied passion with the other. For possibly the first time in his life, he thanked his momentary lack of control. That such a moment should lead to him getting to taste one of the most gorgeous men he had ever laid eyes on was inconceivable to him. As he melded his lips with Cyrus', he silently hoped that he would get at least a few years of this pleasure before the boundling moved on to someone else.

Pulling away from the kiss, both men were panting as they stared at each other. "Know any good spots around here?" Marcus asked, a wicked smile on his lips.

"Actually," the young demon started, his own seductive pout brightening his gorgeous face. "Yes."

Lifting his arms, Cyrus wrapped them around Marcus' neck, gathering his flames and transporting them away.

Cyrus was true to his brat nature, refusing to so much as look at his sister the following morning as he and the rest of the council prepared to meet with Damien for his pledge. Lena had enlisted Titus and two of his boundlings to remain at the house to guard Balo whilst they were gone. To his annoyance, Marcus had been right in the room choice that Balo moved into, silently cursing Lena for her decision to bring the boundling into the house. His interlude with Cyrus in Italy had been perfect to the point where he had wanted to continue it at home and keep the young demon in his bed through the night. They had both agreed, however, that the first night of Balo staying with them was not the time to test that possibility. Leaving Italy, they both flamed to their own rooms, much to their combined disappointment.

Marcus noted that Lena gave her brother a wide berth, casting him some furtive glances as they gathered in the courtyard, readying to descend to Hell, but essentially leaving Cyrus to his thoughts. He knew that the siblings would not be estranged for long, but perhaps this would be a good thing. Force Cyrus to try and see things from a different perspective. Force Lena to see things from Cyrus' perspective. He just hoped that his involvement with the boundling would not delay their reconciliation.

"Everyone ready?" Lena asked as her full council gathered round her.

"What's the plan if Damien doesn't follow through?" Archie queried, watching intently as Balo came out to the lounging area. The boundling stopped in the doorway looking at the group, his face serene even as his eyes burned with anger.

"Then we prepare for another Cleansing," the Prince said bluntly, meeting Balo's gaze.

"The Cleansing two-point-O," Ambrose sniggered under his breath.

"This time it's personal," Cyrus chuckled earning him a glare from Lena and a snort of laughter from the other men.

The cambion was pleased to see a small seed of affection pass between the siblings as Lena's eyes softened, a small smile gracing her features. Cyrus nodded to her, pressing his lips together. They would be fine. Eventually.

Balo shifted in the seat he had taken, evidently having heard them, but as Titus and Jess took a seat either side of him, he remained silent. Marcus studied the boundling from the corner of his eye. He was surprised that he couldn't even find the energy to acknowledge the general beauty of the man. Cyrus had ruined the possibility of that train of thought, which surprised him further, noting that he didn't care. He was almost happy for his desires to be ruined by Cyrus. He reasoned with himself that it would make it easier to keep others away once they stopped whatever it was between them.

"Well," Lena sighed, pulling him from his thoughts. "Shall we? Oh, Cyrus?"

The boundling looked startled at his sister but murmured his acknowledgement.

"You and Marcus swap spots in the formation. I want you to stand by my side. None of this would have been possible without you."

Marcus raised his brows sharing a similar look of surprise as the young demon. He wasn't offended at being moved. Ambrose always stood to her left as her Consort. He normally stood closest to her right side, a position earned from both his history with her and his efforts during the Cleansing. It was right that Cyrus should take this spot for the success with Damien.

"Are..." Cyrus started, before swallowing hard. "Are you sure?"

"Yes," the Prince confirmed. "No objections, I hope, Marcus?"

"None at all," he nodded with a warm smile. How could he object? After all, standing behind Cyrus meant he got ample opportunity to stare at the boundling's perfect arse.

Nodding her approval, she encompassed her council with her lightning, using it to connect them so she could pull them with her through the fires of Hell. Their transformations were seamless as they appeared in a large junction, groups of demons surrounding the room, immediately bowing in reverence as their Prince appeared before them.

Without a word, Lena strode off down a hallway towards the cambion residences, her council in lockstep behind her like a rehearsed procession. The golden rings and chains adorning her horns and clothes glittered under the soft light emanating from the cracks in the walls. She was resplendent in demonic form, her wings raised proudly behind her. Some of the demons that had been waiting for them in the junction followed close behind their group, those within her favour taking the lead.

Damien would bow and pledge his loyalty to her. The cambions would fall into line. Lena would secure her place as Prince of Hell. Cyrus would be acknowledged for this accomplishment. And Marcus couldn't be prouder of them.

# CHAPTER NINETEEN

A fortnight after the pledging ceremony, Cyrus walked through the corridors of Hell. He was heading to his den, having spent the morning in a sister den helping new pups settle in following their separation from their mother.

Everything had gone swimmingly. Damien pledged with little revolt from the cambions. There was still a tension within the house that something was going to go wrong. That something was going to happen that would cause everything to come crashing down. Archie and Marcus still kept keen eyes and ears on Damien, watching for any kind of slip or betrayal from him. So far, he kept his word and Lena - along with the other Princes - was pleased with the ease in which the cambions fell into line.

As Cyrus moved through the corridors, he was both surprised and pleased to note that demons would bow their heads in acknowledgement to him. Of course, not all gazes were kind. Those of cambions not pleased by the deal with Damien, were filled with distain. But none were brave enough to approach him over it.

Recognition had never been something he wanted, content to disappear, to go unnoticed when he had been bound to Zagan. Back then, gaining the attention of others came with dangers of become a 'payment request' for deals with his former sire. Now, it came from a place of reverence. Everyone knew Lena would not trade him in the same way, so he revelled in the attention afforded to him.

Balo was proving to be quite accepting of his fate and had even started to join them at meals. He was still quiet, refusing to speak with anyone and never seemed to relax, especially when Lena was in the room. But he wasn't being difficult so that was something. Damien was due to visit with his first report soon, so most of the council opted to be absent from the house knowing that was also going to be an occasion when the cambion and boundling would be allowed to be alone. No one wanted to hear that. The cuff Balo wore, suppressing his demonic self and powers, could only be removed by Marcus. Damien would be given one to wear whilst at the house, one that only Lena could control, so there was little risk they would be able to do anything or flee whilst alone.

The last two weeks had been bliss for Cyrus. He was still pissed at Lena and they had barely spoken since Damien's pledge, but they were amicable. He wanted to speak with her properly and would find time for it shortly, but in the meantime, he and Marcus had been stealing away to all corners of the globe indulging in their desires. They'd even managed to spend a few nights together, staying at hotels and abandoned houses. Well, not full nights. More often than not, Cyrus either woke to find himself alone, or Marcus roused him early so they could sneak back unnoticed.

Unfortunately, the happiness he was finding in the arms of the cambion was dampened by a heavy pit of dread that had taken up permanent residence in his stomach. The more time he spent with Marcus, the more he knew he was never going to find someone else. He didn't want anyone else. He couldn't imagine ever wanting someone else. The demon knew every inch of his body, every point of pleasure and he knew how to work them to draw the most amazing climaxes from him.

But, one problem at a time and whilst he got to enjoy Marcus' attentions, he was not going to do anything that could jeopardise that pleasure. He'd even managed to hold in some of his more bratty behaviours when around the cambion. However, he wasn't about to complain about the 'punishments' he'd received on the few occasions he'd slipped.

Rounding into the den, he noted that he was alone. Which honestly, suited him fine today. The tension in the house was mentally breaking him. He and Balo had spoken a few times but he made certain not to apologise to the fellow boundling for Lena's decision. If it got back to anyone that Lena's council did not support her decision completely it would not go down well. Balo said he understood and was at least grateful he was still bound to Damien. Cyrus hoped that Damien would find a way to get Lena to trust him soon so the lovers could be reunited, but he would keep that opinion to himself for now.

A few of the hellhound pups bounded over to him in greeting and he checked over them as best he could despite two of the rowdier ones trying to knock him to the floor. His soft laughter rang through the den mixing with the snuffs and whines of the hellhounds. One of the alpha males snapped at the young pups, when once accidentally jumped on the sleeping hound, bringing the boisterous play to an end. The pups scampered off to their alcoves or mothers leaving Cyrus to finish his general rounds.

After a couple of hours in the den, he left hoping to waste a few more hours in the Repository. A library of sorts where newborn demons and boundlings could study the various designs and power methods. It housed endless treasures of knowledge guarded over by one of the most terrifying demons to exist. The Keeper, Morganoth. Or Morgan as she liked to be call now. A titan demon, standing at almost nine feet tall, her black skin and four wings gave the impression of a creature much larger. Try to steal from her Repository and her minions, small black winged-imps, would alert her before you could leave the door. She was also the Consort to the Prince of Gluttony, Belphegor, and one of Lena and Cyrus' favourite demons after she helped them escape Zagan. He knew she could find something to distract him for a while.

Passing through a junction, he paused mid-way as three demons walked through the corridor he had been heading towards. Correction, three *cambions*. Two of which he was unhappily familiar with.

"Well, hey there, twinkle," the leading cambion sneered at him. The ashy tones of his black skin highlighted only by the stark black of his markings that sprawled across his chest and shoulders. His grey horns curled around his ears in an almost perfect circle stopping an inch or so from the starting base.

Cyrus drew in a sharp breath, exhaling slowly to try and keep calm before responding.

"What do you want, Kai?"

The cambion shrugged as he and his companions drew closer. "Just to talk," he said, a jubilant tone to his raspy voice.

"I highly doubt that," Cyrus sighed, placing his hands on his hips.

Like Damien, Kai had once been subservient to Zagan, meaning Cyrus had been sent to him on more occasions that he liked to remember. Of the two other cambions behind Kai, he only knew the other male, Victor. According to reports from Archie and Marcus he was something of a recluse, keeping mostly to himself, but had recently aligned with Kai. He had muddy-red skin with even darker crimson markings.

Cyrus knew the name of the female cambion. Hyacinth. But he had no personal dealings with her. She was young. Sure, cambions age quicker than a human child, but she was young enough that Zagan had no time for her, so neither had Cyrus. Her dark red skin shimmered under the light of the lava veins, pale red markings swirling elegantly over her collarbones and shoulders. He was thankful that like her companions, she sported no wings. If he had to run, the lack of advantage wings gave would work in his favour.

Shifting on the spot, Cyrus eyed up the cambions, gathering his power beneath the surface, ready to use, but not on display.

"Tell me what Lena promised Damien," Kai said bluntly, stepping towards him.

"What makes you think I would tell you anything about what Lena does as a Prince?"

Kai grinned menacingly at him, closing the distance between them as Victor and Hyacinth stayed close behind the lead cambion.

"Let me rephrase," Cyrus sighed, returning Kai's smirk with one of his own. "What makes you think I can tell you anything? I'm Lena's boundling. She could have compelled me to keep quiet."

"Yeah," Kai mused, scratching his cheek with a singular talon, "your bindings would have activated by now if that was the case."

So much for a quiet afternoon in the Repository. The interaction so far was enough for Cyrus to simply want to go back to the house and hide in the library. That would hopefully be enough space between him and Balo's room to not hear him with Damien. But honestly, being subjected to that would be better than dealing with Kai right now.

"Just leave me alone, Kai," Cyrus snapped, making to walk past the three cambions. Hyacinth blocked his path, forcing him back in front of the group with a low snarl. Baring his teeth at her, Cyrus turned his glare on Kai. "I'm not telling you shit and you know Lena won't let you touch me."

"You may be protected by your sire, twinkle, but she's not here right now."

Refusing to back down, Cyrus forced his body to remain relaxed, keeping his unease firmly in check. "I have more than enough power since joining her council to deal with you, Kai," he sighed, keeping his gaze trained on the lecherous brute.

"Maybe if it was just me, sure," the black-skinned cambion smirked stepping forward as Cyrus stepped back. Panic rose like bile in his throat when he felt the coarse rock of the junction wall press into his back. It took all of his control to keep his face blank. Or at least, to not lose his look of disgust for one of uncertainty. "But even that Consort of yours would struggle with the three of us."

"You wouldn't stand a chance against Ambrose and you know it," he taunted them. As much as he hated to admit it, he would be in trouble if he had to try and fend off the three cambions by himself. But one blow to him and Lena would come in all her fury. No matter how pissed he might be with her, or her with him, she would come and Kai and his merry band of idiots would be dead before they blinked.

Victor and Hyacinth rounded on his flanks, caging him in against the wall. He should have stayed in the den. At least there the hellhounds would have protected him. To an extent.

"What did your whore-Prince promise Damien?" Kai asked again, stepping closer.

"Call her that again and I'll rip your throat out with my teeth," Cyrus warned with a low growl, baring his fangs in promise. "She promised nothing but her support. And her word to not repeat the Cleansing. You really want to be the cause for her to break *that* promise?"

"So, what does she have on him?" Victor pushed. Cyrus forced his gaze to remain on Kai. The others were just a distraction. Kai was the real threat.

"Like fuck I'd tell any of you."

"But she does have something on him then?" Kai asked rhetorically, seemingly already knowing the answer.

*Shit.*

Cyrus forced out a harsh chuckle. "If she had something on him, she would have made him pledge on his knees. Or better yet, prostrated for all to see."

Kai grinned cruelly, closing the final distance between him and the boundling. "Oh, you're going to tell us what she has on him, twinkle.

We'll get it out of you. And don't think your *whore*-Prince will save you. She's down with Lucifer at the moment. She won't feel a fucking thing that we do to that worthless, weakling body of yours."

*Double shit.*

He'd forgotten Lena was due to see Lucifer after Damien's report. So much for that plan. A painful lump formed in his throat as Cyrus breathed deeply through his nose, trying to quell the swirling acid in his stomach.

Sensing a rush of movement at his sides, Cyrus attempted to gather his flames as quickly as he could, silently cursing himself for not simply escaping like this sooner, regardless of if they would have been able to follow him or not. Before the fire could reach his hips, a strong fist sunk into his stomach, causing his body to double over from the force. Kai's hand wrapped around his neck, pulling his head back up and slamming him against the wall. Victor and Hyacinth pinned his arms. The female cambion coursed her lightning through his arm, contracting his muscles painfully so they froze in place. Unluckily for them, Lena had done this to him a number of times, training him and the rest of her council in how to deal with demonic-electrocution.

Forcing air into his lungs, Cyrus pulled the pain from their grips into the centre of his chest, letting it mix with his power core. The lightning convulsed his muscles, but his fire was untouched. Exhaling sharply, black fire burst from every pore of his body, exploding out like a wave of molten heat crashing into the cambions. Victor fell to the ground, clutching at his face that had borne the brunt of the explosion. Hyacinth screamed as the skin on her hands bubbled and blistered.

Kai had stepped back, counteracting the attack with his own blue fire. Lunging forward, he slammed his forearm into Cyrus' throat, pushing back into the wall.

"You're going to pay for that, twinkle. I'm going to make you scream until your throat bleeds," the cambion snarled at him, large yellowed fangs snapping inches from his face.

"Are you now?"

Relief hit Cyrus squarely in the chest, knocking out what little air he had left in him.

*Marcus.*

Black smoke swirled around Kai's body, licking out in delicate tendrils against the ashy skin, small cuts left in their wake. The cambion flinched with each touch, his blood trickling down his body, but didn't move to retract his arm from Cyrus' throat.

"I'd let go if I were you, Kai," Marcus said, his large frame emerging silently from the shadows behind them. "You *may* have been able to take Cyrus on his own." He stepped up behind the similar coloured cambion, his wings raised menacingly behind him as he leant forward to whisper in Kai's ear. "But you are sorely mistaken if you think you will survive me. I let you live last year, but I still owe you for that stunt you pulled in London."

Cyrus grinned as he saw pure fear fill Kai's eyes and his throat bob as he swallowed harshly. As quickly as the fear appeared, the cambion shut his eyes and retracted his arm, hardening his face as he turned on his heel and stalked away from the boundling. Victor and Hyacinth scrambled after him, cradling their injuries, no doubt rushing to a healer.

Rubbing his throat even as his power healed any internal damage, Cyrus turned to Marcus intending to thank him, but his breath caught as he took in the thunderous expression on the cambion's face. He had seen the anger and promise of death when Marcus had stepped out behind Kai, but now the black depths of his demonic eyes were pinned on Cyrus and filled with... *fury*? Something was wrong, but he wasn't sure what.

"Ah, thanks," he said softly, hoping the tension he felt radiating from the demon in front of him might ease with the token of gratitude. "Thank you, Marcus."

If anything, the tension increased, vibrating off the cambion in palpable waves. Without so much as a sound, Marcus stepped towards him and grabbed his wrist, flames gathering around them as the older demon transported them through the fires of Hell. Blinking in confusion, Cyrus looked around the room to where Marcus had brought him, instantly recognising Archie's chambers.

Jerking his wrist back, he stared at the cambion indignantly, before immediately giving way to confusion. Among the furious glare, swirled a deep desire, like a flicker of flame against an ink-black sky, devoid of any other light. Marcus stepped towards him, pure animalistic power pouring from his body, reminding Cyrus of a wolf stalking its prey. Although his own body hummed with cautious anticipation, causing him to step back, he realised he was not afraid of Marcus. Something deep within him told him to be careful, or at the very least, to be ready, but it didn't come from a place of fear.

"Are you okay?" Marcus asked suddenly, his voice deeper than he had ever heard it, rasping and... *hot.*

Swallowing hard, Cyrus took another step back and nodded, not trusting his voice as his body flushed with heat. *Fuck, now is not the time,* he chastised himself. How in the hell was being stalked by Marcus arousing? The cambion could kill him in an instant if he wanted to, not that Cyrus believed he did or would, but the danger was there all the same. He should be terrified, shouldn't he? With his elevation onto Lena's council, Marcus was as strong as Zagan had been, if not stronger. They were both cambions and that comparison alone should have Cyrus running for the hills. But he had never been scared of Marcus. Not even in the few encounters they'd had before Lena came to Hell.

He trusted Marcus.

The thought immediately brought his body to life, his cock hardening painfully in his trousers, the tight leather leaving nothing hidden. His breath caught as he saw Marcus' eyes twitch almost imperceptibly towards his groin and back to his face, a wolfish grin spreading on the older demon's lips. The cambion's wings hitched behind him as he now strode purposefully closer.

*Oh shit...*

# CHAPTER TWENTY

"Marcus? What are you doing?" Cyrus asked, stepping back again until the backs of his thighs hit the table.

Marcus felt feral, needing to release some of the pent-up frustration that had been building since he saw Cyrus surrounded by the other cambions. He'd gone to the hellhound den looking for the boundling, but had been distracted by the sounds from the altercation coming from the junction near it. Seeing of all demons, Kai, forcing the young demon against the wall struck a deep and painful nerve within him. How desperately he wanted to make Kai pay for what he did with William, but his desire to make sure Cyrus was safe had completely negated that impulse. Fierce protectiveness mixed with indescribable rage had washed over him, nearly knocking him on his arse at the intensity of it. But he decided to ignore the implications of that for now, just like he was ignoring the shocked look on the boundling's face as he closed the distance between them.

Placing his palms flat on the table either side of Cyrus' hips, he caged the young demon in with his body. Grinning at him, Marcus leant in until his lips brushed the sensitive skin just under his ear.

"Now, this is familiar," he whispered, dragging the tips of his fangs down the length of Cyrus' neck, breathing in his heady smoke and leather scent like he'd been starved for it. "Shall we finally play out how this all started?"

"Marcus," the boundling moaned, as he raised a hand and gripped unsteadily at the cambion's shoulder. The sound sent a wave of heat through Marcus' chest, his abdomen tightening in anticipation. "We can't. Not here. Wh- what if Archie comes back?"

"We can," he said firmly, pressing their bodies together, removing all space between them. "Archie is on an errand for Lena. He won't be back anytime soon. And I remember you saying your moans were mine, *whenever* I want them."

Cyrus made to protest again, but Marcus crashed their lips together, silencing him as he wrapped his hand around the slender throat. The young demon had no right to push him away now after pursuing him so intently. That was not how things were going to work. Licking along the seam of his lips, the cambion growled approvingly as Cyrus parted them for him. Their tongues collided, tasting each other as heat and tension built between them. With a murmured moan, the boundling eagerly lifted his arms to twine around the older demon's neck. Marcus kept one hand on the table, the other moving to Cyrus' lower back before descending to cup the firm roundness of his arse through his leather trousers.

Finally, breaking the kiss, the cambion smiled as he took in the warm flush on Cyrus' face, brightening the usual ashy-red tones of his skin. His eyes were hooded and Marcus found himself missing being able to see the usual warm chocolate colouring of them. However, in demonic form, the boundling's body was tougher and Marcus could allow his cambion nature to indulge itself a little. In the bedroom, Cyrus was a natural submissive, despite his brattish tendencies out of it. Absolutely perfect for a cambion like him. But the boundling had suffered at the hands of cambions before, and he was not about to inflict anything on the gorgeous body that the young demon did not consent to.

"Do you have any idea how furious I was seeing you with those other cambions?" he asked, lowering his mouth to nip at Cyrus' collarbones, ever more prominent as a demon.

"I w-wasn't with them," the demon whimpered, his body trembling against the cambion's, arms still firmly locked around his neck.

"I don't really care, gorgeous," he growled, biting down firmly on one of the boundling's pecs, pulling a shaky groan from Cyrus' throat, hips bucking against his own. "You started this between us, so you're going to be a good boy for me and let me work my frustrations out on that gorgeous body of yours, aren't you?"

"Oh *fuck*. Yes!" the young demon moaned desperately, his head falling back as Marcus' mouth lunged for his neck, biting and licking up its length and along his jaw.

Wrapping his hand around the bounding's throat, he tugged Cyrus forward, forcing their eyes to meet. "Yes, what?"

Cyrus swallowed, his ashy-red skin flushing as he shuddered under Marcus' hard stare. "Yes, sir."

"Good boy."

Pulling away slightly, Marcus moved his hands to the front of Cyrus' trousers, making quick work of untying the stays. The boundling kicked off his boots just in time for the cambion to practically rip the leather down his legs and toss them aside. Marcus coursed power through his vest, making it disappear as he shuffled out of his own trousers, his wings fluttering out behind him, helping to compensate his balance.

"Knees, now," Marcus growled, stepping towards the boundling. With a seductive smirk that almost made the cambion's eyes roll back, Cyrus lowered the floor, hands reaching out to grasp Marcus' thighs. Placing one hand over the boundling's, he grasped under Cyrus' chin, pulling his face up to look at him. "I'm going to fuck your throat, baby." Those pouty lips parted, sucking in a sharp breath, black eyes now swirling pools of desire. Pressing down on Cyrus' hand, he continued. "Hold on. Dig your claws in if you need. I don't care, okay?"

"Yes, sir."

*Fuck.*

Cyrus' voice was sinful as Marcus released his chin, moving his hand to tangle in the boundling's hair, fingers brushing tenderly over the small crown of horns. This time, his eyes did roll as the young demon wrapped his full lips around Marcus' head, tongue pressed flat against the sensitive underside.

The boundling's mouth was impossibly warm as it continued down until his nose pressed against Marcus' pelvic bone, the head firmly seated in the recesses of his throat. The cambion moaned at he looked down at the gorgeous demon, their eyes locked, a silent understanding passing between them. Before he could act, Marcus felt his knees buckle, stunned into silence as Cyrus swallowed around him. He could already feel the tension in his gut rising, ready to snap. Using his grip on the boundling's hair to hold him in place, Marcus pumped his hips, letting himself fall into the perfect suction the young demon created as he hollowed his cheeks.

His need for the demon kneeling before him was becoming all-consuming. All-encompassing. But he was finding it harder and harder to care. Everything about Cyrus was enticing, seductive and formed perfectly to Marcus' desires. He hissed slightly, relishing the slight pain as he felt Cyrus' claws break the skin on his thighs. That sent him over the edge, the pressure in this stomach breaking as he surged forward with a cry, pouring his release down the boundling's throat. He marvelled at the feeling of swallowing around him, not a single drop wasted as he stared at the young demon, his fingers gently massaging the base of Cyrus' skull.

With a gasping breath, the boundling leant back, looking up at him, an indulgent smirk on his now puffy lips. Practically hypnotised, Marcus watched intently as Cyrus' tongue darted out to lick over his lips as if he was savouring the taste now coating them. The cambion's chest heaved as he fought to regain his breath. That had ended quicker than he wanted, but it didn't matter. He had plans for the whole afternoon for this demon.

The last remnants of his self-control fading quickly, Marcus wrapped his hand around the boundling's throat, pulling him to his feet and pressing their naked bodies together. His cock hadn't even softened following his orgasm, his need was so great.

"I won't hurt you, Cyrus," he managed to grind out as his lust haze descended seeing the stark contrast of his black skin against Cyrus' red. He needed the demon to trust him. Once he started like this, he would not be able to stop. Not easily, anyway. "But I will not be gentle. I am still a cambion and I am *very* frustrated."

Those plump lips, with their perfect upturn pout, parted slightly, drawing in a shaky breath. "I know. I trust you."

*Fuck. Me.*

There was no hesitation. Nothing but sincerity in his conviction.

"Fuck, baby," he growled, crashing their lips together, biting down on Cyrus' bottom lip until he drew blood, the warm copper tang coating his tongue. The boundling whimpered at the action but didn't flinch, instead pushing his hips forward to grind against him. "God, you taste so good."

"Marcus."

The soft moan of his name was like warm honey to his ears, serving only to fan the fire that now coursed through his body. Perhaps that is what the boundling had done to him. Poured his fire into him.

Grabbing under Cyrus' thighs, he lifted the young demon in his arms, spinning them until he slammed them into a wall. Cyrus' legs wrapped around his waist, their hard cocks pressed almost painfully together, grinding against the other as their mouths clashed. The tips of his wings embedded into the rock, giving him greater purchase with which to hold the boundling in place.

"Cyrus," he panted, reluctantly breaking their kiss, resting their foreheads together. "Safeword. Give me a safeword before I lose all control."

"Is 'stop' not enough?"

Marcus shook his head. "'Stop' is too instinctive and something said in anger. A safeword is for when things get too much or if I do anything you're not comfortable with. It means everything stops, no questions asked. Use a safeword and I'll take care of you until you're okay again."

The boundling went quiet as he thought, causing anxiety to build in Marcus' chest. He needed to give a safeword now or the cambion was going to have to find the strength to pull away. And he wasn't entirely sure he would be able to do that.

"Za–"

"Don't you dare, gorgeous," he spat harshly, anger rising. "Don't you *ever* dare say another man's name, dead or otherwise, when you're with me."

Cyrus smirked. *Fucking brat.*

"Perfect safeword then," the boundling teased, "because I don't want to use one with you. Show me what you've got, tough guy."

"Cyrus," Marcus warned, his patience running thin.

"Fine," he huffed, causing the cambion to chuckle. Oh, he was going to enjoy this. "'Infernal'."

"Good boy."

Pulling his hips back slightly, Marcus snaked a hand between them and used one of his claws to cut a line in his flesh just above his painfully solid cock.

"Marcus! What are you doing?" Cyrus cried, watching almost in horror as the cambion's blood flowed from the wound, coating his length.

"I said I won't hurt you," he ground out from behind gritted teeth.

"So better to use my own blood."

"But why?"

Locking his eyes with the young demon, Marcus tried to regain some rational thought. "I don't have any lube with me," he said, hoping that would be enough explanation. He didn't have the sense to explain further now, his need to drive inside the demon before him becoming all consuming.

"Lu–?" Cyrus started, before his eyes widened and his lips formed a small 'O', understanding dawning on his face. "Fucking hell..." he groaned, his eyes rolling back as his body trembled with desire.

Smirking at the boundling, Marcus gripped the base of his shaft firmly, lining up with the tight ring of muscle. Once in position, he captured Cyrus' mouth before slamming his hips forward, burying himself to the hilt in one movement, greedily swallowing the young demon's cries as he did so.

"Shit! Marcus!" Cyrus cried into his mouth, his claws digging into the cambion's back. Marcus didn't care, the pain from the boundling's grip mixing with and heightening his pleasure, spurring him on.

Giving the demon little time to adjust, he pulled his hips back before surging forward, setting a punishing pace. Hands tightly gripping Cyrus' arse, Marcus called on his smoke, letting the wisps trail slowly up the boundling's body, smiling as each teasing stroke caused a shiver in its wake. Wrapping around the young demon's neck, the power constricted, pressing in until the Cyrus was gasping for breath, his youthful body convulsing with each thrust. Small dustings of rock showered over them from where Marcus' wings dug in. The soft thuds of their bodies hitting the wall, drowned out by his grunts and Cyrus' delicious whimpers. Even in demonic form, the boundling was tight, squeezing mercilessly around his cock, the painful grip intensifying his own pleasure.

Keeping tight hold of the boundling's body, he mustered a powerful beat of his wings, pushing off the wall. In an instant, he laid Cyrus none-to-gently on the table, a slight crack of the wood echoing through the room. A loud guttural moan pulled from Cyrus' throat, rippling under the pressure of Marcus' smoke, still tightly wrapped around his neck. Placing one hand firmly on the boundling's hip, the cambion gripped with his talons biting into the ashy-red flesh, giving him access to greater depth of the gorgeous body spread before him. Small black flames danced around his fingers. So, Cyrus had the same instinctual healing ability as his sister. *Perfect.*

Cyrus' cock pulsed between them, the head turning an angry shade of purple as he neared his climax. Moving quickly, the cambion grasped it with his free hand, squeezing the base, stroking firmly with each thrust. The carnal sound that pulled from the boundling reverberated around the room, sending a wave of electric pleasure down Marcus' spine.

"Remember, gorgeous," he bit out, his mind barely functioning, but still seeking control. "You don't come until I say you can."

The boundling tried to speak, but the pressure on his neck prevented him from doing so. Demons didn't need to breathe. It was more out of habit that they did so. But they did need air in order to form sound. Easing his power slightly, he allowed Cyrus to draw a shuddering breath that quickly expelled with a loud cry.

"Marcus! I c-can't! Fuck!"

"Yes, you can, Cyrus," he growled. "You can and you will."

Still wrapped around his waist, Cyrus' legs trembled as he desperately held back his release. His clawed fingers dug into the wood by his hips, chipping away at the surface, his chest and abdomen glistening with sweat and his own pre-cum.

"Marcus, please!" Cyrus begged, tears streaming down his face, beautiful anguish etched into his features. "Please, please, please."

"Fuck, baby," he rasped, his jaw clenched painfully until he was sure his teeth would crack. "You sound so fucking good when you beg. Will you be able to keep going? Because I'm not done and I won't stop just because you come."

"Y-yes," the boundling stammered. "Yes, p-please. Fuck, Marcus, please!"

"Then come for me, gorgeous."

Cyrus' shoulders curled, arching his back off the table, his head thrown back as he cried out into the room, his orgasm taking over. Ropes of cum lashed over his stomach and chest, causing Marcus to groan as the pressure around his cock increased tenfold. Forcing his hips to keep moving, the cambion watched with fascination as the boundling twitched beneath him.

Trailing his fingers down Cyrus' chest, Marcus scooped some of the cum up with his fingers, popping them in his mouth as the boundling watched him intently. "Fucking delicious," he growled, grinding his hips against the demon's arse, pulling a long, low moan from him. Gathering more of the salty liquid, he pressed his fingers against Cyrus' pout. "Suck," he ordered.

Obediently, the boundling parted his lips and sucked the cambion's fingers into his mouth, whimpering softly as he tasted himself, his tongue swirling against the digits. His entire body was trembling with the aftermath of his release, causing Marcus to grin with satisfaction. The young demon would be allowed a slight reprieve whilst they changed positions, but the cambion had no desire to be parted from his gorgeous body for long.

Withdrawing, Marcus grabbed the back of Cyrus' neck, pulling the demon with him as they stood up from the table. Without a word, the cambion directed him back to the wall, forcing the boundling to brace against it with his hands. Pressing against his back, Marcus gripped his hips firmly, grinding his hard cock against the young demon's arse. With a low growl that vibrated through his whole body, Marcus sunk his fangs into Cyrus' shoulder as he sheathed himself inside the boundling's warmth.

"W-wait… M-Marcus, I c-ca– Infernal!"

Ice-cold horror crashed over him, instantly clearing the lust fog from his mind. There wasn't just unease in Cyrus' voice. He was afraid. Pure fear radiated from his body. *Shit*, what had he done? Immediately pulling out, Marcus spun the boundling in his arms, wrapping them tightly around him and pulling his wings in close to encase them completely, shutting off the outside world. Cyrus' face buried into the crook of his neck, as he gently guided them back to the table to lean against the edge, continuing to cradle the young demon against him.

"Shh," he soothed as he felt Cyrus' body tremble within his arms. "You're okay. You did so well, Cyrus."

"I-I'm s-sorry," the boundling stuttered, his voice hoarse and breathing ragged.

"Don't apologise. You have nothing to be sorry for," he assured him. "You did so well. I'm so proud of you for using the safeword, gorgeous." He knew Cyrus hadn't wanted to use it, so that he did, meant that he had fucked up somehow. Guilt formed a heavy pit in his stomach making him want to heave against the shame. But he had to take care of Cyrus. Right now, his needs were secondary. "You're okay," he murmured softly, pressing a tender kiss to the boundling's temple. "Do you want to talk about it?"

Cyrus sniffed, the sound like a knife to his heart. He pulled his arms tighter around the lean frame, wanting desperately to make things better.

"I don't want to stop," the young demon said after a moment. "I just... I c-can't like that."

"What? Against the wall?" he asked in a whisper, trying to keep his voice as soft as possible, sensing the vulnerability of the boundling. The small nod was imperceptible but he felt it against his neck. "You were fine at the beginning. What changed? What did I do?"

Chuckling slightly, Cyrus nuzzled into him. "I thought the safeword meant no questions asked."

If he could tease, he was okay. Marcus smiled, dropping a kiss on his shoulder. "Maybe that was an oversimplification," he sighed. "I'm not questioning why you said it and you don't need to explain why, but I need to know what I did so I don't do it again. I don't want to do anything that hurts you, Cyrus. I don't want to scare you. I... I don't want you to be afraid of me."

"You didn't. I'm not."

"Then what happened?"

The boundling sighed heavily, but his body relaxed, melting against the cambion. "It was because I was facing the wall," he murmured, his voice broken and shaking. "Za— *H-he* would hold me like that. My nightmares..."

*Zagan...*

The cambion was dead, for fuck's sake. When would they finally be free of him? A menacing growl built in his chest and it took every ounce of strength in him to stop it from ripping from his throat. But he failed to stop his body from tensing, flushing with anger. Cyrus must have noticed as he lifted his head, worry spreading across his beautiful face.

"Shh," Marcus managed, lifting his hand to palm the back of Cyrus' neck, pulling his head back to his shoulder. The boundling should not be worrying about him right now. "I'm not angry with you. I'm sorry, Cyrus. Fuck, I'm so sorry."

Wishing to provide as much comfort as possible, Marcus ducked his head, burying his face into Cyrus' neck, pressing their cheeks together. Gently and slowly, he rubbed his hand along the boundling's spine, simply allowing their bodies to sink into the other, the soft sounds of their breathing being the only thing filling the room. Cyrus shuddered against him, but pressed closer, the wonderful firmness of the youthful body stoking the fire in him again. He said he didn't want to stop, but Marcus needed to make sure he was truly up to continuing. The cambion could find release later if needed. If he wasn't sure that Cyrus was ready to continue, they would stop.

"I'm okay," the boundling whispered as if reading his mind. "Please don't stop."

Grasping Cyrus' chin between his fingers, lifting his face to his, Marcus brushed a tender kiss over his swollen lips. The young demon moaned and melted into him, further driving his need. As gently as he could, he lifted Cyrus in his arms, carrying him to Archie's bed. They probably should go elsewhere, but what did it matter now? Archie was already going to kick his arse for the damage done to the table. Might as well go all out.

"I'll go gentler now, okay, gorgeous?" he sighed, nestling between Cyrus' warm thighs, nudging the head of his cock against his arse.

"You don't have to," the boundling shivered beneath him, keeping a tight hold on his neck.

"Yes, I do," Marcus nodded, lowering his head and trailing kisses along the demon's jaw. "I need you to enjoy what I do to your body."

"I did enjoy it."

"Until you didn't. And that's fine, baby. I'm not going easier now, because I don't think you can handle it," he murmured, rocking his hips, teasing the boundling until he started to gasp with each movement. "I'm going easier, because I want to leave you with memories that no other cambion has ever given you."

Cyrus moaned loudly as the older demon drove his hips forward, rejoining their bodies. "Yes, please."

# CHAPTER TWENTY-ONE

Pacing around his room, Cyrus silently cursed himself as he tried to find the courage to go and speak with Lena. After his 'session' with Marcus yesterday, he doubted he could continue with his silent treatment towards her. She may have been in the lower rings of Hell at the time, but the things he and Marcus did would almost certainly have fed back to her, even if only faintly. If she had felt the fear that had consumed him when he'd been faced against the wall, she would likely confront Marcus and he needed to prevent that from happening. It wasn't the cambion's fault that Cyrus had nightmares about that, and he shouldn't bear the brunt of Lena's displeasure over it.

"As Lena would say: 'buck up, Cyrus'," he muttered to the room before spinning on his heel and walking out into the corridor.

Archie had been tasked with babysitting Balo today so they were both out somewhere running errands for the Prince. Now the distraction with Damien was sorted, she needed to build her alliances with the other supernatural creatures of Earth in preparation for the Apocalypse.

Cyrus was disappointed to find Lena was not in her altar room. He hoped she was not out following the nephilim. He didn't want to have to track her down, not that it would take much to do so, but he wanted to have this conversation at home. Not on some random street.

Heading downstairs, he sighed with relief, finding her in the kitchen, rifling through one of the cabinets. Ambrose had taken to hiding one of her favourite snacks, mostly because they were also his favourite, and if she found them, they would all be gone before he got one. Didn't matter how many times she pointed out to her Consort that they could always just get more.

"Hey, Lena, can we talk?" he asked, leaning his hip on one of the counters.

"Flaming mother of–" Lena cried, twirling around suddenly and clasping her hand over her chest. Cyrus smirked as he raised a brow at her. Regardless of the fact that their hearts still beat, they were dead. A surprise scare was not going to kill her. Not again anyway. Glaring at him, she took a deep breath before her cool exterior returned. "Of course. What's up?" she answered, returning his grin before dropping her gaze to the floor and shaking her head with a huffing laugh. "You know, I feel like I've been saying that a lot lately."

He chuckled, folding his arms over his chest. "Yeah. Um... I just wanted to say, I'm sorry."

Her head cocked back slightly at his apology, her dove-grey eyes wide. "What for?" she asked quietly.

"For my reaction the other day. With Damien," he forced out, swallowing around the lump that formed in this throat at her reaction. "It wasn't fair of me."

There was a shine to her gaze, filled with unspoken emotion and unshed tears, blinking rapidly as if to hold them at bay. Lena coughed, her eyes dropping momentarily, shifting on the spot. "Don't worry about it," she said, her voice shaky. "I... I wasn't exactly fair on you either." She sighed heavily before walking towards him holding out her hand. He took it quickly, pulling her towards him until she rested on the counter beside him, their shoulders pressed together. "I should have talked to you about it beforehand, but honestly, I really only decided on it that morning. And, I wasn't sure, but I was afraid you wouldn't react well to it so I thought it would be better to just not say anything."

"Look, I get it," he sighed, rubbing his thumb over her knuckles, keeping his eyes fixed on their joined hands. "We both grew up in an environment where it was better to ask forgiveness, but..."

"But what?" she pressed after he trailed off.

Leaning over, Cyrus rested his head atop hers. "I just want you to trust me, Lena. Have faith that I'll support you, no matter what." He paused for a moment before deciding it was better to just lay everything out to her. No more hiding how he felt. "When you were in the lower rings for the anniversary celebrations, I missed you. I really fucking missed you. I need you, Lena. I need you in my life and not just because you are my sire or my Prince. Or even because you are my sister. You are my best friend. I don't want you to think that there is anything, and I mean *anything*, that you can't talk to me about." He shut his eyes as Lena pressed closer to him, hugging his arm tightly against her body. "I've been pissed at you because you trusted me with this, but then sprung your plan on me in a situation where I couldn't react. Where I had to, where I was forced to, play along. I understand why you've made this decision, and honestly, I agree that it is a good one. I just wish you had trusted me enough to talk to me about this."

A comfortable silence fell over them and Cyrus was sure he could hear the wheels in Lena's head turning. But he didn't pull away or drop her hold on his hand. He wanted to be close to her now. The bond held between them was always more than sire and boundling. Simply being with each other was enough for them to sort out any troubles between them. A calmness settled over them, the simple quiet of the kitchen encasing them in this moment.

A distant memory washed over him from their time with Zagan, where he'd held Lena in his arms on the floor of the apartment their old sire used to inhabit, simply cradling her. At the time, she had just endured a round of Zagan's *treatments*, where he tried to force her demonic transformation. Power runes carved into her skin, pulsing with his black lightning, preventing her powers from healing her. Cyrus had done his best to ease her pain, but his own bindings hindered his efforts.

*"I can't do this anymore," she whispered under her breath. "I'm so tired."*

*Tears tracked down his own face as he tightened his hold on her. "I know, little mouse. I know," he choked out past sobs. He hated seeing her like this. He hated that Zagan had claimed her. There was nothing he would not have given in that moment to return her to Ambrose. To get her anywhere but that apartment. "You're so strong, Lena. Stronger than you know. You've just got to hold on a little longer."*

*He was lying to her. He knew he was. She was so young for a boundling. She would be bound to Zagan for decades yet. How long would the cambion subject her body to this? Lifting her from the floor, he carried her to her room, laying her gently onto the bed carved into the stone wall. Kneeling beside her, he stroked her hair, whispering encouraging words to her. Her bindings glowed constantly preventing her from finding rest.*

*Zagan had commanded her to stay awake, no matter what. She needed sleep and he refused to give it to her. Lena had not yet transformed so her human body was bearing the brunt of their sire's frustrations. Slowly, Zagan's power faded from her wounds, her own red lightning overtaking and healing her as it spread over her body. But it couldn't heal her mind. A fragile thing that Zagan chipped away at day by day.*

*"I'm so sorry, little mouse," he whispered to her.*

*"Don't apologise for his actions," she snarled, but due to her exhaustion there was little heat behind her words. "This is not your fault."*

It didn't matter what she said even then. The failure to protect her weighed heavily on his mind. He'd protected her before from their foster father, but he couldn't do anything then. He had been as helpless as she had been in that situation. And it had killed him inside. He'd vowed that night, if they ever made it out from under Zagan's control, to stand by her for whatever time fate would allow him. He would defend her for the remainder of his existence.

Eventually, Lena lifted her head from his shoulder pulling him back from the memory. She looked up into his eyes and he knew she'd felt it. There was a tenderness to her gaze, but he was thankful that the one emotion he had never seen from her was pity. He couldn't take that, not from her.

"I love you, Cyrus," she said softly, barely louder than a breathy whisper as she squeezed her fingers around his arm. "And I do trust you. But I will try harder to show you that."

A tightness in his chest eased and he nodded his appreciation. "I love you, too, Lena. Thank you."

A warm smile formed on her face and he returned it as best he could. His gaze narrowed however, when he saw a hint of concern in her eyes.

"Hey, about yesterday..." she started before trailing off with an awkwardness to her tone. Cyrus closed his eyes knowing full well what she was referring to. "I... ah..."

"I'm okay, Lena," he said hurriedly, holding up his hand, desperately hoping she would not continue on that line of questioning. "You don't need to worry."

She hesitated for a moment, but apparently decided to press on regardless. "Did Marcus do something?"

A loud, barking laugh escaped him. What didn't Marcus do? But that wasn't an answer. He shook his head at her. "Not getting involved, remember," he teased, tugging on her hand slightly in quiet reprimand.

"I know, I know," she huffed defensively despite the coy smile on her lips. "I managed to block you out mostly, but your fear..." Her smile faltered as mild concerned flushed her features. "Do you want to talk about it?"

Sighing heavily, he kissed the top of her head, shaking his. "Marcus and I talked about it. I'm really okay, little mouse. It was just a flashback."

"So, nothing Marcus did?" she pressed.

"No."

"Promise me?"

"I promise," he assured her, nudging her with his elbow. "There's no need to go Prince of Hell on him."

Lena threw her head back with a full belly laugh. The sound of it warmed his heart, joining her with his own chuckle. Wiping a tear from her eye, she dropped his hold to swat at his shoulder with the back of her hand. "Alright, fair enough," she sighed, moving off to finally shut the cabinet door she'd left open.

"Lena, it's time to go."

Cyrus and Lena turned to the kitchen door as Ambrose strode through, a tense expression on his face. The siblings both drew their brows together in confusion.

"Go?" Lena queried. "Go where?"

"To visit Belphegor," the Consort sighed, crossing the kitchen to drop a tender kiss on her cheek. Lena's face simultaneously flushed at the gesture and grimaced at the name of her Princely brother. "He invited us for dinner, remember? With Morgan."

The Prince groaned loudly, her head falling back in the space behind her to stare at the ceiling. "Shit, that's tonight?"

"Yes," Ambrose nodded dejectedly. He didn't look enthused by the idea either

"Do I have to go?" she asked, raising a singular brow at him.

"He's your brother," the demon huffed, folding his arms over his chest. "And, this was *your* idea to get to know him better."

"Yeah, but..." she stared, chewing on the inside of her cheek. "Do I have to?"

Cyrus laughed at her look of defeat as Ambrose rolled his eyes in mock annoyance. The boundling was fairly sure the Consort didn't want to attend that dinner either, but such were the dealings of the Princes and their partners. As far as Cyrus was aware, only Asmodeus did not have a Consort. Something about too much lust to share around.

"Just go, Lena," he said to his sister. "You may actually have a good time."

"With Belphegor?" she quipped, glaring at him.

"At the very least with Morgan," he retorted. "You love her."

"Why in the seven Hells did she have to be Belphegor's Consort? She could do better."

"Please don't say that to him tonight," Ambrose groaned, scrubbing a hand over his face.

Cyrus shook his head, trying to contain his laughter at the interaction before him. "What don't you like about him anyway?" he finally asked.

"I don't know," Lena shrugged, rolling her neck, the soft cracks echoing through the kitchen. "He just... creeps me out. Too many..."

"Chins?"

"Cyrus!"

"What?"

"Don't insult my brother," she snapped at him.

"You were just about to," he said a little too loudly.

"Yeah, but he's *my* brother."

"I'm *your* brother," he reminded her, leaning back against the counter and folding his arms over his chest.

She stared at him for a moment before conceding with a curt nod. "Fair point."

Ambrose had clearly had enough, wrapping his arm around Lena's shoulder, pulling her towards him. "Just come on, my dove," he whispered to her. She instantly melted at the endearment, sinking into his hold. Cyrus knew the Consort had won but Lena wasn't going to go down without the final word.

"Fine," she huffed, rolling her eyes. Pinning her boundling with a hard stare she pointed a finger at him, whilst her other arm snaked around Ambrose's waist. "Be good," she impressed on him firmly. However, her serious expression easily gave way to a mischievous smirk. "Or, you know, good at it."

"Don't worry," Cyrus chuckled. "I won't burn the house down."

"Uh-huh..."

Staring at each other incredulously, Lena huffed in her defeat before gathering her flames around her and Ambrose, leaving the boundling alone.

Glad for the momentary peace and solitude, Cyrus pottered around the kitchen putting together an impromptu meal for himself. He wasn't overly hungry at present, but thought it might be better to head off the need before it came. In fact, he'd been surprised that recently he'd been able to go longer without food or sleep again. His nightmares had been lessening, and save for his unfortunately timed flashback the day before, it had been a while since he'd had one of those too. The few nights he'd spent with Marcus had been blissfully devoid of dreams. Some had even been devoid of sleep, but when he had slept, he'd actually slept and felt refreshed by the morning.

Maybe it had to do with the cambion and the contentment Cyrus felt in his arms. He'd been telling himself it had been because the situation with Damien was finally settled. But then, he'd been plagued by his nightmares well before the cambion had become a problem.

If Marcus was the source of his peace, he was going to have to do something about that and soon. He knew he was falling for the older demon. Desire was no longer his sole reason for wanting to be near him. Cyrus simply enjoyed being with Marcus and the easy conversations they had slipped into of late. Everything felt easy and natural with the older demon, something that Cyrus had never experienced with another, except perhaps Lena, but he wasn't counting her. Not for the purposes of this train of thought anyway.

All of that just meant that it was going to hurt all the more when either he or Marcus were going to have to end things. Unless, they actually formed a relationship, something the cambion continuously reminded him was not going to happen, the casual nature of their... *interludes...*could not continue.

Before he had a chance to delve deeper into those thoughts, the subject of them flamed into the courtyard. Cyrus waved at him from the kitchen window, scooping up the last of his soup with a scrap of bread and shovelling it in his mouth.

"Hey, Cyrus," Marcus greeted him with a small smile as he leant in the doorway. "Have you seen Ambrose?"

Cyrus nodded, quickly trying to swallow the food so he could answer properly. "Sorry," he forced out, covering his mouth with the back of his wrist. "He and Lena just left. They have a dinner date with Belphegor and Morgan."

The cambion's grin grew, a short huffing laugh escaping him. "Oh, to be a fly on that wall," he sighed, shaking his head. "That will be a fun night."

"No kidding."

"Where's Balo?"

"Archie has taken him on an errand," Cyrus shrugged, rinsing his bowl out in the sink before placing it in the dishwasher.

"So, we're all alone then?" Marcus asked quietly.

The boundling felt the warmth of the cambion come up behind him, pressing against his back. Large hands gripped the edge of the counter in front of him and his eyes fluttered shut as Marcus trailed his nose along the back of his neck.

"It would seem so," he answered breathlessly.

"Well, in that case," Marcus gripped his hips suddenly spinning him against the counter, the edge now biting into his lower back. "How about a game of chess? I've been meaning to challenge you to one for a while now."

Cyrus' brows shot up in surprise. With this kind of greeting, he'd been expecting they would immediately go up to one of their bedrooms. But a game of chess actually excited him - not that going to their rooms didn't - and he found a wide smile forming on his lips.

"Alright," he nodded. "You're going down, tough guy."

"Ha!" Marcus scoffed at the taunt, grabbing his hand and pulling them towards the library. "Watch it, gorgeous."

# CHAPTER TWENTY-TWO

Marcus watched enthralled as Cyrus deftly set up the chessboard. They sat opposite each other at the long table that ran through the centre of the library, emerald-green velvet cushioned chairs with intricately carved backs tucked in under the dark-oak wood. Rich red, cream and gold Persian rugs lined the floor under the table, stopping a few inches short of each wall. Every side of the room boasted ceiling to floor bookshelves in which various tomes and scrolls from all periods of time were stored. Artefacts and objects of interest were dotted among the literature at random intervals. Among them rested a relatively small chest which Marcus eyed with fond memories. Lena used to store her conduit in it, a powerful protection spell placed over it so that only she and Ambrose could touch it without harm. Now she stores some of her more powerful cursed objects that she keeps for her own personal use.

"Black or white?" Cyrus asked, pulling Marcus from his thoughts.

Smiling softly, Marcus turned the board so the black pieces were closer to him. "Considering Lena has said she's never beaten you at this, I'll take the advantage of black."

The boundling blinked with soft confusion. "How often have you and Lena played?"

"Not since she became a Prince of Hell," he chuckled. "I played with her and Ambrose a few times after she became a demon. She beat both of us countless times. Even when we teamed up or Ambrose tried to cheat with their binding."

Cyrus laughed under his breath, shaking his head. "Okay then," he sighed, taking the first move.

Thinking he might need some way of distracting the young demon if he was to stand a chance of winning this, Marcus decided to pull Cyrus into conversation. "Tell me more about you."

Looking up through his lashes at the cambion, Marcus could tell the demon knew what he was doing.

"I though you wanted to keep things casual?" Cyrus quipped with a smirk.

"Just because I want to keep the sex casual, doesn't mean I'm not interested in learning more about you," Marcus said pointedly, but couldn't help returning the smile. "You are a fellow councilman after all. I feel like it's time I knew more."

A heavy sigh emanated from the demon as they played a couple more moves before he finally shrugged. "Not much to tell."

"Lena said much the same when I met her, so I no longer believe such assertions."

"Well then, I guess it depends on what you want to know," the boundling said looking up at him. "Are you interested in my human life or my time as a demon?"

"Both," he answered quickly. He was genuinely interested in learning everything about the man. "I know a little of your human life from Lena, but only the period you were together. What about your parents?"

Cyrus went silent for a period, taking a long time before making his next move on the board. Marcus panicked for a moment that he might have hit a nerve, silently cursing his carelessness at, yet again, hurting the boundling. With a small cough, Cyrus finally answered; "They died in a car accident when I was two. I don't know anything about them."

"I'm sorry," the cambion said with genuine sympathy. "Did you go into foster care straight away?"

"No," Cyrus shook his head, his voice shaky with unspoken emotion. The sound of it made Marcus' heart ache. "I lived with my aunt in Italy for a few years, but she got sick when I was eight. She, um..." he drew in a sharp breath, squaring his shoulders before continuing. "There wasn't really anything they could do for her, so she stopped treatment. After she died, with no other close family, I went into the system. Her partner, Brody, at the time tried to get custody of me. He was a good guy, taught me how to stand up for myself. But he had a record and so wasn't deemed a good candidate for a foster parent."

"So, what happened?"

"I got placed with a relatively nice family. Could actually have seen myself settling in there. They even started adoption proceedings."

Marcus noted his distraction tactic wasn't working as Cyrus effortlessly took two of his pawns and a knight before he managed taking even one piece. Pressing his lips together, he focused on the soft hint of pain that had laced each of the boundling's words. "That didn't work out, huh?"

Cyrus scoffed with derision. "No. They always wanted a child of their own and when they got pregnant, I was... forgotten." Everything in Marcus wanted to pull the young man into his arms, to ease the hurt that featured so prominently in his voice. "I lived with them for four years before I was moved to a group home for a bit."

"Lena's told me about the group homes she was in," Marcus said softly, intently watching the morphing expressions on the young demon's face. "They sound almost as bad as the cambion nurseries."

"Ha, yeah..." Cyrus huffed a laugh. The tightness in the boundling's face eased slightly as his thoughts turned to his sister. Marcus hoped that meant that the siblings had finally sorted through the recent distance between them. He made a mental note to ask Cyrus about that later. "Hers were pretty horrific for what they usually are though. You're not supposed to stay in them long. They're meant as a transition place. Lena got the short end of the stick in life really. Probably something to do with that deal her father made."

"No doubt," Marcus chuckled, glad that some of the tension in the room had eased. Focusing back on the game, he managed to take one of Cyrus' bishops. "So, what was your experience like with them then?"

"They were okay," the boundling shrugged. "I got on fairly well with some of the boys I met there. It was in the group homes I figured out I liked guys. Maybe it was a result of nurture over nature in that instance, but I was never attracted to girls."

"I'm not complaining," the cambion grinned wickedly, wondering if this could be his new distraction tactic to try and win the game.

"Careful," Cyrus chastised him with a coy smile. "Might think you're actually starting to care about me."

"What makes you think I don't care?" Marcus asked almost indignantly but coiled back at the demon's pointed glare. "Maybe don't answer that," he sighed, scrubbing a hand over his mouth.

The boundling laughed, shaking his head with badly veiled amusement. "I lived in the group home until just before I turned sixteen. Then Lena and I were placed together in a home with two other kids."

"What was she like then?" he asked, curiosity getting the better of him. As much as he wanted to get to know Cyrus better, he couldn't help wondering more about Lena's history and how it formed who she is now.

"Well," Cyrus started, taking a deep breath and rubbing the back of his fingers over his jaw, pulling at the memories. "She was twelve and had already lived through far too much abuse for a someone of that age. She was so quiet and just let everyone walk all over her. I found it infuriating. My idiot kid brain thought she was just asking to be used. I had never been abused until then so I couldn't understand why she didn't fight back." He fell silent for a moment, shutting his eyes as he shook his head. "God, I was stupid back then."

"Being abandoned by that first family was abuse, Cyrus," Marcus pointed out, keeping his gaze steady on the young demon's face.

"Alright, fine," the boundling huffed, smirking at him. "I hadn't been *physically* abused until then."

"That was the placement you beat up the dad, right?"

"Yeah. Lena slept in the room next to mine," Cyrus continued, scratching the back of his head. "The walls were uncomfortably thin. Pretty sure he thought all of the kids were asleep, but for whatever reason, I couldn't sleep that night. I heard her door open and I heard her start to cry asking him to leave her alone. I felt sick. I knew I couldn't just sit there and listen to what he was about to do to her. I don't think Lena knows just how close I came to killing that man."

"He wasn't a man," Marcus spat vehemently, his conviction in that statement resolute. "He was a pathetic waste of air. We may be demons but abusing children is beyond even my comprehension. I have no patience for anyone that would take advantage of someone who can't fight back." The room was silent and he glanced at Cyrus, his brows raising as he saw a light he not seen before in the chocolate depths of the boundling's eyes. "What?"

"Nothing," the demon coughed, looking back down at the board and taking his turn. Marcus didn't miss the slight blush that spread over Cyrus' cheeks. What was that about? "Thankfully, Lena and I had the same social worker from that point. She made sure we stayed together when we got moved to the next placement. I kind of took Lena under my wing, so to speak. Taught her how to stand up for herself, be assertive. As best I could anyway. I was a hothead back then—" Marcus barked a laugh cutting the boundling off. Smiling, Cyrus continued, rubbing the back of his neck sheepishly. "Ah, still am, I guess. She and I ended up fighting quite a bit over it. But I decided then and there that I was going to protect her for the rest of my life. That's when she became like my sister. I just wasn't expecting my life to be over so soon after that.

"Lena and I were in three placements together. I got moved last minute just before I aged out of the system. Not entirely sure why, but as my social worker explained it, it was the best area she could find to help me get set up. Seemed like a flimsy reason to me at the time. But she was going to try to help me get custody of Lena so I wasn't going to argue with her. But then the family I got moved to sacrificed me to Zagan, so... yeah..."

"Do you know what they wanted from him?"

"Not a clue, and I never wanted to know." Cyrus gave a dejected sigh. "I accepted the binding and that was enough for me at the time. I held out a small hope that I could eventually find Lena again. Take proper care of her. That was, until the non-exposure command, then I was just stuck."

The final word was said with such apathy, Marcus almost flinched at the absence of emotion, something he didn't hear often from the boundling. They played silently for a few turns and Marcus realised he was losing. Cyrus grinned at him as he called; "Checkmate." Rolling his eyes, Marcus reset the board and spun it round. This time he took white and the first turn.

"You are under no obligation to answer," he said as Cyrus took his turn, "but what was Zagan like to you in the beginning? I know how he was towards Lena, but she had already been a demon for a little while by then."

"But then, she hadn't transformed yet," Cyrus reminded him.

"True," he conceded. "The girl you were sacrificed with though, she refused to bind?"

"Yeah," the boundling chuckled. "She made the smart choice honestly. Chose purgatory."

"If you hadn't chosen Zagan, you wouldn't be where you are now."

"Sure. That really helps me through the nightmares," Cyrus teased, his eyes wide with mocking sarcasm.

"You're still having those?" Marcus asked, shocked by the information. The few nights they'd been together, Cyrus had slept peacefully. He'd begun to think the boundling was free of his dreams.

"They're... lessening," the demon admitted. "Zagan left me somewhat alone in the first few weeks. But then I was mainly in the Repository trying to find my design and once I did find it, as the only keeper of the hellhound den, I spent more and more time there away from him."

"So, what changed?"

"He grew bored," Cyrus said with a shrug and a deep inhale. "He wasn't discriminatory in taste, like most cambions. As long as he was in control, he didn't care."

"That I knew," Marcus nodded, making his turn and taking one of Cyrus' pawns. Perhaps playing white had been a good choice. He seemed to be doing better this round. "Ambrose has told me some of what he experienced when he was bound to Zagan."

The young demon hummed, his brow furrowing. Marcus studied him wondering what he was thinking. "Zagan spoke about Ambrose a lot. Part of the reason I was so at odds with Ambrose was that I would be used as Zagan's tool for venting his frustrations on whenever he got pissed off with him."

Marcus felt like the world had fallen away from under him. His stomach dropped into his feet at the confirmation of something he had once suspected, but had never confirmed. "We didn't know," he whispered, wanting to say so much more in apology.

"I know," Cyrus assured him, looking up and giving Marcus one of his gorgeous smiles. He felt his chest ease at the sight, but held the boundling's gaze, still wanting to convey his regret at the knowledge. "Don't worry, I don't hold that grudge now. Zagan would also pass me round between his 'allies' as a form of payment. And it wasn't just sex. Sometimes I was just used as a punching bag."

"An unfortunate fate of most cambion boundlings," Marcus admitted.

"I got used to it," the boundling said with a dismissive shrug.

Something about that irked Marcus. He didn't like the idea that the young demon simply accepted the treatment doled out upon him. The thought of Cyrus being passed around made his throat constrict with raw emotion and his skin crawl with disgust. Swallowing around the lump that formed in his throat, Marcus almost wished that Zagan was still alive so he could subject the cambion to the same treatment. Although he held the belief no one deserved to be treated that way, there were exceptions he would grant. Perhaps he could take his rage out on the demons that accepted Cyrus as payment. That could be therapeutic. Ripping them apart slowly, tearing their flesh from their bones, feeding them piece by piece to the Infernal Pit. He was sure Zamira and Sollis would welcome the snack.

"What were you like to the boundlings you've had?" Cyrus asked, startling him from his dark thoughts.

Pulling his mind back to the present, Marcus tried to focus on the chessboard. "Not like Zagan. I haven't had many and I mostly just let them do what they wanted. I didn't really care about using them for power. I had enough of my own in the beginning."

"In the beginning?"

"Ah, yeah..." Marcus sighed, wondering how to continue, how much he wanted to say, rubbing at his temple. "My father was an exceptionally powerful demon. On parr with Zagan to be honest. He only died because he was tired of living without my mother. He committed suicide about seven hundred years ago."

"I'm sorry."

Surprised by the genuine sympathy in the young demon's voice, Marcus shook his head dismissing the condolence. "Don't be. I helped him."

Cyrus' brows shot up. "What?" he breathed.

"I had eight hundred years with my father," the cambion shrugged. "I couldn't deny him his wish to be reunited in death with my mother."

"I think that is the coldest yet most romantic thing I've ever heard you say," the boundling said leaning back in his chair, looking over Marcus' shoulder at some distant point in contemplation. "That I've ever heard anyone say."

Marcus threw his head back with a loud barking laugh. That had not been what he intended with the statement, but it would be Cyrus to twist that meaning into it.

"So, the boundlings?" the young demon reminded him, extending his arm and moving his knight.

"I've had four in total," Marcus answered finally. "All have moved on to their own factions now. Well, one's dead."

"When was your last one?"

"A thousand years ago," he said quietly, his brow furrowing, dropping his gaze to the board. He didn't want to discuss William. Not with Cyrus. Not with anyone, but definitely not with Cyrus. Cyrus and William were so different and evoked such polar opposite emotions in him. He didn't want his desire for the boundling to become tainted by his loathing for his former lover. Noting that Cyrus was not pushing him to explain further, he felt the need to clarify a little. "They... ah... they betrayed me, and took everything I had built. I've not had any desire for one after that."

"Fair enough."

His gaze snapped up to the young demon, noting the concerned look on his beautiful features, but also the gleam of curiosity in the brown eyes, seemingly held firmly in check. "Not going to press for details?" Marcus queried.

"Oh, I want to," Cyrus nodded with a hint of laughter to his voice. "But I can tell you don't want to talk about it."

"Thank you."

"One question though."

Marcus huffed a laugh, rolling his eyes, but decided to indulge the demon. "What?"

"Did your father not offer a deal to your mother?" Cyrus asked, making his move and taking one of Marcus' rooks much to the older demon's annoyance. "Make her immortal like him."

"He did," the cambion nodded, more than happy to answer this line of questioning than the one he thought the boundling was going to take. "She wouldn't accept. Even when I begged her to."

"Do you know why?"

"My mother loved my father and I more than anything. She was afraid that, by becoming a demon as well, that would change," he explained. "She didn't want to risk it. My father built a cottage for her in the mountains and provided her with whatever she needed. She was happy. We were happy."

"Sounds nice."

"It was," Marcus agreed, even as it dawned on him that yet again, he was losing this match. "Honestly, sometimes I'm surprised my father lasted as long as he did without her."

Cyrus chuckled warmly as he moved his final piece into place. "Checkmate."

Shaking his head in defeat, Marcus slumped back in his chair, folding his arms over his chest. "Well played."

The men smiled at each other for a moment before Marcus pushed to stand and rounded the table to stand next to Cyrus, the need to be closer to him almost overwhelming. Getting to his feet, the boundling met him part of the way, not touching, but close enough their heat began to meld together. The cambion saw the instant the spark of desire ignited in those chocolate eyes and ideas of what he wanted to do to that gorgeous body began to flash through his mind.

"Well, Lena and Ambrose are out for the night," Cyrus said, stepping closer until their shirts brushed against the other. His voice grew husky, lowering to a rich and sultry tone that sent fire through Marcus' lower belly. "Archie shouldn't be back with Balo until the morning either. Shall we take advantage of the solitude?"

Grinning wolfishly at the young demon, Marcus placed his palm firmly against Cyrus' hip pulling their bodies together. Digging his fingers in, his other hand cupped the boundling's jaw, as he sealed his lips over that perfect pout. The boundling melted into him, his eyes fluttering shut as he allowed Marcus to dominate the kiss.

Pulling back slightly, the cambion drank in the heated flush on Cyrus' face. There was no beauty that compared to this man in his arms. "Turn around and bend over," he growled, stepping to the side, placing the young demon between him and the table.

He didn't miss the stiffening of Cyrus' entire body. There wasn't fear like yesterday, but he could tell the demon wasn't entirely comfortable.

"Cyrus?" he questioned, turning the boundling back round to face him. The spark of desire in his eyes had diminished. It was not gone, but it was mixed with uncertainty. Stepping towards him, Marcus perched them against the table, pulling their bodies flush and resting their foreheads together. "That's something Zagan would have said and done to you, isn't it?" he asked, already certain of the answer. The boundling didn't have to answer, but the slight nod he gave tore through Marcus' chest. He'd taken Cyrus bent over his desk the other week so could only assume yesterday had pulled up some latent memories the young demon still needed help moving past. "I'm sorry," he apologised softly before an idea struck him. "Have you ever been in control when it comes to sex? You've been controlled, but have you ever taken someone?" Again, Cyrus didn't have to answer. Marcus saw it in his questioning and pleading eyes. Brushing a gentle kiss over full pout, he stepped back, lacing their fingers together as he led the boundling out of the library. "Come with me."

# CHAPTER TWENTY-THREE

Cyrus could only look at Marcus as he gently took his hand, allowing the demon to lead him up to his bedroom.

He knew he'd been falling for the cambion, but when Marcus spoke with such conviction about the foster father that tried to hurt Lena, that had been it. Everything had clicked into place. Simultaneously, his heart swelled with love for the man and shattered to a million pieces knowing his love would never be returned. He couldn't even process at that point in time, what it would mean going forward. What would happen when things ended with Marcus? He knew he would never want things to end, but they would eventually. Right? They would have to. Marcus didn't want a relationship, although his past and current actions seemed to indicate otherwise. But the cambion was as stubborn as they came and it didn't take much for Cyrus to imagine him simply ending things for no real reason other than 'just because'.

He wanted to think things through. He had to at some point. But the warmth of Marcus' hand around his pushed all reasonable thought from his head, leaving only one ringing loud and clear:

*I love Marcus.*

His body flushed hot with the desire it fuelled, like his own fire snaking through every fibre of his being, coursing down his limbs and making his fingers and toes tingle with both anticipation and anxiety. He was barely aware as Marcus led him into his own bedroom, closing the door softly behind them.

"Marcus?" he queried, not sure what else to say at that point.

The cambion turned towards him, continuing to pull him gently into the middle of the room, stopping at the foot of the bed. Without a word, Marcus gripped his hips and turned him around until his back pressed against the older demon's torso.

"Pleasure when sharing it with someone else should not be selfish," Marcus whispered in his ear, sending shivers down his spine. Deftly, the man ran his large hands down Cyrus' stomach, easily unbuttoning his jeans before slipping a hand inside and wrapping his fingers around his cock. "But in order to learn what you like, sometimes you need to be a little selfish." Marcus began to stroke him inside his jeans. Gasping at the pleasure that radiated from the warmth of the cambion's hand, Cyrus dropped his head back, resting it against the demon's shoulder. Gently, Marcus kissed him on the cheek. "That's it, baby. Give in to the feeling. Right now, only your pleasure matters. Nothing else matters. Not me, not Lena, nothing. Just you."

Marcus' words washed over him like waves of heat from an open flame, rippling across his skin, deliciously warm and inviting. His stomach tightened with desire, warmth flooding throughout his body, overlapping with the fire of his realised love until it burned like an inferno inside him.

"You have been forced into submission for years, but you need to understand that submission is a gift you give to the dominant. Regardless of if you enjoy being submissive or not, if you trust someone enough to submit to them, that is a privilege afforded to the dominant, not the other way round. Submission is a gift that you control and no one should simply take it from you," Marcus whispered against him, his hand stroking tantalisingly slow. "Tonight, I will submit to you. Tell me what you want. And not that you want to be taken, or that you want me generally. Tonight, I am yours to use. Use me as you have been used. Tell me what you want me to do to you. For you. Let me give you this gift."

"Ah, Marcus," he moaned, his hips bucking against the large hand. "I don't... I don't know how to..." He cried out in disappointment as Marcus quickly removed his hand from his jeans. Pulling his head forward, he watched the cambion step around, his eyes widening as Marcus knelt before him.

"I'll help you get started then," Marcus said, pulling Cyrus' jeans down just past his hips so his cock stood proudly before him. "Don't think, just do what you want." With that, Marcus sucked his shaft in his mouth, licking and sucking along the length, his tongue circling the head with enticing skill.

Cyrus moaned loudly as his body tensed, pleasure overwhelming his ability to control himself. Requiring support, he quickly laced his fingers through Marcus' hair, serving to both hold his balance and pull the demon's mouth further down his cock. He felt Marcus smile against him and realised this was his plan. To force his body to simply react to what it wanted, shutting down his mind from analysing what action to take next. His cock throbbed and pulsed within the cambion's mouth, as the warmth and softness of it quickly overtook any hesitation he had been holding onto. He'd loved the feeling of Marcus sucking him off before, but even then, Marcus had been in control of how his mouth was used. Seeing the cambion now kneeling before him, he realised he was truly in control, and for the first time in his life he could take his own pleasure.

Tightening his grip in the blonde hair, Cyrus began to move Marcus' mouth along his length, controlling the speed and depth. With no objection, the demon grabbed his arse, encouraging him to push deeper into his throat. Groaning as his excitement and pleasure mounted, Cyrus thrust his hips in time with his hands pulling at the back of Marcus' head. His cock slipped into the recesses of the cambion's throat, the small space constricting the head of his cock with an intensity he had not felt before. Looking down at his face, Cyrus moaned, "Marcus, I'm going to come." The demon's fingers dug into his backside, but not to pull away or to stop, the grip felt hungry, as if the cambion couldn't pull him close enough. With a cry, the boundling slammed his hips forward, his cock pulsing almost painfully as his release spilled directly into Marcus' throat.

The feeling of the older demon swallowing and the slow licks of his tongue cleaning the remnants of his cum was as pleasurable as the feeling of his throat. Cyrus kept his hands in Marcus' hair, sure he would collapse if he let go, but he eased his grip allowing the cambion to move his head freely. After a moment, he cupped a hand to Marcus' jaw, pulling gently as the older demon got to his feet. Once he was standing, Cyrus claimed his mouth, slipping his tongue inside, tasting his own release on Marcus' tongue. Placing his hands on the demon's hips, he walked them towards the bed, steadily stripping them of their clothes as they went.

"Yes," Marcus sighed into his mouth. "I think you've got this now. What do you want to do to me?"

Pulling his own shirt over his head, Cyrus pressed against Marcus as they fell back onto the mattress. His whole body thrilled as the cambion lifted his legs, letting him nestle between them, their cocks pressing together. Lifting his head, he looked into those sea-green eyes, continuously drawn into their beauty.

"Marcus, I..." he started, still unsure as to what to do next. He wanted the demon more than anything, but he wasn't sure how to proceed in this situation.

"Cyrus," Marcus said, lifting his hand to cup his cheek. "Forget what you've known about sex. Being forced to cater to another with no regard to your pleasure is not sex. I don't care if I'm inside you or if you're inside me, I like it either way. I enjoy being inside you, very much I enjoy that." His seductive grin pulled an involuntary moan from the boundling, as Cyrus dropped his head and claimed another kiss from the cambion. Growling against him, Marcus managed to push him back just enough to continue speaking. "You need to learn what you enjoy more and you won't know that unless you can try everything. In this regard, I am happy to be your test subject. Get out of your head and just let instinct take over. You may be surprised at what happens." His warm smile eased some of the apprehension in Cyrus. "If you are going to fuck me, though, you'll need to go easy at first. It's been a while since I've had someone in my arse."

Hypnotised by Marcus' laugh, Cyrus pressed a warm, tender kiss to his soft lips. Large hands travelled over his shoulders and down his back, pressing their bodies closer. Slowly, they moved together, their cocks rubbing against the other and their hands exploring every inch. Relishing the kiss, Cyrus tried to run through all the things he had imagined with Marcus before they started this affair. But perhaps those were not the things he should be seeking now. Instead, he decided to try something new. Something that had always been done to him, but that he had never been allowed to experience for himself.

Breaking the kiss, they each drew in a loud gasp of air. Marcus' green eyes were almost black with the width of his pupils, desire darkening them beyond anything Cyrus had seen before. The cambion was excited to see what he would do and that gave the boundling all the encouragement he needed.

"Turn over," he rasped, placing a final bruising kiss on the demon's already swollen lips. Marcus smiled and nodded his consent. Resting back on his knees, Cyrus grabbed the lube as Marcus turned over onto his stomach. He briefly considered telling the cambion to turn back foregoing his original plan, but decided the point was to feel how he had felt, or more for him to feel how others had felt when using him in this way.

Pouring some lube on Marcus' arse, Cyrus massaged the tight hole, gently slipping a finger inside. He felt Marcus' body tense briefly before slowly relaxing. Watching his reactions, he slid another finger inside as the older demon gasped and arched his back, taking deep deliberate breaths to ease his muscles. The sensation on his fingers alone was incredible, feeling the cambion clench and tense around them. Stroking his cock as it hardened again, his excitement and anticipation for what was going to happen next grew.

As Marcus' body started to relax, Cyrus slicked his length with lube before positioning himself above the older demon, pressing the head of his cock gently yet firmly against the tight opening. The cambion pulled his knees up, raising his hips and arse into the air, resting on his elbows.

"Ready?" he asked, running his hands over Marcus' firm bottom and up his lower back, coming to rest on his hips.

"Yes," the cambion breathed, pushing back slightly against him.

Slowly, he pressed his hips forward, inching inside as the older demon gasped beneath him. The sensation was extraordinary to him, the tightness and warmth pressing all around him as he slid in further. He groaned with the exertion, closing his eyes, desperately fighting to keep himself in check as his desire threatened to explode immediately when his hips finally hit against Marcus' backside.

"Oh, fucking hell!" Cyrus exclaimed, falling forward and planting his palms onto the mattress either side of Marcus' waist.

The cambion's fists were clenched beside his head, his forehead resting against the mattress, as he took deep breaths, trying to relax his body. Cyrus kept still, the feeling of Marcus pulsing and tensing around him enough to pull a moan from his throat without added movement. Gently, he kissed the back of the older demon's neck, hungrily breathing in his scent of burnt sugar.

"Ah, Cyrus. I knew you would feel good. Fuck, you're big," Marcus moaned, lifting his head to look back over his shoulder. "You can move, gorgeous."

"Are you sure?" he asked, almost wincing as the cambion clenched around him.

Marcus nodded, shifting his own hips to prove his point. Cyrus gasped, a shockwave of pleasure rippled through his abdomen, his hips involuntarily pulling back slightly before pushing forward again. With a low moan, the cambion arched his back, pressing himself against Cyrus' stomach as the boundling picked a steady pace. Drawing out his pleasure from Marcus' tight hole, he pushed himself back up, taking hold of the demon's waist, using it as an anchor for him to more easily control his movements.

The feel of Marcus' body mixed with his moans, quickly pushed him to the edge. Fighting against himself whilst desperately wanting more, he leant forward, reaching underneath Marcus to grab his cock within his hand. The moan that emanated from the cambion was divine, as he began to pump the hot flesh in time with the movement of his hips. The tightness around his own cock increased, contracting and pulsing around him causing a slight, yet enjoyable, pain.

Resting on his free hand, Cyrus kissed and bit lightly at the back of Marcus' neck and shoulders. "Give me your mouth," he groaned, the heat in his body rising to an almost unbearable level. Marcus twisted his shoulder round, turning to meet his hungry kiss. Plunging his tongue into the demon's mouth, Cyrus drank in the scent and taste of the cambion beneath him.

"Tell me how I feel, gorgeous?" Marcus managed to breathe out in between gasps of pleasure, raising a hand to grip at the back of the boundling's neck.

"Amazing," Cyrus moaned without hesitation, claiming another kiss from his lover. "Fuck, Marcus, you feel so fucking good," he said against his lips. "You're so tight and warm and I want more."

"You can go harder, baby," the demon rasped into their kiss. "Take what you want from me."

His mind barely functioning, Cyrus fought to think of what he wanted to do next. What position he wanted to move Marcus into. The cambion was so expert at manoeuvring his body as desired, but he felt completely out of his depth in the moment. Squeezing his eyes shut, he forced the constant chatter in his mind to silence, instead pulling memories of positions Marcus had taken him in that he had enjoyed to the forefront.

Refusing to overthink, he gripped the front of the cambion's throat, pulling him up from the mattress until their bodies pressed together. Removing the hand from his neck, he twisted the demon's arm round and anchored it between them, using it and his throat as leverage to pump ferociously into the warmth of the man before him. Marcus' free arm gripped at his hip, fingers digging in with delicious pressure. The older demon's head rested on his shoulder, vibrations coursing under his fingers as Marcus moaned around his hold. It felt strange having the cambion's large frame in front of his leaner one, but the way the demon eagerly formed into his hold was intoxicating. He bit down on Marcus' pulse point, relishing the loud moan from his lover as he licked over the mark he left behind.

The change of position had increased the pressure around his cock, and he struggled to hold himself in check. With each movement, his body threatened to throw him over the edge. But with the realisation of his feelings for the cambion, he didn't want to end things like this. Releasing his hold, he withdrew from Marcus, growling into his ear: "On your back."

Cyrus was almost surprised by the speed in which the demon complied with his request, watching as he laid back against the pillows, his knees lifting, eagerly inviting the boundling to rest between them. Gripping behind one of the cambion's knees, Cyrus lifted it into the air, draping Marcus' leg over his shoulder. The older demon shifted slightly, adjusting to an accommodating angle. Fisting his own cock, Cyrus drove back within the cambion, sheathing himself in a single movement.

"Oh fuck, baby!" Marcus cried, his shoulders curling up from the mattress.

"You know the rules, tough guy," Cyrus smirked, allowing his bratty nature to take control. "You don't come until I say you can."

The cambion moaned around a laugh. "Fucking brat," he huffed out, his hands fisting the sheets beside them.

"Accurate," he chuckled, rolling his hips at an increasing pace as his body relaxed into the new type of movement.

Slamming forward, both men groaned at the roughness of it, the sounds of their bodies slapping together echoing around the room. Cyrus desperately wanted to draw the experience out, but the only way he was going to be able to do that would be to stop, and he couldn't bring himself to do that. His body felt like it was on fire, burning with overwhelming pleasure. Watching Marcus' face contort with pleasured anguish, his cock bobbing between them with each desperate movement, only drove him closer to the edge. Moving one hand from the cambion's leg, his wrapped his fingers around the pulsing shaft, stroking with each thrust of his hips.

"Cyrus," the demon groaned, his body tensing around the boundling.

"Fuck, Marcus," the young demon cursed from behind gritted teeth. "I want to feel you come around my cock. I want to feel your body pull everything from me. Come for me, now."

Marcus cried out, flinging his head back, his moan echoing into the room as his cock throbbed and pulsed in the boundling's hand, warm strands of cum shooting over Cyrus' fingers and onto the cambion's stomach.

Cyrus thought his cock was going to fall off, as Marcus' walls tightened unbelievably around it. With a roaring cry, he slammed his hips forward, burying himself to the hilt, his own climax rocking through his body. Leaning into the orgasm, his fingers dug into Marcus' thigh, firmly holding him in place as his release emptied into the cambion.

As their bodies stilled, he withdrew from the demon, falling to the side and resting against the pillows. Swiping one of his large hands over his stomach, Marcus scooped his release up and wiped it on the far edge of the sheet before lying beside the boundling. Cyrus shivered as the older demon gently trailed his hand over his smooth chest and stomach.

"That was amazing," he sighed, rolling onto his side to look into those sea-green eyes. He swallowed those three words that he now wished more than anything he could say out loud. But he knew voicing them would end whatever this was between them faster than he could say them. Instead, he bit his bottom lip, forcing a smile to hide his indecision.

Marcus returned the smile with his own roguish grin, resting his head on his arm. "I'm glad you enjoyed it. You were fantastic." He leant forward and pressed a soft kiss to Cyrus' lips before swinging his legs off the bed and standing.

"Marcus?"

The cambion rounded the bed, holding out his hand for the boundling. "Come here," he ordered, his voice a low rasp that set off flutters within Cyrus' abdomen.

Taking the offered hand, he let Marcus pull him to his feet, chuckling as the older demon practically swung him over his large shoulder.

"What are you doing?" he laughed, pushing against Marcus' back, a large hand firmly grasped over one of his read cheeks.

"Taking care of you," Marcus retorted, shifting him slightly as he strode them into the adjoining bathroom.

Unable to see what the cambion was doing, Cyrus heard the shower start, trembling slightly as he was lowered into the warm stream. Marcus stepped in swiftly with him, spinning him round until his back pressed against the cambion's chest, large arms wrapping around his waist. The warmth of the shower cascaded over their sides, pooling between them, as Marcus trailed soft kisses over his shoulder.

"Is this not something I should be doing for you?" he asked cautiously, not wanting to ruin the moment, but unclear on how things stood right now. Was it not the top that should take care of the bottom after sex? Why was Marcus doing this?

"Does it matter?" the older demon rasped in answer, nuzzling his nose into Cyrus' neck.

"I don't understand."

Spinning him again, Cyrus found himself staring into brilliant emeralds, shinning with something that he'd not seen before within them. Knuckles traced down his cheek as Marcus leant down, brushing a tender kiss over his lips.

"You've never topped before, Cyrus," the cambion whispered against his lips. "You were amazing, but I know you won't necessarily believe just words. So let me take care of you and show you instead."

Swallowing thickly, he could only nod in answer and watch as Marcus grabbed the soap, lathering it over his body. Wrapping his arms around the cambion's neck, Cyrus sighed, melting into the warmth of the large body as Marcus' hands trailed over his back, massaging muscles he hadn't even realised were tense.

"That's it, baby," Marcus purred next to his ear. "Just relax. Topping takes more out of you than you realise."

He hummed, nuzzling his face into the cambion's neck, his own fingers tangling into the long blonde hair. Marcus' body shivered as he dug his fingertips into the older demon's scalp, bringing a smile to his face.

"That feels so good, gorgeous."

Cyrus whimpered as Marcus' hand moved to his front, wrapping around his cock, cleaning it with gentle strokes. "So does that," he murmured, pressing closer to the cambion.

Too soon the touch left him, but he sighed contently as the hand landed on his lower back, rubbing small circles over his skin. They simply held each other, the steam from the shower encompassing them. Cyrus didn't want to move. If only time would stand still, he could live in this moment forever. Wrapped in the arms of the man he loved.

He almost groaned in disappointment as Marcus pulled back slightly. But he quickly forgot his frustration as the cambion cupped his face with one of his large hands, a warm smile on those soft lips.

"So, do you prefer to take or be taken?" Marcus asked indulgently.

Cyrus chuckled at the question, but considered his answer. "It was... wonderful, to feel what it's like to be inside someone, and I would definitely be up to trying it again sometime," he said, letting his eyes travel appreciatively over Marcus' frame. "But, I'm pretty sure I prefer to be on the outside of someone," he smiled at the cambion seductively.

Raising a brow, Marcus matched his expression. "Pretty sure?"

"Well," Cyrus said, rising onto his toes and leaning into him, closing the distance between their faces. "I might need a reminder."

With a small laugh, Marcus caught the boundling behind the head and crushed their mouths together, before pinning him against the shower tile. "I think I can help with that," the cambion whispered into their kiss. Cyrus smiled against him, tightening his embrace around Marcus' shoulders, heartily welcoming the older demon to take him.

# CHAPTER TWENTY-FOUR

Something had changed.

In a way, Marcus knew it was going to as soon as he suggested letting Cyrus take control. But he hadn't expected how it would change. The boundling had truly surprised him with how he took the lead. Once he got out of his head, he had come into his own. Fucking the young demon was extraordinary, but being fucked by him had thrown Marcus into a whirlwind of ecstasy. Possessiveness had overcome him to the point he didn't want anyone else to experience what Cyrus had given him. To be his first in that regard was an honour and Marcus wanted to be the only one who ever received it.

Feeling the gorgeous body now sleeping peacefully beside him, spooning it against his own, Marcus shut his eyes trying to focus only on the bliss he now felt. But his mind raced with what this meant. He was becoming attached to the boundling, and the fear that evoked was almost as great as the possessiveness.

As gently and quietly as possible, he extracted himself from the embrace, rising to stand beside the bed. Leaning back down, he paused briefly, hesitating at the implications of his almost instinctive action, before wilfully ignoring it and tucking the covers around Cyrus. Grabbing his clothes, he ducked out of the room, quickly getting dressed in the hall before racing to his room. He needed to test a theory. He could only hope that it would not blow up in his face. But if it did, it would solve his all problems regardless of the result.

Pulling out a mobile from his bedside table, he sent a brief message to an unlisted contact. He chewed on his bottom lip as he waited for their answer. Seeing the reply come through, he quickly deleted the messages and flamed to his new destination.

"I was wondering when I would see you again," the sultry voice behind him carried across the room. "I was beginning to feel neglected, Marcus."

"You know the rules, Kale," he said harshly, turning on the spot, reminded of the pleasurable shivers that had coursed through him when Cyrus had said the same thing to him. Pushing the memory from his mind, he stalked over to the incubus.

The stunning man grinned seductively at him, leaning back against the desk that stood proudly in the centre of the room. Or at least, Marcus used to think he was stunning. Now, he wasn't so certain of that opinion. Chestnut brown hair cropped short at the sides, was slicked back in tousled waves atop a heart-shaped face. Gleaming blue eyes, shone like diamonds in the pale-yellow light from the chandelier above them. His skin was a deep caramel, smooth and supple over gently chiselled muscles. Of course, the demon was beautiful. As an incubus that was his entire reason for being. To be beautifully seductive. But where Kale used to instil immediate lust within him, now Marcus found himself desperately searching for something in the man's features to hold his interest. The open dress shirt and crinkled black trousers indicated to him that the incubus had only recently finished entertaining another client. Not that it mattered to him.

Kale cocked his head to the side, eyeing him speculatively. "You seem... different."

"What did I just say?" Marcus growled, drawing closer.

"Don't worry, darling, I know the rules," the incubus chuckled. "But so do you."

Stopping in his tracks, he glared at the man. Maybe this was a bad idea. A really bad idea. But he had to find out.

"Fine," he huffed out. "Ask away. And *don't* call me 'darling'."

"Transformed or not?"

"Not."

"Powers?"

"Preferably, no."

"Offer?"

"Two souls."

"Generous. Headspace?"

"That's a new one."

"Seems fitting," Kale smirked. "As I said, you seem different. Almost angry. Just want to make sure I'm not in danger. Can risk this brothel's best incubus, can I?"

*This brothel*, Marcus scoffed internally.

It was Kale's brothel. He ran the damned thing. That's why the cambion would go to him. The incubus was only accountable to Asmodeus so it was much less likely that anyone would find out Marcus came here. And tonight, of all nights, he needed the secrecy. There was a risk if Asmodeus found out it would get back to Lena, but he didn't have a choice. Cyrus was quickly invading his every thought. He needed to see if another could find purchase there before he did something he might regret.

Grinding his teeth together, he closed the space between them. Kale's eyes gleamed as Marcus wrapped his hand around the demon's throat. "I'm fine," he said flatly. "I'm not going to hurt you."

"You've said that before," the incubus teased, his hands flat on the surface behind him as Marcus leant them back over the desk.

"I answered your questions. My rules now. So be quiet," he growled harshly, crashing his mouth against the demon's.

Moving his hand from Kale's throat, he tried to focus on the feelings behind the kiss, as his fingers moved almost robotically, stripping the incubus of his clothes. And it was robotic. Nothing like the passionately fuelled encounters he'd had with Kale previously. The kiss was nice, but it did nothing for him. No fire, no heat, just... *just*. Their tongues met languidly, but Marcus honestly felt like he was just going through the motions, with no actual driving need. He could easily continue the experience without even touching lips with the demon again.

Kale's hands slid up his stomach, pulling his shirt along with them. He pulled back from the kiss to assist in tearing it off over his head. The slight break in their contact gave Marcus' mind a moment to assess the situation. The thought struck him as the fabric cleared his head and his eyes settled back on the incubus' smiling face that he was disappointed to not see chocolate eyes looking back at him. It hit him in square in the chest, making him take a small step back, guilt flooding his belly.

His chest heaved as he drew in short, sharp breaths, trying to stem the panic building within him. Thankfully, Kale hadn't seemed to notice as the incubus used the space to let his trousers drop to the floor, stepping out of them and kicking them to the side. Using the opportunity of the demon gazing down his body, Marcus shook his head to clear his thoughts, before stepping forward and slamming the man back against the desk. Kale was now fully bare before him, his hard cock pressing into the cambion's lower stomach.

Unable to bring himself to kiss the incubus again, Marcus gripped at Kale's hips, spinning him around so the demon faced away from him. Planting his hand on the back of Kale's neck, the cambion forced him to bend forward until his chest and cheek rested on the wooden desk. Kale moaned breathlessly as Marcus trailed his hand down the man's back, grazing over the roundness of his arse, before cupping each cheek and spreading them to bare the pulsating hole to his eyes.

His mind assaulted him with images of Cyrus draped over his desk in his office. The boundling had just come to speak with him about an upcoming hellhound race, but Marcus hadn't been able to help himself in sampling the gorgeous body in this way. Cyrus may still have some reservations with some positions to begin with, but overwhelm his body with enough pleasure and he would bend to every whim Marcus had.

*Fuck.*

Desperately trying to focus on the incubus before him, Marcus moved his hand to trail his fingers down the seam of the demon's arse. Teasing the hole slightly, he watched intently as Kale writhed within his hold. But the movements that had once stirred his desire, now felt forced, or well-practiced. Kale was an incubus after all. Adept in attraction and seduction. Even the sounds the man was making did nothing to heighten the sensations of the moment.

Cyrus was so reactive, so responsive to his touch. The slightest brush of his fingers or lips across the boundling's skin would pebble the flesh and course shivers of anticipation throughout his own body. The breathy moans and gasps of pleasure the young demon would make, turned his blood to lava within his veins. Nothing about the boundling felt rehearsed or fake. Everything was effortless. Every touch, every kiss, every sigh and moan and climax.

Squeezing his eyes shut, Marcus tried to force the thoughts from his mind. He knew Cyrus was ruining him, but he'd thought, perhaps hoped, that if faced with one he had previously desired he would be able to lessen the hold the boundling had over him. Lubricating his thumb with his saliva, he pushed the digit inside Kale's hole, listening to the rehearsed gasp that sounded from the incubus. The sensation was underwhelming. Cyrus would pulse around him, practically vibrating with need, his youthful body desperate and eager for everything Marcus could give it.

It dawned on him, that there was no desire in his body for Kale. He wasn't hard, not even a little. His mind couldn't stop from comparing the incubus to Cyrus, screaming at him to return to the boundling and forget that he had ever taken this action, regardless of his intent behind it. His chest tightened with the knowledge that he was risking, truly risking, one of the best things to ever happen to him by being here.

*FUCK!*

Groaning in frustration, he pushed away from the incubus, turning and walking to the other side of the room, needing to put space between him and the demon.

"Marcus?" Kale's sultry voice called to him.

He didn't know what to say. There wasn't anything to say. What could he possibly say? That now of all times, he couldn't bring himself to perform something he had done hundreds of times before. Because to do so would drown himself in shame. Would bury him under a mountain of guilt. Because Cyrus would hate him if he did.

*Cyrus...*

"What's his name?"

Startled by the question, Marcus eyed Kale from the corner of his eye. The demon had no shame, sitting atop his desk, his nakedness on full display. "What do you mean?"

Kale smiled knowingly, tilting his head to the side. "The one who now holds all of your attention. Your desire. There was a time you would have railed me without hesitation, so I can only assume whoever it is must be rather special."

"Don't jump to outlandish conclusions, Kale. I'm just tired."

"Sure, you are."

Growling with annoyance, he turned away, retrieving his shirt from the floor and pulling it over his head roughly. *Damn incubus*, he thought. Great for relieving sexual stress, but they could literally see one's desires. He shouldn't have come here.

"Well," Kale said, drawing in a deep breath. "Whoever he is, he's a lucky guy."

"Oh?" he scoffed. "And why is that?"

Shifting off from his desk, Kale walked over to the cambion, unashamedly swaying as he walked. Marcus smirked at him in exhausted humour. Nearing him, the incubus leant close, his nose barely brushing over Marcus', a playful smile on his lips.

"Because you are one of the best fucks I've ever had. And he gets you all to himself."

"Wow," he marvelled, raising a brow at the demon. "Never thought I'd see an incubus get jealous."

Kale laughed, pulling back and turning to grab his briefs, finally covering himself. "At least, you're not denying there is someone."

Closing his eyes, he cursed internally. He really shouldn't have come here.

"That said, I feel sorry for the kid."

His gaze snapped to the incubus. "How so?"

"Because he's just going to end up hurt with you," Kale said flatly, turning and leaning against the edge of his desk. "Just like all the others you've left in your wake."

Anger flared within him, his chest tightening with quiet rage. "You'd better explain that comment, Kale," he warned softly.

"You know what I mean," the incubus sighed, a knowing grin tugging at his lips. "You never let anyone get close, until Ambrose, and we both know you never wanted him. Not like that anyway. And anyone you did want, you used and tossed aside faster than it took to get my clothes off."

Turning his face away, Marcus stared at the floor, deep, painful sorrow washing over his body, making his limbs feel twice as heavy as they were. "You know why," he said quietly.

"I do," Kale said nodding. "Which is why I never minded being used by you. But you are a cambion at the end of the day. Regardless of your mother's influence, you are made to hurt those around you."

Anger mixed with his sorrow, causing his blood to heat. "You'll shut up if you know what's good for you," he growled, a silent warning in his voice, narrowing his gaze as he locked eyes with Kale.

"You'll listen if you know what's good for you." The incubus didn't shrink or shy away from him, simply shooting him a cocky grin which did nothing but fan the fury in his belly. "You got hurt, you got burnt, so you put up walls that no one can get through."

"Shut up, Kale," Marcus whispered darkly, stalking towards him.

"No," he snapped, pushing off from his desk, rising to meet the cambion's gaze. "I won't. Because you need to hear this." As if to drive home his point, Kale jabbed his finger into Marcus' chest. Breathing heavily, the cambion clenched his fists by his side, ready to lash out if needed. "The rest of us, the ones who actually care about you, we're not William," Kale pressed on. "And whoever this boy is, the boy that has taken your desire for anyone else away, he's *not* William. You cannot paint him with the same brushstroke. If you can't separate the two, you will end up alone and miserable, because he won't stay around forever. He will leave and you will die inside as you watch him move on with someone else."

The incubus' words rung in his ears, growing louder and louder with each beat of his heart. Marcus felt his chest flush cold with fear but couldn't understand why. He couldn't understand what he was afraid of. He wanted to be alone. He'd wanted to be alone for centuries now. Physical needs could be met by anyone, so being alone didn't matter. Or at least, that is what he used to think. Hadn't the whole reason of coming to Kale been to see if he could still be satisfied by others? And hadn't he just realised that was not the case? So, what was he afraid of? Losing Cyrus?

His mind rebelling, refusing to entertain the line of thought further, Marcus glared at Kale, before grunting in annoyance and turning sharply on his heel. "I'm leaving," he huffed.

"Sure," Kale sighed, exasperated. "You always were good at running away."

"Fuck you," he snapped over his shoulder.

"Wish you would," the incubus jeered. "Marcus," he sighed. His voice was so soft and full of genuine warmth, Marcus halted in his strides, turning his head slightly to look at the demon from the corner of his eye. "As an incubus that desperately wants you to come back here one day it pains me to say this, but... don't push him away. Whoever he is, I can see that he's something special to you, even if you're not ready to admit that yet. You deserve more than just errant desire."

A lump formed in his throat as he turned away, unable to face Kale any longer. Taking a deep breath, Marcus gathered his flames and transported himself to his room.

Once in his familiar surroundings, he stripped off his clothes and beelined for the shower. A fucking hot shower to hopefully burn away the floral scent of the incubus. Yet another thing that made his chest ache with longing for the boundling in the other room, his body wishing to replace the floral with Cyrus' smoke and leather. But he couldn't go to him. Not yet. The young demon's senses were keen. He'd pick up Kale's scent with little effort and Marcus knew he wouldn't be able to think up a reasonable excuse for bearing the scent of a sex demon.

Incubi scents were stubborn however, so even after the shower, he couldn't risk sliding back into bed with the boundling, despite how much he wanted to. Cyrus could never know about tonight. He could never know about Kale. It would break him, Marcus was sure about that. If their earlier experience had changed things for the cambion, it most certainly changed things for the boundling as well.

Kale's words rung through his mind. The incubus was wrong. He didn't deserve anything. Much less what Cyrus was offering him. But at the same time, the demon had been right. He didn't want to lose the boundling. Not anymore. He didn't want Cyrus to move on to someone else.

Grinding his jaw until it cracked under the pressure, Marcus rested his forehead on the cool tile of the shower wall, the hot water trailing over his back. Cyrus had crawled under his skin and he wasn't sure he would be able to claw the demon back out. He wasn't sure he wanted to.

"Damn you, William," he ground out under his breath, cursing his former lover for instilling this mistrust and hatred within him. He wanted to let it go. He wanted to move on. But he didn't know how. But perhaps, Cyrus would know. Or could help him.

Perhaps, forming an actual relationship with the boundling, if only to test the waters, could help him finally let go of his past. The idea still flushed his extremities with icy fear. But something told him that no matter how cold his fear ran, Cyrus would be there to warm him.

He owed it to the boundling to at least try... *right?*

Scrubbing a hand over his face, he reasoned he should at least speak with Cyrus. Lay it out. If he could find the courage to do so, even tell him about William.

Maybe he should speak to Lena first. Just in case everything did blow up in his face. Then, hopefully, he could head off any retribution from her on her brother's behalf.

And if he was going down that route, he should speak with Ambrose. Try to enlist his friend's help in buttering the Prince up, which he was certain there was every possibility he would need to do in one form or another.

Groaning, he dropped his head back into the stream of water. This was starting to sound like a loop which would require repeating anytime he and Cyrus even had a disagreement, assuming they did try to have a relationship. Sire or not, Lena was fiercely protective of her brother. She may not be getting involved now, but if it came down to it, she would, and she would side with Cyrus, every time. Of that, Marcus was certain.

*Fuck*, he was in trouble.

# CHAPTER TWENTY-FIVE

An odd churning sensation settled in Cyrus' stomach that morning as he made his way down to the kitchen. He hadn't actually meant to fall asleep last night. He didn't really need the rest, but the warmth of Marcus surrounding him was too strong of a pull into sleep for him to resist. But waking up and finding the cambion gone, whilst simultaneously working through the realisation that he loved Marcus, had set off an uneasy feeling within him that he didn't know how to handle.

Entering the kitchen, he stopped abruptly in the doorway, his gaze pinned on the back of Marcus' head, who sat at the table, sipping a coffee and reading a book.

"Hi," Cyrus greeted the cambion, striding past him to make himself a coffee.

"Good morning, gorgeous," Marcus smiled in response. "Sleep well?"

The boundling studied him from the corner of his eye. He wasn't entirely sure why finding the older demon gone before he woke up annoyed him so much today. It wasn't like it was the first time that had happened, but last night he thought something had shifted between them. Changed. Perhaps it had to do with his realisation that he loved the cambion. Whatever it was, he had been surprised to find himself alone that morning. It took a lot of reminding himself that they were just a casual fling to sate their desires to not go flying off the handle at

Marcus over it. But regardless it didn't make sense. Why cuddle him to sleep to then sneak out?

And why did Marcus' usual scent have a hint of floral to it? Something akin to a succubus. Or incubus. Surely the cambion would not have immediately gone to someone else after they had been together. Would he?

"Yeah, I did thanks," he said quickly, casting the unwelcome thoughts from his mind. "Where di–"

"Could we–" Marcus started at the same time. The cambion chuckled under his breath. "Sorry. You first."

His brow furrowing, Cyrus opened his mouth to continue but before he could say anything, Ambrose flamed into the kitchen, almost crashing into the table as Marcus snatched his own coffee up off the surface to save it from spillage. Cyrus' eyes went wide as he took in his sister practically hanging off her Consort, clearly drunk.

"Heyyy!" she laughed as Ambrose attempted to manoeuvre her into one of the chairs, succeeding only in toppling the seat onto the floor.

"Oh shit," Marcus chuckled, quickly moving to help his friend haul their Prince onto one of the other chairs as Cyrus rushed to the sink to get her a glass of water. "Lena, are you drunk?"

"Oh, absolutely!" she giggled, her arms snaked around both men's necks, holding herself up between them. "Do you know how many bottles of wine Belphegor can drink?" she asked the cambion, smiling sweetly at him, earning her a disgruntled scowl from her Consort. Her words slurred together to the point it was practically a riddle deciphering the question. "I hope you do, cause I lost count after thirteen..."

"Please tell me you didn't keep up with him."

"Oh no," Lena hiccupped, settling into the chair, grasping the sides as if she was afraid she would fall off. She looked like she might fall off. "No, no, no, no..." she trailed off shaking her head.

"She tried," Ambrose sighed, firmly grasping her shoulder to steady her. He looked gratefully at Cyrus as he took the glass of water and tried to get their Prince to drink the clear liquid.

"I wasn't far behind either," she said proudly, taking a few tentative sips of the water. "He can just drink faster."

Watching carefully, Cyrus saw the slight sway in his sister's body as Ambrose moved away from her to place the glass on the table. Stepping swiftly forward he caught her before she fell off the chair, her dove-grey eyes glazed with the vapours of liquor. He'd never seen her like this before and he had to admit it was adorable.

"Oh, fuck me..." she groaned, her head tipping back as Cyrus cradled her against his chest.

Chuckling to himself, he lifted her slightly as Ambrose shook his head in indulgent disappointment. Seeing that she was in good hands, the Consort moved to the kitchen, falling into a hushed conversation with Marcus as he prepared two cups of coffee, presumably for him and Lena. Focusing back on his sister, Cyrus grinned at her.

"Never thought I'd see you wasted, little mouse," he teased, carefully lowering her back into the chair as she gripped at his shoulders to steady herself.

"Never again," she grunted, titling her head forward to rest on his chest. He rubbed his hand up and down her back comfortingly. He was well aware of how her head must be feeling having himself indulged in too much of Hell's liquor a number of times to drown out past memories. "I am never drinking with the Prince of Gluttony again... I can't feel my face."

"Oh my god," he laughed, wrapping his arms around her so her head settled on his shoulder. "Not exactly sure what you were expecting, Lena."

"Screw you, Cyrus," she whispered harshly at him, her nails biting into the flesh on his arms.

"What?" he asked with mock indignation, knowing exactly what she was cursing him for. "What did I do?"

"What didn't you do?" she spat. "If you hadn't gotten so fucking horny, I wouldn't have had to drown you out with wine."

"Yeah," he laughed as Ambrose and Marcus returned to the table. "That's fair."

"You and Marcus seriously need to pick your moments better," she hissed, just loud enough that only he could hear.

Coughing awkwardly, he could only smile at her, or grimace might have been more accurate. His eyes darted to the Consort and cambion, hoping they hadn't heard her. Thankfully, he couldn't see anything on their expressions indicating they had.

"Wait..." Lena trailed off slightly as her brow pulled together, evidently trying to sort out a cohesive thought despite her inebriation. "What day is it?"

Raising a singular brow at his sister, Cyrus cocked his head to the side. "It's Friday, why?"

"Shit," she groaned, forcing her feet to find purchase beneath her. "What's the time?"

"Ten AM."

"Double shit. I'm supposed to be meeting Raphael at two."

"Why are you meeting the arch-angel?" Cyrus murmured with a hint of disgust in his tone. He didn't like the angel. No one in Lena's council did. Especially not after their last encounter with him at the beach.

"He sent me a message. Wants to talk about something," she said, pinching the bridge of her nose. "Probably wants to threaten me some more about staying away from his daughter. Fairly certain he caught me spying the other day."

"Well, we have four hours to sober you up," Ambrose sighed, pushing a cup of coffee into her hand. "Let's get you in a shower." With a small smile, the Consort took her from Cyrus' hold, gripping her firmly around the waist as she clutched the coffee like a lifeline.

Silence settled over the kitchen. Or at least, in reality it was silent. Cyrus felt like the world around him had dialled the volume up to eleven, his heart and blood pumping in his ears so loud he couldn't hear his own thoughts. Turning on the spot, he sought out Marcus, his gaze coming to rest on the cambion, finding him leaning back against the kitchen counter, arms folded over his chest.

"Can we talk?" Marcus asked, before Cyrus had a chance to say anything.

Swallowing around the lump that formed suddenly in his throat, forcing himself to hold the older demon's gaze. "About what?" he all but whispered.

"About us."

The boundling was sure his heart was going to break through his ribcage if it didn't slow down soon. He was finding it difficult to take in a full breath, not that he needed it technically speaking, but he needed it in a stabilising sense.

"Us?" he queried, desperately searching for some rational thought to grasp onto in this moment. Lena usually resorted to humour in these kinds of situations. Maybe he could too? Had to be better than his usual snarky comments, right? "I didn't think there was an 'us'." Nope, that was snarky. His voice sounded small to his ears, hollow and uncertain. Why did he think that was a good thing to say? He wanted there to be an 'us' between him and Marcus. Why did he have to turn into an awkward freak at a time like this?

*Way to go, Cyrus,* he chastised himself.

Panic started to set in. Maybe when Marcus said he wanted to talk about them, he meant ending whatever it was between them. He didn't want that to happen. Not yet. Not before he got a chance to tell Marcus how he felt. And he knew that it was going to be a while before they would be in a position for him to make that leap. He needed time. Things couldn't end now.

But why did Marcus have a sex demon scent on him? A small seed of anger sprouted within the panic. For Cyrus, the sex was amazing. He didn't want or need anyone else. So why did the older demon need to go to someone else immediately after Cyrus had fucked him? Had he been that bad at it? Was the cambion really that unsatisfied? But they were casual, so why did he care so much? He had just assumed that as the agreement was to fool around until he found someone else, Marcus wasn't seeing anyone else.

God, what a fool he'd been.

Marcus sighed, pulling his attention back to the moment.

"I think we both know, that's no longer true."

Well, his heart stopped racing. Cyrus was fairly certain it had stopped beating all together. Surely, he had misheard the demon.

*What?*

Marcus could clearly see the panic in Cyrus' eyes.

Unfortunately, he knew what he was about to do would not help the situation. He'd had every intention of asking the boundling for a chance. A real, proper chance at a relationship. He was even going to tell him about William. Clear the air completely. But he'd heard the whispered exchange between Lena and Cyrus and it made his blood run cold.

He couldn't do it. They were affecting Lena more than either she or they cared to admit. It had to stop.

They walked side by side into his office, Cyrus shutting the door behind them. Marcus could feel the tension rolling off the boundling's body, and he hated that he was about to make it worst.

Standing in the middle of the room, he noted that Cyrus had stayed by the door, hesitation and worry plastered across his gorgeous face. The cambion opened his mouth to speak, but nothing came out.

"Marcus?" Cyrus called softly, and he was grateful to the boundling for breaking the silence. "What did you mean back there?"

Sighing heavily, Marcus dropped his gaze to the floor. This was going to go badly, he knew that. But it had to be done. "I think we need to put some distance between us for a while," he managed to force out. "Calm things down."

The silence in the room was almost unbearable. Risking a glance at Cyrus, he noted that the man's fists were clenched by his side. The boundling was fighting against himself. Trying to keep his emotions in check, and Marcus was surprised that he was proud of the demon for it.

Cyrus took a shaky inhale, his eyes darting to the far corner of the room. "What did you mean by 'no longer true'?" he pressed. "And why then follow it up with 'we need to put some distance between us'?" His tone was measured and controlled, his anger simmering below the surface, but he fought his nature to not let it out. He'd matured so much over the last few weeks. Marcus felt his chest constrict as Cyrus continued his questioning; "To just remind me that you're emotionally unavailable?"

"Cyrus..." he sighed, pinching the bridge of his nose. Just as the boundling was fighting to control his temper, he had to fight against his desire to say 'fuck it' and kiss the hot-headed demon.

"No, Marcus," Cyrus interrupted him, "you don't get to say something like that and then tell me you need fucking space. Especially not after last night. How exactly did you think I was going to react to that?"

"I'm sorry," he said hurriedly, realising he had screwed this up. "I should have phrased it better."

"No fucking kidding."

His stomach churned uneasily. This isn't how he'd imagined the morning going. This isn't how he'd wanted the morning to go. But he had to stick with the plan. The new plan. He had to pull away.

"I still want you to try and find someone else," he almost pleaded with the demon, stepping towards him, ignoring how much it pained him to say it. "This, what we're doing," he said, gesturing between them, "I won't deny that it's been some of the best weeks in a long time for me. But as I've said, I can't give you the relationship you want. The relationship you *deserve*."

Marcus emphasised the last term in a final attempt to make Cyrus understand. He may have thought they could have had something, but Marcus knew he would destroy the boundling. He could try all he liked to have a normal relationship, but he would constantly be afraid of betrayal. He would constantly question every action of the young demon, looking for the first sign that something was wrong. What relationship would that be, if he could never fully trust the one he was with? What relationship would it be for Cyrus, if he felt like he was always being second guessed?

But, yet again, the boundling surprised him.

"I'm not having that argument with you again," Cyrus sighed, scrubbing his hand over his face, the other planted firmly on his hip. "Fuck's sake, Marcus." The vitriol in his voice made the cambion flinch as if it was a physical blow. Chocolate brown eyes zoned in on him, pinning him under their fire. "I don't understand why you're bringing this up. I agreed to the casual fling. I knew this wasn't going to go anywhere. I haven't said a fucking thing about wanting it to go somewhere. So, where the fuck is all this coming from?" the boundling spat. Marcus stared at him helplessly. He didn't know how to answer that without making the situation a million times worse. Cyrus huffed at his silence. "Seriously, you're not even going to answer that?"

"I... I don't know what to tell you."

"How about some of the fucking truth, Marcus?" the boundling practically yelled at him, throwing his hands out to the side. "Explain things to me. Really explain them, don't just make me keep guessing at it. I'm not a fucking idiot. I understand pain and loss."

"It's not that simple."

"Fuck me," Cyrus laughed with derision. "Alright, fine," he sighed, causing Marcus to furrow his brow in confusion. "Maybe we do need to tone things down for a while. Might actually give me time to find someone else. Who knows, maybe Kai's free."

Marcus heard the flat sarcasm in Cyrus' voice, but it didn't stop the red haze that descended over his vision. It wasn't like the demon knew that Kai's name caused a visceral fury to course through him. Cyrus didn't know what had happened between him and the other cambion. But it didn't matter. His pain and anger overwhelmed him. With a loud growl, he closed the distance between him and the boundling, ignoring as those brown eyes widened with fear. Grabbing the young demon by the throat, he slammed them back against the wall, a soft cry emanating from Cyrus as he did so. His other hand punched into the wall beside the boundling's head, the render cracking under the blow.

"Not Kai," he growled from behind gritted teeth, his fingers digging in on the sides of the demon's throat. "Do you fucking understand me, Cyrus? You do not go to Kai. *Ever.*"

The fear that flashed through Cyrus' eyes was quickly replaced with indignant anger. Marcus almost smiled at the sight of his feisty brat. *Shit*, no, not his. *The*. Not his.

"I don't see how that is *any* of your fucking business," Cyrus rasped, his voice barely audible beneath the cambion's hold.

A feral snarl ripped from Marcus' chest as he pulled the brat towards him only to slam him back against the wall with an almost deafening thud. Smoke billowed from his hold, wrapping around the young demon's shoulders. His power wasn't active so no harm was being done, but he couldn't contain it anymore as it encompassed Cyrus within its grasp. He inched his face closer to the demon, their eyes locked, noses almost touching.

"If you even think of going to Kai, I will tear him to fucking shreds," he whispered with deathly promise, his teeth bared as his lip curled. "I will drag him through all of Hell until his blood coats every wall. I will feed him to your hellhounds. Not *fucking* Kai. He doesn't fucking touch you. Do you understand me?"

"Yes," Cyrus croaked, his own hands wrapping around the cambion's wrist trying to ease the pressure on his throat. "Marcus, yes. I understand. I- I'm sorry. I didn't really mean it. I can't stand Kai."

"Promise me, you won't go near him."

"I promise."

Slowly, too slowly, his power receded into his body, as his breathing calmed. His eyes dropped down to the hold he had of Cyrus' throat, seeing the boundling's hands gripping at his own skin, knuckles white. Shame washed through him causing him to loosen his grip, letting his arm fall to his side. He kept his fist pinned to the wall, instinctively leaning into the boundling, pressing their torsos together. With a heavy sigh of regret, he rested his forehead against Cyrus', squeezing his eyes shut, not wanting to see what he fears might be in those chocolate depths.

"I'm sorry," he rasped, knowing he should pull away, give the demon space following his outburst. But his body refused to cooperate, wanting to be close to the boundling, to feel his warmth. "I shouldn't have done that. This is why we need space."

"Okay."

Surprised at Cyrus' quick agreement, Marcus reared his head back, his eyes opening to lock with the boundling's. What surprised him more was the lack of any emotion in them. Cyrus stared at him blankly, like he wasn't even there, slicing through him with their emptiness.

"I've scared you," he whispered, his own darkest fear realised in that moment. He was a cambion and he'd let his true nature out on the one person who never deserved to be subject to cambion treatment again. Marcus swallowed hard against the bile rising in the back of his throat.

"No," Cyrus blurted, emotion returning to his eyes. But there was no light. Only a tired sadness as those doe browns traced over the cambion's face. "I mean, yes," he nodded slightly, before shaking his head. "But, no. You scared me, but I'm not scared *of* you, Marcus."

The older demon blinked, the implication of the words settling over him. His brow furrowed as Cyrus placed his hands on his chest, pushing him away until there was at least a foot of space between them.

"You need to do some thinking, Marcus," the boundling said softly, but his voice unwavering and firm in its resolve. "You need to think about what it is you *really* want. Because if you want to be alone for the rest of your existence then keep pushing me away and maybe one day, I'll get the fucking the hint. But this household, this *family*, that we have, that we are a part of, we don't give up on each other. We didn't last year and we won't now. So, okay, I'll give you some space so you can figure your shit out. But I'm not going fucking anywhere. Do *you* understand *me?*"

Marcus felt frozen under Cyrus' hard gaze, rooting him to the spot. He could only nod his understanding then watch, dumbstruck, as the boundling turned on his heel and walked out of the room, leaving him to his thoughts.

# CHAPTER TWENTY-SIX

*Fuck Marcus.*

Cyrus knew he'd pushed the cambion by mentioning Kai. He wasn't even sure why he did that. Well, he did. His heart had felt like it was breaking within his chest, a painful vice like grip constricting very muscle like demonic lightning. He wanted to hurt Marcus, the same way he was hurting. But he hadn't expected the reaction he got. His breathing was rapid as he stormed up to his room, fire licking over his arms as he fought to gain control of the tide of emotions coursing through him.

*Fucking cambion bullshit.*

He didn't mind being dominated by Marcus, or having his throat held, but this had been different. It actually hurt. And rather than hitting back, he'd just shut down. His vision had almost whited out as Marcus' face morphed into Zagan's and he wanted to throw up as fear swirled in his gut. He'd never been afraid of Marcus until that moment. Hearing the threats the cambion made towards Kai eased the fear into a mix of something akin to confusion and annoyance. The malice dripping from Marcus' tone had confirmed for him that something had happened between the cambions. Something that still caused Marcus pain to this day. Whatever it was, it had to do with the man's aversion to relationships. Cyrus was sure of it.

Detouring from his room at the last minute, he made his way to Lena and Ambrose's wing, taking a deep steadying breath before knocking softly on their door. Ambrose opened the door with a sympathetic smile.

"Hey, Cyrus. Come in. Lena said you were likely on your way," the Consort greeted him warmly, stepping aside for him. "She's still in the shower. Give her a minute."

"Thanks," he muttered, walking past.

Ambrose strode into the room to his dresser. His black hair was wet, likely having just gotten out of the shower himself. He had trousers on but was shirtless for the moment. Not that the boundling cared.

Cyrus wandered over to the couch that sat beneath one of the windows facing the courtyard, falling into the cushions with a heavy sigh.

"That bad, huh?" Ambrose asked over his shoulder, pulling a shirt over his head before turning to face him.

Glaring at the Consort, he huffed in annoyance but not with any malice. He was just beyond caring to control himself. "I'd ask if I'm that obvious, but I already know the answer."

Ambrose chuckled at his response before moving to sit at the edge of the bed closest to him. The room resembled the one that the Prince and Consort had shared in Ambrose's manor shortly after Lena became a demon. Plush burgundy carpet covered the floor, providing a soft fire-like glow to the cream walls. Matching burgundy and cream sheets covered the four-poster mahogany bed.

"Do you want to talk about it?" Ambrose asked, leaning forward to rest his elbows on his knees.

Cyrus studied the Consort for a moment. He liked Ambrose. More now than he used to. But he didn't want to talk about this with him. Not yet. In answer, he shook his head slightly. "No, but thanks. Do you mind if I talk to Lena privately?"

The demon smiled at him. "Of course not. She's your sister. I've got some work to do anyway." Ambrose got to his feet, moving over to the couch to grasp the boundling's shoulder giving it a reassuring squeeze. Staring up at the Consort, Cyrus wondered how much Lena had told him about what was going on with Marcus. It didn't seem likely that she hadn't told him anything. "I am here if you do want to talk with someone who can't analyse your emotions at the same time."

Much to his surprise considering his current mood, Cyrus snorted out a laugh, grinning up at Ambrose. "Might take you up on that one day," he breathed out with a grateful nod.

"I'll be in my office if Lena asks," the Consort smiled, patting his shoulder before walking out of the room.

Now alone, Cyrus hauled himself off the couch, falling onto the bed without fully straightening his spine. He settled into the numerous pillows resting against the headboard. He would never understand why Lena needed so many. They mostly just ended up on the floor at some point or another. The sound of the shower shut off as Cyrus folded his hands behind his head, looking up at the bed's golden canopy, lost in his thoughts as he listened out for his sister.

Although his mind had shut down when Marcus slammed him against the wall, Cyrus realised he'd probably said the most hurtful thing he could have to the cambion. But he'd also realised that Marcus was still holding something back. Holding himself back. Stopping himself from accepting something that seemed so obvious to Cyrus. That they were inevitable. They were meant to be together. And he wasn't going to give that up. Not now.

Marcus needed space. He needed time to realise what was staring him in the face. No matter how pissed Cyrus was in this moment, he could recognise that the older demon was close to just accepting what he wanted. So, he'd give the cambion the space he needed, but he wasn't going away. Maybe it was the brat in him, but he couldn't just walk away. Ignoring the fact that they worked together on Lena's council, he was so unbearably drawn to the man, to walk away now would destroy him. Anything with Marcus was better than nothing.

"Please, make yourself at home."

Grinning at his sister, Cyrus lifted his head slightly as she made her way out of the bathroom, a towel wrapped tightly around her.

"You've never minded before," he teased as she grabbed some clothes out of her dresser.

"I've never been hungover before," she sighed, pinching the bridge of her nose. "Hang on a second."

Ducking back into the bathroom, Lena was barely a moment behind the closed door before she returned in jeans and a loose dusty-pink shirt. Mixing in the flushed tones of her intoxicated skin, she actually looked cute. She wore such a hardened exterior now with her role as Prince of Hell, Cyrus missed this side of her. With a loud groan, she crawled up the mattress from the foot of the bed and flopped down next to him.

"I'm convinced Belphegor tried to kill me with wine," she said, her expression wincing slightly as she rubbed at her temples.

"His wine is rather... *potent,*" he commiserated, rolling onto his side, resting his head on the bend of his arm, his other arm laying in front of him. She turned to him in a similar position as they simply stared at each other for a moment.

Lena smiled weakly at him. "Are you okay?" she asked quietly.

"No."

There was no point in hiding from her. Add to that he didn't want to. He wanted to talk to her about this. Fully. Nothing held back. Not anymore.

"Do you want me to go Prince of Hell on him?"

Huffing quietly, he shook his head, a small smirk on his lips. "No, but I'll keep the offer in mind."

Her eyes narrowed as she studied him. "He hurt you. Like actually hurt you."

"Honestly," he whispered, like he was afraid someone might overhear them, "I'm surprised you didn't come storming in when he did. I half-expected you to."

"I was buck-arse naked," she laughed softly. "Doubt that would have helped the situation."

"Probably not," he agreed. "I'm okay though. About that, anyway. I'm not okay, generally speaking."

With a sigh, Lena reached across the bed and took hold of his hand, interlacing their fingers. "I warned him what would happen if he hurt you."

Smiling at her, he squeezed her hand tightly. "I'm sure you did. And I'm sure he's shitting himself wondering if you're coming for him. Truthfully, that's a nice thought to have at the moment."

They laughed quietly together, before settling into a comfortable silence.

"Can I ask you about Marcus?" Lena asked suddenly, jolting Cyrus from his thoughts.

"You can ask me anything," he said with a nod. "But I thought you weren't getting involved."

"I'm not," she said hurriedly with a small shake of her head. "I'm not getting involved. Getting involved would be saying 'chase him' or 'leave him', neither of which I am doing. But..." She trailed off for a moment, seemingly trying to figure out her next words. Cyrus waited patiently, happy to simply be surrounded by her strength in this moment. "I do need to know what is going on in the lives of my council. And even more so in the life of my boundling. Especially when I get thrown into sexual turmoil or heated rage every other day by him. On top of that, you are my brother, and I worry about you. So… are you and Marcus a thing now?"

"I don't know," he answered honestly and without hesitation. "Yes and no is probably the most accurate answer to your question. Although, today probably leans more towards the 'no' side of things."

"As my brain is not working fully, could you clarify for me?"

"We came to an understanding, but we are not together."

"So, friends with benefits."

"You could say that."

"But you want more?"

"Yes."

"May I ask; why Marcus?" Lena asked, shifting on the bed slightly, settling back into the pillows. "You don't have to tell me if you don't want to. But he is a cambion, as Zagan was. I am well aware that Marcus is different to other cambions, but doesn't it bother you?"

"I know it should, but no," Cyrus sighed, shaking his head. "Zagan would command me to stay still to use me like a flesh-light. It would hurt and I would bleed and after I would wish for the floor to open and swallow me whole. Others would use me the same way except they couldn't force me to stay still so at least I could find some pleasure in it. Marcus cares, in his own way. He makes sure I at least enjoy what we do together."

"Of that I am aware."

"I'm sorry, Lena."

"Why?"

"Never crossed my mind that one day my sister would have to experience my love life with me," he huffed with a laugh.

"At least we're not actually brother and sister," Lena scoffed, rolling her eyes, "otherwise it really would be weird."

Grinning at her, Cyrus kissed the back of her hand. She always knew how to make him feel better, even when everything in him wanted to sink into despair.

"I want to tell you something, Cyrus," she said with a soft squeeze of his hand, "but I will compel you after not to repeat it, okay?"

He stilled, looking into her dove-grey eyes. She didn't generally compel him without good reason, so he understood the gravity of the moment. "Okay," he whispered.

"You remember TJ from my test last year?" She paused briefly, waiting for him to nod his affirmation. "Well, he and I were together just before I aged out of the system. He was... well, I thought he was everything I needed. I never slept with him, but he would push and push and push. One night he drugged me and if his mother hadn't walked in on us, I'm certain he would have raped me." Cyrus paled at her words, remembering what had almost happened to her at the hands of Zagan last year. He had known she and TJ had been together in her life, but he never found out what happened between them. "We fought constantly. He would hit me and I would hit him and round and round we went. But when he wasn't doing that, he was... lovely. He would buy me flowers, chocolates, clothes. Anything I wanted, really. I thought he loved me and the way he treated me, well, it was no better than how anyone else had treated me, excluding you, so I thought it was normal. That I deserved it. So, I would go back, coming up with lies and excuses to cover the broken bones. The bruises. Anything to keep him out of jail. I thought, at least he seemed to care."

"What happened?"

"One day he just left," she said with a half-shrug, as best she could lying down anyway. "Disappeared without a trace. I tried to find him, feeling completely lost without him. I got into cage fighting because I hoped that I might find him again that way. I used to watch his matches then tend to his injuries so I knew he fought the circuits. It was two years before I saw him again and by that point, I was so pissed at him and at everyone else, that I jumped at the chance to fight him in the ring. He beat my arse and put me in intensive care for a week with internal bleeding."

"Shit, Lena," he breathed, instinctively pulling her towards him and wrapping his arms around her. One of her arms hooked over his waist as he buried his face in her hair. He hated that she had been hurt by anyone. Even more so that fate had taken him away from her. From being able to protect her.

"Ambrose only knows part of this, so you do not repeat that to anyone," she commanded softly. Cyrus felt his bindings pulse with their acceptance of the command and he nodded into her hair in acknowledgement. "What I'm trying to say is, just because you think someone cares, doesn't mean they do. It also doesn't mean they don't, but it takes more than just a good fuck to know if they do. I'm not telling you what to do. I just want you to be sure that you know what you are getting yourself into. That you are sure you can live with whatever arrangement you have made with Marcus. You are both part of my council, part of this family, and I do not wish to lose either of you. Just... be careful. I love you, and I don't want to see you get hurt."

Tightening his embrace of her, Cyrus simply allowed her words to settle over him. Holding her close, he smiled as he listened to her breathing slow. She'd fallen asleep, the aftermath of last night evidently catching up with her. He decided to let her sleep for a little, making sure to keep an eye on the clock on the bedside table so he could wake her before she had to meet with Raphael. Whilst she was asleep and he awake, she wouldn't feel his emotions. Not acutely anyway. He could think through things without her questioning him.

He understood what she had been trying to tell him. Pursuing Marcus, trying to potentially force something that wasn't really there, would end up in him being hurt. But he couldn't let go of the feeling that he and Marcus were meant to be together. Every fibre of his being told him he had to try. He would regret it for the rest of his existence if he didn't at least try. His love for the cambion was driving this obsession, he knew that. Having just realised his love, he couldn't throw it away now.

Lena was right. Marcus was a cambion and he shouldn't want anything to do with someone with that kind of nature. Whatever magnetic pull Marcus had over him was likely going to drive him insane. It already was. But for whatever reason, he kept letting the older demon pull him in, despite how much Marcus simultaneously tried to push him away.

His own eyes growing heavy, lulled by the peaceful sounds of his sister in his arms, Cyrus reluctantly shook her gently awake.

"Lena," he called softly. "You have to wake up, little mouse."

Groaning, she rubbed her palms into her eyes. "What's the time?"

"Almost one."

"How bad do you think it would be if I just didn't go see Raphael?"

"You really want him to turn up here?"

Punching him lightly in the arm, Lena pushed up from the mattress. "I hate it when you talk sense. Well," she huffed, throwing her legs off the side of the bed and pushing to her feet. "You're going to hate me."

Cocking his head to the side, Cyrus pushed up onto his elbows, looking at his sister sceptically. "For what?" he asked cautiously.

Pressing her lips together, Lena's gaze was pinned on the floor, unwilling to look at him as she spoke. "I'm taking you and Marcus with me to see Raphael."

"Seriously?" he snapped, annoyance flushing his body. He sprang up from the bed, stalking round the end to glare at her. "Now?"

"I'm sorry," she pleaded, holding up her hands defensively. "But I need Marcus' power and I *need* your sobriety. Seriously, the only reason I'm standing is because I am pulling every bit of balance from you through our bond that I can."

"Hang on, give me a second to go get wasted myself, then you can leave me behind."

"Cyrus," she chastised him, although her tone was laced with apology.

Planting his hands on his hips, he groaned as he looked up at the ceiling. "Could you not take Archie instead of Marcus?" he suggested.

"He's babysitting Balo."

"Ambrose?"

"You saw how he reacted at the beach," she offered meekly. "As I'm expecting a number of colourful threats, you really think taking Ambrose would be a good idea?"

"Fine," he huffed, throwing his hands up in defeat. "I'm not speaking to him though."

"Honestly, that might be for the best," Lena nodded as they made their way out of the room. "Strong silent types could be useful for today."

Barking a laugh, Cyrus ran his hands through his hair as he walked beside his sister down the stairs, heading for Marcus' office. "Well, silver lining," he chuckled to himself, "Marcus is probably shitting himself right now. Can't wait to see his face when you tell him what's going on."

Joining in his laughter, Lena snaked her arm around his waist as he hugged her shoulders. "There's my optimistic brother. Come on. Let's go rattle a cambion."

# CHAPTER TWENTY-SEVEN

Marcus swore he nearly had a heart attack, if that had been possible, when he opened his office door to see Lena scowling at him, Cyrus standing behind her. He would admit he thought for a moment the boundling went crying to his sister, and he hated himself for it. Lena obviously knew what had happened, but she was merely collecting him to meet with Raphael, something he had been expecting. Deep down, he knew Cyrus would never hide behind her. The young demon hated the idea that others only thought he was worthy of something because he was Lena's boundling. The thought, however, proved Marcus' point to himself. He would always second guess moments like that. And that was no basis for a relationship.

After Cyrus had left, he hadn't moved from his spot on the floor for almost an hour, analysing their conversation. It was clear the boundling was not going to give up easily. And for some idiotic reason, Marcus didn't want him to. His conviction to pull away from the young demon was shaky at best. But he had to stand firm. Feeling the coolness and tension coming from Lena and Cyrus as they waited for Raphael, standing on the beach where they first found out about the nephilim, only solidified his resolve. Well, only slightly.

He wanted to say something to Cyrus, but like so many other times around the boundling, he had no idea what. He wanted to apologise further for his actions in his office. But to do so would require explaining something he wasn't ready to admit to yet. Risking a glance at the demon, he caught Cyrus' gaze before the demon quickly looked away. It seemed like whatever it was between them had settled into a perpetual state of needing to talk. He hated it. He wanted things to go back to the effortless exchanges. The blissful interludes. But he knew he'd ruined the possibility of that happening now. Taking a deep breath, he tore his eyes away from the boundling, his body tensing with sorrow and shame over his actions earlier.

Suddenly, Lena huffed turning towards them and pinning both men with a hard glare. "Am I going to have a problem with you two?"

Neither man spoke but Marcus sensed as Cyrus shifted on the spot beside him. Dropping his gaze to the sand, he slowly shook his head.

"No problem," he said softly as he heard the other demon murmur something similar at the same time.

"Good," she said sharply, crossing her arms over her chest. Rolling her neck, she sighed into the air, turning away to scan the beach. "Where the fuck is he?"

Raphael was late and it made Marcus uneasy. He watched as a man with a metal detector strolled aimlessly searching for treasures beneath the sand. Furrowing his brow, he studied the mortal for a moment. Something felt oddly familiar to him about the man, but he couldn't put his finger on it. He was also fairly sure that the man looked at them a few times, despite the fact they were shrouded from mortals. Or should be... So, why was the man looking at them? Was he looking at them? Or looking at something behind them?

Apart from the now suspicious man, the beach was mostly empty, the sun as yet barely reaching over the horizon. They were still exposed, however, and no matter what the situation, Marcus couldn't help but analyse their surroundings, searching for threats against his Prince. Against his family.

That was all that mattered in the end. Protecting his family. Lena and Ambrose were his family. Cyrus was a part of that as well, he knew that. And he was protecting the young demon. Protecting him from... well... *him*. From the destruction that the cambion would reign down upon him if he ever truly lost control around the boundling. He may have wanted to try for a relationship after seeing Kale, but that action alone had been one of the most hurtful things he could have done to the young demon. Cyrus may not know what he did, but if he ever found out...

"Ah, there he is," Lena said suddenly, dragging his focus back to the moment. "Good to see you again, arch-angel," she smirked, her tone dripping with annoyance at Raphael's late arrival.

Although the angel grinned at her, there was no warmth or light in his eyes. "I can't say the same." His body seemed to shudder in and out of existence as he passed through the threshold into the shroud, coming to a stop a few strides from her.

Marcus didn't miss the feral gleam form in the Prince's eyes as she stared at Raphael. He braced himself, knowing that she was about to say something that could light a fuse bomb in its wake.

"How's Hope?"

There it was...

Raphael blanched, his brown eyes wide as he looked at her in horror. "How do you—" he started before catching himself, his fists balled at his side, stepping towards her. His face morphed into one of fury, snarling as he closed the distance between them. Marcus and Cyrus shifted closer to the Prince causing the angel to halt in his stride, glancing at them uncertainly. "I swear, Lena, stay the fuck away from her," he forced out, pinning his gaze on her.

"I didn't think angels were supposed to swear," she quipped, tilting her head to the side.

"Where you're involved it's appropriate."

Lena sighed heavily, rolling her shoulders with impatience. "What do you want, Raphael? I'm honestly not in the mood to banter with you today."

"I'm here about Hope," he said flatly. "Didn't realise you knew her name, but don't think I haven't noticed you skulking around the house. You may be shrouded to mortals, demon, but you cannot hide from me."

The Prince laughed haughtily, throwing her head back in amusement. Her eyes gleamed with mischievous intent, leaning forward from the hips, a cruel sneer on her lips. "Want to bet on that?" she whispered.

"Stay away from them!" the angel shouted.

"I already told you, no!"

"Why the fuck are you so interested in her?"

"Because she's *your* daughter," Lena snapped back. "I won't beat around the bush, Raphael, you know how rare nephilims are. Did you honestly think, I wouldn't want to study her?"

"She is a *child*," Raphael impressed upon her, a desperate pleading tone to his voice. Marcus smirked slightly, enjoying the look of panic encroaching on the angel's fair features. "You cannot drag her into this world."

"I wasn't even born yet when I was dragged into it."

"The sins of *your* father should not affect *my* daughter."

Marcus saw from the corner of his eye as Cyrus shifted next to him. The boundling was as uncomfortable as he was with the interaction between their Prince and the angel. Both of them were aware that Lena's soul had been tied to Hell prior to her birth. Her father had for all intents and purposes cursed her to this life by making a deal with a demon, a deal with Ambrose, to save her mother. Of course, the man had no way of knowing what that would mean for his daughter or the life she would lead because of it, but it boiled their blood all the same. Lena was made to be a demon, quite literally, but that didn't make it any easier for them to accept the path fate had laid out for her.

Lena shook her head violently, her own body vibrating with barely contained rage. "But the sins of *her* father should," she spat.

"Try it, demon," the angel warned, his voice dropping to a low growl, "and I will respond in kind. You may have brought your best weapon with you today," he snarled waving his hand at Marcus as a sneer curled his top lip, "but you also brought your greatest weakness. I know how the connection between a sire and boundling works. How important it is to the sire to protect the boundling."

Marcus heard Cyrus scoff under his breath. The bravado of the demon was simultaneously arousing and enraging. The cambion had no doubt that Cyrus could give the angel a run for his money, but that didn't mean he liked the silent threat Raphael sent the boundling's way. His body flushed with heat, his fingers flexing at his side, wishing to sink into the angel's flesh, to tear him apart and remove any threat, real or imagined, to the young demon.

"I make no secret how important any of my council are to me, Raphael," Lena said firmly, barely flinching at the arch-angel's words. "But all of them are strong enough to take you on."

"Shall we see about that?" the angel taunted, looking over at Cyrus.

The boundling took a step towards their Prince and Marcus saw how he had squared his shoulders, his chest puffed with pride at his sister's faith. He wanted to be able to express the same feeling for the young demon, but to do so would likely give Cyrus cause to outwardly challenge the angel. The thought of the boundling getting hurt in any way made his stomach churn with unease, even though he himself had already harmed him.

Lena smiled, turning her head slightly to look at her brother over her shoulder. "Cyrus? You want to show the angel how strong we are?"

"Absolutely."

"Not happening."

Marcus silently cursed himself for speaking. He shouldn't have said anything. He should have kept quiet. It was not his place to question their Prince and definitely not in front of the arch-angel. But he couldn't help it. The words spilled from his lips before he had a chance to stop them. All gazes snapped to him, as he clenched his fists at his sides and glared at the angel with cold rage.

"You need to learn your place, half-breed," Raphael snapped at him, his eyes narrowed in scrutiny.

Lena spun on her heel and in a flourish of movement closed the distance between her and the arch-angel, shoving against his chest. "You need to learn yours, angel," she snarled at him. "I have warned you before, do not insult my council."

Marcus bristled as Cyrus glared at him, brown eyes glowing with fire, nostrils flared.

"Allow me to teach him," the boundling said, turning back towards their Prince, his voice low with deadly promise.

He was going to get in so much trouble for this. Stepping forward, Marcus grabbed at Cyrus' arm, pulling the boundling back a step. "I said, not happening," he growled, his eyes never leaving the angel.

"Marcus!" Lena snapped, rounding on the cambion.

"What are you doing?" Cyrus hissed under his breath, trying to discreetly wrench his arm from Marcus' hold. But the older demon was not going to let go, digging his fingers in, only easing when he was sure he was about to break skin. His body was screaming at him to stop. To stop Cyrus from making a mistake. It didn't matter how much power Lena gave her council, the arch-angel was dangerous, and he wasn't about to let the boundling get hurt.

"You want someone to teach the angel a lesson, I will," he said in a hushed tone, hoping that the angel couldn't hear him. "He's not touching Cyrus."

"Trouble within the ranks, demon?" Raphael sneered cruelly, his gaze darting back and forth between the boundling and the cambion.

*Fuck.* This was bad. If the angel figured out how protective both he and Lena were of Cyrus, it would make the boundling a prime target. He knew he should back off, let Cyrus go and see how things played out. But he couldn't. He couldn't bring himself to pull away. Everything was so messed up. He'd ruined everything. He'd ruined whatever it was between them and he knew there was no way to fix it. The only thing he could do was protect the boundling. Even if the stubborn brat didn't want him to.

"Quiet, angel!" Lena yelled, her patience evidently running out. Stepping up to the angel, she raised a finger, jabbing him in the chest as she let her fury pour from her body. Marcus was certain Cyrus' emotions were adding to that fire, but so be it. "You and I may not be able to kill each other, *yet*, but I will gladly thrash you into the ground."

"Go near my daughter again and I'll return the favour," Raphael promised, unflinching under her deadly gaze.

"Keep the threats coming, Raphael, and the next time you see me, I won't just be with my council. I will bring my entire inner circle to rain hellfire down upon you."

"Call them now, Lena. I'd welcome the challenge."

The Prince and angel stared daggers at each other, quietly assessing their next move. Lena leant in towards him, her teeth bared in threat. Taking the opportunity, Cyrus wrenched his arm from Marcus' grasp, elbowing the cambion in the ribs. The older demon glared at him, but took the hint and stepped back a pace, taking his position at the other side of Lena, returning his gaze to her and Raphael.

"Tell me, angel," she whispered, "have you thought about what you are going to do when your little human lover dies?" The angel flinched, his nostrils flaring at the thought. "Your daughter is a cancer to her. What will you do with Hope then?"

"That is none of your concern."

Lena paused for moment, forcing her face to relax. "I could take care of her."

"I will never let you near her."

"I highly doubt you could stop me."

She'd broken whatever restraint the angel still had in that moment, as he roared and swung his fist round, aiming for her face. Bright light surrounded his hand, angelic power rippling through the air. Her cool exterior firmly in place, Lena ducked, the blow flying harmlessly over her head as she deftly stepped back between Cyrus and Marcus. The demonic pair snarled in unison, their bodies transforming as they lunged toward their quarry.

Cyrus' claws connected with Raphael's arm, tearing at the flesh, black fire licking over the angel's skin. Marcus ducked to the side, grabbing and pinning Raphael's other arm behind his back even as a bright light emanated from the arch-angel, two feathered wings appearing from thin air, pushing out against the cambion. As Raphael transformed, meeting the two demons with his own power, his body grew in height, still shorter than them, but enough to match them in strength.

Sand mixed with the air as demons and angel grappled with each other, exchanging blows that collided with torsos and shoulders. Marcus' eyes locked with Cyrus as they nodded to each other. Stepping to the side, Cyrus covered his body in fire, propelling forward and slamming into the angel. Marcus shifted his footing, creating a solid barrier of smoke before him, which broke, billowing out and encasing Raphael as he fell into it.

Angelic light burst from the cloud of smoke, forcing it to part and scatter in the air. Raphael spun on his heel, his palm pushed out in front of him, a beam of light shooting from the centre aimed at the cambion. Flaming quickly out of the way, Marcus reappeared behind the angel, his arm wrapping around Raphael's neck, pulling backwards ignoring the dull thuds of the feathered wings as they beat against his body.

Without a word or command, Cyrus flamed in front of the angel, his fist flying before he fully rematerialised, striking firmly against the angel's jaw. Light emitted from Raphael but Cyrus was gone before it had a chance to connect with him. The boundling was quick and used his speed to land a flurry of blows against the angel. Marcus was the strength, holding their target in place, shifting back and forth to keep Raphael from finding his footing.

Something in Marcus' chest eased in that moment as he took in the determined look on the boundling's face. No matter how pissed he might be at the cambion, at least they could still work together as they moved in lockstep coordination, just as they had practiced so many times since joining the council.

"Enough!" Lena shouted, stepping forward, her demonic form radiant under the red aura of her lightning currently coursing over her body. Quickly, Cyrus flamed to stand behind his sister as Marcus abruptly let go of the angel, stepping clear of the feathered wings. Lena's clawed hand grabbed at the back of Raphael's neck, spinning on the spot and throwing him away from her. The angel stumbled over his feet, righting himself as he turned to glare at the demons, his wings rising above him, pure light falling from his body and pooling like mist at his feet. His wounds healed quickly as he brushed down the front of his shirt, straightening it.

"Control your council, demon!" the arch-angel spat at them.

"Leave, angel!" the Prince yelled, spikes of lightning connecting with the sand around them, small divots of glass forming in its wake. "I've had quite enough of you today. You want me to stay away from your daughter, make a threat that actually scares me. Although that would require informing your brothers of her existence. Or maybe, I should do that for you."

"I will find a way to take you down, Lena."

"I'd like to see you try."

With a feral growl, Raphael enveloped himself in light and disappeared. Wasting no time, Lena rounded on Marcus, grabbing his throat and pulling his face towards her, her fangs gnashing at the air.

"What the fuck was that?" she snarled at him.

Fear coursed through his chest as he grabbed at her wrist. Not to pull her away, there was no use in trying to escape her wrath, but to steady himself as she forced him to step back. Their wings beat simultaneously against the air, keeping them balanced as the sand readily gave way beneath Lena's hooves.

"I'm sorry," he croaked, pleading with her to believe him. He knew he'd stepped out of line. He could never make up for that. But he needed her to understand why, to know that he would never do so again. Or at least, he hoped he would never do so again.

"Don't you *ever* undermine me like that again," she hissed at him, pushing him away, her eyes blazing with fire. "Do you understand, Marcus?"

"Yes," he rushed, falling to his knees before her in apology. "I'm sorry, Lena."

Gathering herself, Lena turned away, striding back to her brother. Cyrus glared at him, his arms folded over his chest. The rage of the siblings was palpable, but Marcus knew it was justly deserved.

"Go home," Lena ordered over her shoulder. "I'll deal with you later. Cyrus, come with me."

Silent in his chastisement, Marcus watched as Lena's flames enveloped her and her boundling, taking them to the lower rings of Hell. Once alone, he let his demonic form recede, hanging his head in shame. Guilt and shame were fast becoming his best friends. And he had no idea how to change that.

# CHAPTER TWENTY-EIGHT

"You look like you want to kill someone."

Cyrus looked up from his position on the couch in the library as Balo walked towards him. The other boundling pulled out a chair at the table, folding his arms over his chest as he reclined against the wooden back, his ankles crossed in front of him.

Despite himself, Cyrus felt the small tug of a smile as he let his head fall back against the arm, staring at the ceiling. "That would be an understatement," he muttered.

He and Lena had gone to see Lucifer after leaving Marcus. He'd used the time to analyse the cambion's actions on the beach. Add in his threats towards Kai earlier and you could almost call his behaviour protective. Or possessive? At the very least, he was hypocritical. That alone pissed the boundling off. Coming back to the house, he had retreated to the library to think. He didn't want to go to his room, memories of him and Marcus in his bed distracted the thought process.

"Want to talk about it?" Balo asked. There was a sincerity to his question that made Cyrus pause and genuinely consider the offer. But he decided against it.

"No offence, Bal," he sighed, letting his head roll to the side to look at the man, "but not with you."

"None taken," the boundling chuckled with a nod. "I get it. Want to play a few rounds of chess to distract you?"

Smiling ruefully, Cyrus shook his head. "Not today, sorry."

"Fair enough," Balo said returning his smile. "Not sure my ego has recovered from the last time we played anyway."

He and Balo had played a few times over the last couple of weeks. The other boundling had actually given him a challenge and had even won a couple of rounds here and there. Cyrus was still leading by at least a dozen matches, but he liked knowing there was a possibility he wouldn't win.

"This is about Marcus, right?"

Startled by the question, Cyrus studied Balo from the corner of his eye. "What?" he asked, wondering how in hell Balo had figured it out, hoping that his shock was not plastered all over his face.

"So, yes, then," Balo smiled coyly. "Don't worry. I'm not going to tell anyone," he assured Cyrus, not that it felt like much of an assurance to him. "And Damien's commands don't work whilst we're both wearing these bracelets. Have to hand it to Lena, these things are pretty damn impressive." A small smile graced his lips as he turned his wrist over, studying the cuff. Cyrus nodded pensively, agreeing with the statement. The cuffs were useful. They hadn't been sure if they would suppress Damien's ability to compel Balo. It helped them relax knowing it did.

Pushing up from his reclined position, Cyrus sat forward resting his elbows on his knees. "When did you..." he trailed off, not really wanting to ask the question, not wanting to know if they had been that obvious. He didn't think they had been, but then he would admit they also hadn't exactly been subtle.

"Shortly after getting here," Balo answered with a slight shrug. "I've had nothing but time to observe the way things work around here. Honestly, I'm fucking jealous."

"Of what?" Cyrus questioned, his brow furrowing in confusion.

"The freedom you have here," the boundling said without hesitation, waving around them generally. "You're lucky, Cyrus. In these walls you can truly relax. I don't think there is anyone here that would use what you and Marcus have against you. Here you can just be you, without fear of consequences. Hell, Damien and I are careful to hide things from his other boundlings. Do you have any idea how exhausting that gets when you live with them all the time?"

Sighing, Cyrus hung his head, looking at the floor. Balo was right. They were lucky to be in their position, he knew that. He'd made that argument to Marcus on a number of occasions. Why couldn't the cambion just see that?

"Marcus and I don't have anything," he said after a moment, wishing with everything in him that wasn't true.

"Sure, you do," Balo said confidently. "Whatever is going on, whether it's you or him that doesn't want to acknowledge it, there's something there. I'm sure it will all work out."

"I'm not."

"Do you want it to?"

Hesitating, Cyrus looked up at Balo, seeing nothing but sincerity in the man's eyes. Why he was being so honest with the other boundling, he didn't know. Maybe it was knowing Damien couldn't force Balo to tell him, but he reasoned that the sire and boundling were in a similar position. Wanting to be together, but outside forces keeping them apart. Although with him and Marcus, it was the internal forces. Or, one internal force in particular.

"Yes," he answered finally.

"Then fight for it," Balo nodded, silent reassurance in his tone. "I'm guessing he's the one you want to kill right now?"

Cyrus huffed a laugh, rolling his eyes. Of course, he didn't want to actually kill Marcus, but he wanted to sink his fist into the cambion's proud features.

"Well, you are in the unique position where you could actually take him on."

"Ha!" Cyrus barked, falling against the back of the couch. "I'm no match for him."

"Maybe not power-wise," Balo agreed, pressing his lips together. "But you have Lena on your side. As her boundling, she wouldn't let anything happen to you. And Marcus is no match for her."

"I don't want her to fight my battles for me," he sighed bitterly.

"Fair enough."

"Still," he mused, staring at the ceiling once again, his mind racing with possibility. "You have given me an idea."

"Well, go on then," Balo laughed, pushing up to his feet, moving to one of the bookshelves and grabbing a book, clearly indicating an end to their conversation. He turned back to Cyrus, an amused gleam in his ice-blue eyes. "Go get him."

Smiling with mischievous intent, Cyrus almost jumped to his feet, rushing to the library door. "If this works, I owe you a game of chess," he called over his shoulder.

"Let me win?" Balo teased.

"If this goes badly, no," he said, shaking his head. Pausing in the doorway, hand still on the handle, he looked back at the boundling. "And this could go very badly."

Balo nodded, laying down on the couch Cyrus had just vacated. "All the things worth fighting for could," he said, opening the book.

Silently agreeing with him, Cyrus raced out of the room and up the stairs, headed for Lena's altar room. Balo was right, Marcus was no match for Lena, and the cambion knew it. In some ways, that was Cyrus' advantage. Marcus would never do anything truly harmful to him because he always kept the thought that Lena felt everything through their bond at the back of his mind. On that basis alone, Cyrus could take the cambion on. He could let his frustrations out fully. But he didn't want Lena stepping in the moment she felt the slightest thing, so he needed to make sure that she would stay out of the way first.

Not bothering to knock as he knew she was inside, Cyrus barged through the door, striding over to her with quiet determination.

"Cyrus?" Lena queried, looking up from her conduit. "What's wrong?"

"Nothing," he said quickly, giving her a reassuring smile. "Nothing is wrong."

She looked disbelievingly at him, her brows pulled together. "You sure? You look wild."

He nodded as he neared her, taking both of her hands in his. "Lena, promise you won't interfere," he pleaded, gripping her hands tightly.

"Interfere?" Her head tilted to the side. "In what?"

"I can't explain right now," he said, his plan still forming in his mind. He knew she would try to talk him out of this, but he needed to see this through. "Please, promise me, whatever you feel or see, you won't interfere. *Please?*"

Her eyes widened as if she had figured out what he was about to do. She probably had, but the tightening around her mouth told him she wasn't going to try and dissuade him. "Alright, I promise," she said with a curt nod. "Be careful."

"I will."

Leaning down, he kissed her quickly on the cheek, pulling her into a firm embrace, before stepping back and flaming away. He had two goals tonight. One, get the stubborn cambion to finally tell him what was going on with him. And two, punch Marcus in the fucking face.

Reappearing at the foot of Marcus' bed, he scanned the room looking for his target.

"Cyrus? What—"

He spun towards the bathroom, seeing the cambion standing in the doorway. Marcus' eyes widened, taking him in. The older demon stepped towards him a concerned expression on his face.

"Are you okay?" Marcus asked, a hesitation to his voice.

Without a word, Cyrus closed the distance between them, fisting the cambion's shirt. Flames licked at their feet as he kept his gaze locked with those green eyes that captivated him no matter how much he tried to fight their pull. He wasn't quite sure where he was going to take them, but they needed to get away from the house. Marcus had grabbed at his hips as he transported them through the fires of Hell. Sensing their location, Cyrus realised he'd taken them to a remote area in the Aspromonte National Park in Italy. Although it was night time, the heat from the day lingered in the rocks around them. The small valley and trees surrounding the area would provide them with enough cover from any unwanted eyes.

"Cyrus?" Marcus started, looking around them. "Where are w—"

Before he could lose his nerve, Cyrus pulled his arm back and slammed his fist into Marcus' face. The cambion staggered back, clutching at his face, his expression morphing between shock and anger as his green eyes burned bright with internal fire.

"What the fuck—"

"You need to start explaining things," Cyrus interrupted the demon's snarl with one of his own. "Right now!"

"Explain what?" Marcus shouted, squaring his shoulders, his fists dropping to his sides.

"What the fuck all that was about today. That shit you pulled in front of Raphael," the boundling returned, stepping closer until he could feel the cambion's heat radiating through the air. Marcus' jaw clenched tightly shut, staring daggers at the young demon, but he didn't speak. "Oh, come on, Marcus!" Cyrus snapped. "You can't keep pulling shit like this. You can't keep doing this to me."

"What 'shit' am I pulling exactly?" the cambion spat at him, indignation dripping from his tone.

"This hot and cold bullshit!" he practically yelled at the man. "One moment you fuck me like you can't get enough of me. The next you're pushing me away telling me you can't be in a relationship. And then you flip again by acting all fucking possessive." He didn't miss how Marcus flinched at his words. "Your threats over Kai. Then later with Raphael. You talk about protecting Lena and then you lose your fucking shit in front of the fucking arch-angel. Tell me what the fuck is going on with you!"

Marcus' gaze dropped to the ground but his shoulders tensed, like he wanted to say something but didn't know what. Cyrus had enough. This constant keeping himself restrained, stopping himself from saying or acting on what he was truly feeling, was driving Cyrus insane. He had to push the cambion. Push him until he broke and finally let out everything he was holding back.

"Fucking say something!" he screamed at the demon.

"I don't know what you want me to say!" Marcus snapped back.

"At this point fucking anything!" Cyrus closed the space between them, pushing his face as close to the cambion's as he dared in this moment.

With a low growl, Marcus turned away from him, taking a few deep breaths which only served to infuriate the boundling further. "I'm not doing this," the cambion sighed, shaking his head.

"Of course not," Cyrus ground out from behind gritted teeth. "Because you don't *do* anything. All you do is exist, hiding behind a wall of fucking mystery thinking it will protect you."

"It has so far."

"Has it? Or are you too scared to admit that I cracked that wall a little?" he asked, raising his hand and pinching his fingers together in emphasis. "That you almost let me in and then chickened out."

"I've warned you before about saying I'm scared," Marcus growled, bright green eyes returning to lock with his.

"And you've admitted to me before that you were," Cyrus said, trying to keep his tone even and controlled. "I don't fucking care, Marcus! I don't think less of you because you get scared. Everyone gets scared sometimes. You think I wasn't fucking terrified when Lena and I ran from Zagan? I knew if he managed to get us back, I'd be dead. He would have hurt Lena, but he would have killed me. I still did it."

"Because Lena was worth the risk."

Pure, blinding rage coursed through his body at those words. His body acting before his mind could consider what he was doing, his fist flew out again, clipping the cambion's jaw, sending the man reeling to the side.

"Am I not worth the risk?" he shouted, his pain and anger pouring from his body, his limbs shaking uncontrollably.

"That's not what I meant!" Marcus shouted back, straightening himself and squaring up to the boundling.

"Then tell me what you fucking mean! I'm not a fucking mind-reader, Marcus!"

"I can't."

A roar erupted from his chest as his fist travelled through the air. But the demon was ready for him this time, effortlessly catching his closed fist in his large palm, fingers clamping down on his skin.

"Stop fucking hitting me!" the cambion snapped, shoving his arm back forcing him to stumble a couple of steps away.

"No! Not until you tell me what you mean!" he yelled, his teeth bared as he regained his footing. Stepping forward he shoved against Marcus' chest, needing to force some contact despite the threat of what the cambion could do to him. "You're driving me fucking insane, Marcus. I don't know if I'm coming or going with you and I can't fucking take it anymore! Do I mean that little to you? After everything we have done?"

"It's not like that–"

"Then fucking te–"

"You are worth everything!"

Silence fell over them, their heavy breathing the only sound breaking the oppressive tension that descended. Even the animals that would normally be scurrying through the bushes had fallen quiet, as if they too were aware of the importance of this moment. Cyrus' blood pounded in his ears, his eyes wide with shock as he looked at the demon. *What the fuck?*

"What?" he breathed, unable to muster anything else.

Marcus' body was vibrating. Cyrus could see clearly the fine tremors that shook his limbs. "You are worth fucking everything!" Marcus shouted, his tone at odds with the words leaving his lips. "It's not about you, Cyrus. *I* am not worthy of *you*. *I* do not deserve *you*. I would destroy you. I would destroy everything good about you." The cambion shook his head vigorously, his eyes squeezed tightly shut, pain etched into his features. "I had someone," he forced out, his voice low, broken with sorrow. "A thousand years ago. My last fucking boundling. I loved him and he tried to kill me after he broke from me. He aligned with Kai and they very nearly did kill me. Because of that, I could never trust you fully. Because I don't trust my own fucking judgement. How would that work?" he asked, looking up at the boundling, self-loathing deep within his eyes. "Me constantly questioning everything you do and say? You constantly trying to prove to me I can trust you? What kind of relationship would that be?"

Everything fell into place. Marcus' pain, his distance, his fury. Everything made sense to the boundling. He now understood why the cambion wouldn't let him in. But he wouldn't even give them a chance. A chance to figure it out. To see if they could heal each other. Marcus made all these decisions about them without even attempting to see if Cyrus could understand. Without even trying to help him understand. He'd controlled every aspect of their relationship without giving Cyrus all the information, letting him think that he was the reason they couldn't be together. Because he was Lena's boundling. And that realisation made Cyrus see red.

"You selfish fucking bastard!" he roared, lunging forward, transforming in his rage.

Eyes wide, Marcus quickly brought his own transformation to the surface, meeting the boundling halfway. Swinging through the air, Cyrus landed a hit directly on the side of Marcus' face. The cambion recovered quickly, grabbing at his wrist and twisting it behind his back. The older demon was stronger than him, he knew that, but he was faster and his anger gave him an edge. Shifting his feet, Cyrus pulled his elbow of his free arm back sharply, sinking into Marcus' stomach, just below his solar plexus. The demon gasped, leaning forward instinctively to escape the pain. Wrenching his wrist free of the cambion's hold, Cyrus spun on the ball of his foot, his left fist slamming into Marcus' jaw.

Marcus roared against the pain, pushing out one of his wings, the taloned bend clipping Cyrus' shoulder, tearing at the skin. The boundling hissed from behind his teeth as the sharp talon sliced through his flesh, but his fire quickly healed the wound. The cambion took the opportunity to swing his own fist, hitting Cyrus square on the cheekbone. It was a reactive move as Marcus reared back, shock on his face, realising what he had done. But Cyrus didn't want him to hold back. They needed to get this out and if he had to get hurt in the process, so be it. His power would heal him before the cambion could do any real damage. The same could not be said for the older demon.

Snarling at him, Cyrus pressed forward, his talons sinking into

Marcus' bicep as he flung his head forward, his forehead connecting with the cambion's nose with a satisfying crunch. Marcus cursed as his head snapped back. Lena could heal that later. Cyrus pulled his free hand into the air, bringing it down to hit the same spot his head had just damaged. With a powerful flap of his wings, Marcus pulled himself from Cyrus' hold, landing a few feet away. Simply following his forward momentum, the boundling raced towards the cambion, fangs bared as his fire coursed over his arms.

Shifting his footing, Marcus held up his arms and deftly grabbed Cyrus by his shoulders. A loud cry echoed through the valley, as the cambion swept his foot out, knocking the young demon off balance, sending him to the ground. His stomach pressed into the rocks beneath them, Cyrus struggled against Marcus as the older demon pinned his arms behind his back, straddling his hips. Black smoked smothered him, forcing his entire body to lie still.

"I said to stop fucking hitting me!" the cambion snarled at him, talons painfully digging into his wrists.

"I may hit you with my fists," Cyrus snapped over his shoulder, "but you fucking gut me with your words! Get off me!"

Marcus pulled away, quickly putting some space between them as Cyrus scrambled to his feet. Black fire coursed over his entire body as he rounded on the cambion, stepping closer but keeping his distance.

"I want you, Marcus," he said, his breathing harsh as he forced his fire to recede. "I want there to be an 'us'. I'm sick of hiding that fact. And if you gave us a chance, gave me a chance, I would fight for us every day for the rest of my existence. I would never give up on you. Tell me you don't want that. Tell me you still want me to find someone else."

"You're a fucking idiot if you think I still want that!" the cambion yelled at him, stepping towards him, smoke snaking around his arms, lashing out like whips against the air.

"Then what do you fucking want?"

Wind rushed around him as Marcus flew forwards, their bodies colliding in the air. The sound of wood cracking echoed through the valley as they crashed into a tree, Cyrus' back pressed painfully against the rough bark. But he didn't care. Marcus' lips were on his before he could draw breath, taloned fingers tangling in his hair brushing against his crown of horns.

# CHAPTER TWENTY-NINE

He couldn't take it anymore. He couldn't take the pain in Cyrus' eyes and voice, knowing that he had caused it. He'd had to tell the boundling that this was not about him. The young demon had been right all those weeks ago. Lena and being her boundling was an excuse, but it was not the reason he held back. He thrived on the pain from William's betrayal. It was what made him a good assassin, a good spy, a great demon. Pain and anger. He'd spent a thousand years honing that into his skillset, into making those around him afraid. Ambrose had been his only comfort because he had always been able to keep him at arm's length. They were friends, but Ambrose never questioned him or his methods. And neither did Lena. They simply accepted him for what he was.

But Cyrus dug in, burying his claws and his fire within his very being and made him want to be someone else. To let go of the pain. If only he knew how, without compromising everything he was. But still the boundling wanted him. Still the demon wanted to be with him. And Marcus was losing the fight.

Breaking their kiss, he pulled his head back, staring into the endless black pools of Cyrus' demonic eyes. Desire laced the pain, dulling it, but it was still there. He knew it wouldn't leave. Not yet. Maybe not for a long time. If ever. Guilt stabbed him in the chest at the sight of it as he silently wished he had the strength to erase it completely. All he could do for now, was ease it slightly.

Crashing their mouths together again, Marcus' hands clung

desperately to the boundling's hair and neck, pressing their bodies together, revelling in the melding of their warmth.

"Marcus," the boundling moaned into his mouth, spurring him on. "I–"

The cambion thrust his tongue inside Cyrus' mouth, silencing him as he ran his hand down the gorgeous body, gripping at the band of his leather trousers. Coursing his power over their clothes, he quickly bared both their bodies to the warm night air.

"Open up for me, baby," he growled into the kiss, his hand travelling down further, grasping under Cyrus' knee and lifting it up to hook over his hip. The boundling shifted his body, one hand moving to the tree to dig in his claws, pulling himself up slightly. His other hand gripped at Marcus' horn, fingers brushing against the cambion's jaw as he did so. The sharp tug on the side of his head heightened his desire, their cocks pressed together as Marcus rocked his hips against the demon.

Pulling back, he moved a taloned finger to his abdomen, making to slice his skin as he had done so before.

"Wait," Cyrus panted, his hand that had been wrapped around the cambion's horn flying to grab his wrist, stopping him. Letting go, the boundling brought his hand to his mouth, biting down on his palm until his skin broke.

"Cyrus, no," Marcus blurted, grabbing at the young demon's wrist, watching horrified as blood pooled on his ashy-red skin.

"It's alright," the demon said softly, gently pulling his wrist free and wrapping his fingers around Marcus' hardened length, coating it in his blood. "I heal. You don't." Marcus groaned at the warm feeling of Cyrus' hand, his head wanting to tip back despite his eyes being firmly locked on the boundling's work. Taking his hand away, Cyrus held his palm upwards showing his fire licking across it, healing the wound.

A low growl pulled from the centre of the cambion's chest, taking hold of the demon's wrist and pulling it up to his lips. Kissing the palm, he licked at the remnants of blood, cleaning his skin.

"Don't you *ever* do that again," he whispered. Raising Cyrus' hand back up to his horn, he wrapped the long fingers around it. "And don't let go."

"Okay," Cyrus breathed, his grip tightening as Marcus lined himself up with the boundling's entrance.

With as much care as he could muster in his current state, he pushed inside the gorgeous body, swallowing Cyrus' gasp as he sealed their lips together. The boundling cursed as Marcus rolled his hips, quickly bringing himself and Cyrus to a pinnacle. Pulling his wings around them, he dug the taloned tips into the other side of the tree, using it as an anchor for him to drive into the boundling. The young demon responded as he always did, clinging desperately to the cambion, his breathy moans surrounding them like a melody. It wasn't enough for Marcus. It would never be enough. But it had to be.

His chest tightened with grief, knowing this had to be the last time. He couldn't keep doing this to the boundling. He couldn't keep doing this to them. It was selfish of him to do this now, but he knew Cyrus needed this as much as he did. He reasoned that made this okay. He was doing this for Cyrus.

"Come for me, gorgeous," he growled, his arm wrapping around the boundling's waist, a driving need to pull him closer. "Come for me and scream my name like the good fucking boy you are. Let the world hear who makes you feel this good."

"Fuck, Marcus!" Cyrus cried out, his shoulders curling into the cambion, his head tipping back against the tree. The warmth of the boundling's release coated Marcus' abdomen as he quickly fell from the cliff alongside him. Roaring his pleasure, his embrace of the young demon tightened, his wings contracting simultaneously. The wood of the tree splintered, leaves and twigs raining down around them. The top of the tree crashed to the ground with a loud thud, startled creatures scurrying away from the sound. Sharp points of splintered wood dug into his forearm as Marcus wedged it between Cyrus and the tree, not wanting it to hurt the boundling.

Panting together, he tucked his head into the crook of the young demon's neck, breathing in his scent like he had been starved of it, listening to the racing of Cyrus' heartbeat.

"I'm sorry," he rasped, still sheathed inside the demon.

"For what?" Cyrus asked, the hand that had been clinging to the tree now wrapped around the back of the cambion's neck, the other tangled in his hair. "Fucking me? Please, Marcus, please don't say this was a mistake. I couldn't take it."

"I won't," he said quickly, shaking his head slightly so the boundling could feel it. "I'm not. You are not a mistake, Cyrus. You were never a mistake. I need you to understand that. I do not regret anything we have done."

The young demon was silent for moment, his fingers stilling in their movements. Marcus felt Cyrus withdraw into himself, steeling himself from the rejection he knew was coming. Swallowing hard, Marcus forced himself to lift his head, knowing he needed to look the boundling in the eyes. He owed him that courtesy at the very fucking least.

"You still want me to find someone else?" Cyrus whispered disbelievingly, his hands releasing Marcus' hair and trailing down to rest on his shoulders.

"You need to," Marcus said softly, resting their foreheads together. "It doesn't matter what I want, Cyrus. You need to find someone else. I cannot be the one for you. I do not regret this, but I would if I ever truly hurt you."

The boundling bit his bottom lip, breathing in heavily before speaking. "Why do you always assume you're going to hurt me?" he asked, his warm breath washing over Marcus' face.

"Because I'm a cambion. It's in my nature," he replied with firm resolve.

"You've overcome it once before for me."

"Just because I have once, doesn't mean I'll be able to again. Cyrus, please. *Please* stop fighting me on this," he pleaded with the demon.

Firmly, Cyrus pushed at his shoulders, putting space between them. Leaving the gorgeous body felt different this time compared to others. This felt final and a heavy, indescribable pit formed in the cambion's stomach. He was surprised at how much it hurt to be pushed away by Cyrus in this moment.

Black fire coursed over the boundling's lower body, his clothes reforming on his skin as he straightened and looked Marcus directly in the eye. "I told you, the only way I will give up is if you tell me there is no hope for us."

Knowing this was the moment where everything would end, Marcus squared his shoulders and hardened his gaze. His own clothes rematerialised as his smoke flittered around him. "There isn't," he said, desperately trying to keep any emotion out of his voice.

Stepping towards the cambion, Cyrus brought their noses to almost touching, his own eyes narrowed with scrutiny. "I don't believe you."

Despite himself, Marcus chuckled, a small grin forming on his lips. "You're such a brat," he breathed, knowing he'd lost the argument. If you could call it an argument.

A wide grin formed on the gorgeous face as Cyrus leant forward and pressed a fleeting kiss to his lips. "And proud of it."

Before Marcus could respond, the boundling flamed away leaving him alone in... well, Cyrus knows where.

Cyrus avoided him for the next few days. Yet again, Marcus wanted to speak with him, although he had no idea what he would say the young demon. At least they weren't shouting at each other anymore.

Lena still tore him a new one after his actions in front of Raphael, and he didn't blame her for it. The conversation had been warranted but after the tongue lashing, she had embraced him, the comforting action healing him somewhat. He'd been most grateful when she actually healed his nose after the head-whipping he'd received from Cyrus. He knew the boundling had a thick skull, but... *damn.*

Sitting in his office, Marcus was pouring over some accounts he and Ambrose had been dealing with recently. Ambrose was better with the figures than him, but the Consort had gone to bed a few hours ago, needing some rest. Well, needing some time with Lena anyway.

With a sudden start, his chair clattered to the floor as a loud bang echoed through the house. Barging out of the room, he raced up the stairs and into Lena and Ambrose's wing, the source of the sound becoming instantly evident to him.

Red lightning crackled around the room, snapping loudly at the walls and floor. A bolt raced towards his head as he dived out of the way, catching himself against the doorframe.

"Lena!" he shouted, trying to find her. "Ambrose!"

Dread made his stomach drop to the floor as he spied his friend laying on the ground by the bed, motionless, lightning coursing over his body. Something wasn't right. Lena would never do this to Ambrose. She would never lose control like this.

"Lena!" he shouted again as he attempted to get to Ambrose, lightning driving him back.

"Marcus!" Lena's voice carried through the room. Finally, his gaze landed on her, huddled in the corner of the room, her whole body encased in her red aura. Her arms were firmly locked over her head as she cowered on the floor, face pressed into her knees.

*What the hell?* he questioned internally. This wasn't like her. Not since she first became a demon.

"Lena, what's happening?" he yelled, summoning his smoke around him, trying to shield himself from the onslaught of power before him.

"You need to wake Cyrus, now!" she screamed, a singular bolt of lightning whipping from her centre and crashing into the bed, bits of fabric and feathers scattering into the air on impact.

Escaping in flames, Marcus appeared next to Cyrus' bed, his jaw dropping at the sight. The boundling writhed in the centre of the bed, black fire and red lightning lashed over his body, his face contorted in pain as he cried out into the room.

"Cyrus!" Marcus bellowed, trying to wake the young demon. Getting as close as he dared, he tried again. "Cyrus! Wake up!"

The demon couldn't hear him, his back arching as he screamed, pure terror lacing the animalistic sound ripping from him. Panicked and unable to reach the boundling, Marcus punched out with his smoke, a condensed ball hitting Cyrus on the side of the face. Those doe-brown eyes snapped open on impact.

All power in the room receded immediately as Cyrus sat bolt upright, chest heaving as he looked around his room bewildered, taking in the damage to his bed. His gaze landed on the cambion, confusion overtaking his features.

"Marcus? Wha—"

Unable to explain and desperate to get back to check on his friend, Marcus simply spun on his heel and ran out of the room. He barely heard Cyrus throwing the covers off and racing after him.

Rounding the corner back into Lena and Ambrose's room, Marcus exhaled sharply noting the erratic lightning had stopped. Cyrus came up beside him, practically collapsing against the doorframe as they both surveyed the scene.

"Please, Ambrose," Lena sobbed as she cradled her Consort in her arms, her hand over his torso, fluid like plasma licking over his skin, healing a charred wound in the centre of his chest. "Please, wake up."

"What happened?" the boundling asked, pushing off from the doorframe, his eyes wide with shock.

"You happened," Marcus snapped, instantly regretting it, but unable to hold his concern for his friend in check.

"Marcus!" Lena chastised him, her furious gaze pinning on him.

Ignoring both her and Cyrus, he focused on the slight rise and fall of Ambrose's chest. His friend was alive at least. "Cyrus, this is not your fault," the Prince said calmly, turning to her boundling. "Your dream got too much for me, but this is not your fault."

He could see from the corner of his eye the way Cyrus' body stiffened beside him.

"I- I'm sorry..." the young demon stammered, before a shuddering breath punched out of him as he turned and ran away.

Relief washing over him as Ambrose began to come to in her arms, Marcus nodded to Lena, before he raced after the boundling.

"Cyrus, wait!" he called out, flaming ahead to close the distance between them, grabbing roughly at the demon's arm.

"Get off me!" Cyrus shouted, turning to face him, ripping his arm from his grasp. His torso and hair were plastered with sweat, visible vapour rising from his shoulders as his body heated with rage.

"Cyrus, please," the cambion pleaded as gently as he could. "I'm sorry. I didn't mean to sound like it was your fault. It was an accident, it happens."

"Are you fucking kidding me?" the young demon snarled at him. "I have been a demon for eleven years. I shouldn't be having these dreams anymore and now they're feeding back to Lena, and Ambrose is— Ambrose is—" Cyrus looked like his whole body simply wanted to collapse in on itself as he looked past Marcus back towards Lena and Ambrose's room.

Seeing movement in the opposite direction, the cambion spied Balo standing in his doorway, a panic stricken look on his face. Cyrus saw where he was looking and following his gaze over his shoulder, cursing under his breath as he did so.

"Balo, go back in your room. Now!" Marcus barked at the other boundling. Balo jumped but complied without argument. Once the door was shut, he turned back to Cyrus, reaching for him. "Cyrus?"

"Don't touch me!" the young demon shouted, jerking away from him. "Don't you get it? What the fuck is wrong with me?"

"Nothing," he said earnestly, shaking his head. "Cyrus, nothing is wrong with you!"

"Oh yeah?" Cyrus spat harshly at him. Pressing his lips together, he grabbed Marcus' wrist, pulling him into the boundling's bedroom, slamming the door shut behind them. "You sure, because the only thing you want to do with me is fuck my arse," the demon said haughtily as he rounded on the cambion. "You can't even admit to yourself how you really feel about me or even spend just a normal fucking night with me! Do you honestly think I didn't pick up the scent of an incubus on you the other day? As if sneaking out in the middle of the night like some guilty fucking secret wasn't bad enough, you did it to be with a fucking sex demon! Evidently, I'm just not enough for you."

*Shit.*

He knew there had been the possibility that Cyrus would find out he went to Kale. Shame washed over him, not knowing what to say, how to explain. How desperately he wanted to simply take the boundling in his arms and never let go.

Seeing he wasn't going to say anything, Cyrus sighed with exhaustion, hanging his head in defeat.

"Do you know why my dream likely got to Lena so much?" he asked quietly. "Because tonight, instead of seeing Zagan's face, I saw yours. Instead of hearing Zagan's voice, I heard yours. That cambion bullshit you pulled the other day."

The boundling might as well have punched him directly as Marcus staggered back a step, his skin feeling too tight.

"Cyrus–"

"Stop," Cyrus interrupted, his voice breaking with a painful plea. "Just stop. Stop saying my name like it has some meaning to you. I don't mean anything to you."

"That's not true," he said, knowing he hadn't really done anything to indicate otherwise.

"Just admit it, compared to the rest of you, I'm nothing. I'm worthless, just a waste of fucking space!"

"You know I don't think that!"

"Yes, you do! Everyone does!" Cyrus cried, tears forming in his eyes as spoke. Marcus wanted nothing more than to erase the pain in those chocolate depths, but knew no matter what he said or did tonight, the boundling wouldn't believe him. Might never believe him. "You may not say it out loud, but the way you all look at me is perfectly clear! Like I'm some kind of liability that needs to be coddled. And as you so kindly keep reminding me, anything I do might affect Lena! All I am can be boiled down to her, to being her boundling! Without her, what the fuck am I?"

"Cyrus!"

The door behind them rattled as it slammed against the wall, Ambrose striding through, his angular face set in hard lines. Although he was healed, he looked like he'd just gone twelve rounds in the training pits. His hair flung wildly around his shoulders, his hazel eyes glowing with a determined light. Lena was close behind him but stayed still in the doorway.

"Ambrose… I- I-" Cyrus stammered, stumbling back, shock and sorrow plastered on his face.

Without looking at Marcus, the Consort closed the distance between him and the boundling, grasped Cyrus' hand and laid it on the centre of his chest, where the majority of the damage had been. The boundling's brown eyes were wide with fear as he looked at the contact between them.

"I'm fine," Ambrose said softly but with an unwavering firmness. "Look at me." Swallowing hard, Cyrus finally lifted his head to look at the demon. "I'm fine. This was not your fault, do you hear me? I'm fine. Lena is fine. We can fix the rooms. Everything is okay."

All fight left the boundling at once, a breath punching out of him as he stepped towards Ambrose, his head falling onto the demon's shoulder. His shoulders shook with silent sobs, as the Consort wrapped his arms around them, whispering gently to him.

"It's alright, Cyrus. You are a part of this council. You are a part of this family. You are not worthless. You mean everything to your sister. To me."

Not for the first time, Marcus felt out of place. The siblings and the Consort were more of a family between just the three of them. He didn't belong.

With a start, he turned to look at Lena, as she came up beside him, sliding one of her small hands into his.

"You too, Marcus," she whispered to him, resting her head on his arm.

Unable to describe what he was feeling in that moment, he simply squeezed her hand, looking on as Ambrose continued to comfort Cyrus, wishing he could do the same. He wanted to be so much more for the boundling. To be everything he needed. But he couldn't. And Kale was right. It killed him inside.

# CHAPTER THIRTY

The rooms had been fairly easy to repair. For a few days after his nightmare, Lena and Cyrus spent the time locked in her altar room, carrying out various rituals to try and dampen the connection between them. Almost all rituals had backfired, merely resulting in more damage to be repaired later. Those that didn't backfire, did... nothing.

Refusing to resign to their fate, Lena went to discuss matters with Morgan in the Repository, to see if the Keeper had any information that would assist them. Cyrus tried to hide in his room, or the hellhound den still feeling immensely guilty over what happened, regardless of how many times his sister told him it wasn't his fault. He hadn't seen Marcus since that night as the cambion took over babysitting duties of Balo, giving Archie a much-deserved break. But he was due back to the house at some point today.

Cyrus was going out of his mind trying to figure out how to fix things between him and the older demon. Trying to find a way to convince Marcus to give them a chance. He needed to figure out what he wanted to do before the cambion got home.

Finally working up the courage, he left his room in search of Ambrose. Surely, he would know how to help. Knocking on the Consort's office door he waited to be called in. It wasn't like Ambrose would have minded if he had just walked in, but he didn't want to be rude.

"How are you feeling?" he asked as he closed the office door behind him, moving to one of the chairs opposite the desk.

"I'm fine," Ambrose replied, giving him a warm smile. "Please, Cyrus, stop worrying about me. I'm fine."

Slumping down in the chair, Cyrus crossed his arms over his chest. "I don't understand why you and Lena aren't pissed at me."

"Why would we be pissed at you for having a nightmare?" the Consort asked, cocking his head to the side, genuine confusion over his face.

"A nightmare that fed back to Lena, blew up your room and almost killed you?"

"It wasn't your fault, Cyrus."

"But it was."

"No, it wasn't," Ambrose said firmly, holding up a finger as if chastising a child. "You don't control what feeds back to Lena." He got up from his chair and moved to the one next to the boundling, leaning forward on his elbows. "You know she destroyed her room on her first night as a demon."

Brows shooting up, Cyrus straightened, looking at the demon in surprise. "She accessed her powers on the first night?" He knew that Lena was powerful and had defied almost all demonic norms, but even that seemed unbelievable.

"Yep," Ambrose nodded, a fond melancholy smile on his lips, small strands of his dark hair that had escaped the tie at the nape of his neck falling in front of his face. "Scared Marcus and I half to death. If we weren't already dead that is."

Cyrus huffed a laugh, shaking his head in amusement. He hadn't realised that Marcus had also been aware of Lena's exceptional power right from the beginning. It began to make sense why he felt so loyal to the Prince. Not that they didn't all feel loyal to her.

"Another time," Ambrose continued, "she had a nightmare about her mother. When she woke up, she flamed out of the manor and into the middle of the ocean."

"Seriously?"

"Mm-hm. Swears she saw a shark," the Consort chuckled. "What I'm trying to say, is that the dreams you experience have a way of messing with you. Pulling out your worst fears and thoughts. I may not know what you see in your dreams, but I can guess. Zagan was adept at creating and building on the smallest insecurities."

Looking away, Cyrus shut his eyes tightly, trying to keep the memories from resurfacing. He didn't want to remember what Zagan did to him. He didn't want to admit to Ambrose that his dream had morphed to Marcus inflicting such horrors on him. He swallowed hard as he felt Ambrose reach out and take hold of one of his hands.

"Hey, look at me," the demon requested gently. Taking a deep breath, he forced himself to face the Consort. "You are not worthless," Ambrose said, emphasising his belief in that statement. "You are incredibly smart, fiercely loyal and a wonderful brother. And I do think of you as a brother. Do not for a minute think that you don't belong here."

Staring at the man in disbelief, a lump of emotion formed in his throat as he held tightly to Ambrose's hand. For so long he had held animosity towards the demon, hating how Zagan had used him to vent frustrations whenever he and Ambrose clashed within their roles in Hell. But the Consort had been nothing but patient with him, accommodating without complaint the rebirth of his sibling relationship with Lena. Now, hearing that Ambrose thought of him as a brother, he realised that he did indeed feel the same way. He couldn't imagine his life anymore without Lena and Ambrose in it. And he didn't want to imagine it without Marcus.

Forcing a steadying breath past the lump in his throat, Cyrus squeezed Ambrose's hand in thanks.

"I'm glad Lena met you," he said softly, smiling at the Consort.

Ambrose coughed, his gaze dropping to the floor as he choked on a flood of emotion. "Thank you," he said gruffly. "That means a lot coming from you. So..." he trailed off, dropping Cyrus' hand and leaning back in the chair. "What's going on with Marcus?"

"What?" he asked breathlessly. Did everyone in the house know? Maybe it had been naïve to think that, even though she said she wasn't going to get involved, Lena wouldn't have talked to Ambrose about it a little. After all, considering the number of times that his emotions would have fed back to Lena during times she had been around Ambrose, he would have noticed something was going on. The Consort could read her like an open book.

"You and Marcus?" Ambrose said pointedly with a nod.

Realising there was no point in denying anything to the demon, Cyrus sighed in defeat. "There is no me and Marcus."

"Uh-huh..."

"What has Lena told you?" he asked, unsure he wanted to know.

"Nothing. Do you honestly think I didn't notice whenever your desire fed back to her? I didn't know for sure it was with Marcus, but I have eyes and could guess," the Consort chuckled good-naturedly. "So, is there something at all?"

"Marcus doesn't want there to be."

"I see," Ambrose sighed, folding his hands in front of his chest. "Do you want there to be something?"

"Yes," he nodded. "Very much so."

"Well, Marcus has always been very private about his personal life, even with me," the other demon shrugged. "I've never met any of his previous lovers." Cyrus flinched at the thought, internally berating himself for it. "Sorry."

The boundling shook his head, dismissing the apology. "I have no right to be jealous of things that happened before I met him," he said flatly. He wasn't even annoyed by the thought that Marcus had been with others. The cambion was fifteen hundred years old, after all. But the memory that Marcus had the scent of an incubus on him the morning after they had been together still stabbed at his chest. The cambion hadn't denied it the other day, either.

"Fair enough," Ambrose huffed a laugh, pausing briefly before speaking again. "What I do know, is that he has never been with anyone long and usually never more than once. So, considering how long you two... '*haven't*' been a thing," he said, using his fingers in emphasis of quotation, "I'd say it's safe to assume there is something there, even if he won't admit it."

"Even if there is," Cyrus said letting his head fall into his hands, "I'm not sure I can survive the process to find out."

The pair were silent for a moment, both lost in their own thoughts. The boundling had hoped that the Consort would be able to help him figure out what to do. He knew Marcus was a private person, but he hadn't realised how private. He had thought that the cambion would have been more open with his friend. In some ways that made their time together all the more meaningful to Cyrus. He had gotten closer to the demon than anyone. But he didn't know what to do with that information.

"Well," Ambrose said suddenly, pulling him from his thoughts, "at the end of the day, Marcus is still a man. If he can't appreciate what he has, let him see what he might be losing. Oh and," he said quickly, looking slightly panicked at the boundling, "please don't tell your sister that I told you that. She hasn't given me any details but she did tell me not to get involved, and I prefer to keep my skin on my body."

"I won't," Cyrus chuckled, getting to his feet. "I'll just flay you myself if this blows up in my face."

"Yeah," the Consort said softly, rising next to him. "Well, you know where to find me," he smiled, clapping Cyrus on the shoulder before heading back to his chair.

Leaving Ambrose to his work, the boundling quickly checked on Zamira and Sollis whilst forming his plan before heading back upstairs. It was a bad plan. A *really* bad plan. Probably worse than his plan to fight the stubborn cambion the other week. But that had ended on somewhat of a good note, all things considered. So maybe, this one would not completely blow up in his face. And if it did... well, that would solve everything.

There really were only two outcomes to this plan. Either, he and Marcus finally ended up together. Or, it goes horribly wrong and Cyrus would be left to lick his wounds with a broken heart. Absolute worst case, they kill each other, which would solve Lena's problem.

Firming his resolve, he made his way to Marcus' room, knocking softly, listening for any indication that the cambion was inside. He hoped that the demon was back by now. His stomach dropped with dread as he heard the door begin to open, stepping back slightly to hide that he'd had his ear pressed to the surface.

"Cyrus," Marcus said with a soft smile, "come in." The cambion waved him inside, shutting the door behind him.

"Hey," the boundling returned the greeting, even as his chest tightened and his resolve started to weaken.

The cambion looked at him puzzled, tilting his head to the side. "Are you okay?" he asked, closing the distance between them. "Do you need something?"

"Ah, no," Cyrus said shaking his head and taking a deep breath.

"Oh?"

Lifting his gaze to look at Marcus, he locked with those sea-green eyes that caused his belly to constrict with desire. "I came here to tell you, I, ah..." he started, trying to keep his focus even as he wanted to launch himself into Marcus' arms and kiss the stubborn cambion until he forgot everything. "I've met someone else. I'm going to try... I'm going to try and be with them. So, I'll leave you alone now."

"I see," the older demon said slowly, his brow furrowing and his gaze hardening with something Cyrus didn't recognise. "Why did you feel the need to come and tell me? I told you I wanted you to find someone." His tone was measured, his words clipped. Something twisted in the boundling's stomach at the sound.

Cyrus nodded, returning his gaze to the floor. "I know, I just..." This really was a bad idea. He should stop now. "You said we could, fool around, I guess, until I found someone else, so..." Why wasn't he stopping? Why did his mouth carry on talking? "And with everything that's happened recently... I- I don't know." *Shut up, Cyrus!* "I just... I thought you should know." Well, too late now. Might as well follow through. "I'll see you round."

As he turned to leave, he gasped as Marcus grabbed his wrist, preventing him from moving. Looking over his shoulder, he saw the demon's expression changing, yet consistently unreadable.

"Marcus?" he asked quietly, a small seed of fear planting within his stomach at the darkness on the cambion's face, telling him to be cautious. The last time he'd seen that expression had been after he teased the demon with Kai. He doubted it was a good sign.

Without a word, Marcus pulled Cyrus towards him, grabbing the nape of his neck roughly and crushed his mouth over the boundling's. Pinning his arms behind his back, the older demon forced them round until they fell onto the bed. Cyrus closed his eyes, simply allowing the assault on his lips, parting them as Marcus' tongue delved into his mouth, meeting it with his own in ferocious passion. The cambion bit at his bottom lip, grinding his lips against his teeth, until he could taste his own blood on his tongue. The pain radiating from the kiss was bittersweet, as the boundling whimpered beneath the older demon, wanting more yet fearing what was to come. His hands still pinned under him as Marcus' fingers dug painfully into his wrists.

"Is this what you want?" the demon growled against his lips, pushing Cyrus' legs apart with one of his own, grinding their hips together. "One last fling to get me out of your system?" His lips were brutally hard as they ground into Cyrus' with a renewed tenacity. Ensuring the boundling's wrists were adequately pinned with one of his hands, Marcus moved the other to wrap around Cyrus' throat, pressing down firmly, forcing the young demon to gasp against the hold. "Why else would you have come here, if not to flaunt yourself in front of me one last time?"

Opening his eyes, Cyrus looked up at the cambion, his eyes wide as fear and lust mixed together within his belly. "Yes," he panted, raising his hips so his cock rubbed against Marcus, cursing the fabric that separated them. "Yes, Marcus, this is what I want." The reaction of the older demon was not quite what he had expected when he came to his room, but it meant everything to him.

Letting go of his wrists, Marcus pushed up onto his knees and pulled at the boundling's shirt, ripping it to bare his chest to the open air. Cyrus found he couldn't move, leaving his arms under him, as Marcus' green eyes wandered over his body. His skin shivered under the intensity of the cambion's gaze, causing his nipples to harden with anticipation. Marcus lowered himself back over the young demon, capturing one of the buds within his mouth, licking and biting as Cyrus writhed beneath him. Cautiously, he pulled his arms out and tangled his fingers within the demon's long blonde hair.

Marcus gently pressed his fingers into the boundling's stomach, dimpling the flesh as his hands travelled down his body, his mouth continuing its work on his chest. Cyrus moaned breathlessly as Marcus slipped a large hand within his jeans and wrapped it around his cock, sending waves of pleasure skittering up his spine. His hips bucked upwards against Marcus' hand, as his fingers gripped the blonde hair, holding the cambion's head in place.

With expert familiarity, Marcus quickly stroked him into a quivering pool of desire. "That's it, gorgeous," he sighed, returning his mouth to Cyrus' now swollen lips, claiming them as his hand continued to pump the hardened shaft. "Don't hold back. Come for me."

Cyrus thrilled at the endearment that now had become so precious to him. Digging his fingers into the older demon's shoulders, his back arched as he cried out into the room, the pressure in his abdomen burst, coating the inside of his jeans with his release. "Marcus!" he cried, intense pleasure coursing through his veins as the cambion kept tight hold of him, pulling his climax to its fullest extent. "Marcus, please," he begged, "I need you. I love you."

He was barely aware he had spoken those words, or of Marcus' body stiffening above him. Suddenly, the cambion pulled away and rolled off the bed, getting to his feet and retreating to the other side of the room, placing his hands on his hips. Feeling utterly exposed as pain raged through his chest, Cyrus pulled the ripped edges of his shirt over his chest. He sat up in the bed, staring at the demon's back, as he tried to regain control of his breathing.

"Marcus?" he called softly, as he scooted to the edge of the bed.

"Get out."

Marcus' voice was deathly quiet to the point where Cyrus almost didn't hear him over the blood rushing through his ears. Swallowing hard, he got to his feet, buttoning his jeans. Feelings of hurt and anger began to swell within him as he felt the cold of his release stick to him.

"You bastard," he spat at the older demon. "You fucking bastard. What the fuck did you do that for?"

"I didn't hear you complaining," Marcus snapped turning to face him. "You came to me, remember."

"I came here to give you what you wanted," he said as calmly as he could. "At every turn you have pushed me away. Yes, you've fucked me, but you have reminded me constantly that you don't want anything more than that. I came here to make it easy for you, to tell you I'm done chasing you. You were the one who pushed me onto that bed!"

"I hope whoever it is you've met can satisfy you, because do not for a minute think you can come back to me if they don't."

"Fuck you!" Cyrus shouted, his anger boiling within his veins. "I am done being used by you. Pulled along like a fucking piece of string. You want to be alone, fine. Be alone!"

With that he turned on his heel and left Marcus' room, ignoring as the demon called out after him. Once the door was shut behind him, he ran to his room, nearly tearing his door from its hinges as he raced inside.

Cursing ever meeting the cambion, he ripped the tatters of his shirt and peeled his jeans off his body, throwing them both in the bin. After cleaning himself in his bathroom, he pulled some briefs on and threw himself onto his bed, burying his face in a pillow. Taking a deep breath, he screamed into the fabric, hurt and despair mixing within his chest, constricting his heart, as it threatened to tear him apart from the inside. He hadn't meant to say those words. He hadn't wanted to say them out loud. Marcus had become so skilled at pulling everything from him, even his innermost thoughts. But he had meant them, with every fibre of his being, he had meant them.

Minutes passed before he collapsed onto the bed, his throat hoarse, tears soaking the pillow pressed against his face. He didn't hear his bedroom door opening, or the soft footfalls as Lena walked over to him. His body stiffened as he felt the mattress beside him dip with her weight to finally relax as he felt her hand in his hair.

"Oh, Cyrus," she sighed, his pain and sorrow mirrored in her voice. "I'm so sorry."

He couldn't bring himself to lift his head. He didn't want to see how he was feeling reflected in her eyes. But he needed her comfort. Swallowing hard, he crawled to her, letting her gather him in her arms, burying his face into her lap as her hands stroked gently across his back. His tears flowed freely as he let the sobs rack his shoulders, wrapping his arms around her waist, desperately needing her warmth and presence to ground him. To stop him from falling into the dark pit forming in his heart.

# CHAPTER THIRTY-ONE

The slamming of the door echoed through his mind after the boundling left his room. What had he done? Everything in him screamed at him to race after the young demon. To apologise for his outburst.

Instead, he ran.

Flaming to his mother's cottage, he roared into the night air, screaming into the silence, pouring his pain and sorrow into the void. Smoke billowed out of his body, lashing out at the space around him, erratic and uncontrollable as his emotions took over. Lightning flashed in the sky, thunder rolled over the rise of the mountains, rain falling from the heavens, soaking the world below.

The rain beat down upon him as he closed his eyes, the feelings of guilt and shame pervading his every sense. He'd tried so hard not to hurt Cyrus, and in doing so he'd let himself get too involved with the boundling. When Cyrus had told him he'd found someone else, Marcus had seen red and all he wanted to do was to stop the young demon from leaving. From leaving him. What possessed him to take such actions was beyond him.

Over the years he had meticulously built walls around his heart. He knew they had begun to crack as he got closer to the young demon but they were still intact for the most part. He'd already prepared himself to have to push Cyrus away, he'd attempted it more than once, but he hadn't imagined it would go like this. He hadn't imagined that the boundling would actually fall in love with him. There was nothing special about him. Nothing worthy of love. So why did this hurt so much?

He'd never felt such pain within his being as when Cyrus declared his love for him. To say such a thing after telling the cambion he'd found someone else, ripped through him like a tsunami. It felt worse than William's betrayal, finally making him realise what he had been denying for so long.

He loved Cyrus.

Fear lanced through his chest, knowing that his heart was about to break for the second time in his existence. He loved someone he had pushed away. That he had encouraged to find someone else. And instead of declaring it at the same time, instead of begging the boundling to stay with him, he lashed out, wanting to drive away the source of his agony thinking that would help.

But it didn't. It couldn't.

Nothing could ease this pain now.

Cyrus was gone.

The one thing that could have helped him was gone. The one thing he wanted. And he only had himself to blame.

Whatever this meant for his position on Lena's council, he was beyond caring about. He'd been so concerned about protecting her, about keeping his position, but it no longer mattered to him. He should have listened to his uncle. He could have had both. Love and power. But now he was certain he'd lost both. All because he refused to allow the boundling in. Because he refused to acknowledge the young demon had clawed his way in with or without his consent.

A thought occurred to him. Perhaps, he could still salvage something. Cyrus declared his love, maybe, if he did the same, he could win the boundling back. But what would that make him? If Cyrus had found someone else who made him happy, someone who didn't push him away from the outset, did Marcus have any right to get in the way of that? After everything he had done to the young demon?

The thought of begging the demon to forgive him, to give him a second chance made his skin crawl. He didn't want Cyrus to be with him that way. But he wanted the boundling. He wanted to wrap the gorgeous body in his arms each night. He wanted to kiss and hold and love every inch of the young demon. He wanted to tame the stubborn brat and simultaneously allow the boundling to tame him. To claim him. Even if

Cyrus had found someone else, Marcus knew there would never be anyone else for him. He was well and truly ruined for anyone else. No one would ever compare to Cyrus. No one could.

He had to try speaking with him. To try and explain. Even if it meant begging. He needed Cyrus. He needed the boundling more than he needed the fires of Hell. Steeling himself for the young demon's anger, he flamed back to the house, appearing in the courtyard. Although it was now late afternoon, the desert heat bore down on him, making his wet skin prickle at the sudden change in temperature.

"I told you!"

Turning his head, he saw Lena striding towards him, a darkness in her eyes he had never seen directed at him or anyone in her council before. He couldn't react, frozen in his pain and fear as she came up on him, her fist swinging through the air and slamming into his jaw, red lightning crackling across his skin. Pain vibrated through his body from her hit, his brain rattling within his skull from the force and electricity. He fell to the ground, his shoulder crashing against the granite. He deserved this. He deserved her fury.

"Lena, I–"

"Shut up!" she screamed at him, reaching down and grabbing the front of his shirt, turning his face towards hers. Forced against the ground as she towered above him, he stared into her grey eyes that had darkened to pools of unfathomable and terrifying rage. He wouldn't fight her. She could kill him if she wanted and he wouldn't even try to stop her. At least then the pain would end.

Lifting him by his shirt, Lena lowered her face to his until there was barely room for air to move between them. "I told you, if you hurt him..." her voice was deathly quiet, her anger and fury mixed with pain.

"I didn't mean to," he said, his voice shaking, barely able to form the words. "I didn't want to."

Nothing else was said as Lena continued to grip his shirt. Marcus couldn't bring himself to move even the slightest, fear constricting every muscle in his body. He knew she would be able to smell his fear of her, but it didn't matter. Not anymore.

Suddenly, she closed her eyes and with a sharp exhale, pushed him down against the ground. He simply lay there, closing his own eyes, allowing his sorrow to envelope him.

"Get up," she ordered, turning away from him.

"I'm not going to fight you. If you want to kill me, just do it," he sighed, letting his head fall to the side.

"I'm not going to kill you."

His eyes flew open to stare at her back. Slowly he pushed himself up to his knees, sitting back on his ankles. "Why not?"

Lena sighed heavily as she turned to face him, her hands on her hips. "I could kill you, but that would end your suffering too quickly," she said flatly. "Killing you would put you out of your misery. The guilt you are feeling, is more punishment than I can mete out."

Marcus' head fell forward in defeat. She saw right through him. Grunting with the effort, he got to his feet, standing before her, broken and in unbearable pain.

"I need to speak with him," he said, his voice shaky and uncertain. He didn't want to tell Lena about his feelings before he got to speak with Cyrus.

"You won't go near him," she spat harshly. "If you think I'd allow the potential for you to inflict more pain on him, you are sorely mistaken."

"I need to try and fix this," he pleaded, taking a step towards her with his hands outstretched in surrender.

"Fix this?" she screeched, throwing her arms out beside her. "There is no *fixing* this, Marcus. I said I wasn't going to get involved, but I never expected something like this to happen."

"Lena, please," he begged. "I need to see him."

"No!" she yelled, such vitriol in her voice, his jaw clamped shut. Sighing, her shoulders slumped as she pinched the bridge of her nose. "I wish it were that simple, Marcus. But Cyrus doesn't want to see you. Regardless, he's not here. He left about half an hour ago. I'm sorry, but his anger and pain are almost too much for me to bear. I can barely stomach looking at you right now."

Of course, she would be feeling everything Cyrus was. If her rage was anything to go by, it wouldn't matter whatever he might have said to the boundling. He'd truly ruined any chance he had to be with him.

"Lena," he whispered, choking on his words as he spoke. "I'm sorry. I'm so sorry."

"Go get dry and clean up. You're coming with me." Turning on her heel, she strode off towards the canopied area.

"Where are we going?" he asked, forcing himself to follow her, even as he wanted to the ground beneath him to swallow him whole.

"We're going to see Lucifer. I need to talk to him about Raphael. He's been spotted around other demonic compounds recently," she said, stepping inside, never looking back as she walked away.

Closing his eyes, Marcus swayed on the spot for a moment. He had expected her initial reaction, but not her mercy. Not that it was really mercy. She left him to be racked by his guilt and his shame. Which, as she said, was the worst punishment he could receive.

"You're a fucking idiot."

He spun on his heel at the voice, coming almost face to face with Archie. His gut reaction was to snap back at the demonic-trainer, but all fight had left him, leaving him devoid of fire. Archie's face was one of pure anger as he stepped towards the cambion.

"I should beat the crap out of you for what you did to and in my chambers, but I let it slide because I thought finally, you had allowed yourself to open up to someone," Archie continued, closing the distance between them, his black eyes burning with rage. "I don't know what you did or what you said to him, but Cyrus was the best thing to happen to you. And you are a fucking idiot for pushing him away."

A distant fire managed to spark in him at Archie's words. The trainer knew what had happened with William. He'd been there as one of Marcus' only alliances that had survived the betrayal. Much like everyone else he may not have understood the full extent of what happened, but he knew.

Stepping up to the demonic-trainer, Marcus pushed against his chest, shoving Archie out into the courtyard. "You honestly think I don't know that?" he spat harshly.

"Then what the fuck are you doing here?" Archie snapped at him, pushing back, squaring up to the cambion.

"Lena won't let me see him."

"Bullshit," the demon snarled, his face mere inches from Marcus. "There is nothing stopping you from going after him. Lena may say some shit when she's pissed off. You should have heard the things she said to me about Ambrose after their fight last year. But she wouldn't actually stop you."

"It's not that simple."

"Of course it fucking is!"

"Shut up!" Marcus yelled, his fists balling at his sides. In human form, Archie had a good six inches on him in terms of height, but the cambion no longer cared if he was at a disadvantage. "You don't know what the fuck you're talking about."

"Don't I? I may suck at relationships, Marcus, but don't forget I was there after what happened with William," Archie shouted. "I saw what he did to you. What Kai did to you. I thought you had finally put all of that behind you." Exhaling sharply, the trainer threw his hands up in the air in exasperation before planting them firmly on his hips. "Cyrus is a fellow council member, for fuck's sake! Please tell me you didn't compare him to William, even in that stubborn arse mind of yours."

With a frustrated roar, Marcus swung his fist through the air, aiming for Archie's face despite the upward reach. Changing his stance instantly, Archie reared backwards, Marcus' fist missing him, but only just. The trainer braced himself, his fists coming up to cover his centre. Lunging forward, the cambion recovered quickly, swinging his other fist, his smoke coiling around his forearm like snakes, sharped points aiming for their target. Blue flames coursed over Archie's body as he ducked out of range, allowing Marcus' rage to make his movements erratic. Dodging another blow, the trainer took the opportunity, stepping forward and slamming his fist into the centre of the cambion's torso.

Reeling backwards, Marcus clutched at his chest, smoke billowing out of his body, forming a pool of shuddering trails around his feet. "How dare you?" he rasped, glaring at the other demon. "Of course, I fucking didn't!"

"Oh?" Archie pressed, a haughty expression on his face. "Then why are you still denying him?"

"I'm not!"

"Aren't you?"

"Fuck you!"

Marcus rushed at Archie, grabbing him around the waist and slamming them into the ground. Their bodies collided with the gravel of one of the flower beds. Their fists flying, both men grunted and snarled as they landed blows on other. Pain radiated from Marcus' back and shoulders, blue fire searing his skin in various places as his smoke cut and slashed against the trainer.

"You're a fucking coward, Marcus!" Archie snarled as the demons scrambled to their feet. "Cyrus deserves fucking better than you!"

"I'm warning you, Archie, shut up!" the cambion growled, connecting his fist with the trainer's jaw.

Laughing darkly, Archie slammed his elbow into Marcus' shoulder, gaining some space between them. "Not everyone is as blind to a good thing as you, friend." The term was laced with derision fuelling the cambion's rage as he raced forward. Stepping back, remaining just out of reach, Archie sneered at him. "But hey, if you won't fight for him, maybe I'll take care of him."

Faltering in his advance, Marcus' body shook, the trainer's words slicing through him. He knew Archie was goading him, but that didn't stop the possessive fury that now bubbled to the surface.

"You touch him, I'll fucking kill you, *friend*," he breathed, returning the veiled insult.

"Tell me," Archie grinned cruelly as they glared at each other. "Is he as tight as I think he is? Is he as good in bed as he looks?"

Roaring, the cambion surged forward with an explosion of power, colliding with the demon, slamming them into the house wall. Blood pounded in his ears as he pressed his arm into Archie's throat, teeth bared, ignoring the jabs of pain against his ribs.

"What the fuck are you two doing?"

Marcus barely heard Ambrose shout as he continued to grapple with the demonic-trainer. Archie's fist connected with his stomach as he tried to band his arm around the demon's neck. The cambion groaned at the contact, stumbling back slightly even as Archie launched at his mid-section, sending him hurtling back against the solid granite tiles for the second time that night.

"Knock it off!" Ambrose yelled at them, his voice drawing closer.

The cambion and trainer refused to listen, Marcus sending out a wave of smoke to wrap around Archie's arm, pulling the demon back off him. Archie cried out as the smoke constricted around his bicep, pushing a fireball from his free arm which collided with Marcus' shoulder. With a ferocious roar, the cambion shot forward, his fist swinging through the air at his target.

Pain radiated up his arm as his blow connected. But not with the demonic-trainer.

"Shit, Ambrose!" Marcus blurted, his body sagging with horror as he watched his friend clutch at the side of his face. "I'm sor—"

The Consort held up his hand, silencing him, a murderous look on his face. Straightening, Ambrose looked between the men, their chests heaving as Archie continued to glare with fury at the cambion. "I don't know what the fuck is going on with you two," the demon spat coldly stepping between them. "But knock it the fuck off!"

"Fine," Archie shrugged his shoulders, relaxing his body. "I've got shit to do anyway."

Without another word, the trainer gathered his flames and disappeared, leaving Ambrose and Marcus alone in the courtyard. His stomach churning, the cambion looked desperately at his friend.

"Ambrose, I–"

"Don't bother, Marcus," Ambrose interrupted, pinning him with a cold look. "I don't know what you've done, but I suggest whatever it is you find a way to fix it. Lena's waiting for you."

The Consort's face told him there was no point in arguing. His body ached from his encounter with Archie, but he didn't think there would be any point in asking Ambrose or Lena to heal him right now. It didn't matter, the pain grounded him, mixing perfectly with his guilt and shame over Cyrus.

Clearly dismissed, Marcus shut his eyes before turning and walking away from his friend. Or at least, he hoped Ambrose was still his friend.

# CHAPTER THIRTY-TWO

Cyrus was grateful that Archie let him hide out in his chambers for the moment. He hadn't said anything to the trainer, but the feral gleam that had entered those red-glowing eyes did give him some concern. Archie left quickly after he arrived and Cyrus was glad to have somewhere quiet that he could retreat into his own thoughts for a while.

He felt like such an idiot for what he said. For not being able to hold back the words. He knew they would be explosive for the cambion, but he hadn't been able to stop himself. And now, he'd lost everything.

After his eyes had run dry, he'd pulled away from Lena, ignoring her questions as he dressed. She picked up pretty quickly that he didn't want to speak with her, so simply grasped his hand between her own and kissed his shoulder before leaving him alone. He was thankful that she hadn't compelled him to answer her.

He left soon after that.

Archie had still not returned a few hours later and Cyrus was becoming jittery. He needed to do something. He wanted to hit something, or *someone*, but decided that he would likely just end up getting himself hurt. His mind wasn't functioning properly, replaying the events between him and Marcus on an endless loop. He very much doubted he would be able to anticipate a sparring partner's moves right now. Archie would likely keep an eye out for him, or spar himself, but Cyrus didn't want to be treated like a breakable object right now.

It didn't matter how many times Marcus told him to find someone else, he wouldn't. That cambion, *his* cambion, was the only one for him. And Marcus was his, whether he liked it or not. Whether he accepted it or not. Whatever it was between them may be over, but in Cyrus' mind, Marcus would always be his. It didn't matter what the cambion said, he'd let Cyrus in, if only a little. And from everything the boundling could glean, that was more than Marcus had ever let anyone get.

Sighing with resignation, he left Archie's chambers heading for his den. Throwing some bales of hay and stacks of meat around for the hellhounds for a bit should help relieve some of the tension in his body. At the very least, playing with some of the pups would distract him from the pain in his chest.

The den was quiet. Most of the hounds were sleeping or simply lazing within their alcoves. After looking in on a few of them, Cyrus made his way to storage area, opening the faux wall with a wave of his hand.

"Hey, Cyrus."

Stopping mid-way, he spun around spying Jess walking through the den entrance. He really wasn't in the mood to deal with anyone. But he supposed that Jess would be the most agreeable to engage in conversation right now.

"Hey, Je—" His stomach dropped as he took her in, his eyes locked on her arms which she hugged tightly around her waist. "What happened?"

Her bindings had changed. The soft coils of Titus had been replaced with sharp flicks of black. He didn't recognise the pattern, but the power emanating from them felt familiar. It would take an older demon than him though to recognise her new sire from that alone.

"It's alright," Jess said softly, rubbing her arm. "I chose to change."

"Why? To who?" Cyrus questioned, stepping towards her.

"Please Cyrus," the young boundling said, stepping closer to him, "just hear him out."

"Hear him out?" His mind was racing. Who had she bound to? Why did she leave Titus? He knew she was young so didn't know how a lot of Hell worked as yet, but surely even she could see the benefit of staying with someone in a Prince's inner circle. Stepping back as she neared him, Cyrus realised he was backing himself into a corner in the storage area, but he needed to keep space between him and Jess. "Hear who out? Jess, what is going on?"

"He just wants to help you."

"With you being so cagey over who he is, I highly doubt that," he growled under his breath. "Who the fuck is he, Jess? Why did you leave Titus?"

The boundling looked panicked taking in his building anger. Holding up her hands, she paused in the doorway to the store area, a pleading look in her eyes. "I swear, Cyrus, he wants to help you. To help you and Marcus."

His eyes widened at the cambion's name. He could accept that those within Lena's council and even Balo had figured out what was going on between him and Marcus, but no way, absolutely no way, did Jess know. Even granting the possibility that Titus had figured it out, he wouldn't have said anything to his boundlings about it. He was far too loyal to Lena.

"What the fuck does Marcus have to do with this?" he snarled at her.

"He said that he owes Marcus for something in London."

"Lond—" Cyrus desperately tried to calm his mind, to hold onto a rational thought even as panic sunk its claws into his chest, gripping at his ribs, labouring his breath. Marcus had said something about London, a debt owed. But he'd said it to... *No... It couldn't be. She wouldn't have aligned to him.* "Jess, please tell me you didn't bind to Kai."

"Oh, she has, twinkle."

The black-skinned cambion stepped up behind Jess, almost tenderly curling his hand over her shoulder. The ash-tone of his colouring was further dulled by the brightness of the boundling's red. Cyrus almost laughed at the disparity, dimly recognising he and Marcus had a similar contrast.

Swallowing against the bile rising in his throat, Cyrus stared down at the cambion, stubbornly refusing to show fear. "What lies did you tell her?"

"I only told her the truth," Kai responded, his grip on Jess' shoulder tightening until the female boundling flinched under the pressure. Cyrus' eyes locked on the movement, quickly returning to the cambion, not wanting to give Kai any form of opening. "That day at the beach, Marcus was just trying to protect you from the arch-angel and how did Prince Lena respond? By nearly killing him." Kai placed a hand over his heart, his features morphing into something akin to sorrowful sympathy.

Jess looked at the cambion like he'd hung the moon. Cyrus wanted to hurl at the sight. "What kind of Prince is she where she doesn't let two of her own council be together?"

The gleam in Kai's fire-like eyes gave Cyrus pause. It was deadly. Unfeeling yet full of loathing. A sight all too common in cambions. And his red-gaze was firmly fixed on Cyrus.

He dug his claws into his thigh, hoping the pain might get Lena's attention. If she could see what was happening through their bond, she would come. He knew she had been planning to see Lucifer so he could only hope that she was not still in the lower rings of Hell. Silently cursing himself, he resolved to never again go to Hell unless he knew for certain she was top-side.

"I told you, Cyrus," Jess said, turning her gaze back to him, a hopeful gleam in her eyes. She stepped towards him, Kai allowing her to move forward, out of his grasp. "He just wants to help you and Marcus. So, you don't have to hide from Lena."

He shook his head emphatically. Of all people, Kai would find a hopeless romantic to manipulate. "Jess, he's lying to you," he spat vehemently. "I'm begging you, run, go get Titus. Now!"

"She's not going anywhere," Kai said calmly, closing the distance between him and Jess. "And neither are you. Actually," he laughed, tapping the side of his head as if he had just remembered something. "You are. But you won't like where you're going."

Jess' face fell as she looked over her shoulder at her new sire. "Going? You said you were going to talk to him."

The sinister sneer that formed on Kai's lips was terrifying as he stopped in front of the female boundling. "Young demons really are too trusting."

Before he could even blink, Cyrus' breath caught in this throat as he watched Kai's talons sink into Jess' chest. The sounds of cracking bone echoed off the walls, her ribcage caving in around her heart. She didn't even have time to scream before Kai pulled his arm back, his talons piercing the organ's surface as he crushed it within his hand.

"Jess!" Cyrus cried for her, knowing he was unable to do anything to save her in that moment.

Her body collapsed to the floor as Kai tossed her heart into a corner. The fires of Hell licked over her form, burning and destroying her flesh, claiming her for the final time.

Without a shred of remorse or feeling, Kai shook the blood from his hand. "She served her purpose."

He was in trouble. He already knew that. But something was very wrong. Kai should not have been that powerful. And now he effortlessly took out his own boundling. Without even flinching at the pain that would have fed back to him.

Knowing he needed to run, Cyrus tried to pull his flames around him. But nothing happened. No fire licked at his feet. He could only look at the cambion, unable to hide his confusion. "What—"

"Yeah, that's not going to work right now," Kai laughed.

Stepping back, Cyrus' tried to analyse his surroundings without looking away from the cambion. The demon stood between him and the exit to the store area. Hellhounds were beyond that, but they wouldn't help him. They might have if they were out in the main den, but they didn't serve him so were unlikely to come to his aid. They were made to protect the demon they bonded with, which was not him. Without a demon they had no powers, and until then their instinct would be to hide. There were a number of crates in the store area that, in ordinary circumstances, could be used as cover, but they wouldn't stand up to demonic powers.

"Cyrus, get back!"

He had never been so happy to hear Damien's voice as he was right then, dashing behind a large crate as a golden fireball flew through the entrance to the store area, aimed directly for Kai. The black-skinned cambion roared in frustration, barely managing to throw himself out of the way, landing roughly against the ground. The heat from the fire filled the room, clashing with the shelving on the far wall, incinerating all that it touched.

Racing into the room, Damien surveyed the scene, his gaze landing on the boundling, a wild look to him.

"About time someone showed up," Cyrus growled, fighting to contain a manic laugh that wanted to escape.

"Yeah, yeah," the cambion huffed, rushing over to him. "You okay?"

Nodding in answer, he jumped to his feet, quickly throwing his black fire alongside Damien's gold towards Kai. "How'd you find me?"

"You got lucky. I was looking for Kai, not you. Titus confronted me, saying he'd lost Jess and thought I had taken her. I'd seen her around with Kai recently so... Where is she?"

Cyrus didn't have time to answer as he spied Kai from the corner of his eyes, snarling at the interruption and hurriedly pushing to his feet.

Spinning on the spot, Kai held up his palm, his skin illuminating from within, a burst of white tearing through the air towards the two demons. Shoving against Damien's chest, Cyrus pushed the cambion away so the power passed between them.

That power didn't belong to the cambion who wielded it. It had no place within Hell. A power within that Cyrus had recently become familiar with.

"You're dealing with angels?" he spat at Kai, ignoring the menacing growl that emanated from Damien at the question. "That's low even for you." His skin prickled at the heavenly power rippling through the air. If Lena was top-side that would definitely have gotten her attention. But still nothing. Reaching out for her through their bond, he couldn't feel anything. Taking a deep breath, he resigned himself to the realisation that she wasn't coming.

"Actually, I'd say it's rather high for me," the cambion sneered, turning towards him.

"Lena will kill you for this."

"That *whore* will never know what happened," Kai snapped, raising his hand, pure light shooting from the centre of his palm, aimed solely at Cyrus.

"Cyrus, get out of here, now!" Damien shouted, throwing a gold fireball at the other cambion.

"I can't!" he cried back, narrowly avoiding the beam. It connected with a crate behind him, splinters of wood and hay raining down over him as he scrambled to his feet. "He's done something. I can't flame!"

Snarling, Damien stepped between Kai and the boundling. "You're not getting Cyrus. Prince Lena will kill us all if you do anything to him. You really want to start that war?"

"Absolutely," Kai growled. "She took everything from us! Cambions should rule Hell. A bonded demon like her should *never* have been made a Prince. It's an insult to true demons!" With a cry, Kai launched forward, colliding with the cambion.

The pair met with a furious intensity that Cyrus had not seen from either cambion before. Stepping back, he determined it was best to stay out of the way as much as possible. He had not practiced fighting alongside Damien and as he seemed to be Kai's target, he would only distract or hinder the cambion trying to protect him.

A sickening thud echoed through the room and Cyrus stared in horror as Damien collapsed to the ground. White light emitted from Kai's fist as it landed on the side of Damien's temple. Flinching for the now unconscious demon, Cyrus realised he was well and truly alone. Although he could sense his other council members, they couldn't call to each other in the same way Lena could call them.

Fire pooled in Cyrus' belly as he stared at the demon, refusing to back down. Rage contracted his muscles, coiling his body tighter as he prepared to defend himself. It wasn't just fear for himself or his desire to prove himself to his sister that caused this reaction, but the knowledge that Kai had done something to Marcus. That the cambion aided in the betrayal that caused Marcus to close off from everyone around him. That Kai was directly responsible for why Marcus wouldn't let him in, wouldn't entertain the connection they shared. Forget wanting to hit Marcus, he wanted to murder Kai. A red haze descended over his vision as he allowed his fire to lick like black snakes up the length of his arms.

Snarling, he threw as large a fireball at the demon as he could, even as white light enveloped him, ironically pulling him into darkness.

His head hurt.

Honestly, everything hurt, but his head felt like it wanted to split in two. Something akin to how it would feel after a night full of his dreams and terrors. But he hadn't been dreaming. Or had he? He remembered voices in amongst the darkness that had consumed him. But he couldn't place who they belonged to.

Trying to concentrate, he squeezed his eyes tight until small bursts of light appeared in his vision, his mind tugging at the faint voices before they lost purchase.

*"I told you, I wanted Ambrose," the first voice said flatly, distain and malice dripping from every word.*

*"And I told you, I couldn't get Ambrose," the other hissed with displeasure. This voice was the most familiar but it still alluded immediate recognition. "Neither he nor Lena go anywhere alone. But you are failing to see the bigger picture here."*

*"Oh really? Enlighten me then."*

*"Cyrus is her boundling. She will feel everything he feels."*

*"Only if she remains on Earth."*

*"She will. She won't risk his life. He's more than just her boundling. He's her brother."*

*"Really? Well then. Maybe you weren't so useless after all."*

*"Whatever you are going to do to him, wait until Lena gets back top-side. He'll die if you take him to Heaven now and she won't feel anything whilst she's in the lower circles."*

Grunting at the effort, the voices faded from memory, retreating back to the recesses of his mind.

His eyes felt heavy, but he forced the lids to crack, hissing as bright light assaulted them. His body tensed providing him with the dim realisation that his arms were tied behind his back. Likewise, his ankles strapped painfully to something solid. A chair? Whatever it was, he couldn't move. Rope or something bit into the skin around his wrists, another burning mercilessly across his bare torso, holding him upright even as his head hung forward. Although he recognised he was back in human form, he wasn't entirely sure he was wearing anything as his lower body felt numb, refusing to acknowledge any mental input from him.

"He's awake."

The cold voice caught his full attention, his eyes snapping open as he finally lifted his head, ignoring the twinge in his neck as he did so.

The room, or at least it appeared to be a room, was completely white. Every surface was unbearably bright, like it was illuminated from within. Something about them caused Cyrus' mind to rebel, trying to figure out what he was seeing, convinced it was some sort of illusion. The texture of the walls and floor seemed to shift in and out of existence, alternating between transparent and opaque. A constant flux of visual energy forcing his eyes to continuously refocus. Flexing his toes, he could feel the floor beneath him like it was hardwood, unyielding to his touch, although its appearance was to the contrary. He was actually grateful for the chair he was bound to as the sight of the floor seemingly disappearing and reappearing instantaneously gave him vertigo.

Continuing his study of the scene before him, his eyes came to rest on a most unwelcome face.

"Raphael," Cyrus spat, grinding his jaw in renewed anger.

"How nice of you to finally join us," the arch-angel sneered at him. "I was beginning to think Kai had gone over the top in collecting you."

*Kai.* He'd been the other voice he remembered hearing. Fucking cambion.

Taking a breath, Cyrus attempted to summon his fire. The walls around him pulsed, a flicker of darkness within their luminance, before it faded, overcome by the brilliance that blinded him. Shivers coursed over his skin like ripples across a pond, cold and all consuming, threatening to pull him into an abyss of nothingness.

Frowning, he focused on feeling his power core, noting it was diminished. His fire felt small, cool, like a small flickering candle rather than its usual roaring bonfire. He attempted to build it again only for the room to have a similar reaction as before, shattering his concentration as his spine constricted with displeasure.

Raphael smiled, evidently noting his struggle, exchanging a quiet word with another angel before they rushed away, passing seemingly without effort through the fluidic walls. No... there was a door, but it pulsed like the walls, seamlessly melding with the room when closed.

Studying him for a moment, Cyrus realised the arch-angel and the other angels in the room were all dressed in the same clothes. A loose fitted white shirt, white trousers and white... loafers? He huffed in amusement at just how bright they were. And their ridiculous choice in footwear.

"Why can't I use my powers?" Cyrus asked, looking around the room as he tested the restraints on his wrists. Whatever it was burned at his skin, but didn't yield to his efforts.

Raphael looked at him, a disdainful look on his face. "You are in Heaven, as abhorrent as it is to have you here. The light within these walls will prevent you from accessing the power you possess in your own right. Nor will you be able to access the collective powers of Hell. You are cut off from Hell, so to speak."

"If I'm cut off from Hell, how am I still alive?" he queried, tilting his head to the side. "I need my connection to Lena to survive."

"Lena is on Earth," Raphael said, turning back to take something from one of the other angels in the room. "So, your connection to her is not affected. For now. Better hope she doesn't go to Hell looking for you."

A wave of panic coursed through his chest. If Lena wasn't aware that he was missing...

Stamping down that thought before it could take purchase, he drew in a steadying breath, lifting his gaze to glare at the arch-angel. He may be hurting, his heart may be bleeding in his chest, but he wasn't going to die. Not here. Not now. He may have lost the only man he ever truly loved, but he still had his family. And no matter what, he was getting back to them. One way or another.

"What the fuck do you want, angel?"

"Lena's warded her compound from angels," Raphael explained over his shoulder. "From me. You're going to tell me how I get in."

A dark chuckle escaped him as Cyrus shook his head in disbelief. "If you think you can get to Lena through me, you're wrong. There is nothing you can do to me to make me betray her," the boundling spat at the haughty angel.

"Whether you betray her or not is of no real consequence," the archangel said softly, turning towards the demon. "Having you is as good as getting to her. Causing you pain will cause her pain."

"Ha!" Cyrus laughed cockily. "Trust me, she and I are very accustomed to pain. It will barely register with her."

"That might be true if we were only hurting your body. Which we will still be breaking. But hurting your soul might have more of an effect, don't you think?"

"I'm curious what it is exactly you think will hurt my soul."

"Experiencing the loss of a loved one perhaps?" Raphael sneered stepping closer. "Over and over until your mind breaks."

*Fuck... that might do it.*

# CHAPTER THIRTY-THREE

The meeting with Lucifer had been relatively short in comparison to how long they had taken in the past. Still hours, but the last meeting had taken almost a day, so he was thankful for that small grace. Lena remained tense around him when they got back to the house, and Marcus didn't blame her for it. He hated himself, a mutual feeling between them he suspected. She hadn't let him out of her sight, insisting that he stay with her at all times. The constant scrutiny felt unnecessary, but likewise he didn't want to be alone. Being alone would allow him to fall into his own thoughts, into the darkness consuming them, and he wasn't ready to face that yet. He wasn't ready to fully realise what he'd lost. What he had thrown away.

Sitting in the kitchen as Lena flittered around the counters, cooking dinner, he simply watched her, wondering instead what she was thinking. He wasn't sure he really wanted to know, but until Ambrose and Balo joined them to distract him, it was better than his own mind. He didn't know if Cyrus would join them tonight. He hoped the boundling would. He hoped he could get a moment, just a moment, to speak with him. To try and fix things. Even if fixing only meant creating a situation where they could continue to work together on Lena's council.

Although, he wasn't entirely sure he could survive even that possibility.

"So, you want to finally talk about what's going on with you and

Cyrus?" Ambrose asked, sitting down next to his friend.

Marcus looked at him shocked for a moment before turning his head to shout; "Lena!"

Jumping at his cry, Lena turned quickly towards the men holding up her hands defensively in front of her. "I didn't tell him anything!" she said loudly, her eyes wide.

"What?" Ambrose chuckled, looking between the two. "Is it supposed to be a secret?"

"It's not supposed to be anything," Marcus sighed, fiddling with the corner of his napkin before him on the table.

Ambrose scoffed, patting his friend on the back. "You two have not been very good at hiding it then."

"There isn't anything to hide!" the cambion cried indignantly, throwing his hands in the air and falling back against the booth. "There is nothing between Cyrus and I." The lie fell so easily from his lips and he flinched at the words, hating himself for still clinging to it despite his desperate wish for the opposite.

"Could've fooled me," Ambrose sighed, folding his arms across his chest.

Marcus swallowed, before looking at his friend from the corner of his eye. "How long have you known?"

With a knowing smile, Ambrose shook his head slowly. "Long enough," he said warmly. "You're a cambion so it wasn't a stretch to think your preferences would swing that way. I don't care. It doesn't change who you are. You're still my friend."

Marcus looked at him bewildered. No matter how many times he'd told himself not to be, he had always been afraid that Ambrose would pull away from him if he knew. That he might assume Marcus desired him in some way, regardless of what assurances the cambion might give to the contrary. Some part of him relaxed knowing that his dearest friend accepted him despite this. The same way Cyrus had so readily accepted him, despite having been so mistreated by other cambions.

"So why is there nothing between you and Cyrus?" the Consort continued, pulling Marcus back from his thoughts. "It doesn't seem like either of you want it to be nothing."

Marcus sighed and hung his head. "This, this is why I asked you to let me leave your council," he directed at Lena, knowing he was merely avoiding the question.

Ambrose coughed into his drink, grabbing his napkin quickly to cover his mouth. "You asked to leave the council?"

"He did," Lena said flatly from the kitchenette.

"She refused," Marcus scoffed.

"You refused?"

"I did."

"Okay, now I need to ask you why?" Ambrose said turning towards her.

The cambion raised a brow looking at her as well. "I'd like to know that too."

Lena stared dubiously at the men, shaking her head at them. "Because being part of my council has nothing to do with whatever relationships you may or may not entertain," she explained, turning back to the stove and tossing the cooking food in front of her. "It only has to do with helping me prepare for the Apocalypse. And in that respect alone, I need you," she sent a pointed look towards Marcus. "As I said to you before, I don't care if you are with Cyrus or someone else. And, as I said to Cyrus, being with him would mean you don't need to keep secrets from each other."

Looking at the table, Marcus leant forward and rested on his elbows. "Well, that doesn't matter anymore, anyway. I don't... *didn't* want to be with anyone. And I'm pretty sure I've just ensured that I never will be."

Ambrose sighed, his head falling back as he stared at the ceiling. "I'm getting sick of asking 'why', but... why?" he asked, gentle annoyance creeping into his voice.

"Because Cyrus..." he coughed, unable to bring himself to finish that statement. Shaking his head, he forced himself to explain a different way. "If there was going to be anyone, it would be him," Marcus said so quietly he almost didn't hear his own voice. Denying it to his closest friends would serve no purpose, so he decided to be fully open with them, no longer fearing their judgement. "But I... I had... someone... almost a thousand years ago. A boundling. *My* boundling. I loved him but, he... he betrayed me and destroyed everything I had built, leaving me with nothing. If it hadn't been for my father, I would have been killed by the demons that tried to take advantage of the situation. It took until just before I met you," he said, motioning to the Consort, "for me to rebuild. To be able to protect myself again. I didn't want to put myself in that position again."

Lena turned off the stove and walked over to the table, pulling out a chair and lowering herself onto it. Marcus looked up at her as she searched his face, warmth and care in her eyes. So vastly different to how she'd looked at him earlier in the night. "Have you told Cyrus that?" she asked softly.

Marcus shook his head. "Not exactly," he whispered in response. "And please don't tell him. I…" he trailed off, unsure of what it was he really wanted to say.

"You know," she continued, leaning forward and holding one of his hands between hers, "Cyrus is not your former lover."

"I know," he breathed, holding tightly onto her hand, silently thanking fate for giving him such devoted friends. "Trust me, I am very aware of that. But it doesn't matter anymore. He's with someone else."

Lena looked taken aback, as her eyes widen and she tilted her head. Letting go of his hand, she leant back in her chair. "What?" she asked, looking over to Ambrose then back to the cambion.

Marcus furrowed his brow at her reaction, unsure as to what it meant. "He told me, he's met someone."

Both Lena and Ambrose were staring at him, dumbfounded looks on their faces. Marcus twisted his head between them, waiting for someone to speak, annoyance building within him.

"What?" he snapped at them.

"Ah, Marcus," the Prince said hesitantly, shaking her head softly, "he hasn't found someone else." Something akin to shock slammed into Marcus' chest with an intensity that he felt the air in his lungs expel suddenly. His stomach turned, making him feel sick as the events from earlier in the day replayed in his mind, his eyes glued on Lena. "Of all people," she continued gently, "I would know if he had."

Sucking in breath, Marcus managed to force out, "But why would he say that, if he hasn't?"

Lena kept her expression gentle, but her eyes grew firm. "How long do you think someone can take rejection before they just give up?" she asked, holding his gaze with her own.

"I haven't been rejecting him," he whispered, even though he knew it wasn't true.

"You haven't been accepting him either," she said shaking her head. "You may have been taking him into your bed, but you've been keeping him at arm's length."

She was right of course. He knew she was right. He could lie to himself all he liked that he had been letting the boundling in, but that was the complete opposite to the truth. The closest he had come was that night in the national park, but even then, he had held back, closing himself off from Cyrus, ever again denying what it was he really wanted. *Who* he wanted.

Looking at Lena, Marcus felt a desperation overcome him. "I need to talk to him," he whispered.

With a soft smile, she nodded, looking into the kitchen for a moment. "Cyrus," she called, waiting for him to appear. He should have responded to her summons within only a few moments. After a minute Lena shifted in her seat, bracing her arm on the back. "Cyrus?" she repeated a slight hint of concern in her voice. Marcus felt his spine stiffen, his eyes locked on his Prince. Ambrose leant forward, resting his elbows on the table. "Cyrus!" Lena shouted, practically jumping up from the chair as if it had burned her. He should have responded by now. There was no reason he wouldn't. He had to. All members of her council were forced to come when she called. Where was he?

"Lena?" Marcus asked raising to his feet, his hands balled into fists, digging into the table surface. Ambrose stood as well, placing a hand on the cambion's shoulder in comfort.

"What's wrong?" the Consort asked, looking at their Prince.

"I don't know," Lena said, panic fully set within her tone. "I can't feel him."

Marcus rounded the table before he knew what he was doing, coming to a halt before her. His heart was pounding loudly within his ears, drowning out all rational thought. "What?"

"Cyrus," she said, turning to him, her eyes pooling with worry. "I can't feel him. I can't sense where he is."

"What does that mean?" he managed to grind out, his fingers flexing by his sides, restraining himself from grabbing her arms and shaking her.

"I don't know," she said gently, shaking her head. "I need my book."

They made for the hallway before pausing suddenly as the alarm sounded through the house, noise from the courtyard grabbing their attention.

"Lena!"

Marcus reached the door to the courtyard first, throwing it open with a loud crash, fury coursing through him.

"Damien?" Lena said puzzled, pushing past Marcus as he loomed in the doorway. "What the–"

"I'm sorry," Damien blurted as his body slowly reverted to human form, shuddering in pain as he did so. Something was very wrong. A cambion as old as Damien should not be having difficulties in transforming. "I tried to stop him."

"Stop who? Wha—"

Lena froze as she stepped towards Damien, as if she had hit an invisible barrier. A moment passed where no one moved. No one breathed. Marcus locked his eyes on his Prince, barely noting as Ambrose came to stand behind him.

Her scream ripped through the silence as her hands flew to her head, her body lurching forward, doubling in pain. Heat washed over Marcus' back as Ambrose flamed to her side, catching her in his arms as they fell to their knees, her fingers digging into her scalp.

With a growl, Marcus rushed at Damien clutching the other cambion's shirt in his fist, hauling the man towards him. "I'm guessing that had to do with Cyrus," he snarled, baring his teeth, his lips curling in disgust. "Where is he?"

"I don't know," Damien said, a note of fear in his voice, his trembling hands held up in surrender. "Marcus, I swear I don't know! I was looking for Kai. He'd cornered Cyrus in the den and I tried to help. I tried to stop him. Kai must have knocked me out and I can only assume took Cyrus. But I don't know where. I swear it!"

"Why should we believe you?"

"Because if you don't, I know you're going kill Balo. Please... I'm begging you," the other cambion pleaded with him. "I came here as soon as I woke up."

The screaming had stopped but Marcus didn't look away from Damien, relishing the strong scent of fear rose from the man. From the corner of his eye, he saw Balo step into the courtyard, halting in front of the alfresco panelled wall.

"Marcus, what are yo—" Balo started, his gaze darting between the cambions and Lena and Ambrose.

"Balo, stay out of this!" Damien barked at the boundling, his brown eyes never leaving Marcus' face.

"Marcus, let him go," Lena huffed, still cradled in Ambrose's arms, her hands clutching at his shoulders. She struggled to get to her feet, Ambrose holding onto her elbows, assisting her. She was unsteady, pain etched into her face, her body vibrating as she looked towards the cambions.

"Lena?" Ambrose questioned, pulling her body towards his.

Marcus didn't move, unable to look away from Damien.

"He wouldn't risk Balo's life," she said firmly. "Let him go." Marcus eased his grip on Damien but didn't release him, relaxing only enough for the other cambion to finally look towards Lena. "Cyrus is with the angels. I can see Raphael's face."

"If he's with angels and you can't find him, he's likely in Heaven," the Consort said, continuing to hold her against him as she shifted on her feet. "You need to go to Hell, now!" Flames began to lick at their feet, a horrified look on Lena's face as she pushed against Ambrose, stumbling away from him.

"No!" she cried, catching herself against the canopy railing. "If I leave Earth, he dies. In Heaven he's disconnected from Hell. He needs my connection to keep him alive."

"If they are using him to get to you, he would want to die," Ambrose pleaded, his hands reaching for her, although there was a soft apology to his tone. "He would not risk your life for his."

Tearing his gaze from Damien, Marcus shoved the other cambion away from him, turning to face his Prince. Balo raced forwards, clasping at Damien's shoulders as he staggered back under the force of Marcus' anger. "He's right, Lena," he said, a heavy sorrow causing his shoulders to fall, knowing the grief he was about to bring upon himself with his advice.

Her grey eyes snapped to him, confusion barely visible within their depths, clouded by the pain she was feeling from Cyrus. "Marcus?"

His chest constricting to the point he wasn't sure he could draw in enough breath to make sound, he shook his head, stepping towards her. "Don't think of me," he rasped, his voice sounding hollow to his ears. "Cyrus would rather die, than cause you this pain."

"No," she stepped away from him, her eyes gleaming with fire even as she winced, her hand flying to clutch at her temple. "I'm not leaving him to die. Archie!" she shouted, turning as the demonic-trainer flamed in beside her. "Go to the other Princes. Tell them, Heaven has taken my boundling."

"What?" Archie stepped towards her, his eyes darting briefly to Marcus, concern and worry flashing through them. "How?"

"Not now. Go!" she ordered, her body collapsing back slightly. Ambrose caught her quickly, holding her firmly against his chest, his face barely concealing his own agony seeing his love in pain.

Knowing there was no use in questioning further, Archie merely nodded, his flames coursing over his body as he left to do her bidding.

"You may deny him," Lena hissed, turning back towards Marcus, malice in her voice. "But he is my brother. I *will* save him."

"I am protecting you, Lena," Marcus said emphatically, waving a hand towards her. He'd been telling everyone, including himself, that protecting her was the sole reason he did anything recently. Might as well continue to stick to that line now. If he didn't, he would break, wholly and so completely that he knew he would never crawl back out of the darkness.

"I do not need your protection!" she shouted at him, her words slamming against him like storm. "When will you understand that? I can protect myself. What I do need, is your counsel. Damien!" The other cambion stepped forward, nodding his acknowledgement to the Prince. "You said it was Kai, right? Kai took Cyrus?"

"Yes," Damien answered immediately, his hand firmly clasped with Balo's, holding the boundling behind him as if to shield him.

"How would Kai even know to work with Raphael?" Ambrose questioned, running a hand through his hair, not bothering to hide the distress on his face. "Not even the inner circle knows about what's been happening with him."

Marcus felt like the ground gave way beneath him, memories flooding his mind. "The beach," he breathed, his chest constricting with panic. "He was at the beach. That day... you, Cyrus and I... the man..." Looking at Lena, the cambion saw she realised what he was talking about, horror spreading over her features. "I didn't recognise him. I haven't seen him in human form for centuries. It was him. Kai was there."

"But how did he know?" the Consort said softly. "How did he know you were even there? Only your council knew you were going. And none of us would have told him."

"Titus knew," Lena said, swaying on the spot. "He was meant to be looking after Balo that day before Archie swapped with him."

"Titus wouldn't betray you."

"No," she agreed. "But one of his boundlings might."

"Jess," Damien said suddenly, pulling every demon's gaze to him. "Jess changed her binding to Kai."

Clenching his jaw, Marcus shut his eyes for a moment, forcing himself to breathe. Forcing himself to remain calm. Rage burned in his chest, beating against his ribs, as the inner darkness he had locked away since the Cleansing tried to fight its way to the surface. Nostrils flaring, he looked to his Prince, waiting for her command.

Lena turned her gaze to him, their eyes locking, an understanding passing between them. "How do you feel about hunting down Kai for me?"

He had no idea if she knew his history with Kai, and in that moment it didn't matter. His body came alive, desire to inflict pain and suffering against his enemy, such that would make Satan, the Prince of Wrath, fear him. "How many pieces do you want him in?"

"As long as he can still talk."

He didn't need more. Nodding at the command, he gathered his flames and headed to Hell.

It was time for the assassin, the monster within the shadows, to hunt.

# CHAPTER THIRTY-FOUR

Passing only fleetingly through a junction, Marcus flamed immediately to the hellhound den. It didn't take much for him to pick up on the scents of Cyrus, Damien and Kai within the store room. Looking at the floor, he saw the charring on the rock surface. The remaining scent was faint, almost overcome by the fires of Hell, but he recognised it. *Jess.*

Closing his eyes, he fought against the memories trying to claw their way to the surface. Marcus had been fairly sure that Jess liked Cyrus, so struggled to understand why she would do anything that would bring him to harm. He could only imagine what lies the other cambion would have told the young demon to get her to sway to him.

But there was another scent intermingled with the others. Something... *pure*, like the smell of clean air after a heavy rain. A smell he had only scented on three occasions before now.

*Angels.*

But there was no way that angels could get into Hell. Not undetected at least. And multitudes of demons would have swarmed on any that dared to enter. So how was their scent here? How did it permeate every surface? To the point where even the hounds avoided coming near the entrance to the store area. He spied one of Zamira's pups, Orion if he remembered correctly, studying him before gingerly stepping towards him. Holding out his hand, he waited patiently for the hound to approach him, letting Orion's snout dust over his knuckles.

Marcus took the moment to collect his thoughts, wondering where he should start looking for Kai. It didn't seem logical that the cambion would be simply walking around the corridors of Hell, more than likely knowing that Lena would be sending someone after him. That Marcus would volunteer to go after him even if he hadn't been ordered to do so. But then, Kai was not necessarily known for being logical, so it was still entirely possible he would be sauntering around somewhere, thinking himself untouchable.

It had been a while since he'd been allowed to let the beast within him out like this. It was already growling within his chest, waiting for the perfect opportunity to pounce. To take control. But he had to be smart. Letting it out now would not end well. At the time of the Cleansing, it had been after a public declaration by Lena for the cambions to fall into line. Tearing through the corridors of Hell for a singular cambion would cause disruption. Chaos and speculation that Lena could ill afford at the moment. He had to think things through. Properly and not simply react.

If only Cyrus were there, he lamented to himself, scratching under Orion's snout. The boundling could think through anything. He saw everything, remembered every detail. But then, if Cyrus were there Marcus wouldn't be hunting down Kai.

Turning away from the hellhound, he surveyed the store room one last time, focusing on Kai's scent. Smoke trailed from his fingers, licking out into the open air, snaking across the ground and melding with the other cambion's scent. He could feel the traces of angelic power interlaced with Kai's scent. So, that was how it was here. Kai had allowed angels to fuse their power with his, giving him the advantage he would have needed to counteract the power Lena fed Cyrus and Damien. That the cambion would degrade himself in such a manner actually surprised Marcus, but it made his mouth water with anticipation as to what Lena would do when she found out.

Keeping his power active, Marcus walked out of the den, following the trail his smoke pointed out to him. It led him to a junction where the scent then disappeared.

Pulling what power he could from his connection to Lena, he locked on the trail and followed it through the ether, appearing in a forest somewhere in a northern continent. Here the scents of Cyrus and Kai separated. Cyrus' lingered for a moment and Marcus hovered his hand over the patch of ground the boundling had lain on. Images of the young demon lying unconscious, likely bound, ripped through his mind, further fuelling the hate and fury within him. His chest hurt, wishing more than anything he could hold Cyrus in his arms, shielding the boundling from this fate.

How bitterly he regretting his actions. How desperately he wanted to wind back time and change things. As if driven by some unseen force, Marcus flattened his hand on the ground, a low growl vibrating from the centre of his chest, his lips curling away from his teeth.

"Mine."

The word ripped from his throat as he silently vowed, if he found Cyrus, if he got him back, he would give the boundling everything. And he would never let anyone or anything take Cyrus from him again. The young demon was his. Would always be his. No matter what came next. And everything he was belonged to Cyrus.

Pushing to his feet, he fought to push those thoughts back to the recesses of his mind. It wasn't that he didn't want to acknowledge them. He wanted nothing more than to give into them completely. But he had to focus on Kai. He had to find the cambion. Find Kai, and he would find his way into Heaven. His way to Cyrus.

Breathing in deeply, he caught Kai's scent, turning and walking off through the trees. A few strides into the tree line he lost the scent, noting that Kai must have flamed somewhere else. Closing his eyes, he found the trail easily. The angelic power was fading so the cambion's advantage was diminishing.

A bloodlust took hold of him. Something he hadn't felt since the Cleansing. Since he killed William. His breath came rapid, his chest falling and rising in time with the beating of his heart. He wanted to kill Kai. Kill him for poisoning William against him. For taking Cyrus from him. For taking everything he had ever loved.

But Lena needed him. The bloodlust, although tantalising, was inopportune for keeping a clear mind.

Taking a steadying breath, Marcus flamed to the one person he hoped would help him now. It was time to call on the last of his family for help.

"Henry!"

His body was wired, coiled tightly, ready to fight as his gaze desperately sought out his uncle, flames receding. Hearing nothing, he called for the demon again. There was a crash from the upper floor as Marcus whirled round to face the direction of the sound, finally seeing his uncle rounding the corner into his entrance hall.

"Marcus?" Henry looked puzzled even as he raced towards him. "What's wrong?"

"I need your help," the cambion said hurriedly, noting that he was still in demonic form but beyond caring.

Henry's blue eyes took him in, his face setting into hard lines as he obviously noted the urgency in Marcus' stance and tone.

"What's happened?"

"It's Cyrus. He's been taken by angels."

"Cyrus? Who–" Henry questioned even as his eyes widened with shock. "Prince Lena's boundling?"

"Yes."

"Angels took him?"

"Yes. Please, Henry. I don't have time to explain."

"Wait, is Cyrus who you..." Marcus knew what Henry was asking him. He also knew he didn't need to answer. That his silence would be enough to confirm what it was his uncle was questioning. "Fuck," Henry breathed, running his hand through his blonde hair. "What happened?"

"Kai happened," Marcus spat harshly, malice dripping from each word, his hatred for the other cambion firing through every nerve of his body. Henry drew in a sharp breath, his body tensing as Marcus' words settled over him. "Kai handed him over to Raphael. I need your help finding him."

"You're a better tracker than I am, Marcus," his uncle said shaking his head slightly.

"Let me rephrase then," Marcus said, stepping towards Henry, his wings rising behind him. "I need you to stop me from killing him before Lena can speak to him."

Henry smiled at him, a feral gleam entering his blue eyes as he allowed his body to transform. Sharp pointed horns broke from his temples, rising into the space above his head as his skin darkened to a deep red, muted with tones of black that wrapped around his hands and feet. Red and black veined wings sprouted from his back, rising with barbed talons towards the ceiling. His suit burned away, replaced by wrappings of black cloth around his shoulders and hips, leaving his hard-planed stomach bare. Two horns emerged from his hips, curving back behind him with a lethal quality.

"That I can do," his uncle growled, stepping towards him as they clasped hands, talons digging into each other's forearms. "Let's go."

*He couldn't breathe.*

*A weight bore down upon his chest, forcing all air to vacate his lungs.*

*"Please, stop," he begged, his eyes pleading with the black demon looming over him.*

*The face of the demon morphed continuously before his eyes, evoking feelings of fear, hate and sorrow to blend within him. Zagan, Kai... Marcus...*

*"You're worthless..."*

*"You're nothing..."*

*"You're not enough..."*

*The pain shifted down his body, searing through his hip and thigh, his bones cracking under the weight.*

*His vision spun and the world gave way beneath him, spiralling into a void of nothingness. He could hear voices, distant and ethereal, tugging at his mind, at his memory.*

Gasping, he rubbed his fingers against the abrasive surface of the chair he was bound to, using it to centre his consciousness.

"Don't lose the connection!" he heard someone shout.

Cyrus swallowed against the dryness of his throat, remembering where he was as blinding light assaulted his senses. *Fucking angels...* he cursed silently. But it would take more than that to break him. The images were nothing new. Showing him his own nightmares would accomplish nothing.

A dull pain radiated up his side. He shifted in the chair, hissing as the pain became tearing, ripping through his body like fire. So, the breaking of his bones had been real, then. Mixing mental torture with physical stimuli. Something Zagan had been quite adept at. Cyrus smirked with a fleeting thought that some demons could learn a thing or two from the angels.

But his powers should have been healing him. A small seed of dread planted in his stomach as he came to realisation, he wouldn't be able to rely on his healing ability to survive the torture. He had to protect his mind. Close it off, if he could.

"Move aside!" the voice shouted again, a flurry of movement behind him.

Warmth course through his scalp and Cyrus used it to push his mind to his mornings spent with Lena under the canopy, her power arcing gently through his hair, easing the pain in his mind. Ambrose and Marcus training in the courtyard.

The canopy...

Lena...

Ambrose...

*Marcus...*

*His back slammed into the coarse surface of the wall, a thick black arm pressing into his throat.*

*"I'm going to make you scream until your throat bleeds," Kai snarled at him, large yellowed fangs snapping inches from his face.*

*"Are you now?"*

*Black smoke swirled around Kai's body, licking out in delicate tendrils against the ashy skin, small cuts left in their wake. The cambion flinched with each touch, his blood trickling down his body, but didn't move to retract his arm from Cyrus' throat.*

*"I'd let go if I were you, Kai," Marcus said, his large frame emerging silently from the shadows behind them. "You may have been able to take Cyrus on his own." He stepped up behind the similar coloured cambion, his wings raised menacingly behind him as he leant forward to whisper in Kai's ear. "But you are sorely mistaken if you think you will survive me. I let you live last year, but I still owe you for that stunt you pulled in London."*

*There should have been fear in Kai's eyes. Now they gleamed with delight.*

*A loud snap echoed in his ears as he screamed, pain rippling from him in waves, the arm at his throat bearing down on his collarbone, bending it until breaking.*

*Kai was torn from him, flying across the cavern until he slammed into the opposite wall.*

*Large arms encompassed him as he fell forward, collapsing into a broad chest, the scent of burnt sugar comforting him.*

*"I've got you," Marcus murmured in his ear. "You're okay."*

*But it wasn't okay. This wasn't right. This wasn't how things were supposed to go.*

*Looking up at Marcus, Cyrus fell into the warmth he saw even in those black depths.*

*"This isn't right," he murmured, wincing as the movement of his jaw jostled his broken clavicle.*

*Marcus' large hand cupped the side of his face, his thumb tenderly stroking across Cyrus' cheek.*

*"Of course, this is right," the cambion replied. "Everything is alright now. I've got you."*

*His breath caught in his throat as he stared at the demon who now meant more to him than anything.*

*"I love you," he whispered, again not meaning for the words to leave his lips.*

*"My gorgeous Cyrus," Marcus sighed, lowering his lips to the boundling's, brushing a gentle kiss along them. "I love you."*

*Something told him to not believe it. To not give in to the cambion. But his body refused to listen. Snaking his hands up the broad chest, he held tightly onto Marcus' shoulders, ignoring the pain in his neck.*

*Love...*

*All he wanted was for the cambion to love him. To hold him and never let him go. To be complete together. They both held pain inflicted by shadows of their past. But when Marcus held him, when the cambion kissed him, his shadows meant nothing. They simply faded away.*

*Suddenly, Marcus' body went still and a sharp pain stabbed into Cyrus' chest.*

*Crying out, he looked down, seeing a black hand protrude from Marcus' torso, talons at the end of long fingers digging into his own skin.*

*"No!" he cried, his hands clutching at Marcus as the cambion spluttered, blood pooling from the corners of his mouth.*

*Kai's face emerged from behind Marcus' shoulders, a cruel sneer on his face.*

*"I told you I would take everything from you," Kai hissed, glee and malice mixed in his tone.*

*Cyrus' mind was screaming.*

*No, no, no...*

*NO!*

*This was wrong. This wasn't what happened.*

*This wasn't real!*

*This wasn't real...*

A laugh burst from his throat as he shook his head, clearing the images from his mind. "I would have thought that angels would have better torture methods," he said, glaring from the corner of his eye as Raphael stepped around him. The arch-angel's face was twisted with rage and Cyrus drank it in like a healing balm. "That was pathetic."

Two other angels were in the room with him and the arch-angel. One moved quickly around him, removing the vice that had been firmly strapped to his shoulder, evidently the tool used to break his collarbone. The other was hunched over a table, fussing over another instrument

Cyrus couldn't get a good look at. More than likely something else that would be used to inflict physical harm.

"I knew demons were depraved, but still…" Raphael shook his head with disgust. "You lie with a man?"

Chuckling despite the pain in his shoulder as he did so, the boundling sneered at the angel. "After everything, your problem is that I'm gay?" The torture was worth the look of horror on the arch-angel's face at his question. "Do you want to know what really happened after that? Do you want to know how Marcus made me scream out his name, begging him to fuck me harder?"

Raphael's top lip curled away from his teeth, a faint growl building from his chest.

"Maybe you'd learn a thing or two," he continued. "Learn how to properly satisfy that human lover of yours."

The room stilled and the two other angels looked towards Raphael. The arch-angel didn't even blink but pinned the angels with a hard glare.

"Demons lie," he scolded them. "Never forget that."

The angels quickly lowered their gaze and carried on setting up their next device. Now Cyrus could see what they were handling. A large studded leather strap was fitted around the circumference of his knee, holding a contoured iron plate over the front. A long T-handled screw protruded from the plate with the other end forming a blunted wedge that dug into the centre of his bone. He was well acquainted with such a device. It could cleave through bone, muscle and nerves without breaking skin, leaving the joint to swell with internal bleeding. Inescapable pain with no relief. A favoured tool of most demons within the pits.

"Only one of us is lying, angel," Cyrus spat, a metallic tang clinging stubbornly to the back of his tongue. He was hurting, his entire body wincing with only the slightest movement. But this pain meant nothing. It was nothing compared to the pain Marcus had already inflicted on him. And there was no way the angels could conjure a vision that would even come close to that pain. Or so he hoped.

"Oh?" Raphael hissed, stepping back behind the bounding. "Let's go again, shall we?"

"Go as often as you want, arsehole," Cyrus growled, squaring his shoulders as best he could considering his restraints. "Keep showing me things like that and you'll get fucking nowhere. Kai is no fucking match for Marcus."

"We'll see."

*His back slammed into the coarse surface of the wall, a thick black arm pressing into his throat...*

# CHAPTER THIRTY-FIVE

They found Kai quickly, strolling through Hell like he didn't have a care in the world. Like he didn't just conspire with angels. Like he didn't just hand the single-most important person to the one who now hunted him to an unknown fate.

Marcus used his smoke to conceal their presence, hiding within the shadows, as they stalked him through the corridors, waiting for their opportune moment. Like Lena, Henry manifested lightning, and would be invaluable to subduing the other cambion.

A sinister smile formed on his lips as he watched Kai enter a junction, alone. A lamb to slaughter. His power vibrated around them, eager to lash out at his prey. To watch the life drain from Kai's red eyes. The image in his mind hardened his body, fuelling his malicious intent with a hint of desire. He was so close, he could almost taste the sweet scent of death in the air. The cool relief of revenge. The warmth of spilled blood between his fingers. A low, rumbling growl built within his chest, causing Kai to pause and look behind him, despite not finding anything.

He paused as he felt a taloned hand fall on his shoulder. Looking back, he saw his uncle, his throat constricting as he fought to rein in his impulses. This was why he brought Henry after all. The one person that could stop him from doing something that would prevent him from getting Cyrus back.

"Stick to the plan, Marcus," Henry hissed under his breath.

Slowly, he nodded, letting his uncle step in front of him. Bright golden lightning coursed up Henry's arms as Marcus coiled his smoke around the walls, swiftly moving to both entrances of the cavern. Forming around the entrance sides, his smoke waited patiently for his silent command, small wisps snaking up from the floor.

Glancing over his shoulder, Henry nodded subtly as his lightning charged, mixing with the smoke around them. Marcus' mind cleared all thought, focusing on his target, his vision narrowing on the other cambion before them.

With a loud snap, impenetrable smoke walls formed within the entrances. Kai jumped back, his body spinning to face them as their cover retreated and Henry's lightning shot out across the floor. With a short-lived scream, the cambion's body seized, convulsing as the electric current overtook him. Light burst from his body, the last remnants of angelic power forced to expel. Both Henry and Marcus hissed against the light filling the room, their skin searing under its weight.

As the light receded, Marcus spied Kai lying limp on the floor. Checking their own bodies, he noted the light had not done any physical damage but his skin tingled like it was healing from a sunburn.

"Angel power?" Henry questioned as he stepped towards Kai's unmoving body. He prodded at the unconscious cambion with the toe of his boot, his lip curled away from his top teeth in disgust. "How did he not burn up, holding that within him?"

"Who cares right now?" Marcus snarled, gathering his smoke to pull Kai's wrists behind his back, binding them together.

Henry knelt down and sparked some lightning against the cambion's temple. "He'll be knocked out until we wake him."

"Let's get him to Lena. I can't fucking wait to see what she does to him."

His uncle chuckled darkly as Marcus stepped up next to Kai, reaching down and grabbing the unconscious form. With minimal effort, he slung the demon over his shoulder, straightening to look at Henry.

"Think she'll let me watch?" his uncle asked, a hint of glee and hope in his voice. "I know she and I aren't on the best terms, but I'd love to see her in action."

"Come back with me and this vermin," he said, bouncing Kai on his shoulder, "and I'm sure she could be persuaded."

Matching Henry's sinister grin with one of his own, Marcus gathered his flames around them and took them to the house.

Lena's scream ripped through the night air as they appeared. Without second thought, Marcus dropped Kai on the granite tile, racing into the house towards the sound, his demonic form receding as he ran. He found her and Ambrose in her altar room as she clutched at her neck and shoulder. Bruises formed on her creamy skin as her panicked eyes locked onto him.

"Kai?" she asked, her voice gasping and laden with pain that was not her own.

"Downstairs. Henry's keeping him unconscious."

"Henry? Your uncle?"

Marcus nodded stepping further into the room. "Cyrus?" he asked, unsure he really wanted an answer.

Lena shook her head, tears brimming in her eyes as Ambrose cradled her in his arms. "He can't heal," she whispered. "His powers are suppressed. I'm taking what I can from him, but..."

Her voice broke as she winced within the Consort's hold, her body buckling under the weight of the pain being forced upon her. Marcus stepped close falling to his knees before her.

"Henry has lightning powers, right?" She was whimpering as she spoke, pulling long, ragged breaths into her lungs.

"Yes."

"Get him to bring Kai up here."

Dashing from the room, Marcus collected the demons, ignoring the worried look on Henry's face. They bound Kai to a chair, placing the cuff Lena made for Damien on his wrist.

Events moved rapidly after that. Henry settled into his position as head-torturer under Lena's instruction, electrocuting and convulsing Kai's muscles until his screams echoed through the house, seeping into the walls. Ambrose sliced through the cambion's skin with his tendrils, his power probing into the wounds, snaking under the flesh, inflicting damage internally. Marcus' smoke surrounded Kai's head, cutting off his air, forcing a path down the demon's throat, filling his lungs until the expansion cracked ribs from the inside. Damien and Balo stood in the doorway, looking on at the scene with equal parts of fascination and horror on their faces.

However, Kai was stubborn and he held his tongue. If she had not been focusing on lessening Cyrus' suffering, Lena would have delved into his mind with her book, tearing him apart mentally until nothing was left. But that was still rather humane, and perhaps her own rage made that a non-option. Marcus was certain, like him, she wanted to see the other cambion suffer.

A soft sound drew all their attention to the hallway as Archie strode purposefully into the room, pushing past Damien and Balo. Upon seeing Kai, a loud snarl ripped from his throat, his blue fire licking over his fingers. Fingers that flexed with desire to join in the torture. Marcus' chest swelled at the sight, despite his recent encounter with the trainer. Cyrus always doubted his importance to this council. What he wouldn't give to show the boundling how his abduction affected those left behind.

With long strides, Archie made his way to Lena's side, bending down to whisper in her ear. Her eyes darkened, fury etching into her features. Marcus felt the seed of her power within him pulse. Both Ambrose and Archie straightened as the same happened to them. Her demon roared within them, their connection beating like a drum, sounding like the footfalls of an army marching to war.

"Enough," Lena coughed as she leant heavily against her workbench. "Leave us. Henry, stay."

Marcus wanted to protest. It wasn't enough. He could see the pain his Prince was in, knowing it was only a fraction of what was currently being done to Cyrus. He wanted to mirror that pain in Kai. He wanted to tear the other cambion apart, his vision clouded with black rage. But he'd learnt his lesson with Raphael. He wouldn't question her. Especially not in front of his uncle. Growling as he stepped around the beaten demon, he paused by Henry, looking him in the eye.

"Make it hurt," he snarled.

Henry's blue eyes gleamed with delight. He was in his element, adding to his swelling pride at currying favour with a Prince of Hell. Reaching out, he clasped Marcus' shoulder firmly. "I swear it."

Nodding approvingly, Marcus begrudgingly left, taking a small moment to jostle Kai's shoulder, making the cambion flinch as pain flashed through his body. He smiled as he heard Lena chuckle indulgently behind him, knowing he was not going to be reprimanded for the action. The door shut behind him, the click sounding like a hammer sealing his fate. Ignoring the others, he strode to his room, needing a moment of solitude. He needed to collect himself. To calm himself before he lost all control.

Slamming the door behind him, he stood in the centre of the room. His body was vibrating, needing to further unleash the monster within.

Logically, he understood why Lena dismissed them. Alone with Henry, she could focus on instructing the lightning within them, the power she was most accustomed with. He reasoned she also needed Marcus in particular out of the room to avoid a loss of control. But that didn't ease the tension in his body.

"Fuck!"

His roar bounded around the room as his power pulsed out of him in a shockwave, rattling the furniture its wake. Small cracks formed in the plaster at the blast, barely symbolising the turmoil within him. He felt a presence push back, protecting themselves from the onslaught. Spinning round, he found Ambrose standing by the door, a sympathetic look on his face. Ordinarily, an expression like that would have angered him, but now, he simply felt defeated, letting his shoulder's slump with exhaustion.

"I get it now," he murmured quietly, dropping his gaze to the floor.

"Get what?" the Consort asked, stepping towards his friend.

"Why it was so hard for you, when Zagan had Lena. I get it and I'm sorry I didn't understand fully back then."

"Marcus, we are going to get Cyrus back."

He shook his head, wanting to believe his friend, but unable to dispel the feeling of foreboding forming in the pit of stomach.

"This is all my fault, Ambrose," he sighed, turning away, squeezing his eyes shut to stave off the tears threatening to fall. "If I hadn't pushed him away. If I hadn't..." His hands raised in front of him, attempting to grasp at something that wasn't there. Something he couldn't reach, no matter how much he wanted to. "He wouldn't have gone somewhere he wasn't protected. He would be safe."

He felt the Consort step up behind him and place a comforting hand on his shoulder. "Lena is pissed, beyond pissed, and she loves Cyrus. She is not going to let anything happen to him."

"Something is already happening to him!" he snapped, turning on his friend, although he knew his anger was misplaced. "They are torturing him!"

"I know. I'm sorry," Ambrose quickly apologised, holding up his hands defensively. "I didn't mean to say otherwise."

Sighing, Marcus looked over at the bed, memories of the day before assaulting his mind with renewed vigour. Guilt and shame had become his only friends of late. He knew, if he didn't get Cyrus back, if the boundling was not brought home safe, they would never leave. "He told me he loved me yesterday," he admitted finally. "And I threw him out."

"Marcus–"

Whatever the Consort had been about to say was cut short as a piercing scream ripped through the house. They both raced into the hallway, stopping in their tracks as Lena strode towards them, her eyes dark, a new bruise forming over her upper arm. Others might have missed it, but they saw how her body winced with each movement. Looking past her, Marcus spied the faint outline of Kai still strapped to the chair in the altar room, his head slumped forward against his chest. Evidently, whatever Archie had told her pressed matters for her to break Kai's mind.

Marcus realised that he didn't care. He should have. He should have wanted to hear and see Kai suffering for days. That need he used to have, paled in comparison to his need to get Cyrus back. Nothing else mattered now.

"Ambrose, it's time to go," she rasped, striding towards them, her voice strained and broken. "Henry has gone to Lucifer. He'll be back soon. How poetically ironic that Lucifer cannot come to Earth and currently, I cannot leave."

Clapping Marcus on the back, Ambrose took a step forward. "Come on."

"No, he stays here."

Her words might as well have been a physical blow, causing the cambion to step back, conflicting emotions gripping at his chest. *What?*

"Lena?" the Consort queried, looking at her, his brows drawn together.

"He stays here," she spat, turning on her heel, heading for the stairs.

"Lena, please," Marcus breathed, ready to drop to his knees and beg her if needed. "Let me help."

"Help how?" she snarled over her shoulder, pinning him with a glare that could have set him ablaze with the fire in their depths. "Help in the way that you pushed Cyrus away? Help in the way that you broke his heart?"

His own anger flared. Not at her. But at the truth behind her words. "That's not fair," he ground out, although he knew he deserved it.

"Now that sounds familiar," Lena chuckled, turning back and stepping closer to him, her fists clenched tightly by her sides. "You made a similar statement when I refused to release you from my council. You want to know what's not fair, you riling my boundling up to the point where I haven't been able to think straight for the last few weeks and then turning round and crushing him. It's not fair that I have to suffer his pain with him, pain caused by someone else that I love. That I trusted! From what I have seen, Cyrus is being tortured with fabricated memories of losing someone he loves. Of losing you. Do you honestly think I will risk causing that fabrication to become a reality? No, you will stay here with Henry and I where you are protected."

"Lena, don't do this," he begged, reaching for her but keeping his distance. "Don't shut me out!"

"You wanted out of my council! So be out!" she shouted, her rage and pain pouring from her body in palpable waves.

Marcus' body reared back as the connection that bound him to her council snapped, punching the air from his lungs. His knees buckled as he slammed to the floor, a deafening crack surrounding them. An agony that he had never felt before crashed in on him, pulling him down into helpless desolation as he stared at his Prince, silently begging her to take him back.

"Lena." Her name fell like a plea from his lips, not caring as tears began to stream down his face. "Please. Don't do this."

Glaring at him, she scoffed before once again turning her back on him. Her body stiffened as she took a singular step, her hands flying to her neck as she choked and gagged on nothing, collapsing before the men. Ambrose ran to her, falling to his knees as he skidded along the floor, wrapping his arms around her. Marcus crawled forward, grasping at her hands, preventing her from opening her skin as she clawed at her throat. Her face was red, tears coating her cheeks as she looked panicked at the cambion, eyes wide, trying to form words, gasping for breath.

"Lena, please!" Ambrose begged, holding her tight. "Go to Hell. This needs to end. I can't see you like this!"

Marcus couldn't bring himself to hate Ambrose for his plea. Knowing that both their loves were suffering was unbearable. He would gladly swap places with either of them, a sentiment he was sure Ambrose mirrored.

The Prince shook her head violently as she finally drew in a full breath, her body shuddering with the relief of it. "No!" she sobbed, lurching forward and clutching at Marcus' shoulders. Ambrose supported her even as the cambion held her arms, their eyes locked together. "Do you love him?"

Marcus stared into her grey eyes, his grip tightening for a moment before relaxing, remembering the bruising on her arms. "Lena..."

"Do you at least care for him?" she rushed, panting with the effort.

His head shook, but not in answer. In uncertainty. He didn't want to admit to his feelings to her before saying them to Cyrus. But if he wanted the Prince to let him back in, he didn't have a choice. He swallowed harshly, moving his hands down to grip her elbows, squeezing slightly in firm resolve.

"Yes," he said finally. "Lena, I... I do... I love him. I can't lose him. *Please*, you can't leave me behind. I'll go insane."

Slowly, her hand travelled from his shoulder to the centre of his chest, laying it flat against his thundering heart. Red lightning sparked around her fingers, entering his being, warmth coursing through his limbs as the seed of her power resettled, joining him once again to her. To her council. But it grew, flexing within his chest, expanding like roots wrapping around his veins and filling his entire body. She poured her power into him through her touch, their bodies glowing momentarily with their mixed auras.

"Save him, Marcus," she breathed, her fingers digging desperately into his shoulder. "Bring him home."

"How?"

"Henry will be back shortly with a token from Lucifer. One of his feathers. It will take you to Heaven. He is the only Prince that has ever been there, so he is the only one that could enter. Take Archie and Damien with you. I've already shared my power with them."

"Are you not coming?"

"I can't. Princes of Hell can't actually go to Heaven. Not yet, anyway. I can't go anywhere even if I wanted to," she sighed heavily, sinking back into Ambrose's hold, her hands falling from the cambion. "I'm sorry, Marcus. I had to see how much you cared."

Leaning towards her, Marcus cupped her face between his hands, resting their foreheads together. Her eyes closed at the contact, a breath of relief escaping her.

"I will bring him back," he swore, the words laden with solemn promise.

She nodded against him, opening her eyes again to look at him. "As soon as you find him, bring him to me. I will need to heal him."

Rising to his feet, he nodded to his Prince and Consort. Even as they knelt on the floor before him, clinging to each other, they were regal in their presence. Hellish purpose and resolve surrounded them and he basked in it. He could think of no better demons to hold their position in both the rule of Hell and in his heart. His closest friends had the faith in him that he would bring Cyrus home.

Now he had to have faith in himself.

# CHAPTER THIRTY-SIX

He was in so much pain.

He hadn't felt such pain in a long time and he knew he'd become accustomed to the comfort of his current life. Add in the fact that his powers were being suppressed, the inability to heal himself was wearing on his endurance.

Gasping for air as the bind around his neck released suddenly, the black spots in his vision retreating slowly. That shouldn't be possible. He didn't need to breathe. Why was he suffocating? Sure, he would gasp when choked during sex, but that was more a performance than actual need. Now he needed air. His throat was raw from his screams. Blood pooled within his mouth, coating his tongue and cheeks. It was like he'd become mortal and he supposed for all intents and purposes he was. In Heaven it was as if everything demonic in him had been stripped away.

How long had it been? How long had he been here? It felt like days, weeks, his mind devolving into an incoherent stream of broken thoughts. He'd lost all reason. All sense of time or presence of mind.

But he could feel *her*.

He could feel her rage, her hate, her power.

She was reaching out for him. The presence of her power throbbed within his soul as the searing pain in his shoulder eased to a dull throb. He knew she was coming. She would stop at nothing to get him back. He knew that. He just had to hold on until she did.

The loud crack of his ribs snapping within his torso echoed through the room, his head flinging back, a raw, stuttering scream ripping from his throat. Droplets of blood sprayed into the air as the bind around his throat tightened once more, cutting the sound short and removing his ability to draw breath.

"Again."

The voice was so distant as it broke through the pounding in his ears, but he heard it, his mind rebelling at the sound.

Retreat.

Disappear.

Hide.

*Darkness.*

*Shadows swirled around him, encasing his limbs within its cold grasp.*

*Shadows?*

*No, smoke.*

*Marcus?*

*"Marcus!" he cried, turning with the pool of smoke, his eyes desperately seeking the one he wanted. "Marcus!"*

*A faint voice called back, but he couldn't see its origin. He couldn't make out the words, his heart thundering in his ears. His chest burned, heaving against an invisible force. Vision blurring, he strained to see through the encroaching darkness.*

*"Marcus!" The strain in his voice grated against the silence surrounding him. Everything was silent except for the beating of his heart, threatening to drown him in the opposing void it created. "Help me!"*

*"Cyrus!"*

*His name was quiet. Almost like a whisper on the wind. But there was no wind to carry it. No breeze to calm the pain in his soul.*

*Grabbing at his hair, he screamed into the void, his voice breaking, choking as smoke filled his lungs. Sharp pain pierced through his shoulder, causing him to stumble to the side, trying to escape it.*

*He fell into something solid. Warm. Large arms banded around him, lifting him out of the smoke as the billowing waves became more erratic. The scene shifted around him to something he recognised. Something comforting. Yet simultaneously painful.*

*"That's it, gorgeous," the shadowed warmth above him sighed. His eyes snapped open, relief punching him in the gut as he stared up into ocean green eyes. Their mouths danced together as he sunk into the soft sheets beneath them. "Don't hold back. Come for me."*

*He was too warm. A searing heat coursing through his body. Burning him from the inside causing his back to arch as, what should have been pleasure flooding his body, was replaced by panic.*

*No.*

*No!*

*Please!*

*Don't show me this!*

*Don't make me live through this again!*

*His stomach tightened, pained pleasure forcing its way through his chest. He couldn't stop the words from falling from his lips.*

*"Marcus, please. I need you. I love you."*

*Wide horrified eyes tracked as the man, who morphed between solid and smoke, rose from the bed, turning away. His heart shattered in his chest before those words even met his ears.*

*"Get out."*

*He broke, crying out into the shadows.*

*Black fire coursed over his body, pulsing out like bushfire over dry grass, encompassing the bed, overtaking the room. The scene shifted again as the fire dissipated. Falling to his knees, he clutched at his throat, unable to breathe, unable to speak.*

*"I told you!"*

*Her voice roared across the distance, his eyes frantically seeking her. She was his salvation. He needed her. He tried to scream for her, crawling over the stone beneath him trying to ignore the pain in his knees as he did so. Again, he was surrounded by smoke as it formed two figures before him. This time solid, with faces.*

*Marcus!*

*Lena!*

*He couldn't shout out for them like he wanted, the pressure around his throat preventing all speech.*

*"Lena, I–"*

*"Shut up!"*

*Her rage washed over him, knocking the last of the air from his lungs. Gasping uselessly, his vision narrowed as he stared in horror at the scene before him.*

*Lena's taloned hand descended through the air, slashing through Marcus' throat. Red lightning enveloped the kneeling man, tearing him apart, tearing the courtyard apart.*

*No!*

*No!*

"NO!" Cyrus' head reared back as he screamed into the room, the bind around his neck loosening again. Slumping in the chair, he drew in ragged breaths, the pure air burning his throat as he did so. Vision spinning, his head fell forward, his chest heaving with draining effort. "It's not real," he whispered to himself. "It's not real."

"Oh, I assure you, demon. It is very real."

Forcing his eyes to open he spied the toes of those obscene loafers. His stomach knotted, wanting to hurl its non-existence contents straight onto those damned shoes. *Fucking loafers.*

"Screw you, angel," he rasped, hating beyond belief how small and broken his voice sounded.

Raphael's hand fisted his hair, ripping his head back until their eyes met, causing the boundling to hiss through bared teeth. "How do I get into the compound?"

*Compound... it's our fucking home, dickhead!* "Like fuck I would ever tell you!"

"Your sister has killed your lover. Why protect her?"

"Because that wasn't fucking real, arsehole!"

The arch-angel snarled at him. It would have been funny under any other circumstance, seeing an angel of all beings try to be intimidating, but Cyrus was struggling to keep his bravado up. And Raphael was intimidating. Angels were warriors after all.

"Lena is not the only one with a conduit that can see through the various realities," the angel sneers at him, leaning down until their noses were almost touching. "We are counterparts after all. She painted the courtyard with his blood."

"She wouldn't."

"But she did."

"Liar," the boundling snapped, relishing the sight as bloody spittle sprayed over the angel.

Raphael recoiled, wiping roughly at his face. "Do you need to see it again to believe it?"

How many times had seen Marcus die? He'd lost count at this point. His mantra helped in the beginning but his belief in the words was failing. Kai, Zagan, Lena... Ambrose... they all ripped the cambion apart. His cambion. His nightmares had come to life and he couldn't escape them. Icy fingers dug into the far recesses of his mind, tearing down the walls he had hidden them behind, clawing at them as they were pulled forcefully to the surface.

The seed of Lena's power pulsed again within him, like she was trying to pull him to her. He had never prayed in his life, but he prayed for that. He prayed for her. The ache of his ribs lessened and he was able to draw in an almost full breath. Was she healing him through the bond? Could she? Was that even possible? Closing his eyes, he tried to focus on her power, trying to reach out to her.

She was there, he could feel it. Her presence traced over him like fingers skimming the surface of a pond. Barely there, yet enough to send ripples over his skin. With each touch something in him hurt less. Not healed. Shared.

Lena didn't kill Marcus. He was sure of it.

"Show me whatever you want, angel," he croaked, shaking his head slightly. "Lena would never kill Marcus. No matter what he fucking did."

"Last chance," Raphael said quietly as he crouched before the demon. "How do I get into the compound?"

"Fuck. You."

The angel's head cocked to the side, a cruel, twisted smile forming on his lips. "How about I show you what really happened to your parents?"

Cyrus chuckled, wincing as the movement jolted his broken ribs, molten pain coursing through his body. "I know what happened to them. It was an accident."

"An accident?" Raphael tapped his chin, a sinister gleam in his dark eyes. "No Cyrus, it was your fault. Your parents were arguing because you wouldn't stop crying. They didn't see that they veered into the wrong lane because they were trying to shut you up."

"So what?" he spluttered, coughing as bile burned the back of his nose. "I was two years old!"

Before he could even finish his sentence, Raphael's hand snapped out, wrapping around his throat, squeezing mercilessly. His eyes rolled back as darkness enveloped him, plunging him into memories he never wanted.

*A flash of light broke overhead, thunder rolling over his senses as he slammed his hands over his ears. Sirens broke through the buzzing in his brain, pulling his attention to the chaos before him. Silver and black metal mangled in the centre of a long stretch of road. White and blue police cars block off the area.*

*The scene spun and his body was pulled back into the memory. The metal reformed into the cars they used to be, reversing up the road like the scene was rewinding. In a flash of lightning, he blinked, finding himself sitting in the back of the silver car. Rain beat down against the car as it sped down the highway, light lining the side of the road flashing past with increasing pace. A baby cried in the car seat next to him.*

*Looking at the baby, he was struck by the dark blonde hair. Chocolate brown eyes darted frantically around the car, tears streaking down the flushed red cheeks.*

*"Cyrus, sweetheart," a woman cooed from the front seat. "Please sweetheart, shhh," she soothed, her hand reaching back to rub on the baby's stomach. "We're almost home, I promise."*

*He squeezed his eyes shut, not wanting to look at her. Not wanting to see her face. He'd seen pictures. That was all he needed. Not this. Not this fresh pain.*

*"Why won't he stop crying?" a male voice snapped, the car swerving slightly at the sharp irritation in the voice.*

*"He's a baby, George," the woman snapped back, her own annoyance sparking through the car, causing louder shrieks to come from the child.*

*"Well done, Amelia. You made it worse."*

*"At least, I'm trying!"*

*He couldn't take it. Peeling his eyes open he glanced to the front of the car, his breath catching in his throat as he took in the woman's features. His mother's features.*

*Dark brown hair fell across her sweetheart face, almost covering her chocolate eyes. His eyes. She was beautiful. Pictures didn't do her justice. There was a softness to her eyes that calmed his soul. Eased the pain rooted in his core.*

*He couldn't look away. His father was right there, but he didn't want to look. He wanted to soak in every line, every curve of her beautiful face.*

*"Mum," he said softly, but she didn't respond, her hand continuing to rub soothing circles on the baby's belly.*

*"It's alright, Cyrus," she breathed. "It's alright."*

*"Oh, for fuck's sake, shut him up!"*

*The spell was broken and his eyes snapped to his father, dark eyes filled with rage beneath blonde hair. The man reached back, his hand flying through the air towards the baby.*

*"No!" he screamed at the same time as his mother, his hands flying forward to grab at his father's wrist.*

*There was a screech of tyres. A horn sounded. Everything slowed as he watched, devastation creeping in as the lights of an oncoming car pierced through the front window. He launched forward, stumbling as he found himself standing once again on the road, watching the two cars essentially meld together.*

*He couldn't move, couldn't breathe. The pressure in his skull brought him to his knees as the baby's cries broke through the blaring horn. Lightning flashed in the sky as if the heavens were aware of what had happened. As if they cared for the loss of life. The loss of family.*

*Ripping at his hair, he could only watch as, finally, police cars raced to the scene. Bodies moved around the two cars, frantic and loud. Shouts between them echoed over the expanse of the road as they tried to reach the baby. The only sound of life coming from the carnage.*

*"No!" he screamed, his body caving in on itself as he sobbed into the night. "It's not my fault! It's not my fault!"*

*A taloned hand caught him around the back of his neck, pulling him to his feet before crashing him forward into coarse rock. Darkness pressed into him, those sharp talons digging into his flesh as fear threatened to drown him.*

*"It is your fault," a voice whispered in his ear. That voice... no, please... "It's always your fault. Your parents died because of you. Lena was taken by Zagan because of you. She is hurting now because of you. I left because of you."*

*A choking sob left him as the scent of burnt sugar washed over him. Not this. Not him. Black and silver-grey wings encompassed him, their talons digging into the rock above him, showering him with the small shards.*

*Fear ripped through him as the talons at his neck sunk into his flesh, a similar pain at his hip, tearing at him, pulling him apart.*

*"You are worthless," Marcus whispered. "You are nothing. This is all you are good for. This is all I wanted you for. All anyone wanted you for."*

*He felt the sting fire up his spine as his body was slammed into the wall repeatedly, a steady rhythm that only caused pain. He couldn't breathe again. There was nothing. No air, no light, no peace for him to cling to. The rock tore through the skin on his fingers, his blood coating the sharp surface.*

Something snapped. Or banged? Exploded. He wasn't sure. The grip on his throat was unrelenting but the images faded. There was shouting. Footfalls echoed around him, but he didn't know why. He couldn't even acknowledge the pain he was in as his body slumped in the chair, his head raised only by the hand beneath it.

He was frozen in fear, unable to fight, unable to move. Because Marcus was right. Zagan had been right. There was nothing special about him. He was worthless. He was the reason everyone left. No one fought for him. Even when he and Lena escaped Zagan last year, demons fought to protect her. Protecting him was only an extension of protecting her. She was what was important. Not him. He wasn't important to anyone.

His father was going to hurt him because he was crying. His aunt refused treatment, wanting to die more than wanting to take care of him. Brody let him go into foster care. Marcus...

*Marcus...*

And now Lena would leave him. She would leave him here to die. Because that was easier than fighting for him. He wondered dimly if she could feel his pain.

Some distant thought fought its way to the surface. She could feel his pain. He knew that. Her rage had touched him briefly. Her power had taken some of his pain away. She was taking on his pain.

*No!*

He screamed in his mind, shouting his sister's name, begging her for relief.

*Go to Hell!* he cried. *Go to Hell! Please! Let me die...*

Her voice barely pierced through the darkness descending over him, broken and distant, as if trying to reach him from across a vast canyon.

*Cy... rus... we're com– hol– on...*

His vision faded as the hand around his throat tightened. He welcomed the darkness, wanting to sink into its comfort. As the shadows began to greet him, Raphael's fingers flexed, letting a sliver of air pass into his lungs, pushing them back.

*No, please... I want to die...*

But there was something... Something that called to him, like a beacon trying to pull his attention. Letting the feeling settle, he rolled his eyes to the far side of the room, darkness seeping into the light of the walls. The roaring cry jarred his mind, causing his body to flinch as his eyes shut, the heavy strain of his broken form finally overwhelming him.

"CYRUS!"

*That voice...*

His name cut through the raging thoughts of his mind, trying desperately to pull him back from the darkness. To pull him back to centre. But like so many times before, it wasn't real. It couldn't be real.

*He* wasn't coming.

No one was coming. Not for him.

The sounds grew louder, a loud bang forcing its way through his body, vibrating his very being despite the burning in his chest. There was someone else in the room. A presence that pulled him forwards like a magnet. Something... *familiar.*

He strained to open his eyes, his vision blurred as he took in the dark shadow by the door. The power emanating from it was terrifying. All-encompassing and furious, pulsing against the light around it. After everything he should be scared. But he wasn't. He'd never been afraid of that looming shadow.

A final sound reached his ears even as he drowned in darkness.

"Get away from him!"

# CHAPTER THIRTY-SEVEN

The air within the house was tense. So unbelievably tense.

Tension that held everyone on the end of a fraying piece of string, waiting for the final thread to snap.

Just over a day had passed since Cyrus had been taken and Marcus was more than ready to get him back.

Lena was barely keeping it together. New bruises formed on all parts of her body as she pulled more and more of the damage being done to the boundling through their bond. She could ease his pain, but she couldn't heal him. She couldn't stop the turmoil of his thoughts or the darkness slowly pulling apart his mind. Healing her own body from the aftermath was becoming exhausting. Even her instinctual ability was having difficulty keeping up.

Marcus was sure he cracked a few teeth when her latest scream ripped through the courtyard.

Ambrose held her close as they sat under the canopy, his usual bright hazel eyes darkened with his own torment seeing her like this. After a few minutes of pacing, Marcus joined them, clutching her hand tightly in his in some broken hope that the comfort of it might feedback to Cyrus. But it wouldn't. That wasn't how a bond worked. But maybe...

All eyes turned to the centre of the courtyard as Henry appeared in a flourish of flames, clutching a black feather in his hands. Abaddon stood at his side, a worried expression on her face as she looked at Lena, taking in the damage being done. As their flames disappeared the feather began to change, shifting with a light that cast long shadows over the tiles and flowerbeds. Flowing from the centre, each strand of the feather slowly turned white, the black seemingly melting away, like ink under a drop of water.

"Bring it here," Lena croaked, forcing her body to straighten.

Henry rushed over to her, placing the feather reverently in her outstretched palm. Slowly, she stoked down the centre stem of the feather, languid strands of plasma wrapping around the surface, intricately weaving and knitting together. Soon, the centre glowed red, illuminating the now completely white barbs.

"Everyone ready?" she asked, as she struggled to her feet, Ambrose and Marcus holding either elbow. Abaddon rushed over with a powerful beat of her large black wings, taking over from the cambion, immediately pouring her power over Lena's back, trying to help ease the pain.

"I'm going with them."

Marcus' and Lena's eyes shot to the Consort, shock prevalent on both their faces.

"Ambro–"

"Lena," he cut her off with a stern look. "I'm not letting Marcus go without me. He helped me get you back last year. I'm going to help him get Cyrus. Not only that but Cyrus is our family. And I can't just sit here watching…" His voice trailed off as he looked away ashamed. The words didn't need to be said. "I will stay if you ask. I will always stay with you. But I want to help alleviate your pain. And I can only do that by helping to save Cyrus."

Gently, Lena reached up and cupped his cheek, pulling his gaze back to her. He leant into her touch, a tortured sigh leaving him. "I can't share my power anymore. I don't have enough to give you. Abaddon?"

"Not without affecting his connection to your council," the other Prince said softly, shaking her head. "Apologies sister. Even the Princes have limitations."

"He can stay close to me," Archie spoke up, stepping forward. "All respect Lena, but Ambrose can take care of himself and he may see something the rest of us don't. And he's a healer. May be the difference between all or only some of us coming back."

Marcus chewed the inside of his cheek, blinking against the flow of tears that suddenly welled in his eyes. For so long he had welcomed the safety of isolation. Letting Ambrose in, becoming his friend, had been his only solace from crippling loneliness. But now, seeing the way the council, his friends, his family banded together to save Cyrus, to help him, was more than he could have ever hoped for.

"Let me go, too."

His gaze snapped to Balo as the boundling stepped forward.

Damien growled from his position, moving swiftly to grab Balo by the shoulder, tugging him back. "Not happening."

"Damien, I like Cyrus. Hell, I'd even consider him a friend now. And besides, the more demons you have with you the better chance you'll have in getting him back." Shrugging off the cambion's hold, Balo moved closer to canopy, squaring his shoulders as he did so. "Prince Lena, please. Let me go with them. If Ambrose sticks with Archie, I'll stay close to Damien. Or Marcus if you'd prefer. Please, just let me help."

The courtyard was silent for a moment. It wasn't long, but long enough for Marcus to shift on the spot, desperate to get underway, but calm enough to wait for the order.

And he was calm, or at least his mind was. Settled into the bloodlust, it waited patiently for the first kill. His body vibrated in anticipation, knowing the wait would be worth the reward. As long as that reward was combined with the return of Cyrus to his arms.

"Marcus." Lena's voice pulled him from his thoughts and he straightened, turning to look at her. "Take the cuff off." With a curt nod he strode quickly to Balo, grabbing at the cuff roughly, pouring his power through the runes waiting for the leather to respond. "Damien, if you get Cyrus back," Lena continued, "we'll talk, *really* talk, about returning Balo to you and bringing you in, properly, to the inner circle."

Marcus didn't miss how the other cambion squared his shoulders at the promise, now given a personal reason to help.

The leather of the cuff finally loosened and Marcus slipped it from the boundling's wrist. "Stay close to Damien," he growled, stepping back as Damien moved to stand beside them. "I'm getting to Cyrus one way or another and I don't need you under my feet."

Balo stiffened at the underhanded insult but simply nodded. "Fine by me."

Lena sighed, wincing as she clutched at her temple. Ambrose rubbed her back for a moment before she waved him off, directing him and the others into a formation at the centre of the courtyard.

"Please try not to kill each other in the process," she said as forcefully as she could, considering her current state. "I would prefer *all* of you get back. I can't go to Heaven, so once you're there, you're on your own. I've divided my power as much as I can. Take these." She came to stand before each of them, placing a crystal in their hands. "Smash these to come home." Lingering in front of Marcus, she gently closed his fingers around the crystal. "You can't kill Raphael as much as I know you will want to."

Her voice was soft, like she was scared of his reaction at the statement. Furrowing his brow, he dipped his head, trying to encourage her to look at him. "Why?"

"Rules of the game, unfortunately," she said with a shrug. Finally looking at him, Marcus realised she wasn't afraid, but saddened by the need to tell him. "He and I must survive to the Apocalypse."

Leaning down, he pressed a reverent kiss to her knuckles, acknowledging the command. "I can still hurt him, right?" he whispered, moving back with a sinister smirk on his lips.

Lena smiled and nodded. "That you can."

With everyone in position, the demons transformed, a mix of black, grey and red skin shining in the afternoon desert sun. Lena moved towards them, holding Lucifer's feather in her hands.

"The longer you are in Heaven, the harder it will be to retain your demonic forms," she explained, her lightning lifting the feather to float in the middle of the group as she stepped back towards Henry. Stumbling back, Abaddon caught her, encasing her sister in her purple tendrils, gently tracing over the bruises on Lena's skin, healing what she could.

"I cannot stay up here for long. I am not made to walk on Earth. Not yet," the Prince of Sloth said pointedly. "So, try to be quick. And be ready for anything. Good luck."

With that, Abaddon threw a dart of her power towards the feather, shattering it. Light encompassed the five demons, pulling them into Heaven.

Marcus clamped his hands over his ears, his horns seeming to vibrate against his skull, a blaring alarm jarring through his brain. Glancing around him, he saw Ambrose and Archie in a similar position. Damien and Balo behind him.

"Think they know we're here?" Archie shouted over the alarm, a cruel sneer forming on his lips, wings thrashing out behind him.

Marcus barked a laugh, his senses quickly adjusting to accommodate the sound. Gathering his smoke, he blasted it out like a wave, easily passing over the other demons as it rippled down the corridor they had arrived in. The alarm died, replaced by cracks of power as his smoke smothered the detection systems. It wouldn't last long, but at least they could hear again.

Taking the reprieve to study their surroundings, Marcus narrowed his eyes against the glaring light that seemed to emanate from every surface. The floor, walls and ceiling of the corridor almost seemed like they weren't there. Swirling masses of light and mist that looked trapped behind glass without reflections. *Clean.* Everything was so clean. And bright. It gave him a headache.

"Are we sure this isn't Hell?" Damien chuckled, rubbing the back of his hand over his eyes. "This is a literal eyesore."

"They're coming," Ambrose said, drawing their attention towards his end of the corridor.

Turning his head, Marcus heard footsteps from the other direction as well. "They're surrounding us."

"More the merrier, I say," Archie growled, stepping closer to the Consort as they flanked the sides of the walkway.

Damien cracked his neck as he and Balo took up position behind them. "We'll need to keep one alive to find out where Cyrus is."

Grinding his jaw, Marcus allowed an annoyed rumble to vibrate through his chest, his fingers flexing by his sides. "Someone else will have to take care of that. I'm killing any angel I see."

He heard one of the others say something, but he wasn't listening as the first of the angels rounded the corner, gleaming armour over their bodies, their feathered wings beating behind them.

*How cute,* he thought to himself, *they think armour will protect them.*

In an instant, all five demons threw concentrated forms of their power at the angels, red, blue, black and gold auras intermingling through the air. The angels threw up shields of light, only fragmented shards of power breaking past to rebound off the armour. Maybe it wasn't entirely useless.

His vision flushed with red, Marcus roared as he beat his wings, charging forward to clash with the nearest angel. The scent of fear reached his nose as his taloned hand pushed the shield aside with ease. Black smoke swirled around him, grabbing at the angel's wrist and arm, constricting around the armour plating. The angel screamed, the metal crushing against his flesh, wings shuddering behind him in pain. Marcus felt someone at his back, an arm wrapped around his throat, pulling as if they had a chance at breaking him away from his current victim.

Twisting his body, his wing beat against the one behind him, the barbed talon ripping through the flesh of the angel's face. Shifting back to the one before him, his closed his hand around the angel's throat, digging his claws in before ripping back. With his smoke holding the angel in place, his neck tore with ease, blood spraying over Marcus' chest, the warmth fuelling his bloodlust.

The angel fell to his knees, clutching his throat as Marcus rounded on the one at his back. A feminine face stared at him in horror, but he didn't have capacity to care as he slashed at her chest armour. She recovered quickly from her shock, pulling up a shield of light before her, a radiant lance in her other hand. He caught the lance as it swung towards him, ignoring how it burned against his palm as he ripped it from her grasp. Marcus' claws dragged uselessly over the surface of the shield, but his smoke curled and covered the surface, crushing it against the angel's hand with a satisfying crack.

Her scream ripped through the air as he stepped forward, punching out with his fist and power, slamming into the centre of her chest, caving the armour plating as she hurtled into the wall behind them. She slumped to the floor, cradling her hand, white light emanating from it in a way that he could only assume was trying to heal her. Not giving her a moment to recover, he raced forward, gripping the sides of her jaw, planting his foot on her hip pressed into the floor and jerked her head to the side. The snap of her neck was harmonious to his ears as her flesh tore and her head rolled to a stop beside her body.

Taking a moment to look around him, he took note of his companions. Blood splattered the walls and floor already, the light within illuminating the ruby colouring covering them. Damien and Balo subdued the two angels flanking them, with the boundling essentially cooking an angel as his lava oozed from his fingers coating the angelic armour in its molten heat. Ambrose had taken a spear to his shoulder, but the scrape over his flesh did not hinder him as he threw darts of his red tendrils through the air, two embedding themselves in the eyes of the angel charging him. Archie's hands were encompassed with his blue fire as he clasped an angel's face firmly between them, the screams and sizzling flesh echoing through the corridor.

"There'll be more soon," Ambrose snarled, kicking the now lifeless angel away from him. As he did so, bright light enveloped each fallen angel, forcing the demons to shield their eyes. Surveying the result after the light receded, there was no evidence of the recent struggle, except for what remained on the five demons. "Well, how about that," the Consort almost chuckled. "Easiest clean up ever."

Damien wiped his arm over his brow, attempting to clear the blood from his eyes. "So much for leaving one alive. Which way?"

Marcus shut his eyes, breathing steadily through his nose as he focused on Lena's power. He felt Archie and Ambrose, turning his face to them momentarily to centre himself. There was a faint pulse coming from his left.

*Cyrus.*

"This way," he growled, turning swiftly and heading down the corridor.

"Can you sense him?" Ambrose asked, staying close to his side.

The cambion nodded grimly. "It's faint, but he's here."

"What's faint?" Balo was panting as he came up on the other side, Damien close behind him. It seemed the boundling was already struggling with the pressures of heavenly power on his form.

"Lena's power," the Consort explained. "A Prince's council are connected. We can sense each other."

"Like boundlings," Damien chuckled as they rounded a corner.

Archie barked a laughed. "Not the first time that joke's been made."

The laughter quickly died as the five demons dove to the floor, a blinding wave of light passing over them. Archie hissed as the tips of his wings connected with the power, searing the flesh, quickly pulling them tightly against his back.

"Fuck!" he spat, shuddering as he pushed to his knees. "Screw being tall."

Spinning on his knees, Ambrose rounded to Archie's back, trailing his hands over the burnt flesh, strands of his power licking over the wounds, healing quickly. The others sprang around them, forming a barrier with their powers. Marcus' smoke swirled around them as Damien fed in his flames to create an inferno protecting the Consort as he worked.

Shrouded behind their power, Marcus could feel, and intermittently see sharp spikes of light bound off in broken shards, trying to find a weakness that he would not give them. His fury fed his power, building its mass until his power core began to throb in his chest, stretched to its limits but desperate to carry on.

Archie grunted between them, forcing himself to his feet and stepping closer to the cambion. "We need to separate," he shouted over the raging fire and smoke. "Create a distraction to give you time to get to Cyrus."

"Balo and I can take the ones behind us," Damien yelled, sweat pooling off his brow as his own limits were tested. "Force them away from here."

Marcus nodded over his shoulder. "As soon as you're clear, use the crystal. Don't get yourself killed."

The other cambion laughed as Balo stepped up next to him, feeding his own power into their cover, alleviating the strain on Damien. "Feel like I should be saying that to you!"

"I wouldn't listen anyway," Marcus grinned, pushing a final pulse out. "On three!"

Covering his body in flames, Archie stepped in front of Marcus, wings beating out behind him despite the only partially healed skin. The cambion felt Ambrose at his back, waves of his red power licking out at the air around them. Counting down, Marcus braced himself. They would surge forward together until he could find a moment to veer off.

Breaking the cover, the demons took off in their formations, cutting through the angels around them. Shining arrows of power flew towards them, radiating heat against their skin as they dodged the luminous attacks. Not daring to chance looking back, Marcus could only trust that Damien and Balo could take care of themselves. With him and Archie flanking the Consort, they drove forward, blue fire and black smoke mixing in pulsating orbs of power, colliding with the angels' chest plates, pushing them back.

Ducking to the side, narrowly avoiding a sharpened spike of angelic power, Marcus stared horrified as his companions were not so fortunate. Archie fell forward, pure light slicing through his side, leaving a large gaping wound beneath his ribs. Dark red blood poured from the opening as an expelling gasp left the demon.

"No!" he cried, sliding to his knees and grabbing the demonic-trainer by the shoulders, stopping him from crashing into the ground.

Red tendrils whipped out across the floor like snakes, wrapping around the ankles of the two angels closest to them. With a roar, Ambrose pulled them up into the air, his fist clenching, the snap of bones ringing through the corridor as he flung his victims back into the angels behind them.

Gritting his teeth, Marcus pushed his smoke out of every pore, blasting it out around him and the other demons, shielding them within.

"Don't you dare, Archie. I still have to beat your arse for your comments about Cyrus," he gritted out, clutching his friend to him.

"I didn't mean any of it, friend," Archie smiled weakly, grabbing his wounded side. "Just wanted you to admit how you felt about him..."

Ambrose fell to his knees beside them, quickly taking Archie's weight from the cambion. Holding his hand over the wound, the Consort attempted to heal it, even as small sparks of light fought against him.

"He needs Lena," Ambrose growled, cradling the demon against him as Archie's breathing grew shallow.

Rising to his feet, Marcus clenched his fists, stepping away from them. "Take him back."

"What?"

"Go," he snapped, turning to head back into the awaiting battle.

"Marcus, stop!" the Consort shouted, reaching out for him.

Shaking him off, the cambion snarled his frustration even as he immediately regretted the words. "You wouldn't stop if it was Lena."

"Dammit, Marcus!"

Before he could react, he felt Ambrose's power wrap around his leg, ripping it from under him. Crashing to the ground, he managed to catch himself on his hands, quickly spinning on his knees, his wings raised menacingly behind him.

"The fuck was that?"

"I'm not going to stop you," Ambrose snapped at him, "just take a fucking second to assess the situation. We're cut off from Damien and Balo. Archie is hurt and we're fucking surrounded. Think it through for a fucking moment!"

He had thought it through and he was done playing games. He had one goal and working around others was holding him back from reaching it. But he wasn't stupid enough to ignore what his friend was trying to impress upon him. Taking a deep breath, he pushed up onto his feet.

"Take Archie and head back."

"Marcus?" the Consort looked up at him uncertainly, but the cambion knew he wasn't going to argue further.

"I mean it, Ambrose," he said with a firm shake of his head. "I won't risk you or Archie. Go back."

Ambrose nodded, pulling the demonic-trainer closer to him as he fished the crystal out of the band of his trousers. "What about you?"

Stepping towards them, Marcus knelt beside his friends, clasping both their shoulders in parting. "Either I'm leaving here with Cyrus or I'm not leaving," he said softly, resting his forehead against Ambrose's. "I'm sorry, my friend. But I won't go through losing him for good."

The Consort nodded in understanding, gripping his elbow firmly. "Good luck, my friend."

Moving away, Marcus turned back towards the barrier of his smoke, listening as Ambrose crushed the crystal beneath his palm, the crackling of power pulling the Consort and trainer away from Heaven. Closing his eyes for a moment, the cambion searched his surroundings, reaching out for Cyrus. The hum of Lena's power had dimmed further, barely there as he tried to hold onto it.

Rage building within him, he squared his shoulders, snapping his power back into his body in an instant. The shouts of angels filled his ears, storming towards him as he stood his ground. Waiting for the opportune moment, he tracked the movements of five angels surrounding him. Seeing his opening, he punched out, enveloping the angels completely in smoke holding them immobilised as he closed his eyes and probed with his power along their armour, looking for a weakness.

The armour was near perfect, each seam sewn together with angelic light, malleable yet unyielding to his power, refusing to break. Even around the opening of the face, light emanated around the edge refusing his smoke passage beneath. But like water, his smoke was unrelenting, gliding over the surface of the armour, feeling every rise and fall. With a breath, he found his mark, a small gap beneath the arms, where the light stretched so thin it broke under the pressure of his power.

Smoke delving beneath the plating, Marcus' eyes snapped opened, sharpened points digging into each chest, piercing through the angels' hearts, wrapping them in darkness and squeezing until they burst. There were no screams, no cries of terror or pain. The angels slumped within his hold as he lowered them silently to the floor.

Racing forward, he cleared the bodies as light began to take them, rounding the corridor to the point he felt the last pulse of Lena's power. He was waylaid by a door, locked and refusing to open as he gripped the handles. Taking a moment, he traced his palm over the surface, trying to feel for what lay beyond. Reeling back, he ground his jaw, concentrating his power and slamming it against the surface, watching intently as it began to buckle. His love was within and he wouldn't let a door stand in his way.

"CYRUS!" he shouted, pouring as much power as he could summon through his body and out against the door.

The shifting surface cracked, crumbling to his intent as it swung inwards with a percussive force, baring the room beyond to his eyes. His stomach dropped to the floor as he took in the boundling's broken form, tied to a chair, Raphael's hand wrapped around his neck.

# CHAPTER THIRTY-EIGHT

"Get away from him!" Marcus roared.

"Or what, demon?" Raphael spat, eyes narrowed in disgust, his hand still clamped around Cyrus' throat. "What will you do? You are nothing compared to me. Even with your Prince's power which you have wasted."

Marcus felt it as soon as he stepped past the threshold into the room. His power seemed to just... vanish. It hurt to maintain his demonic form, but he fought against the pain, refusing to lose his advantage. So, that was why Cyrus wasn't healing.

Snarling, he stepped back into the hall, his eyes never leaving the arch-angel.

"That's right, half-breed," Raphael sneered, his fingers curling tightly around the boundling's throat. "You can't do shit to me in here."

Outside of the room, Marcus felt his power return, the pain within his limbs eased. Lena's seed of power pulsed angrily within him. He realised everyone must have made it back to the house and she had diverted all her power to him. Smirking at the knowledge, he placed his palm flat on the surface by the door.

Smoke sped from his fingers, quickly encompassing the outside wall, seeping into the spells and wards within. His power smashed through the barriers like glass until he held the entire room within his grasp. Relishing the sight as Raphael's eyes widened with horror, Marcus squeezed, the floor shuddering under the force, cracks running along the shifting walls, light and smoke pouring out in waves.

A deafening bang echoed as every surface exploded into the room, shards of power raining down on the two occupants. At last, Raphael let go of Cyrus, raising his arms to shield himself from the onslaught. Beating his wings, Marcus surged forward, slamming into the arch-angel with such force, he felt his own spine compress.

The angel recovered quickly, light emanating from his being as his wings thrashed around him. A blow landed on the side of Marcus' face even as the cambion found his footing, sinking his own fist into Raphael's stomach, an explosion of smoke forcing space between them. Pain radiated down his neck, but it didn't matter. Nothing mattered but keeping the angel away from Cyrus.

Glancing over his shoulder, he spied the slumped form of the boundling in the chair. He hadn't moved. His chest was barely rising with each small breath. Turning back to the angel, Marcus shook his head slightly. He had to focus.

Pulling what was left of Lena's power within him, Marcus covered his body in smoke, his aura pulsing menacingly against the light around them. Raphael looked panicked, stepping back slightly as he took in the expanding form of the cambion.

"You can't," the arch-angel breathed, backing up against the wall, the haemorrhaging power washing over his shoulders. "This isn't possible."

Marcus snarled, his talons itching to rip through the angel's throat. "I know the laws of the Apocalypse. I know your death should only come at Lena's hands. So, this is your only warning, Raphael." Stepping forward, he ducked as a spear of light aimed for his head, missing him by an inch. The radiant heat burned over his skin, but he ignored it, punching out with his power. Smoke enveloped the arch-angel, wrapping tightly around Raphael's neck. Desperate hands clawed at the bind giving Marcus untold pleasure as he closed the distance between them. "You can leave now or I *will* kill you. Consequences be damned."

Releasing his power, Marcus grabbed Raphael's neck with his own hand, slamming the angel back against the wall. The angel clawed at his arm, trying to push him away. But it was no use. The cambion was fuelled by rage, by his need to remove the threat to Cyrus. He would endure anything to accomplish that.

"Fine," Raphael gasped, flailing in Marcus' hold. "Fine!" Letting go, the arch-angel slumped, rubbing his throat, hate glaring from his eyes. "Take the abomination and leave, half-breed. But this is my warning to you. Come here again, go near my daughter again, and I'll do worse than hurt a fucking boundling."

"*That* boundling," Marcus snarled, stepping closer, "is worth more than any angel in Heaven."

"And yet, you broke him so easily."

Roaring as his fist swung through the air, his blow landed on the wall, punching through the shimmering pulse that Raphael disappeared into. His mind pulling back to the moment, he spun on his heel, running to Cyrus. Falling to his knees, he took the boundling's face between his hands, his eyes wide as he took in the damage done to him.

Every part of the young demon's body was covered in bruises. Harsh red marks against his lightly tanned skin, deepening to pools of mottled purple where blood pooled beneath. Marcus' throat closed as he took in the broken collarbone and dislocated shoulder. Forcing himself to breathe, to calm the renewed fury ripping through him at the sight, he tenderly stroked the dark blonde hair.

"Cyrus," he called to him, "Cyrus, wake up." Brown eyes fluttered open briefly, as they tried to focus on the scene before him.

"Marcus?" the demon croaked, his voice barely audible.

"I'm here, Cyrus," Marcus assured him. "I'm here."

Working quickly, he slashed at the bindings on Cyrus' wrists and ankles, pulling him from the chair and into his arms.

"Ah!" Cyrus cried, his body convulsing with pain.

"I'm sorry," he said quickly. "I'm sorry."

"Is it really you?"

"Yes, it's me," he answered, cupping the gorgeous face with one hand, the other hooked under his shoulders. "I'm really here, baby. I'm taking you home."

"No, you can't," the boundling said panicked, his hand shooting out and grabbing at Marcus' vest, his entire being flinching against the sudden movement.

"Shh," he soothed. "It's alright now. I've got you, you're safe."

"No," Cyrus shook his head feverishly. "No, please. You'll die. You always die. I can't see that again. I can't lose you again. No more, please. Please, just let me die."

"Cyrus, listen to me," Marcus said softly, rubbing his thumb over the young demon's cheek. "That wasn't real. None of that was real. I promise you, nothing is going to happen to you or me. Lena's waiting to heal you."

"Marcus... I..." Cyrus' voice faded as his eyes unfocused. To his horror, the cambion watched as those brown eyes closed and his hand fell limply to his side.

"Cyrus!" he cried, shaking the boundling slightly. "Please, no!" Quickly, he smashed the crystal against the floor, cursing even his small delay, transporting them to the courtyard where Lena and Ambrose were waiting for them. "Come on, baby, please, open your eyes. Cyrus!"

Lena ran over to him, falling to her knees beside the men. "Marcus, quickly, give him to me," she said gently, placing a soft hand on his back. "He's not dead, but he is dying."

Marcus looked up at her, a pained expression on his face. Her grey eyes were so gentle and warm, he had to have faith in her. In her strength, because his faith in his own vanished. "Lena..." he breathed, "please, don't let him die."

She smiled softly and moved her hands to grasp just underneath Cyrus' shoulders. "Give him to me."

Carefully, he lifted the boundling into Lena's arms, shifting back as he felt Ambrose's hands on his shoulders, pulling him to his feet.

"It's alright, Marcus," Ambrose assured him. "Come on."

He allowed the Consort to pull him away, his demonic form slowly receding, feelings of hopelessness and despair robbing him of his power to fight. He could only watch silently as Lena pulled Cyrus' lifeless body closer to her, pressing her cheek against his, her lightning enveloping them. The red glow of her power flashed across the courtyard, highlighting the space with a sinister yet awesome aura. Archie stood in a doorway, looking on as Lena fought to heal her boundling, holding the side where he had been wounded.

"Is Archie..." Marcus asked quietly, turning his head to Ambrose.

"He's fine," his friend nodded. "Lena has already healed him, but angel powers leave residual pain. Damien and Balo made it back too, a little worse for wear, but nothing detrimental."

Turning back to Lena and Cyrus, he tried to swallow the feeling of dread rising in him.

"Why is it taking so long?" he snapped at no one in particular.

"I don't know," Ambrose answered, placing a comforting hand on his back. "Lena said the damage is severe. It may just take a while. Trust in her, Marcus. She has him now. She won't let him die."

The lightning enveloping the sire and boundling branched out, arcing towards the ground and walls. No damage was left on contact, seeking only to offload latent energy from the process within its centre. Slowly, the lightning subsided, withdrawing back inside its creator. Marcus took a step forward, seeing that Cyrus' body was cleared of all damage done to it by the angels. He was healed, he was safe. So why didn't the tension in his chest ease?

"Why isn't he waking?" he asked, noting that no movement returned to Cyrus' body. Even his breathing had stopped. Falling to his knees beside Lena, Marcus touched his fingers to Cyrus' cheek, trying to feel some form of life from the young demon.

Lena shook her head sadly. "They broke his mind," she whispered. "He may not want to wake."

"No!"

Marcus grabbed for the boundling, pulling him from Lena and pressing him against his chest. Lena did not resist in any way, helping to support Cyrus' head as the cambion wrapped his arms around the lean frame.

"Marcus," Lena sobbed, her own grief sounding in her voice. "I'm sorry. I cannot heal his mind. Only he can do that."

Burying his face in Cyrus' neck, Marcus shook his head in denial. He'd fought against his feelings for too long to give up now. The young demon had been so patient, so willing to be with him and he had forced him away. He had forced the boundling to lie that there was someone else, simply because he needed to be released from Marcus' callous and constant rejection of him. And he had been too selfish to care. Seeing Cyrus' gorgeous body broken and abused had torn at his heart, pulling out his stark realisation that never again would he allow those events to repeat. Cyrus was his. His to protect, his to love. All the boundling wanted was his love, and Marcus would give it, endlessly, if it meant that he would stay.

Raising his head, he looked down at Cyrus' beautiful face, his Adonis-like features still managing to take what little breath he had left from him. From the corner of his eye, he saw Lena get up from the ground and move towards Ambrose, covering her face with her hands. He knew her grief would mirror his own, but he had no capacity to console her. Gently he pressed a soft kiss to those full lips, lingering on the perfectly upturned top lip.

"Cyrus, listen to me," he whispered against his mouth. "It's you. It's fucking you! You are the only one I will ever want. I belong with you, I belong to you. I look at you and I know you are all that is good with me. You are the only thing that matters to me now. I need you to the point where I don't know how I will exist without you in my life. I know I pushed you away, but I was wrong. I was so wrong. I spent my entire life, my entire existence, hoping to find someone like you. So don't you think for a second, that I would ever give up on you. Not today. Not tomorrow. Not for the rest of our fucking lives whatever they may be. So don't you dare give up on me now!" Cupping the back of his head, Marcus pulled Cyrus against him, falling back to the ground, desperately holding onto the young demon who held his heart. "Please, come back to me," he begged, whispering into the boundling's ear. "Please. I love you."

Cyrus' body rested limply against his own as he rocked on the ground, cradling his love in his arms. A strangled cry pulled from his throat as he buried his face into the slender neck, breathing in the smokey-leather scent, praying to anyone who might listen to bring Cyrus back to him. He would pray all night if he had to. Nothing in Hell, Heaven or Earth could make him let go.

"Marcus?"

His breath caught in his throat, his heart racing, as he heard that soft voice in his ear. Barely daring to believe it was real, Marcus raised his head to stare at Cyrus' face. Those beautiful brown eyes were open, hooded in a daze, but open. A touch of pink flushed his cheeks, matching the soft lips that parted with confusion.

"Cyrus, I'm here," he whispered, stroking his thumb across Cyrus' cheek, staring into his eyes. "I'm here, gorgeous. And I'm never letting go."

"I'd ask if this is Heaven, but well, there'd be more pain."

Marcus chuckled slightly, relief washing over him as Cyrus smiled at him. "Too soon, my love. Too soon," he breathed, the fresh memories of seeing the demon's broken body unsettling his stomach.

"Love?" the boundling asked, his eyes widening.

"Yes," he nodded. "I love you, Cyrus. I love you so much."

With that, Marcus brushed their lips together, ignoring the shock on the gorgeous face. They could talk later. Right now, he needed to feel the young demon, to reassure himself that he was safe.

"Cyrus!" Lena cried racing forward as she crashed into the men, gathering them both into her embrace. "Thank all that is, you've come back to us!"

Twisting away from Marcus, Cyrus wrapped his arms around Lena, holding her close to him. The cambion removed himself from their reunion. There would be time later for him and Cyrus. He knew that the boundling needed his sister and sire now, more than ever.

"Lena," the boundling sighed. "I'm sorry. I'm so sorry. I didn't tell them anything, I swear."

"Hush," Lena soothed, tightening her embrace. "I know. It's alright." She pulled back and cupped her brother's face tenderly between her hands. "You are safe now. We'll need to talk later, but for now you need to rest."

"No," he shook his head. "I don't want to rest."

"Cyrus, please," she pleaded with him. "I've healed your body, but what they did to you will resurface if you push yourself. Even Archie cannot transform at the moment and he took much less damage than you. Do not make me compel you." Cyrus let his gaze drop, as he leant forward, resting his head on her shoulder, surrendering to her request. "Rest now," she repeated, placing a tender kiss to his temple. "Later, when you're feeling up to it, we will go speak with the other Princes."

With a heavy sigh, Cyrus tried to get to his feet, but the trials he had endured caught up with him as his legs proved too weak to hold him. Lena caught him even as Marcus rushed over, grabbing one of the boundling's arms and bringing it over his shoulder.

"Let me help," he said softly, raising Cyrus from the ground and supporting his weight.

The young demon looked at him hesitantly from the corner of his eye but made no protest as Marcus led them in to the house. Heading for Cyrus' room, Marcus helped him inside and gently laid him on the bed. The boundling watched him silently the whole time as the cambion pulled back the covers and tenderly laid them over the lean frame. With a sigh, he sat on the edge of the bed and took hold of the young demon's hand, rubbing it between his own, his fingers brushing along the base of his bindings. He could feel Cyrus' gaze boring into him, but found he was unable to meet it yet.

Everything he wanted to say to the demon suddenly eluded him, unsure of where to start. Taking a deep breath, he forced himself to speak, figuring it was better to start anywhere than not at all.

"I'm sorry, Cyrus," he said softly. "I'm sorry for everything I have put you through. For every cruel thing I said to you. I'm sorry for pushing you away. I wa—"

"Infernal."

Marcus snapped his head up, caught off guard by the pained look on the boundling's face, guilt racking his body. The young demon shut his eyes, drawing in a shuddering breath as he slowly pulled his hand from Marcus' hold.

"Cyrus?"

The boundling stayed silent, his eyes still closed, unmoving on the bed. Dread washed over the older demon, settling in his stomach as he watched the thoughts in Cyrus' mind play out over his gorgeous face.

After what seemed like an age, Cyrus opened his eyes, but wouldn't meet his gaze, simply staring at his hands folded on top of the covers.

"I can't do this, Marcus," he said finally. "Not now. My mind is..." The heavy sigh that left the boundling tore at the cambion's heart. It was a sound of defeat, of pain and heartache. Cyrus scrubbed a hand over his face, shaking his head slightly. "I don't even know how long it's been since I was taken."

"Just under two days," Marcus answered even though it hadn't been a question.

The young demon huffed, pressing his lips together in a hard line. "I'm broken, Marcus. Please just go. Don't break me further."

His throat constricted, unable to draw breath as he looked at the demon, shoulders slumped in sorrow. His mind raced, trying to find something, some way, of reaching the boundling, of convincing him of his love.

"Cyrus, I–"

"Just go."

Tears stung in his eyes as he took in the broken expression on Cyrus' face. Nodding silently, Marcus pushed to his feet, standing beside the bed.

"I'll go. But we're not over, Cyrus," he said softly, keeping his gaze locked on the boundling. Brown eyes shot to him, uncertainty in their depths as they searched his face. "You want me to leave, I'll leave. For now. But I know that's not what you need. And I will always give you what you need. Anything you need." Despite the pain lancing his chest, Marcus forced himself to turn and walk towards the door, acutely aware of the eyes boring into his back. Stepping through, he paused, gripping the frame as he looked over his shoulder. "You're mine, gorgeous," he whispered, loud enough for Cyrus to hear him. "And I'm not giving up on you."

Closing the door behind him, Marcus let himself fall against the wall, dropping to the floor as he pulled his knees into his chest. That wasn't how he had expected things to go, but he deserved it. His head fell back with a thud against the wall, delving into his mind for what to do, what to say, to fix this. To find his way back into Cyrus' heart. Because without the boundling...

"Hey."

Snapping out of his thoughts, Marcus turned his gaze to look at Lena. She was holding two cups of tea in her hands, offering him one which he took gratefully.

"Hey," he nodded to her as she slid down the wall to sit beside him.

"He's asleep," she sighed, rubbing her eyes, looking as exhausted as he felt.

"You should get some sleep, too."

"I will, in a minute." She sipped at her tea for a moment, before placing the cup on the floor. "It's going to be a long night. He's already dreaming."

Glancing at the door, Marcus' mind was assaulted with images of Cyrus writhing in the bed, as he had the other night before all of this happened. Before he'd pushed the boundling away, possibly for good.

"Go to bed, Lena," he said, turning back to her. "I'm staying here."

A soft smile formed on her lips. "Good," she hummed approvingly before pushing up from the wall. "Damien and Balo are staying the night. They're okay, so once we've talked in the morning, they'll go back to Hell. Archie is going to stay a few days. I hope you don't mind, but if you're going to stay here, I'll tell him to sleep in your room for tonight."

"That's fine. Is he okay?"

"He will be," she nodded. "It takes longer to heal from angelic wounds. The '*purity*' of their power rips us apart from the inside in ways we don't fully understand. Cyrus will take the longest to heal."

He nodded in understanding, digging his palms into his eyes.

"He's scared, Marcus," Lena breathed, sorrow lacing her words. He looked up at her as she wrapped her arms around her waist. "The things he's been shown... he's scared that it's going to come true. Prove him wrong."

He didn't need to say anything as his Prince turned and walked away, the weight of her words settling over him. In that moment he realised what he needed to do. Cyrus always felt like he came second. Like others were more important than him. The young demon needed someone to fight for him. He'd already fought to save the boundling, but now he needed to fight for his heart. And Marcus would fight for it.

Taking a deep breath, he got to his feet, quickly dashing to his room to grab a pillow and blanket before returning to Cyrus' room. As quietly as possible, he cracked open the boundling's door, the sleeping form stirring only slightly. Sneaking inside, he set up beside the doorframe, listening intently to the sounds coming from the demon. Cyrus may have told him to go, but he wasn't leaving. The young demon needed him, and he would be there.

Always.

# CHAPTER THIRTY-NINE

As soon as Marcus shut the door, Cyrus wanted to call him back. To ask the cambion to simply hold him. Everything in him screamed at him, telling him not to let the demon leave. But his voice wouldn't work. His body wouldn't listen. Sinking into the pillows, his eyes drifted shut. He didn't want to rest, but the exhaustion was overwhelming so he knew he needed it. And he couldn't relax with Marcus in the room.

His body had instantly reacted when Marcus kissed him in the courtyard, so attuned now to his touch, but his heart had been caught in a vice, squeezing until he thought it might burst. He'd barely been able to draw a breath, heat flushing through his body under the cambion's intense gaze. Hearing the older demon say he loved him, tore at his very being, threatening to drag him into both joy and despair. He couldn't handle it. With everything he had seen, everything he had been shown, he couldn't let the cambion in that easy. He couldn't suffer that pain again. His mind wouldn't take it.

Letting out a shaky breath, he let his limbs grow heavy, pressing into the mattress beneath him.

Sleep came quickly. So too, did the dreams.

Darkness, fear, pain... Everything melded together, overwhelming his senses.

Crying out, pain ripped through his body, jerking him awake even as powerful arms wrapped around him.

"Shh, baby," a warm voice soothed as he thrashed blindly against the hold. "It's alright. You're alright. You're safe."

"M-Marcus?" he stuttered, burying his face into the broad expanse of the cambion's chest.

"I'm here, Cyrus," Marcus whispered, pressing a kiss to his temple. "Go back to sleep, baby. You're okay."

"I-I… I told you t-to leave." It wasn't a statement or a question. He wasn't sure what he meant by his words. Something in him needed assurance, confirmation that Marcus was really there.

"I'm not going anywhere," Marcus said, his tone like a reverent promise.

"Why?"

"Because I love you. Go back to sleep, gorgeous."

Cradled in the cambion's hold, a sob ripped from Cyrus' throat even as his body relaxed, melting into the warmth and falling back into darkness. His sleep was fitful, getting barely more than an hour between wakings. But each time he felt strong arms band around him, rocking him back to sleep, whispering sweet nothings in his ear. His sheets were soaked both from sweat and tears as his mind warred between reality and fiction.

As morning light drifted through his window, Cyrus shivered within his bed, the cool of sheets sticking to his skin. There were no arms around him. No warmth at his side. Sorrow pierced his heart as he squeezed his eyes shut, fighting against the tears that threatened to spill. He'd cried enough. He didn't want to cry anymore. Expelling a quiet breath, he pushed against the mattress, forcing himself to sit. He needed a shower. And to change the sheets on his bed before falling back into it. Maybe Lena could help him with that though, as he wasn't entirely sure his legs would hold him up for long.

Finally sitting with some effort, his eyes shot wide as he stared at the form resting against the wall by his bedroom door.

*Marcus?*

The cambion was still there. His knees drawn up, elbows resting upon them as his head hung forward, soft sounds of rest emanating from him. A pillow was tucked between him and the wall, a blanket strewn over his legs.

Cyrus felt like he couldn't breathe, his body humming with an unfamiliar feeling. Why was Marcus still there? He'd half expected the moments of comfort he'd received from the demon during the night to turn out to be dreams. It seemed so unbelievable that the cambion would have actually stayed. Would have actually been there for him. Had he really stayed there all night?

As if sensing he was awake, Marcus stirred, looking up from his position, green eyes illuminated in the soft light. Seeing that the boundling was awake, the cambion surged to his feet, but didn't make a move towards the bed.

"You're here..." Cyrus said in disbelief, his body shaking with both fear and longing. It would be too easy to fall into Marcus' arms and forget everything. He wanted to. God, how he wanted to. But he also felt an overriding need to protect himself. His mind and body were too fragile to survive further rejection.

"I told you," Marcus said softly, taking a step towards him, "I'm not going anywhere."

"Why?"

The cambion sighed, a look of deep exhaustion on his face as he rubbed the back of his neck, shoving his other hand into his trouser pocket. "Because I love you."

He couldn't accept the words. Not yet. His heart wanted to, but his mind wouldn't let him.

Swallowing around the lump in his throat, he tore his gaze from Marcus, looking at the state of his bed in dismay.

"I need a shower," he stated simply, moving to throw the covers from him.

"I'll help you."

"I'd rather you didn't," he snapped, his body flushing with anger. What right did the cambion have to act like this after throwing him out? After breaking his heart?

A shadow fell over him as he slid his legs over the edge of the bed. Marcus crouched down in front of him, their eyes locking together.

"Be a brat all you want, Cyrus," the cambion said firmly, his voice low and commanding, sending ripples of excitement over the boundling's skin. "Say whatever you want to hurt me. I deserve it and I can take it. But don't for a minute think that you can push me away. I didn't fight my way through Heaven to lose you now."

Unable to breathe, Cyrus felt his resolve begin to fade. Marcus' large hands gripped under his arms, helping him to his feet as they shuffled into the bathroom. Turning the shower on, the cambion stripped him of the last of his clothing, holding him steady as he stepped into the stream.

"Can you stand?" Marcus asked, looking at him with earnest concern. Not trusting his voice, Cyrus merely nodded, bracing himself with one hand on the wall. The cambion looked at him with such longing that he wanted to beg the demon to stay, to throw his arms around those broad shoulders and never let go. Evidently seeing his uncertainty, Marcus leant forward and pressed a soft kiss to his cheek before stepping back. "I'll be right back. I'm going to change your sheets. Call out if you need help."

Nodding again, he watched as the older demon walked out of the bathroom, leaving the door open. Gingerly, he brushed his fingers over his cheek, still feeling the fleeting touch of Marcus' lips.

Sighing, he dipped his head into the warm water, as if it could wash away the darkness of his thoughts. He couldn't understand what was going on. Marcus had thrown him out. Shattered him. Why was he being so… attentive? That didn't seem like the right word, but he didn't know what else to call it.

His limbs were shaky as he grabbed the soap, washing himself as best he could. A dull throbbing radiated over every inch of his body, threatening to make him buckle under his own weight. He was panting from the effort by the time he finished washing away the sweat and grime coating him. Falling back against the wall, he simply allowed the water to beat down on him, welcoming the heat as it eased his joints. Taking a deep breath and focusing his mind, he could feel his power coursing through him, healing what it could, even as its efforts were dampened. Lena had healed all the physical damage, but his body still needed to purge the lingering remnants of angelic power. And who knew how long that would take.

"Are you okay?"

Turning his gaze to the bathroom door, his eyes fell on Marcus. The cambion was tense, concern etched into every line of his proud features.

"No," Cyrus said truthfully. Nothing made sense to him right now. He had wanted to die. He'd wanted his pain to end. Only now to be subjected to more, afraid that after everything, even this moment of tenderness and care from the older demon, would be ripped from him.

Again…

Hurt flashed through Marcus' eyes as he took in Cyrus' trembling form. Grabbing a towel, the cambion stepped towards him, turning off the shower and wrapping the boundling in the soft fabric.

"What are you doing?" he asked as Marcus lifted him into his large arms, cradling him against his firm chest.

The older demon smiled at him, green eyes still laced with sorrow and pain. "Taking care of you."

Cyrus shook his head, rejecting the notion even as Marcus gently lowered him to sit on the edge of the bed, clutching the towel tightly around him. "Why?"

"Because I love you," the cambion repeated.

Grinding his teeth together, he pushed a hand against Marcus' chest, needing to put space between them. The older demon didn't fight him, simply resting back on his haunches, waiting patiently for the boundling to speak.

"You keep saying that, but why?" Cyrus snapped, his brow furrowed in anger, hand still pressed flat against the cambion. "You have shown me, time and time again, that I don't mean shit to you. I didn't mean to say it to you the other day, but I meant it when I said it and you threw me out. You threw me away like trash. So why the fuck do you keep saying it now?"

The air in the room was heavy, bearing down on him like a tidal wave. It was almost too much when Marcus reached up and covered his hand with his own, pressing down until Cyrus could feel the beating of the demon's heart.

"Cyrus," Marcus started, leaning forward and cupping the boundling's face with his free hand. The action caused his own eyes to mist with tears, caught by the pull of those green depths. "I was an idiot. A fucking idiot. When you came to me saying you'd found someone else, everything in me hurt in ways I didn't know was possible. I was jealous even if I couldn't figure it out at the time."

"Don't," he breathed quickly, shutting his eyes unable to look at the haunted expression on the older demon's face. Unable to look into those sea-green eyes that had captivated him so many times before. "Unless you mean what you are about to say, please just don't. I watched you die enough times over the last day. Don't torture me further."

His breath caught in his throat as the cambion pulled closer, resting their foreheads together. He could feel the warmth of Marcus' breath caressing his lips as he kept his eyes firmly shut.

"You need to rest, baby," the cambion said softly, but the command in his voice was clear. "I mean every word I say. But you're not ready to hear it. So, I'll show you until you are."

Daring to look at the older demon, Cyrus' throat closed at the burning fire in Marcus' eyes. With a firm hand, the cambion helped him pull on fresh briefs before guiding him to lean back against the headboard, tucking the clean covers around him, just as he had the night before.

"Ambrose brought some food up for you." Marcus moved towards the dresser, lifting a tray filled with toast, various pastries, fruit and some water.

"I'm not hungry."

The cambion sighed heavily as he walked back to the bed, resting the tray next to the boundling. "Punish me all you want, Cyrus," he said sternly, squaring his shoulders as he looked down at the boundling. "But I won't let you not take care of yourself. So be a good boy and eat something."

Looking away from the man, Cyrus huffed trying to cover up the way his body shivered at the dominance of Marcus' tone. He cursed his traitorous reactions to the demon. Studying the food as if it had personally offended him, he picked up a slice of toast, tearing a small bite off with his teeth.

"Good boy," the cambion smiled as he settled on the foot of the bed, simply watching as Cyrus ate in silence.

As soon as the butter melted on his tongue, the young demon felt his stomach growl with appreciation. Refusing to look at Marcus, knowing the demon would have a smug-arse grin on his face, Cyrus forced himself to eat slowly, taking small sips of water between mouthfuls. Three slices of toast, an almond croissant and an orange later, he pushed the tray away slightly, feel all kinds of better for it. Not that he would admit it.

Nodding approvingly, Marcus put the tray back on the dresser before returning to the foot of the bed. Cyrus stared at him, folding his arms across his chest, stubbornly denying how tired he felt.

"You should get some more sleep, baby," the cambion said softly. "Don't push yourself."

"Are you going to leave?"

Licking his bottom lip, Marcus' mouth pulled up into a half-smirk. "Do you want me to leave?"

"Yes," Cyrus said bluntly, even though he knew it was a lie.

Huffing a quiet laugh, the cambion shook his head. "Go to sleep, Cyrus," he said pushing to his feet and heading back to his spot by the door. "I'm not going anywhere."

Glaring at the infuriating demon, Cyrus shuffled down on the bed, his need for sleep overriding his desire to argue further. He took some solace that he didn't have a couch or chair in his room so at least Marcus had to sit uncomfortably on the floor. The demon could do to be a little uncomfortable after what he put the boundling through. Pulling the covers over him, he let the comfort of sleep wash over him, secretly grateful that *his* cambion would be there when his dreams began.

Like he had during the night, Cyrus tossed and turned, fighting against his dreams, needing rest but afraid to fully relax. The scent of burnt sugar enveloped him, strong arms holding him tight as he tried to escape the terrors that chased him. Comforting words were whispered into his ear, helping him find what little respite he could.

Jolting awake a few hours later, he drew in a steadying breath, realising he was pressed firmly into a solid warmth. Marcus was holding him, his own face peaceful with sleep. Cyrus grimaced as he realised both his sheets and the cambion's shirt were damp with his sweat. He twisted away from the demon, trying to extract himself from the arms holding him tightly.

"Cyrus?" the older demon asked, suddenly awake and lifting onto his elbows. "Are you okay?"

"Fine," he ground out, continuing to struggle against the strong hold. "Let go."

The growl that vibrated from the cambion's chest was oddly comforting as Cyrus managed to get himself free of the sheets. Not free of Marcus, but the sheets were something at least, no longer chilled by the dampness of them.

"No."

Stilling in his movements, Cyrus looked at the demon holding him, almost shocked by the angry tone of the word. Marcus' gaze was hard as he tightened his embrace, pulling the boundling closer to him.

"I told you, I'm not going anywhere," the cambion growled, leaning over the young demon, pressing him into the mattress. Cyrus melted into the warm weight of the man above him, revelling in the comfort of it as it sunk deep into his bones, easing the latent pain. "I meant it, Cyrus."

His voice failed him as Marcus lifted him from the bed, carrying him to the bathroom. He shivered with pleasure as the heat of the water washed over him, again bracing himself against the wall. After again kissing his cheek, the cambion left quickly to change the sheets, repeating the same routine from the morning.

Staring at the door, Cyrus attempted to use the time to analyse his thoughts. His mind was barely functioning, or at least, not to the same capacity it had before recent events. He didn't know what to make of the way Marcus was taking care of him. Or what the cambion meant by fighting his way through Heaven. There was so much that Cyrus didn't know. What happened after he was taken? He knew what happened to him, but what did the others do?

His memory was... fuzzy. But he remembered the looming shadow in the doorway. He remembered the rage coming from the figure and the comfort that had brought him. He remembered feeling safe when he saw the shadow. A feeling he only had when the cambion was near. Marcus had come for him. Saved him. But was it because he wanted to or because he was ordered to by Lena? Did it matter? Even if Lena ordered him to save Cyrus, Marcus was still here, taking care of him.

And he remembered that firm, commanding voice, calling to him as he drifted between life and death.

Closing his eyes against further tears, he wrapped his arms around himself, wishing it was someone else holding him.

"Marcus," he called softly, his voice low and broken, giving evidence to how close he was to further tears.

The cambion was there in an instant, a panicked expression on his face as his gaze searched every inch of the boundling. "What's wrong?"

Simply looking at the older demon, Cyrus shook his head, unable to form words. As if sensing his inner turmoil, Marcus stripped his clothing, before stepping into the shower and wrapping his arms around the young demon.

Falling into the strong embrace, a broken sob ripped from Cyrus' chest. He broke, so completely as tears and pain poured from his body, relinquishing to the arms that held him together. A large hand wrapped around the back of his neck, possessively cradling him against the solid frame. Soothing words whispered, melding with the sound of running water that continued to spray against his shuddering body.

"Why are you here?" he sobbed, needing answers. Needing something to calm the raging thoughts in his mind.

"Because I love you," Marcus said simply, pulling back slightly so their eyes could meet. "Cyrus, listen to me. Really listen, please?"

Swallowing harshly, he nodded, staring up into those green eyes.

"After I threw you out, I tried to find you. I realised what a massive fucking mistake I'd made and I wanted to fix it. I had no idea how, but I had to try. Damien told us you had been taken by Kai and I'm honestly surprised I didn't kill him for not protecting you better. When Lena said that angels had you, I went a little insane. I tried to be rational. I tried to be detached but I was just lying to myself, again. When I saw you—" Marcus closed his eyes and the boundling watched silently as pain and fury fought across the cambion's proud features. "When I saw what Raphael had done to you, I lost myself. I would have killed them all to save you. I almost did." Cyrus felt hot tears rising within him again as he searched Marcus' face, his chest tightening, making it difficult for him to breathe as the older demon continued. "I love you, Cyrus. I don't know when it happened, but it did. You stole my heart and I don't want it back. I don't just want your body anymore. I want you. I want your heart and soul. I want everything with you. And I want to give you everything. Everything I am, is yours."

"Marcus," he rasped, lifting his hands to hold onto the cambion's neck. "Do you really mean it?"

"Every word. I love you."

He thought he'd run dry, but the tears flowed freely as Cyrus flung his arms around Marcus' shoulders. The demon caught him, wrapping those strong arms around his waist and pulling their bodies tightly together.

"I love you," he cried, burying his face into Marcus' neck, nuzzling against his cheek.

"I love you too, gorgeous," the cambion repeated, tightening his hold of the young demon. "Don't be so aggressive, baby. We're in no rush."

Cyrus pulled at Marcus' face and crushed their lips together, wanting to taste his warmth, his strength. The cambion growled into the kiss, cupping the back of his head to pull him closer. Flicking his tongue out, sweet joy coursed through him as Marcus sucked it into his mouth, meeting it with his own. His body was singing, relief and warmth flooding every part of him with an indescribable happiness. Marcus loved him. Marcus had pulled him back from the brink of death after battling the angels just to save him. An otherwise insignificant boundling, meant enough to this demon to risk everything. He desperately wanted to show Marcus how much that meant to him.

Pushing up on his toes, Cyrus thrilled as Marcus gripped under his thighs, lifting him into the cambion's arms. Suddenly, pain shot up his spine causing him to break the kiss and cry out into the room.

"Cyrus!" Marcus cried, quickly turning off the shower and stepping out. Deftly he wrapped a towel around them, cradling the whimpering boundling against him. Laying him gently against the pillows, the cambion sat back, stroking Cyrus' cheek tenderly, worry in his green eyes. "You need to rest. There is time for everything else later."

Cyrus shook his head. "I don't want to rest. I'm sick of resting. I don't..." he took a deep breath not only trying to fight against the pain, but the fear that gripped at him still. "I don't want you to leave," he finally admitted staring up at the demon above him.

Marcus' face softened as he stood up from the mattress, lifting the covers and crawling into the bed beside him. Cyrus' heart raced as Marcus came closer and gathered him into his arms. With a sigh of contentment, he rested his head on the cambion's chest, laying his hand over his beating heart, something in him easing at the feeling. At the reminder that Marcus was there. That he was alive.

"I'm not going anywhere, Cyrus," the older demon said softly, placing his hand over the boundling's. "As long as you'll have me, I will stay right here. With you."

He relaxed into the cambion's warmth, his heart filling with love for this man. The tightness in his chest finally releasing as he laced his fingers with Marcus', continuing to rest over the cambion's heart.

"I love you," he sighed as he slowly drifted off to sleep, feeling safe and secure in the older demon's arms. Now that it had been said, he didn't want to stop saying it.

"I love you, too," Marcus declared warmly, tightening his hold as Cyrus' breathing slowed to a steady rhythm of sleep.

# CHAPTER FORTY

The next morning, Cyrus woke as the soft rays of sunlight broke through his curtains and flickered across his face. He must have turned in his sleep as he found himself curled around Marcus' arm, his back resting against the man's stomach. The cambion's free arm was draped over his waist, pinning him in place where Cyrus could feel his bottom pressed into the older demon's abdomen.

A thought struck him that he'd managed to sleep through the night without dreams. Or at least, without nightmares. Shivering at the warmth at his back, he dimly realised that in Marcus' arms, he felt safe, protected. His fears forgotten. He doubted it would last forever. The dreams would return. But for now, he'd take the comfort those large arms brought.

Blinking as he grew accustomed to the light, he shifted his body, stretching lazily as he turned towards the one holding him.

"Good morning, gorgeous," Marcus sighed, dropping a row of light kisses along his shoulder.

"Good morning," he smiled, lifting his leg to hook over the cambion's hip, entangling his fingers into the soft curls on his chest. "Did you get any sleep?"

"A little," Marcus said returning the smile, trailing his fingers lightly over the boundling's back. "I wanted to make sure I was awake when you were. How are you feeling?"

Cyrus looked up into Marcus' face, surprised to see such concern and devotion in his eyes. Instinctively, he raised his hand and traced his fingers along the cambion's jaw, his own lips parting with desire for the demon who had completely overtaken him. "I'm fine," he whispered. "I doubt I'm up to a round in the pits, but I'm fine."

Marcus tightened the embrace, leaning his head down to brush a soft, gentle kiss to his lips. The young demon sighed into the kiss, arching his back to press himself closer to the warmth of the large frame. He needed to feel Marcus, to touch and hold him, to remind himself that he was really there. He wanted to give himself to Marcus, completely, regardless of any residual pain he might feel. There was no urgency or haste in the kiss, but he wanted more, as he snaked his arms up to pull on the older demon's neck, deepening the embrace between them.

Doubt crept in as he felt Marcus' body stiffen, large hands gripping painfully into the boundling's waist and hips. Drawing back from the kiss, Cyrus looked at his face, shocked to see the cambion's brows furrowed with pain.

"Marcus?" he asked hesitantly, brushing a strand of blonde hair from his face. "What's wrong?"

A long moment passed as they merely held each other, Marcus' jaw clenching as he seemingly wrestled with his inner demons. "I was so scared," the cambion admitted finally. "I was so scared that I was going to lose you. After Lena healed you and you didn't wake straight away, I..." he swallowed hard and shook his head. "I can't lose you, Cyrus. I don't know how I would live without you."

Overcome with love and joy at the sweet words, Cyrus pressed himself closer to the man. "I heard you, Marcus. When you held me, I heard you." The demon's eyes widened with shock as he held his breath. Moving his hands to cup his face, Cyrus rubbed his thumb over those soft lips, tracing the faint lines at the corners of his mouth. "I will never give up on you."

Marcus hesitated for a moment, only a moment, before pushing Cyrus onto his back and raising above him, crushing their mouths together. This kiss was hungry, passionate and full of need, but the boundling wanted more. Grabbing at Marcus' shoulders, he shifted his hips until the man sat snuggly between his thighs, the hardness of their bodies pressing together. The cambion traced his hand over Cyrus' side, his fingers leaving a trail of fire behind them, exciting the young demon to the point of wanton abandon.

"Tell me if I hurt you," the older demon managed as he turned his affections to Cyrus' jaw and neck, biting softly into his flesh. The boundling moaned under him, arching his back as he clawed at Marcus' neck, wanting to pull him closer. "I need you, Cyrus," the cambion growled against his skin. "I need to feel you."

"I'm yours, Marcus," he sighed, lifting his hips to grind against him. "Take me. Show me how much you need me."

Reclaiming Cyrus' mouth, Marcus began to shift his hips, rubbing their cocks together in slow yet deliberate movements, their pre-cum mixing together against their bellies. Cyrus moaned into the kiss, his hands travelling down the older demon's back, revelling in the pleasure that coursed through his body after having been subjected to so much pain.

Lena's back straightened suddenly as she practically jumped out of her chair, her face flushed. Ambrose and Archie startled, looking up at her as her breathing became ragged and unsteady. "Oh, for fuck's sake!" she spat, turning on her heel and making for the kitchen door.

"Lena?" Ambrose asked. "Are you okay?"

"I'm fine," she snapped over her shoulder. "I'm going to take a shower. A cold shower!"

Archie snorted into his coffee, descending into uncontrollable laughter. The Consort smiled and shook his head. "Do you want company?" he called after her.

"No, the last thing I want is to have sex knowing it's only a result of Cyrus' horny arse!" she shouted slamming the door behind her.

"Fair enough," Ambrose laughed as Archie practically fell off his chair, holding his side.

After a moment, the demonic trainer gathered himself, sitting back in the chair an amused smile on his face. "This house was bad enough with just you two," he smiled at Ambrose. "It's going to be unbearable now."

"Is that why you live in Hell and not here?" the Consort asked.

"Why else do you think?" Archie responded raising a brow at him.

Ambrose chuckled, taking a sip of his coffee. "Want a roommate?"

Cyrus writhed under Marcus as the latter worked down his body, kissing and biting over his chest and stomach, a large hand firmly wrapped around his cock, stroking and twisting until he felt like putty in the cambion's hold. "Marcus," he moaned, squeezing his legs against the older demon's hips.

A low growl rippled from the man, as he descended further down the boundling's body. "I love hearing you say my name," he whispered against Cyrus' abdomen. "I want it to be the only name you call for."

"No one else," the young demon said, throwing his head back on the pillow. "There is no one else."

"Oh, I know, gorgeous," Marcus said softly, placing a delicate kiss to the head of Cyrus' cock, pulling a soft whimper from the boundling. "And as long as I have any say in the matter, there never will be."

The older demon sucked Cyrus' cock into his mouth, laving it with a passionate kiss, his tongue licking along its length and pressing against the sensitive skin under the head. The young demon's hips bucked upward, pushing his cock further into the cambion's throat. Marcus grabbed under his hips, pulling him up from the bed, sucking him in deeper.

"Marcus!" he cried, grabbing at the demon's hair, unsure if he wanted to hold him in place or pull him back up to his mouth. He loved feeling the warmth of Marcus' mouth wrapped around him, the movements of his tongue heightening his pleasure. His stomach tightened and he knew the cambion would have no trouble pushing him over the edge. "Marcus, I'm so close."

If the older demon heard him, he made no indication of it, other than his fingers digging into the soft flesh of the boundling's arse. Cyrus moaned into the room, his cock throbbing and pulsing, begging for release. Marcus moved one of his thumbs to press against the flesh between his balls and hole, sending a shockwave of pleasure into his stomach, breaking the pressure within. Arching his back, unable to make any sound, Cyrus' body convulsed with his climax as the warm ropes of his cum pooled into the back of Marcus' throat. Panting he collapsed against the pillows, his fingers still entangled in the blonde hair as the older demon crawled over him.

Cyrus kept his eyes locked on Marcus' face, enthralled as his sea-green eyes darkened to a tidal storm, full of desire. With a wicked grin, the cambion took hold of his softening cock and held it against his own, rubbing them together between his large hand. Cyrus' body twitched as his over-sensitive flesh craved more, taking but a moment to harden again under the touch.

"That's it, gorgeous," Marcus growled. "My god, you're beautiful."

Lifting his arms, Cyrus' heart skipped wildly as Marcus willingly fell into his embrace. Claiming his mouth, he wrapped his arms around the cambion's neck, his body cooling from the mist of sweat now covering him. Moving his lips to Marcus' ear, he whispered, "I want to taste you."

Chuckling against his neck, the older demon obediently rolled onto his back, pulling Cyrus with him. Smiling, the boundling scurried down his body, trailing kisses down the broad chest, pausing briefly to lick at the cambion's nipples. Positioning himself, between Marcus' legs, Cyrus took hold of the cambion's cock in his hands, stroking it gently as he sucked the head into his mouth. His hand guiding his movements, he bobbed his head, swirling his tongue around the head, listening intently as the demon sighed above him. Looking up through his lashes, he saw Marcus propped up on some of the pillows, his eyes shut, one arm resting lazily above his head. Reaching for the other hand, Cyrus laced their fingers together, as he breathed out and sucked the full length into his throat.

"Ah, Cyrus," the cambion moaned, his hips bucking at the sensation, fingers tightening around the boundling's. "Your mouth feels amazing. So warm and inviting."

Emboldened by his words, Cyrus licked up the line underneath Marcus' steely shaft, paying particular attention to the soft skin under the head. Discreetly, he lathered some saliva on his finger, before taking the hot flesh again into his mouth. He moved his moistened finger and inserted it slowly into the cambion's arse, curling it within to press and massage against his prostate.

A loud groan of pleasure pulled from Marcus' chest as he arched his back, the arm above his head suddenly reaching to cup the boundling's cheek. "Oh hell! Cyrus..." he cried, "where did you... ah!"

Marcus' cock throbbed within his mouth, stretching his lips around its expanding girth. Cyrus grinned, pleased that he too could cause the older demon as much pleasure as he received from him. Releasing the cambion's hand, he fondled his balls as his head furiously bobbed, sucking and licking along the pulsing shaft.

"I'm going to come," Marcus ground out through gritted teeth as his hips bucked up, slamming himself against the back of Cyrus' throat. Pressing against Marcus' prostate, revelling in the feel of his arsehole clenching around his finger, he sucked hard, encouraging the cambion to let go. The hardened cock in his mouth twitched and pulsed as he heard Marcus groan above him. Without warning, the cambion grabbed the back of his head, pulling down forcefully against him, his release flooding the boundling's mouth. The young demon moaned as he drank and swallowed every bit of cum given to him, the saltiness pleasantly stinging against his tongue. As he felt Marcus' cock start to ease, he withdrew his finger, resting his hand atop the older demon's thigh, rubbing gently as he licked every last drop of release from his love's shaft.

With a gasp of surprise, Cyrus found himself on his back, Marcus pulling him up on the bed to lie atop him. Tenderly, the cambion stroked his cheek, looking lovingly into his eyes, before leaning down and placing a tantalisingly slow kiss on his lips. The young demon shut his eyes, pushing up into the kiss, knowing he would never get enough of this man.

"I love you," Marcus said against his lips, his voice full of love and caring, robbing Cyrus of all remaining rational thought.

"I love you," the boundling sighed, wrapping his arms tightly around the older demon's neck. "I need you, Marcus. I need you inside me, now."

The cambion chuckled against him. "Give me a minute, gorgeous. That was intense. I'd ask where you learnt that, but I don't think I want to know."

"Jealous?" he teased with a smile, pressing a soft kiss to his lips.

"Yes," the older demon admitted, smiling as Cyrus pulled back in surprise. "I'm jealous of everyone who got to enjoy your body before me. And angry that it had been so carelessly used for others' pleasure disregarding your own." Cyrus' skin shivered as Marcus slowly traced his hand down his side, gently pressing their bodies closer together. "I don't want to just fuck you, Cyrus. I want to love you. I want to show you how much I love you."

He swallowed as he looked up at Marcus. "I never thought I would hear you say those words. Not after you..."

The cambion's gaze grew serious as he reached up and cupped Cyrus' cheek in his hand. "I will never be able to make up for the hurt I caused you," he said softly. "When you said you loved me, I was reminded why

I kept everyone away. I lashed out, desperate to protect myself. I never wanted to hurt you."

"You said your last boundling..."

"Yes," Marcus nodded, gently interrupting him, "but I don't want to talk about him. Not right now. I will tell you everything in time. Suffice to say, I thought I loved him. But what I felt for him, is nothing compared to what I feel for you." A tear escaped Cyrus' eye at the sweet words. This was more than he could have hoped for. More than he ever dreamed possible when it came to loving the demon above him. Marcus brushed the tear away with the pad of his thumb and smiled sadly. "I should never have pushed you away. I will spend the rest of my existence atoning for that error. I promise to spend every day showing you how precious you are to me. I will spend every day loving you and earning your love."

Placing his fingers over Marcus' lips, Cyrus drank in the sight of the beautiful man who bore his soul to him. "You don't need to earn something freely given," he whispered, lifting his head to dot gentle kisses over Marcus' cheeks, jaw and lips. "My love is yours. It always has been and always will be."

"My gorgeous Cyrus," the cambion purred, lifting himself over the young demon, pressing him into the mattress. "I love you."

"Show me," the boundling whispered into his ear.

"Gladly."

Cyrus reached between them fisting Marcus' cock, stroking as it hardened within his hand. With a growl, the older demon reached for the bedside table, pulling out the bottle of lube from the drawer, emptying some onto his hand before rubbing it over his length. Pressing the head of his cock against the boundling's tight hole, Marcus rested on his hands, leaning down to capture his mouth in a passionate kiss.

"Ready for me, gorgeous?" he asked, smiling against Cyrus' lips.

"Yes," the young demon sighed. "Yes, Marcus, I'm ready. Please."

"Please?"

Cyrus grinned, arching his back to press into the cambion's chest, before answering; "Please, sir."

No further encouragement needed, Marcus pressed his hips forward, sinking into the demon, smiling as the boundling gasped beneath him. Cyrus' body opened for him, eagerly welcoming the slight pain as his arse stretched to accommodate Marcus' size. Pain that was soon replaced with overwhelming pleasure as his head dropped back onto the pillow, his mouth agape, his moans echoing throughout the room.

"You're still so tight," Marcus rasped, dropping his head to kiss the boundling's neck. "Your arse is incredible, Cyrus. Fucking perfect. I will never get enough of you."

Cyrus could barely concentrate on his words, as waves of pleasure coursed through his body, heating his stomach with blinding pressure. "Marcus. Sir," he moaned, "I'm yours to take whenever you want. I love you."

"I love you," the cambion whispered.

Capturing Cyrus' mouth with his own, Marcus quickened his pace, holding the boundling's face tenderly between his hands as their mouths danced in slow abandon, simply feeling and exploring the other in delicious detail. Cyrus wrapped his legs around the older demon's waist, pulling him deeper into his body as his nails dug into the board shoulders.

Having both recently found their release, there was no haste in their lovemaking, simply reacquainting themselves with the other's body. Cyrus felt whole, his heart full and content as Marcus held him in his arms, their breath combining as they moved together. The cambion's hands were everywhere, coaxing further pleasure from his body, turning his mind into a wild frenzied state that could no longer remember what it was like before the demon claimed him. He felt like an extension of the older demon, needing him like he needed the powers of Hell to survive. Three times Marcus brought him to the edge, only to ease back waiting for his body to calm, before fanning the flames of desire within him to greater heights than ever.

"Marcus!" he cried, desperately clinging onto the demon atop him, his face buried into his shoulder. "I can't take anymore!"

"Yes, you can, gorgeous," the cambion growled into his ear. "You can take everything I give you. And I will give you everything."

Marcus arched his back to reach between them, wrapping his fingers around Cyrus' cock, rubbing the slickness of his pre-cum over the head and along the shaft. The boundling's head dropped back, deep guttural moans tearing from him as the older demon began to furiously pump his throbbing length.

"Come for me, gorgeous," Marcus groaned, his own cock pulsing within the young demon's body.

Cyrus practically roared into the room, his arse clamping down tightly, his climax dissolving his body into a pool of spent desire as his release fired up his stomach, coating his chest and neck. Marcus released his hold on him, leaning down and licking the drops of cum from his neck, biting softly along his jaw, hips still moving in a steady rhythm.

"Marcus, please!" he begged, tightly gripping the blonde hair of the demon driving into him.

"Tell me again," the cambion requested, nuzzling his mouth into Cyrus' neck. "Tell me, you love me."

"I love you!" he cried, his body continuing to convulse as the older demon slammed against him. "I love you more than anything."

With a low, powerful moan, Marcus rammed his hips forward, burying himself to the hilt, as his cock pulsed and throbbed, coating the walls of the boundling's arse with his release. Their bodies entangled, they held each other, slowly descending from the throws of their passion. As their breathing returned to normal, Marcus lifted his head and kissed every inch of Cyrus' face. His mind blissfully blank, the young demon could only smile as he held onto Marcus, sure that if he let go, he would fall from reality. The cambion brushed the back of his fingers along Cyrus' jaw, inviting the boundling to open his eyes. Brown met with green, as he looked at Marcus with pure amazement and love for the experience they had just shared.

"I love you," he said softly, touching his forehead to Marcus'. "Never leave me."

The cambion smiled, cupping his face with his hand. "Never," he promised. "Like you would let me anyway." Chuckling together, Marcus rolled to the side, pulling Cyrus into his arms, pressing soft kisses to his cheeks, jaw and lips. "Did you feel any pain?" he asked, running his fingers up and down the boundling's back.

"No," Cyrus said shaking his head. "I probably will later. I'm not sure I'll be standing any time soon."

His embrace tightening, Marcus pressed Cyrus closer to him. "I'll help you," he teased, though there was a sincerity to his offer. "Let me know when you're ready to get up."

"Not yet," he said quickly. "I just want to stay with you right now."

"Fine with me."

"Marcus?"

"Hm?"

"I'll never hurt you."

Marcus' arms tightened almost painfully around the boundling's body. "I know," he said softly.

Relaxing together, Cyrus allowed himself to find peace within the cambion's arms. Fate had thrown them together and tested them in unfathomable ways. But in that, they had found something more, and he vowed he would never let it go.

After a moment, they raised their heads as someone knocked at the door.

"Marcus, Cyrus," Lena called through the door. "We need to talk. When you've recovered from your morning... '*exercises*', can you meet me in my altar room, please?"

"Think she's pissed?" Cyrus sighed, nuzzling his cheek into the solid chest, his head bouncing as Marcus laughed.

"I'm sure she's fine," the cambion chuckled, dropping a kiss to the top of his head. "Come on. Think it's probably best we don't keep her waiting."

# CHAPTER FORTY-ONE

Marcus paced his office, obsessively dragging his hands through his hair, trying to quell his anxiety. Ambrose lounged casually in one of the chairs, his head resting in his hand as he smiled in amusement at his friend.

"You're going to wear a hole through the floor, Marcus."

Glaring at the Consort, he huffed in frustration, earning a low chuckle from the other demon.

It had been almost a month since they, *he*, got Cyrus back. Although they spent a few days and nights in Cyrus' room, Marcus insisted that the boundling move into his wing immediately. He refused to spend a single night without the young demon safely wrapped in his arms. Cyrus didn't protest, eagerly delving into the process of moving his things in, including the massive record collection he'd acquired over the last year. Marcus didn't mind, as most evenings they now spent curled up together on the bed, listening to the various genres of music, simply holding each other and talking.

Slowly, Cyrus opened to him, telling him the things he'd been made to see. The cambion was desperate to take all the memories from him and erase them. To take on his pain and carry it for him. But he knew that wouldn't help. Cyrus needed to come to terms with it all. To accept the truth and not fall into the lies forced upon him. Following Marcus' encouragement, Cyrus agreed to let Lena delve into his mind with her book. The boundling and their Prince were currently locked away in her altar room doing just that, just as they had done for the last fortnight.

The problem was Cyrus always came out of it exhausted, frustrated and just... not himself. It set the cambion on edge as it felt like the young demon was pulling away from him after; as if he still needed to protect himself from the things that Raphael had shown him. As if he was still afraid that something was going to happen to Marcus. To them.

He'd noticed how, whenever Lena came into the room, Cyrus would instinctively step between them, as if he could protect the cambion from the Prince. Obviously aware of how the boundling was feeling, Lena gave Marcus a wide berth, staying on the other side of room, or sitting down swiftly to reduce her presence. She tried to help with his fears, using her conduit to show him the past, to show him what really happened the night of his parents' death.

They hadn't been arguing. Cyrus hadn't even been crying. The rain had been intense and visibility had been minimal at best. But it was difficult for the boundling to accept what he saw. There was too much for his mind to sort through. Too much left uncertain.

And then there were the nightmares.

Cyrus had slept almost every night since he got back, his body still needing to recover, and every night he woke up screaming, sweat dripping from every inch of his skin. He'd torched their bed twice when he woke tangled in the sheets and panicking, unable to escape the binds of the fabric. Without fail, Marcus was there, holding him and soothing him back to sleep, but he didn't know how to ease the pain. He didn't know if it ever would.

Today, he was particularly nervous waiting for Cyrus and Lena to emerge. He had a plan. Something that, hopefully, would finally allay the boundling's fears and prove that Marcus wasn't going anywhere. That he was all in.

But there was something they had to do first. And the wait was killing him.

"How much longer are they going to be?" he asked, finally taking the seat opposite Ambrose.

"As long as they need," the Consort smiled at him. "Of all people you know how difficult the last few weeks have been. They need time. You need time."

"I need Cyrus." He no longer held any reservations in admitting this to Ambrose. His friend understood better than anyone the need to be with the one he loved.

The smile on the other demon's face grew at the statement. "I used to wonder when you would finally settle down with someone. I'm glad it's with Cyrus. You're good for each other."

Huffing a laugh, Marcus shook his head slightly. "Makes me wish I'd spoken to you about him sooner."

Ambrose simply hummed in agreement.

The alarm sounded through the house, their heads turning to the door. A grin crept over Marcus' face as he and the Consort pushed to their feet.

"Show time," he chuckled under his breath, Ambrose clapping him on the shoulder, heading for the door. Hardening his gaze, they stepped out into the corridor, the alfresco windows fully open, letting the arid air fill the house. Ambrose's hand fell from his back and his body flushed with rage as he took in the arrogant form of the figure standing in the middle of the courtyard. "What the fuck are you doing here?" he snarled, rushing forwards. "Get out!"

Raphael sneered at him even as Marcus fisted his shirt, bringing their faces close together, teeth bared in warning. "I was invited, demon."

"If you were invited, you're an idiot for accepting," he growled, malice dripping from every word. "I should kill you for what you did."

"Marcus! Stand down."

Snapping his head to look over his shoulder, his breath caught momentarily seeing Lena and Cyrus walking towards them. The boundling looked wreaked, like he'd gone ten rounds in the pits. Marcus' heart plummeted to his feet, wanting to simply wrap himself around the young demon and never let go.

"Lena?" He swallowed sharply, turning back to glare at the arch-angel, forcing himself back into the moment. "Please do not tell me you invited this bastard here? Not after everything he did!"

"I said, stand down!"

His grip on the arch-angel's shirt tightened, the fabric tearing slightly under his grip.

"Marcus..."

Cyrus' soft voice washed over him, pulling him back like magnet, soothing his rage in the way only the boundling could do. Closing his eyes, Marcus shoved the angel, smirking as Raphael stumbled a few steps. Slowly retreating towards the sire and boundling, he reached for Cyrus' outstretched hand, lacing their fingers together.

"Are you okay with this?" he said in a hushed tone, fully aware that the sound would carry through the courtyard regardless. "He tortured you."

Those chocolate eyes bore into him, as if searching for something. He felt the slight squeeze on his hand as Cyrus tightened their grip of each other.

"Trust her, please," the boundling implored, raising his free hand to grasp at Marcus' bicep. Subtly, the cambion nodded, inching closer, placing himself as a barrier squarely between Cyrus and the angel.

"You need to better control your council, Lena."

The Prince snarled at the arch-angel, stepping in front of Marcus and Cyrus. "My council is not your concern, Raphael."

"Why have you asked me here?" the angel huffed, folding his arms over his chest. "Surely not to simply cause dissent within your circle."

"Hardly. I want to offer you a deal."

Marcus' eyebrows shot to his hairline. From the corner of his eye, he saw Ambrose step forward, coming to a stop a few feet beside them. Almost inadvertently, they stood in formation behind Lena, standing as witness to the discussion between the arch-angel and Prince of Hell.

Raphael threw his head back with a barking laugh, his eyes cold at he stared at Lena. "What deal could a demon offer an angel? And why would you think I would entertain such a thing anyway?"

"You already made a deal with one demon," Lena sneered. The angel flinched but didn't look away. "Kai is not much use to anyone now, but I still got enough from him to make your life within Heaven very difficult."

The cambion bit his bottom lip, fighting to contain a laugh as he watched the morphing horror on Raphael's face. The angel deserved to be taken down. To be stripped of everything he had and loved for what he did to Cyrus. Tightening his hold of the boundling's hand, Marcus watched silently, putting aside his rage for now.

"What do you want?" Raphael asked, his tone clipped.

"Your daughter."

"I told you, leave her out of this!"

Lena's head tilted to the side as the angel shouted, her lips curling into a tight smile. "And I told you, leave me and my council alone. You stole and tortured my boundling. I threatened your daughter. We could go round and round hurting the other, but all that will result in is us both losing something we love. Or, you could listen to my offer."

The sound of a pin falling could have been heard in the courtyard as Lena and Raphael stared at each other. Marcus felt Cyrus press into his back, as if he needed support to keep standing. The cambion had no idea what the boundling was feeling, but he was itching for them to be alone. Needing to hold the young demon tightly against him.

"Alright," Raphael murmured finally, his hands falling limply at his sides. "I'll listen, but that is all."

"Fine," the Prince smiled. "I want information about Heaven. I want to know everything about your brothers. From arch-angels to seraphim. I want to know their powers, their strengths and their weaknesses. Any time one of them moves or walks on Earth, I want to know. And you are going to tell me."

"And why would I do that? Why would I betray Heaven like that?"

"Nephilims are highly sought after by both sides are they not? Their blood is potently powerful."

"What are you trying to say?"

The tone in Raphael's voice told everyone that he knew exactly what Lena's was implying.

"I know that if your brothers found out about her, they would drain her dry to feed their own agendas. I also know that my siblings would likely do the same." Marcus bit the inside of his cheek to stop the smile that wanted to form on his lips. Her threat was a good one, especially knowing the other Princes of Hell were already aware of the nephilim, but hadn't made a move, trusting Lena and her judgement. They knew that. Raphael didn't. "As would any other angel or demon," Lena continued with a dismissive wave of her hand. "You know I am more powerful than you. You know I can protect her. I will protect her. I will stop anyone from finding out about her." She stepped closer to the angel, lowering her voice to one of hushed understanding. "I know you love your daughter. I saw it in your eyes that day on the beach. As her father, do you not wish to protect her?"

The arch-angel swallowed at her words, his eyes darting around the courtyard, glancing over the other men before settling back on her. "What assurances do I have that you will not use her blood?"

"I will never hurt a child. Believe me or don't," she huffed, leaning back and folding her arms. "I lived a mortal life and was abused constantly. I will not allow a child under my protection to suffer as I did. I will keep her safe. Think about it if you need, but this deal won't be on the table forever. I made you this offer before. I will not do so again."

Grinding his jaw, Marcus squared his shoulders, taking a small step forward, but not enough to let go of Cyrus' hand behind his back. "Lena, what are you doing?" he snarled, putting as much vitriol into his voice as he could.

"Back off, Marcus," she snapped, looking over her shoulder at him. "It is not your place to question me."

"You convinced me to stay on your council," he ground out, pointing his finger accusingly at her. "And now you want to deal with the angel who hurt Cyrus? What makes you think I would stay after this?"

Lena simply shrugged, turning away and back towards the angel. "Cyrus agrees with me."

"What?"

He felt Cyrus' hand settle on his lower back, pulling his gaze back to the boundling.

"She's right, Marcus," the young demon whispered, exhaustion lacing every word.

"Are you insane?" he asked, stepping away from demon although it tore at his chest to do so. Shaking his head, he looked over at Ambrose briefly, turning pleading eyes back to Cyrus. "This is a bad idea—"

"Marcus, enough," the Consort sighed, pinching the bridge of his nose. "This has nothing to do with you."

"The hell it doesn't," he snapped, throwing a death glare at his friend.

"Lena. I accept your terms," Raphael said with a smile, bringing all eyes to settle on him. "If only because it is clear that it will tear your council apart."

The Prince smiled cruelly, flipping a strand of hair over her shoulder. "They're replaceable," she stated simply.

One of Raphael's eyebrows shot up, a look of almost respect forming on his face. "So callous."

"We are demons after all."

"Yet, in contradiction to the assault you made on Heaven to get your boundling back."

"Key difference," Lena said with a click of her tongue. "He's my boundling. As you said before, it is important for a sire to protect their boundling."

"And you said everyone on your council was important to you," the arch-angel smirked, folding his arms.

Marcus shifted uncomfortably, his feet restless against the hard granite beneath him. The conversation between the angel and Prince was becoming too casual. This needed to end, now. *Come on, Lena.*

"Things change."

"Then how do I know you will keep your word?"

"I think you know I will," Lena smiled reassuringly, holding out her hand for the angel. "Do we have a deal?"

Licking his lips, Raphael huffed in defeat, extending his arm and clasping her hand with his. Red lightning sprang from Lena's fingers, wrapping around both their wrists, snaking up their arms before stopping at their elbows. Likewise, Raphael's light radiated softly from his touch, seeping into Lena's flesh, highlighting the veins beneath their skin.

As their powers receded, Marcus choked on a gasp as he saw faint lines, almost like Cyrus' bindings, snaking up Raphael's arm. The arch-angel looked at his skin, his face morphing into a picture of shock and fury.

"I'd stay clear of Heaven for about an hour," Lena chuckled, releasing their hold. "The markings should have faded by then."

"You bound me to you?" Raphael snapped, almost lunging at her. Ambrose growled at the angel, moving closer to Lena. The arch-angel faltered, stumbling in his steps as panicked eyes snapped between the Consort and Prince.

"Not quite," she said, retreating enough to take herself out of arm's reach. "Think of it as an insurance policy. If I am going to protect you, I need to know where you are."

This time, Marcus didn't try to suppress his grin, letting a small laugh bubble from his chest, amused by the expression on Raphael's face. Dangerous eyes pinned him for a moment, causing his smirk to widen. Like hell he was scared of the arch-angel.

"The deal was to protect my daughter, not me," Raphael snarled, rubbing at the skin on his arm as if he could get rid of the marks that way.

"You are about to give me endlessly useful information," Lena shrugged unapologetically. "You have become an investment, and I protect my investments."

Realising the true extent of his fate, Raphael's shoulders slumped in defeat. The sight was pure vindication to the cambion as he mentally burned the image into his memory. It was certainly one to cherish.

Sighing, the arch-angel scrubbed a hand over his face. "I'll bring you what I can in a week."

"I look forward to it," Lena smiled, nodding her head in dismissal of the angel.

Light encompassed Raphael as he disappeared, evidently too caught up in the crashing reality of the deal he had just agreed to, to bother insulting any of them further. Once gone, an audible sigh of relief escaped every demon.

Taking a deep breath, Marcus let his shoulders relax, turning his gaze to look at Cyrus as the boundling stepped closer to him. He smiled lovingly, wrapping his arm around the young demon's waist, pulling the lean frame firmly against his. "That went well."

Lena chuckled warmly, turning to face the pair, her eyes soft and motherly as she took them in. "Fabulous display, Marcus," she complimented.

"Performance of the century, I'd say," Ambrose smiled, clapping Marcus on the back as he made his way to the Prince, stepping behind to wrap his arms around her. Lena sunk into his hold, and Marcus didn't miss the way Cyrus' body relaxed slightly at the sight.

Looking at his love's face, Marcus cupped the boundling's jaw, encouraging their eyes to meet. The gorgeous demon nodded slightly to him, his chocolate eyes guarded, but full of love. Slowly, Cyrus lifted his hand and placed it over the centre of Marcus' chest, two fingers slipping between the buttons of his shirt to touch the skin above the cambion's heart. It was so simple, such a small action, but the older demon saw the comfort it brought the boundling. To be able to feel the beating of Marcus' heart. To remind him that he was fine, that they were fine.

"And now, we have the constant location of Raphael and a nephilim," Lena continued, her voice distant to Marcus as he tightened his hold on Cyrus, content to forget the world around them.

"And soon, everything we need to know about angels," the Consort mused.

"As I said, fabulous display."

Cyrus smiled, leaning into Marcus' embrace, resting his head against the cambion's shoulder. "Here, here," he sighed, his fingers tracing teasing circles over Marcus' heart.

Chuckling softly, the older demon pressed a lingering kiss to the boundling's temple. "Careful, gorgeous," he warned, placing his hand over the boundling's, stilling the movements.

Lena laughed, the sound soft and bell-like throughout the courtyard. "I get it now," she mused, looking up at Ambrose. "Why Archie doesn't live here."

The Consort smiled at her, planting a kiss on her lips. "Shall we visit him?"

"Absolutely!" she grinned, clapping her hands together, flames already encompassing the pair. "We need to bring him up to speed anyway. See you lovebirds later."

Finally alone, Marcus turned fully into his embrace of the boundling, banding both arms tightly behind his back. Cyrus still kept his hand over the cambion's heart, the other fisting the back of Marcus' shirt as he shuddered in the hold. Burying his face in the dark blonde hair, the older demon breathed in deeply, drinking in the smoke and leather scent that felt like home to him now. His heart ached as he heard Cyrus sigh, the last of the tension in the gorgeous body finally easing as they simply held each other.

Lifting his head, the cambion ran his hand through Cyrus' hair, staring at his very reason for being. The very reason his heart still beat.

"Are you okay?" he asked, placing a tender kiss to that perfect pout.

The boundling hummed, nodding his head slightly. "I am now. Today was... intense."

"Do you want to talk about it?"

"No," Cyrus murmured, nuzzling into Marcus' chest. "Not yet, anyway. I just need you."

Marcus smiled, cupping the young demon's face with his hand, closing the distance between them. "And you will always have me," he promised as his mouth finally sealed over the boundling's. Cyrus leant into him, tangling a hand in his hair as he parted his lips, allowing Marcus access to taste him. As much as the cambion wanted to deepen the kiss, to take his love to their room and never leave, he had a slightly different plan. Grinning at Cyrus' disappointed groan, he tore his mouth away, tightening his embrace reassuringly. "Come with me."

Brow furrowing, Cyrus stared at him, a small seed of fear in those chocolate depths. Marcus swallowed harshly around the lump that formed in his throat at the sight, needing more than anything to remove that fear completely.

"Where are we going?"

Placing a gentle kiss to the young demon's cheek, Marcus dropped his arms, clasping Cyrus' hand firmly within his. "Just come on, Cyrus.

It's a surprise."

The way the boundling pressed his lips together in contemplation was adorable to the cambion. "I'm not sure you and surprise should be in the same sentence."

Chuckling, he tugged the young demon closer, grabbing his chin between his fingers. "Oh, you're bratting it today, are you?" he asked, loving how those brown eyes darkened impossibly, drooping with desire.

"No, sorry," Cyrus apologised quickly, his breath hitching as he melted into Marcus' hold. "I'll be good."

"Then come with me."

# EPILOGUE

As the flames around them subsided, Cyrus drew in a sharp breath, taking in their surroundings. Vast mountains rolled over the horizon around them, small patches of snow decorating their peaks. The air was cool but a warm breeze drifted up the landscape to meet them. However, it was the small cottage that stole all of his attention. Vines curled around the stone walls and the thatched roof was overrun with moss. Various flowered shrubs trailed along the base of the walls, skimming the underside of the window sills. To Cyrus, it looked like something out of a child's storybook, cozy and inviting.

"Marcus?" he questioned softly, tightening his hold of the cambion's hand. "Where are we?"

"A cottage," Marcus said with a mocking tone.

Rolling his eyes, Cyrus nudged his shoulder into the older demon. "I can see that. But why?"

"Because," the cambion said, making his way to the front door, pulling the boundling along with him. "It's ours."

"Ours?"

"Well, it's mine, I guess," Marcus chuckled. "But I want it to be ours." They walked inside, Cyrus' eyes darting everywhere as he took in the homey interior, his mouth parting slightly in shock. Stopping suddenly, Marcus squeezed his hand, drawing the boundling's gaze back to him. "Don't look so worried, gorgeous."

"I'm not worried," Cyrus said softly, his brow furrowing, "I'm confused. You want to move out of the house?"

The older demon smiled but shook his head. "No. For one, you have to stay close to Lena, and I don't want to go too far from her or Ambrose in case we need to get to them quickly. Also, we just finished moving the last of your things into my wing, *our* wing, and I do *not* want to move your record collection again." Smiling sheepishly, Cyrus let Marcus pull him deeper into the room, coming to stop in front of the window above the small kitchen. The cambion turned towards him, still holding his hand, a loving smile on his face. Raising his free hand to brush the back of his fingers along Cyrus' jaw, Marcus tilted his head to the side, his gaze studying the boundling. "I just wanted somewhere we could go when we want to be just us. Somewhere we don't share with anyone else. This is the cottage my father built for my mother," he said, looking around them briefly. "I've kept it magically intact since he died, but I rarely come here so it needs some work. It's shrouded so there's no risk of mortals finding it. Not even Lena or Ambrose know about this place."

Staring at the older demon, Cyrus felt overcome with happiness. He knew what this meant for Marcus, to bring him here, to bring him into this part of his life. Of his past. And it meant everything to him.

He was exhausted. His time spent with Lena was draining, although it helped. He didn't feel as nervous around her anymore as he had when he first got back. But some of his reactions were beyond his control. Fear and anxiety followed him like a plague, ready to crash through any small moment of happiness he might find. The first few days had been fine. Then one day Lena and Marcus were training in the courtyard, nothing strenuous or out of the ordinary. But when the Prince's fist connected with the cambion's jaw, the panic that consumed the boundling in that moment pulled everything to the surface.

Taking a deep breath, he closed his eyes momentarily. He would be fine. He would heal. He knew he would. He also knew that his family, Lena, Ambrose and Marcus, would be there for him at every turn. And this, bringing him to *this* cottage, only proved that.

"Marcus, I..." Cyrus looked at the cambion, his heart feeling heavy in his chest, overflowing with his love for this man. "I don't know what to say."

Smiling warmly, Marcus stepped towards him, encircling his arms around the boundling's waist, pulling their bodies tightly together. "Tell me you like it."

"I love it," the young demon sighed, snaking his own arms around the cambion's neck, breathing in his scent of burnt sugar. "It's perfect," he whispered, planting a brief kiss on those soft lips. "You're perfect."

"I'm here, Cyrus," Marcus said softly, his eyes swimming with sincerity. "I'm all in. No matter what happens next, no matter what is waiting for us, I'm here. I'm never giving up on you and I'm never leaving you. I love you," he declared, claiming a firm kiss from the boundling.

"Marcus, I love you, too..." he breathed into the kiss, hesitating as he gingerly let his tongue play with an endearment, "babe."

Pulling his head back slightly, but not letting go, the cambion held a pensive look on his face. "Hm, no," he mused with a soft shake of his head. "It's okay, but... let's not settle on 'babe', just yet."

Pressing his lips together, Cyrus tried desperately to hold his bratty nature in check. He should have known better even as a coy half-smirk formed on his lips, the word spilling from his mouth before he could stop himself.

"Daddy?"

Thankfully, Marcus threw his head back with a loud, barking laugh. "Fuck, no," he said emphatically, a wide smile on his face. "Are you after a spanking?"

His mind may have been exhausted, but evidently his body had not gotten the memo, as it hardened in anticipation, shivering at the question. He wasn't entirely against the idea, his grin growing as Marcus' large hands travelled down his back to cup his arse, grinding their hips together. Head tipping back with a moan, the cambion took the opportunity to kiss and nibble along the length of his neck. Pleasure skittered over his skin, coursing down his spine as his arms tightened around the older demon's shoulders.

"How about 'love' then?" he sighed, his fingers moving to tangle in the cambion's long hair.

Marcus hummed against his skin. "I like that."

"My love."

"Even better," the demon whispered huskily, biting along his jaw until their mouths met in a languid, all-consuming kiss. Emotion welled in Cyrus' chest, constricting around his heart as he clung to the cambion, afraid to ever let him go. As if sensing the change, Marcus pulled his head away, concern in his green depths, staring intently at the boundling. "Hey, what's wrong?"

"Nothing," he blurted quickly, cupping the cambion's face between his hands. "Nothing's wrong. I'm just happy. I- I..."

"What?"

Taking a deep breath, he swallowed around the lump forming in his throat. Marcus had spent almost every minute of every day since his rescue proving to him that the cambion wasn't going to leave him or push him away again. Cyrus still had nightmares, now mixed with what the angels did to him, but each time he woke with a start, Marcus would hold him, whispering words of love, lulling him back to sleep. But he still couldn't help the small seed of fear in his gut that something would take this happiness away from him.

Bracing himself for possible rejection, he leant forward brushing a tender kiss to his love's lips. "I want to bind to you, Marcus."

"Oh, gorgeous," the cambion breathed, launching forward to crash their mouths together. Colliding with the wall behind them, Cyrus revelled in the warmth of the body pressing against him, holding him securely within large arms. The cambion really had a thing for pushing him up against walls and he loved it. Pulling back, Marcus' eyes were almost black with desire. "Nothing would make me happier," he rasped. "I can only imagine what it would feel like to share in your joy, your love, your pleasure."

Cyrus' chest was heaving with breathlessness as he melted into the heat of the cambion's gaze. Possession and love shone from the depths of the demon's soul and he couldn't get enough of the sight. But mixed within was a sorrow, or regret, that gave him pause.

"But?" he queried, rubbing the back of Marcus' neck with his fingers, wanting to keep as much contact with the demon as possible.

"But," Marcus said with emphasis, "Lena is the perfect sire for you right now. As much as I think she would love to not feel your emotions anymore, you need her. Besides," he sighed softly with a slight shake of his head, "even with your consent, I'm not strong enough to overcome her bindings. She would need to relinquish you and I'm pretty sure she wants to keep an eye on how I treat you at the moment. And I'd rather not be on the receiving end of another one of her right hooks again anytime soon."

Groaning as Marcus chuckled, Cyrus' head fell back against the wall with a thud. "I hate it when you talk sense."

"Maybe we can revisit the idea another day," the cambion murmured, leaning into the boundling.

"Fine."

"Oh, come on, gorgeous," he breathed, dropping light kisses along Cyrus' jaw. "Don't pout. Smile for me, baby."

Grinning despite himself, he kept his head turned upwards to hide his mirth. "Make me," he whispered, knowing full well he was asking for trouble.

Huffing a laugh, Marcus dropped his hold of the boundling, stepping back. Cyrus looked at him panicked, missing the contact between them. "We are bratting it then," the cambion smirked, immediately allaying the young demon's fears. "Lena is going to kill me when I'm finished with you." Slowly, Marcus rolled up his sleeves, Cyrus tracking every movement of those large hands with his eyes, intrigued as to the meaning behind the cambion's words.

"If I were bound to you," he quipped, "you wouldn't have to worry about that anymore."

"Oh, I'm going to enjoy this," the older demon chuckled darkly, shaking his head. "You're going to need to transform for this, baby."

Smiling widely, Cyrus allowed his demonic form to surface, black fire flicking over his body as he did, removing his clothing. Marcus followed suit, smoke billowing out from his arms, snaking towards the boundling. Cyrus gasped as the cambion's power enveloped him, tracing along the lines and ridges of his body. The power was warm and sparked points of electric pleasure to ripple through him, wrapping around his spine, vibrating his very being. Smirking at the man he loved, his anticipation grew like a wildfire.

"Bring it on, tough guy."

# Bonus Epilogue

*Six months later...*

“Hey, babe.”

Marcus sighed as he looked up from his desk, his green eyes sparking with desire as Cyrus shut the door to the office behind him, resting back against the door.

“We're sticking with ‘babe’, then?” the cambion asked, leaning back into his chair, folding his hands over his flat stomach.

“Not all the time,” the boundling smirked, tilting his head to the side. “Only outside the bedroom. I think ‘sir’ suits you better in it.”

Those sea-green depths darkened at the term, the older demon's breath hitching as he pushed back against the desk, putting some space between him and it.

“Come here,” he ordered, a challenge in his tone that made Cyrus' skin shiver with anticipation. The boundling hadn't come into the office for sex, but he was never going to turn down the opportunity. Didn't always mean he wanted to make it easy on the cambion. Where most times his bratty nature slipped out, today he truly wanted to brat for his demon.

Biting his bottom lip, the young demon straightened against the door, pressing back into it, not missing the flash of warning across Marcus' face as he did so. “And if I don't?” he asked cautiously.

“You really want to find out?” the cambion's voice was low, growling with laden promise.

"Maybe."

"Last chance, gorgeous."

Firming his resolve, Cyrus pressed his hands flat against the door, grinning at the older demon. He swallowed as he tracked the movement of Marcus' tongue licking along his lips. Suddenly, flames enveloped the cambion, transporting him directly in front of the boundling, large hands punching into the wood either side of his shoulders, caging the young demon in. The older demon smirked at him, his head lowering until his nose could trail up the column of Cyrus' neck.

"You had your chance, baby," Marcus growled against him. "You want to be a brat, I'll treat you like a brat. You're going to wish you'd listened to me." Cyrus gasped as a large hand fisted his hair, jerking his head back, fully exposing his throat as Marcus dragged his teeth over the sensitive skin above his pulse point. "You have two choices, gorgeous. You can walk over to my desk and bend over it for me, or I can drag you to it and put you in the same position. I'm going to punish your arse either way, but the choice you make decides if I use my hand or my belt. Make your choice, brat."

He really should have known better than to provoke Marcus. Even though both choices served to fan the fire within him, desperation overtook his senses, wanting to see how far the cambion would go if he refused.

"Make me," he whispered, shuddering as the hand in his hair tightened, a sharp tugging pain serving only to skitter waves of pleasure down his spine.

Marcus bit down hard on his shoulder, a low moan escaping his throat at the sensation. Such actions used to make him feel disgust for the one inflicting them upon his body, but with Marcus it didn't matter. Even in his punishments, all the cambion focused on was overwhelming Cyrus' body with pleasure. And he wanted more. He wanted it all. He wanted Marcus to control him, to own him, to love him, and now that he had it, he was never going to let it go.

The cambion's free arm banded around his back, pressing their bodies together as flames overtook them, reappearing behind the desk. In a flourish of movement, Cyrus felt his clothes melt away under Marcus' power before he was spun on the spot, a firm hand placed between his shoulders, pushing him down to the desk's surface. Old memories threatened to overwhelm him as his cheek pressed against the cool wood, but the warmth at his back sunk deep into his bones, easing the tension within him.

"Relax, baby," Marcus soothed him, knowing like he always did, what was going on in the boundling's mind. "There is just you and me. You have your safeword if you need it and I will always take care of you." Breathing deeply, Cyrus forced his body to calm, recalling the times Marcus had taken him like this before, remembering the pleasure he'd felt then. "That's it, gorgeous. Good boy," the cambion praised, running his large hands soothingly over the boundling's back.

Shivers spread from the touch, knowing the gentleness of the moment was about to end. His breath caught in his throat as he heard the unbuckling of Marcus' belt, feeling the shift of movement behind him. Slowly, his hands snaked over the surface of the desk, gripping the far edge, awaiting his punishment.

"Remember to breathe, Cyrus," Marcus instructed, rubbing the smooth leather against the skin of his arse. "I promise you'll enjoy this."

He knew he would. He always did. Marcus was right, he had his safeword if he really needed it. Over the months he'd used it a few times as memories of both his time with Zagan and the angels clawed their way to the surface. And every time, the cambion had taken such good care of him, soothing and comforting him until they could either continue or simply be content in each other's embrace. But the older demon wanted to push him, to prove to him that he was stronger than he believed. And he loved Marcus all the more for it.

The first smack was from the cambion's hand, causing him to jut forward trying to escape the sting, his harden cock hitting the desk edge. Cyrus gasped in both shock and pain, his back arching into the air. Marcus' hand stayed where it landed, rubbing soothing circles to chase away the bite. No sooner had the cambion's hand left him, then it returned with increasing force. This time the pain gave way to pleasure as the older demon leant over him, kissing the nape of his neck.

"The day you break from your bindings, I'm going to ruin your perfect little arse," Marcus growled against him. "I'm going to make you come over and over until we lose track and then I won't have to hold back with you."

Cyrus huffed a weak laugh as another smack landed on his rear cheek. "You've been holding back?"

"You have no idea how much I hold back with you," the cambion whispered near his ear. "I told you I'd destroy you, gorgeous. I didn't say how."

The first lash of the belt landed across his skin, the searing bite travelling up his spine, pebbling his flesh as he half cried, half moaned into the room. "Oh, fuck!"

A slight wave of fear tightened his chest, forcing his eyes shut as he tried to draw in a full breath. But Marcus was right there, his large hand soothing the area as his weight pressed into Cyrus' back.

"Well done, baby," the cambion praised, kissing along his shoulders and down his spine. "You did so well. Can you take more?"

He nodded, his desire to please the demon overriding his fear. His chest heaved as he sucked in a lungful of air, his grip tightening on the edge of the desk. "Y-yes," he stuttered, pushing up into Marcus' chest, sagging back against the desk as the warmth at his back disappeared.

The sound of the belt ripping through the air met his ears before his mind could recognise the sting of the leather. His moan was loud, echoing off the walls as his head lifted, rearing back against his spine. It was quickly followed with another lash and then another, his body covering in a fine mist of sweat as his mind fought to reconcile the pain and pleasure vibrating through this body. Again, Marcus pressed into him, comforting his shuddering form, grabbing under his chin to hold his head up. He felt the cambion's hot breath against the shell of his ear even as his mind entered a daze of desire.

"When I tell you to 'come here', what do you do?" Marcus questioned, nipping against the curve of where his neck met his shoulder.

"Go to you," Cyrus panted, grinding his hips back into the older demon's groin. The cambion growled as he did so, biting harder on his shoulder.

"When I tell you to bend over for me, what do you say?"

"Y-yes."

"Yes?"

"Yes, sir."

"And why is that?"

"Because I'm yours," Cyrus rasped, knowing exactly what it was his demon wanted to hear.

"Damn fucking right."

Within a moment, he felt the bareness of Marcus' body against his, the cambion's hardened length throbbing against the now raw skin of his arse. There was a sound of a hand rummaging in a draw before he felt the cool slick of lube running between the seam of his rear cheeks. The older demon wasted no time, planting his hand on the back of Cyrus' neck, pressing him into the desk as he lined up the head of his cock with the boundling's tight hole. The sting of Marcus entering him in a single thrust barely registered after the lashing, but he gasped and writhed within his love's hold all the same.

"Fuck, baby," Marcus groaned, holding himself still as they both adjusted to the sensations. "You look so fucking good stretched around my cock. I love seeing you like this. Desperate and needy, begging to be fucked."

"Marcus," Cyrus moaned, his breath running rapid as the cambion's words fuelled his intense desire.

"What do you want, gorgeous? Beg me for it."

"Oh fuck, please, Marcus," he begged, no longer caring about anything but the feel of the demon inside him. "Please, fuck me. I need you so badly it hurts. Just fuck me."

"You want me to fuck you, baby boy?"

"Yes!"

"What do you say?"

"Please, sir! Please, fuck me!"

"Good boy."

Slowly pulling back, Marcus teased his hole with the head of his cock before slamming back inside him. Cyrus' back arched into the air as his hands pulled back from the edge of the desk to form tight fists either side of his head. The cambion's pace was as punishing as his belt, the boundling's cock slapping against the desk with each thrust. Large hands moved to grip his hips, aiding in the brutal assault on his arse.

It wasn't long before he was panting, pushing back against the demon, needing more, needing everything. Marcus' hand travelled down his hip, lifting his leg to rest it on the desk, opening him up further for the cambion. Holding it in place, the demon's other hand moved round, gripping Cyrus' cock and pumping in time with each thrust. He was so close, biting down on his arm to hold himself back, no longer needing to be told to wait until Marcus allowed him to come.

A warmth washed over him and he cried out in frustration as Marcus stilled suddenly, their hips pressed together.

"Oh shit," the cambion cursed, his fingers digging into Cyrus' flesh.

Barely managing to summon the strength, he looked over his shoulder, concern coursing through him at the expression of fear on the older demon's face.

"Marcus?"

A clearing cough drew his attention into the middle of the room, a mix of anger and horror flooding his body as he saw his sister standing there. Her neck flushed red as she kept her hand firmly clamped over her eyes, the other held up defensively.

"If you could extract yourselves from each other for five minutes, we need to talk. I can't take this anymore," she ground out, her teeth bared as her jaw pulsed with invisible effort.

"Lena!" Cyrus snapped, pushing up from the desk as Marcus hurriedly withdrew from him. "What the fuck?"

"I'm sorry!" she cried quickly. "But I can't do this anymore! I can't keep feeling this shit!"

Their powers coursing over them, Marcus and Cyrus glanced worriedly at each other as their clothes reformed. The boundling's mind was barely functioning, but he could still muster the energy to be pissed at his sister.

"You couldn't have fucking waited?"

"No!"

"We're dressed, Lena," Marcus said softly, placing his hand on Cyrus' chest, attempting to calm him.

"Thank Lucifer," she sighed, dropping her hand from her eyes. "Look, be pissed all you want, Cyrus. I don't really care right now. Or, you can let me transfer your bond to Marcus."

Both male demons went totally still, simply staring at her, mirrored expressions of shock on their features. Lena huffed with impatience, planting her hands on her hips as she waited for their reactions.

"A-are you serious?" Cyrus finally managed to force out, his hand rising to clutch at Marcus' wrist. They had asked a few weeks ago but Lena had refused at the time. Screw the sex, this is what he wanted more than anything right now. Well... maybe not completely screw the sex. If his bond was truly going to be transferred, he had every intention of riding the cambion for the rest of the day.

"Yes," Lena confirmed with a sharp nod. "I honestly cannot take this anymore. So, if you want to and Marcus is still willing, I will relinquish you."

"Yes!" he blurted, making to step towards her before pausing and looking back at the cambion. "Marcus?"

The older demon turned to look at him, his face still a picture of shock. As those green eyes met his, relief washed through him, taking in their burning brilliance, a complementary smile overtaking those proud features. "Do you even need to ask, gorgeous?"

"Wonderful," Lena said flatly, clapping her hands together. "Don't think this gets you off the hook though, Marcus." The cambion's head snapped to look at her, a solemn expression taking over. "I can always take him back if needed and I *will* kill you if you hurt him again."

Cyrus wanted to argue with her, to chastise her for the threat, but was silenced as Marcus gripped his arm tightly in silent warning.

The older demon nodded to their Prince. "I understand. I won't."

"Great," she muttered, stepping towards them. "Well, the sooner we get this done, the sooner you two can get back to..." she trailed off, waving her hand absently through the air, "you know."

Deciding to let his anger at her interruption go considering what she was doing for him, for *them*, Cyrus stepped quickly around the desk, pulling her into his arms, hugging her tightly against him. She sighed softly as her arms wrapped around his waist, returning the embrace.

"Thank you," he whispered to her. "I love you."

"I love you, too," she returned, tightening her hold on him. "I will still always be here if you need me, okay?"

"I know."

Releasing her, he straightened, looking at Marcus over her head as the cambion came to stand beside them. Again, Lena held out her hands for them, each taking one with their own, their free hands lacing together, closing the circle. Lena's power coursed up their arms as Marcus' smoke swirled around his hold of the boundling. Still fascinated by the process, Cyrus watched as his bindings for the second time in his existence, shifted and morphed across his skin, settling into their new pattern. Now faint wisps with sharp points traced around his wrists and arms, layering and fanning over his shoulders and down his spine. It seemed even with his new sire, the power he'd gained bound to Lena had not diminished.

Marcus' grasp of his hand tightened to almost crushing, pulling Cyrus' gaze to him. The boundling drew in a sharp breath as he saw the intensity of those green depths, swimming with barely contained emotion.

Without a word, Lena flamed out of the room as the new binding settled into place. As the last of her fire disappeared, Marcus pulled

Cyrus towards him, his hand grabbing the back of the boundling's neck, crushing their mouths together.

The moment their lips met, Marcus was plunged into bliss. Pure, unadulterated bliss as Cyrus' love and pleasure coursed almost violently through his chest. The moment the binding settled, the moment he knew they were alone, he was overcome by the emotions blending with his own. It felt like his heart was too big for his chest, it was so full, overflowing with what was being fed to him. He knew instantly that what he'd had with William wasn't love. Because it wasn't *this*. It wasn't the overriding need to become an inseparable part of the demon before him. The other half of him. Yes, the binding was not forever, but he would cherish every moment, every feeling, for as long as it lasted.

"I love you," the cambion rasped into the kiss. "Fuck, Cyrus, I love you so fucking much."

The boundling's arms flung eagerly over his shoulders, whimpering as he leant into the kiss. Greedily swallowing the sound, Marcus banded his own arms around the slim waist, desperately wanting to pull the young demon closer, needing to eliminate all space between them.

"I love you, Marcus," Cyrus panted.

Marcus' head was spinning with the overload of affection as he refused to part their lips for long. "I know," he moaned, his tongue sliding against the young demon's in desperation. "I can feel it. If I knew this is what it felt like..." The thought trailed off as the cambion lifted the boundling onto the desk, stepping between his thighs, his hands moving to cup Cyrus' face between his palms. "Never leave me," he begged. "Never stop loving me."

"Never," the boundling promised. "Never, Marcus."

"Cottage, now," the older demon ordered, lifting Cyrus in his arms, encouraging the young demon to wrap his legs around his waist. "I need you. I need to feel you. Right fucking now."

"Yes." Cyrus' head tipped back with a sigh. Seizing the opportunity, Marcus grazed his teeth over the slender neck, barely holding back his desire to devour the boundling. "Yes, Marcus. Sir. I *need* you."

"No holding back now, baby." Marcus tightened his embrace as his flames coursed over them. "You're mine. Completely." They fell onto the bed, their clothes disappearing as black smoke engulfed them. "I want to feel everything."

"Even the spankings?"

The cambion chuckled darkly into their kiss. "Want another one, brat?"

"No," the boundling breathed, even as his body shivered against Marcus' at the threat.

"No?"

"No, sir."

"Good boy. Now let me take care of you."

Making his way down Cyrus' stomach, Marcus marvelled at the wealth of pleasure feeding back to him. He always knew the boundling was responsive to him, but this was more than he ever realised. Every touch, every lick, every bite. It was like there was nothing he could do that didn't cause the young demon's body to spark with desire. But in amongst it all, he could discern what actions his lover liked the most.

Using the freshness of the bond to memorise each blazing point of pleasure, he focused on Cyrus' chest, kissing over his sternum, grazing his teeth down those firm pecs, licking over the hardened peaks of his nipples. Each action brought forth a louder gasp, a louder moan, than the one before it and the cambion quickly became addicted to the sounds.

When he finally wrapped his lips around the boundling's cock, he felt the sparks in the depths of his own belly, his own abdomen tightening, balls drawing up into his stomach. He wasn't going to last long with how Cyrus' desires overtook his own.

"Grab the lube, baby," Marcus ground out, lifting his head only long enough to get the words out, before returning his attentions to the boundling's shaft.

Cyrus writhed beneath him, stretching his arm to grab at the bottle on the bedside table, tossing it down onto the mattress. Falling back against the bed, the boundling's breathing was ragged as his long fingers laced in Marcus' hair. The cambion hummed with approval as Cyrus' hips bucked upwards, sinking his cock deeper into his throat. Keeping his head pressed down, Marcus swallowed, listening intently to the young demon's breathy moan at the sensation around the head of his cock.

"Fuck, Marcus!" the boundling cried, his body coiling tighter with each movement of Marcus' tongue around him. "Please, fuck me! Sir!"

With the overwhelming pleasure hitting him through the bond, Marcus crawled eagerly up Cyrus' body, sitting back on his knees as he lathered a generous portion of lube over his length. Words escaped him as he grabbed under the demon's knees, pushing them up to Cyrus' chest, practically folding the young demon in half. Sinking into the gorgeous body, both men groaned simultaneously at the wondrous sensation. He felt the building tension within the boundling, gritting his own teeth, fighting desperately to hold himself back.

"Don't you dare fucking come, gorgeous," he rasped, rapidly finding a pace that fuelled their combined pleasure. "Not until I say you can."

"Yes, sir!"

"Fuck, baby!" His voice was unbelievably hoarse. Completely foreign to his ears. Broken and desperate. And he was desperate. Desperate for everything he could give to and take from the demon laid before him. "You always take me so fucking well. You were made for me, weren't you? Made to take my cock."

"Yes, Marcus," Cyrus moaned, his back managing to arch despite his knees pressing into his shoulders. His hands flew above his head, bracing against the headboard, holding himself in place for the cambion. "Fuck, yes! Harder, please," he begged. "I need more!"

"Anything, Cyrus," Marcus breathed, increasing his pace obediently. "Anything you need, I will give to you."

The sounds of where their bodies met, slapping together with a pleasured fury, echoed through the cottage. The rocking of the bed thudded against the wall, small sounds of rattling ceramics from the vases on the window sills joining in. Marcus smiled, remembering the vase that interrupted their first kiss. How far they had come since that day. How much further he wanted to go with this demon. His demon.

*His.*

His Cyrus.

His gorgeous Cyrus.

*His boundling.*

The thought hit him like a freight train, barrelling through his chest with an intensity and fury that his ribs ached. Cyrus was his, had been his for months now. But now, he truly was, in every possible way. In every way that meant absolutely everything to the cambion. The binding solidified that final connection they needed, he needed, to truly comprehend that this was it for him. Cyrus was it for him. He'd thought it before. He knew he was ruined for the demon. But now he felt it. Deep within the very core of his being. Without warning, the tension in his stomach broke, ravaging his body at the realisation.

"Fuck!" Marcus roared as he surged forward, Cyrus' pleasure sending him over the edge, spilling everything he had into the youthful body. Collapsing onto the boundling, his body twitched with the aftermath of his release. The young demon's legs lowered, their fine tremble fluttering against the cambion's sides.

"M-Marcus?" Cyrus stammered, his breathing coming hard and fast, his cock throbbing mercilessly against the older demon's stomach. "I haven't..."

Groaning plaintively, Marcus silenced him with a kiss. Like he wasn't painfully aware that the boundling's body still hummed with a broaching orgasm. "I know, baby," he sighed against that perfect pout. "Do you want to fuck me, gorgeous?"

The young demon's breath caught in his throat, his body tensing, pulling a low moan from the cambion. "Yes," he breathed.

"How do you want me?"

Looking into those chocolate depths that continued to captivate him, Marcus' body shivered with anticipation as he saw the shifting blaze behind them. Quickly, Cyrus' submissiveness gave way to his bratty nature, giving him the confidence to take over. They had only switched a handful of times, but Marcus was eager to feel this. He tried to tell himself that they had plenty of time to explore everything together, but the bond would never be as fresh, as intense, as it was right now. He refused to waste this opportunity.

"On your back, tough guy," the boundling rasped, his pout quirking to a seductive smirk. The cambion groaned aloud at the sight, soaking in the feeling of excitement coming from his brat.

Quickly rolling to the side, Marcus grabbed the bottle of lube, tossing it to the demon. Climbing between the cambion's thighs, Cyrus caught his mouth, their tongues sliding lazily against the other. Breaking the kiss, the boundling moved down his body, biting along his jaw and neck as he went.

"I love your body," Cyrus sighed, licking down the centre of Marcus' chest. "Since the moment I met you, I wanted to touch it. To touch you. To lick and kiss every inch of you."

Threading his fingers through those dark blonde waves, the cambion smiled as he allowed his lover to play. He felt the truth of those words, the heated intent behind them branding him from the inside.

"I refused to look at you when you were bound to Zagan, but I always thought you were gorgeous," he admitted, melting into the chocolate eyes as they snapped to him. "I fought it for so long, but I've always wanted you."

Grinning, Cyrus bit his lip, hooking his hands under Marcus' knees, pushing them up to the cambion's chest. With a low groan, the older demon took over holding his legs, curling his body, knowing exactly what it was his boundling wanted to do. His body flinched at the first swipe of Cyrus' tongue over his hole, long fingers kneading his arse, spreading his cheeks to allow for long, slow strokes. He gasped as Cyrus breached his entrance, the firm thrust of his tongue causing a wave of blood to return to his own cock.

"Oh, fuck, Cyrus!" he moaned, curling further into the mattress as the boundling licked up his taint before sucking one of his balls into his mouth. A slicked finger swirled around his entrance, sinking inside, immediately curling to stroke his prostate.

Cyrus hummed with approval, the vibrations against his balls shooting through Marcus' body, threatening to send him over the edge yet again. His fingers dug painfully into the back of his knees, desperately trying to keep hold, to keep himself open for the young demon. The pleasure his boundling was getting from this was divine as it coursed through the bond. He didn't want to stop, or be the cause for it to stop.

Without warning, a second finger entered him, stroking and stretching as Cyrus licked up the underside of his length. The boundling moved up the bed, continuing his work with his fingers, draping his body over the cambion's. Dropping one knee, Marcus grabbed the back of Cyrus' neck, crushing their mouths together.

"Fuck me, baby," he begged into the kiss, relishing the feel of Cyrus' smirk against his lips.

"You want me to fuck you, tough guy?" the young demon teased, swiping his fingers over Marcus' prostate one last time before removing them.

The cambion huffed. His brat was certainly out to play, but that's what he wanted. He wanted Cyrus to seek his own pleasure. "Yes, gorgeous," he moaned, watching as the boundling coated his length in lube. "I need you."

Rubbing the head of his cock against Marcus' hole, Cyrus looked at him, a searing heat burning from his brown eyes. The cambion melted into that heat, wanting to live in this moment.

"Are you mine, Marcus?"

The older demon blinked at the question. To him it wasn't a question that needed asking, but he heard the hint of vulnerability in Cyrus' voice. Reaching up, he cupped the gorgeous face, running his thumb over that perfect pout.

"Yes, Cyrus," he breathed, swallowing around the lump forming in his throat. "Yes, baby, I'm yours. I'll always be yours."

The smile was blinding, stealing all his focus, even as the young demon pushed inside his body. The slight burn was quickly overcome with pleasure as Cyrus settled over him, his hips rolling in a tantalising rhythm, their mouths locked in a salacious kiss. Marcus drank in every moan, every gasp, every sound that fell from his love.

Running his hands over Cyrus' bindings, the cambion's body sang with happiness to share this connection with the boundling. To see his marks, his bindings, claiming the young demon as his, filled him with joy. There would be questions as to why Lena relinquished Cyrus, but they would figure out some explanation. Any consequences didn't matter to Marcus in that moment. He had his gorgeous demon, he had his love, and nothing else mattered.

He groaned as Cyrus pulled away from the kiss. A groan which quickly turned into a whimpering moan as the boundling rested back on his knees, grabbing at Marcus' hips and setting a punishing pace. His strokes were long and firm, shooting waves of pleasure up Marcus' spine causing it to arch up from the bed.

"Cyrus!" he cried, fisting the pillow next to his head as his other hand gripped his own cock, squeezing the base, holding himself back.

"Oh fuck, Marcus!" Cyrus groaned around his name. "You feel so fucking good."

"Come in me, gorgeous. Please!"

Cursing from behind gritted teeth, the boundling buried himself in Marcus, his cock pulsing as his release spilled inside the cambion. Following close behind, the older demon stroked his cock, white lashes of cum shooting up his stomach.

Cyrus immediately fell into his arms, their bodies resting together as they fought to regain their breath. Hearts beating in furious union. As the boundling slipped from his body, Marcus pulled the gorgeous demon up further onto the bed, wrapping his arms around him. Cleaning up could wait, he needed another kiss.

Claiming the smile on Cyrus' face, Marcus tenderly stroked along the boundling's jaw, their lower limbs tangled as they held each other.

"I love you, Cyrus," he whispered into the kiss. "So fucking much."

"Marcus," the young demon sighed, his fingers burying into the soft curls on the cambion's chest. "I love you too, babe."

"Brat."

"Your brat."

Marcus smiled, his heart overflowing with love for the man nestled into his side, running his hand along Cyrus' back to further press their bodies together. Sighing with contentment, he brushed a tender kiss to his boundling's temple, whispering a promise against his skin. "And I'm never letting you go."

# AFTERWORD

Dear Reader,

Thank you for reading Demon's Faith. I really hope you enjoyed reading it as much as I enjoyed writing it.

It was the creation of Marcus and Cyrus and their story that formed the idea for the Demons of the Apocalypse series. Initially, I was only going to write Lena and Ambrose's story, but I fell in love with Cyrus as I was writing him. A fleeting interaction between him and Marcus towards the end of Demon's Choice spurred me to write their story, to write their love for each other.

And thus, the rest of the series was also born!

I hope that you love Marcus and Cyrus as much as I do. And if you want to see more of them, make sure to read the rest of the series and the novellas as they come. Cyrus has a greater role to play as the Apocalypse draws nearer.

With my deepest gratitude!

Much love,<br>Jasmine

# DEMONS OF THE APOCALYPSE

## THE WORLD NEEDS TO RESET. HEAVEN AND HELL NEED TO RESET. THE APOCALYPSE WILL DECIDE THE FATE OF MORALITY.

Book 1: **Demon's Choice**
*"My whole life someone, or something else has been pulling the strings… I never had a choice until I died."*

Lena moved to town to disappear, but found herself drawn to a man that could do anything but…

Sacrificed to a demon she finds herself thrown into a world where she is the centre of attention, completely dependent on the man she longs for. Others now covet her and her growing power, seeking to tear her apart from the only person who has truly cared for her. The one she chose to be with.

Can she find the strength to save both her and her heart?

Book 2: **Demon's Faith**
*"Just admit it, compared to the rest of you, I'm nothing. I'm worthless, just a waste of fucking space!"*

A year after becoming the boundling to both his sister and Prince of Hell, Cyrus struggles to find his place among his fellow council members. He would do anything for his sister to trust him, to have faith in him. Whilst also trying to prove to Marcus that they are meant to be.

Family has meant little to Marcus for centuries, betrayed by one he trusted. But now that he has one, he will do anything to protect it, even deny his own heart. Although a certain boundling may yet test his resolve.

Can they overcome their pain to find peace with each other?

Book 3: **Demon's Hope** – Coming out – November 2024

Book 4: **Demon's Right** – Coming out – 2025

Book 5: **Demon's Wrath** – Coming out – 2026

Spin-off Novellas:

**Demon's Lust** – Coming out – 2025

**Demon's Peace** – Coming out – July 2024
Tegan loves her job, guiding and ushering sacrificed souls beyond the void, but the life of a Reaper Demon can be lonely. After all, who wants to hang around someone who deals in death? Her one comfort is when she sits atop her hellhound and races through the corridors of Hell, the cheers and roars of the demonic crowd spurring her on.

But when she's not reaping or racing, she falls into bliss, cradled in the arms of her English Rose. Her Charlotte, a sweet bookshop keeper in the curving side streets of Devon. Only she knows that Charlotte has a wild side behind closed doors.

So, when a dark shadow from Charlotte's past descends on their peace, Tegan grapples with the decision to expose what she is.

What lengths she will do to, to protect her human love?

Printed in Great Britain
by Amazon

4cee3f18-b529-4f3a-b78d-0dc1affdd3bcR01